"Wonderful historical whodunit . . . Rome comes to full life."

—*Midwest Book Review*

"Enjoyable."

—*Ellery Queen Mystery Magazine*

"Food, fashion, festivals—Davis tucks countless details of daily life in among the red herrings."

—*Charlotte Observer*

"This series is a wonderful ground-zero introduction to life and death during the Roman empire."

—*Rockhill Herald* (SC)

"With the passing of Ellis Peters, the title Queen of the Historical Whodunit is temporarily vacant. Lindsey Davis is well suited to assume it—and she is funnier than Peters. . . . Davis's books make old Rome sound fun. . . . It is all so enjoyable."

—*Times* (London)

"The cast of characters is as various, corrupt, nasty, and gnarled as the best of Dickens, described with similar scope and loving attention."

—*Mail on Sunday* (London)

❖ ❖ ❖

Also by Lindsey David

THE SILVER PIGS
SHADOWS IN BRONZE
VENUS IN COPPER
THE IRON HAND OF MARS
POSEIDON'S GOLD
LAST ACT IN PALMYRA
TIME TO DEPART

A PROCLAMATION FROM THE CRITICS OF TWO CONTINENTS—
LINDSEY DAVIS'S SERIES FEATURING MARCUS DIDIUS FALCO IS "ONE OF THE BEST HISTORICAL SERIES."*
AND NOW THEY PRAISE HER NEWEST NOVEL,
A DYING LIGHT IN CORDUBA

❖ ❖ ❖

"Solid detail and vivid insights that bring ancient Rome alive. But the plotting, though leisurely, is nicely suspenseful and the ending worth the wait."

—Library Journal

"A fascinating peek at everyday life in the colonial Roman empire, and the usual loopy cast of eccentrics that make Lindsey Davis novels such fun."

—Detroit Free Press

"Ancient Rome, busy and grand, bursting with passion, greed, and social ambition, provides a perfect setting for political intrigue—and for murder."

—Rocky Mountain News

SPECIAL FOR THIS EDITION!
An Excerpt from Lindsey Davis's Newest Novel,
Three Hands in the Fountain

**Detroit Free Press*

Please turn the page for more reviews . . .

"Corrupt cops, nasty political intrigue, bloody conniving over natural resources-they're all there in A DYING LIGHT IN CORDUBA . . . but it's the droll and personable Falco who supplies most of the fun."

—***Washington Post Book World***

"Mayhem, murder, humor, a lively fresco of shady characters, and a colorful re-creation of the bad old days in Rome, seasoned with a soup—on of biting satire, all combine to give Lindsey's latest a flavor all its own."

—Bill Sweeney, "Redwood Empire Bookbeat"

"The best historical mysteries combine scrupulous period detail with a modern sensibility. It's a tricky proposition. . . . Through eight novels in her Marcus Didius Falco series, Davis has managed to walk this tightrope flawlessly."

—***Booklist* (boxed review)**

"Murder most slick . . . rollicking good fun and high adventure. . . . Davis is a master of characterization and local color."

—***Roanoke Times (VA)***

"As usual, Falco is more slippery than an eel in a vat of Baetican olive oil, and a lot more entertaining."

—***Alfred Hitchcock's Mystery Magazine***

"Irreverent and deft, cynical to a fault . . . Falco is back in a new adventure with his smart-aleck attitude and steady resourcefulness intact. . . . Highly recommended—a romp through ancient Rome with a shrewd, resourceful, and entertaining guide."

—***Mystery News***

LINDSEY DAVIS

A DYING LIGHT IN CORDUBA

WARNER BOOKS

A Time Warner Company

WARNER BOOKS EDITION

First published in Great Britain in 1996 by Century Books, Random House UK Ltd, London

Cover design by Richard McClain
Cover illustration by Stanslaw Fernandes

Warner Books, Inc.
1271 Avenue of the Americas
New York, NY 10020

Visit our Web site at
http://warnerbooks.com

A Time Warner Company

Printed in the United States of America

Published in hardcover by Warner Books
First Paperback Printing: March, 1999

10 9 8 7 6 5 4 3 2 1

In Memory of
Edith Pargeter

Romans, in or out of Rome

M. Didius Falco	a frantic expectant father; a hero
Helena Justina	a thoroughly reasonable expectant mother; a heroine
D. Camillus Verus	her father, also quite reasonable, for a senator
Julia Justa	her mother, as reasonable as you could expect
A. Camillus Aelianus	bad-tempered, self-righteous, and up to no good
Q. Camillus Justinus	too sweet-natured and good to appear
Falco's Ma	who may be spooning broth into the wrong mouth
Claudius Laeta	top clerk, and aiming higher
Anacrites	Chief Spy, and as low as you can get
Momus	an "overseer"; the man who spies on spies
Calisthenus	an architect who stepped on something nasty
Quinctius Attractus	a senator with big Baetican aspirations
T. Quinctius Quadratus	his son, a high-flyer grounded in Baetica
L. Petronius Longus	a loyal and useful friend
Helva	a short-sighted usher who can look the other way
Valentinus	a skillful gate-crasher; on his way out
Perella	a mature dancer with unexpected talents
Stertius	a transport manager with inventive ideas

The Baetican Proconsul	who doesn't want to be involved
Cornelius	ex-quaestor of Baetica; leaving the scene hastily
Gn. Drusillus Placidus	a procurator with a crazy fixation on probity
Nux	a dog about town

Baeticans, out of and in Baetica

Licinius Rufius	old enough to know there's never enough profit?
Claudia Adorata	his wife, who hasn't noticed anything
Rufius Constans	his grandson, a young hopeful with a secret
Claudia Rufina	a serious girl with appealing prospects
Annaeus Maximus	a community leader; leading to the bad?
His Three Sons	known as Spunky, Dotty and Ferret; say no more!
Aelia Annaea	a widow with a very attractive asset
Cyzacus senior	a bargee who has barged into something dubious?
Cyzacus junior	an unsuccessful poet; paddling the wrong raft?
Gorax	a retired gladiator; no chicken!
Norbanus	a negotiator who has fixed a dodgy contract?
Selia	an extremely slippery dancer
Two musicians	who are not employed for their musical skills
Marius Optatus	a tenant with a grievance

Marmarides	a driver whose curios are much in demand
Cornix	a bad memory
The Quaestor's clerk	who runs the office
The Proconsul's clerks	who drink a lot (and run the office)
Prancer	a very old country horse

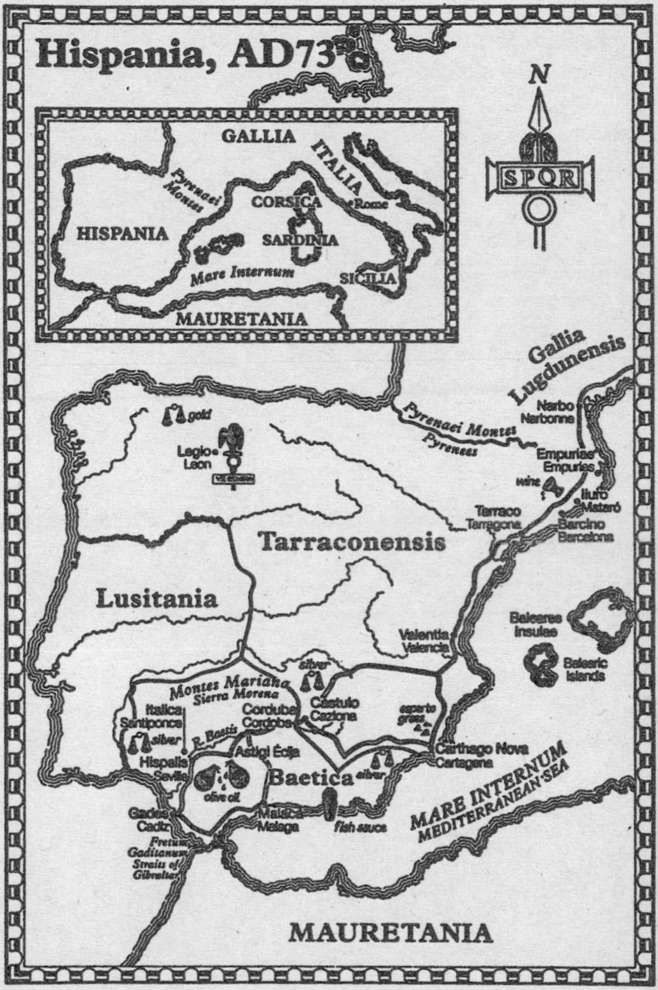
Hispania, AD73
N
SPQR
GALLIA
ITALIA
Pyrenaei Montes
CORSICA
Rome
HISPANIA
SARDINIA
Mare Internum
SICILIA
MAURETANIA
Gallia Lugdunensis
gold
Legio
Leon
Pyrenaei Montes
Pyreneas
Narbo
Narbonne
Empuriae
Empuries
wine
Iluro
Mataró
Tarraco
Tarragona
Barcino
Barcelona
Tarraconensis
Lusitania
Valentia
Valencia
Baleares Insulae
Balearic Islands
silver
Montes Mariana
Sierra Morena
Italica
Santiponce
Corduba
Cordoba
Castulo
Cazlona
esparto grass
silver
R. Baetis
Astigi Écija
Carthago Nova
Cartagena
Hispalis
Seville
Baetica
silver
olive oil
Gades
Cadiz
Malaca
Malaga
fish sauce
MARE INTERNUM
MEDITERRANEAN·SEA
Fretum Gaditanum
Straits of Gibraltar
MAURETANIA

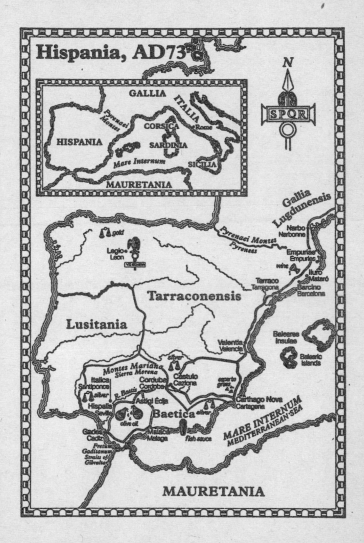

PART ONE:

ROME

A.D. 73: beginning the night of 31 March

Cordobans of any status surely sought to be as Roman as the Romans themselves, or more so. There is no evidence of a "national consciousness" in the likes of the elder Seneca, although there was presumably a certain sympathy among native sons who found themselves in Rome together . . .

Robert C. Knapp, Roman Cordoba

ONE

Nobody was poisoned at the dinner for the Society of Olive Oil Producers of Baetica—though in retrospect, that was quite a surprise.

Had I realized Anacrites the Chief Spy would be present, I would myself have taken a small vial of toad's blood concealed in my napkin and ready for use. Of course he must have made so many enemies, he probably swallowed antidotes daily in case some poor soul he had tried to get killed found a chance to slip essence of aconite into his wine. Me first, if possible. Rome owed me that.

The wine may not have been as smoothly resonant as Falernian, but it was the Guild of Hispania Wine Importers' finest and was too good to defile with deadly drops unless you held a *very* serious grudge indeed. Plenty of people present seethed with murderous intentions, but I was the new boy so I had yet to identify them or discover their pet gripes. Maybe I should have been suspicious, though. Half the diners worked in government and the rest were in commerce. Unpleasant odors were everywhere.

I braced myself for the evening. The first shock, an entirely welcome one, was that the greeting-slave had handed me a cup of fine Barcino red. Tonight was for Baetica: the rich hot treasurehouse of southern Spain. I find its wines oddly disappointing: white and thin. But apparently the Baeticans were decent chaps; the minute they left home they drank Tarraconensian—the famous Laeitana from northwest of Barcino, up against the Pyrenees where long summers bake the vines but the winters bring a plentiful rainfall.

I had never been to Barcino. I had no idea what Barcino was storing up for me. Nor was I trying to find out. Who needs fortunetellers' warnings? Life held enough worries.

I supped the mellow wine gratefully. I was here as the guest of a ministerial bureaucrat called Claudius Laeta. I had followed him in, and was lurking politely in his train while trying to decide what I thought of him. He could be any age between forty and sixty. He had all his hair (dry-looking brown stuff cut in a short, straight, unexciting style). His body was trim; his eyes were sharp; his manner was alert. He wore an ample tunic with narrow gold braid, beneath a plain white toga to meet Palace formality. On one hand he wore the wide gold ring of the middle class; it showed some emperor had thought well of him. Better than anyone yet had thought of me.

I had met him while I was involved in an official inquiry for Vespasian, our tough new Emperor. Laeta had struck me as the kind of ultra-smooth secretary who had mastered all the arts of looking good while letting handymen like me do his dirty work. Now he had taken me up—not due to any self-seeking of mine though I did see him as a possible ally against others at the Palace who opposed promoting me. I wouldn't trust him to hold my horse while I leaned down to tie my boot thong, but that went for any clerk. He wanted something; I was waiting for him to tell me what.

Laeta was top of the heap: an imperial ex-slave, born and trained in the Palace of the Caesars amongst the cultivated, educated, unscrupulous orientals who had long administered Rome's Empire. Nowadays they formed a discreet cadre, well behind the scenes, but I did not suppose their methods had changed from when they were more visible. Laeta himself must have somehow survived Nero, keeping his head down far enough to avoid being seen as Nero's man after Vespasian assumed power. Now his title was Chief Secretary, but I could tell he was planning to be more than the fellow who handed the Emperor scrolls. He was ambitious, and looking for a sphere of influence where he could really enjoy himself. Whether he took backhanders in the grand manner I had yet to find out. He seemed a man who enjoyed his post, and its possibilities, too much to bother. An organizer. A long-term planner. The Empire lay bankrupt and in tatters, but under Vespasian there was a new mood of reconstruction. Palace servants were coming into their own.

I wished I could say the same for me.

"Tonight should be really useful for you, Falco," Laeta urged me, as we entered a suite of antique rooms in the old Palace. My hosts had an odd choice of venue. Perhaps they obtained the cobwebbed imperial basement at cheap rates. The Emperor would appreciate hiring out his official quarters to make a bit on the side.

We were deep under Palatine Hill, in dusty halls with murky histories where Tiberius and Caligula once tortured men who spoke out of turn, and held legendary orgies. I found myself wondering if secretive groups still relived such events. Then I started musing about my own hosts. There were no pornographic frescoes in our suite, but the faded decor and cowed, ingratiating retainers who lurked in shadowed archways belonged to an older, darker social era. Anyone who believed it an honor to dine here must have a shabby view of public life.

All I cared about was whether coming tonight with Laeta

would help me. I was about to become a father for the first time, and badly needed respectability. To play the citizen in appropriate style, I also required much more cash.

As the clerk drew me in I smiled and pretended to believe his promises. Privately I thought I had only a slim hope of winning advancement through contacts made here, but I felt obliged to go through with the farce. We lived in a city of patronage. As an informer and imperial agent I was more aware of it than most. Every morning the streets were packed with pathetic hopefuls in moth-eaten togas rushing about to pay attendance on supposedly great men. And according to Laeta, dining with the Society of Baetican Olive Oil Producers would allow *me* to mingle with the powerful imperial freedmen who really ran the government (or who thought they did).

Laeta had said I was a perfect addition to his team—doing what, remained unclear. He had somehow convinced me that the mighty lions of bureaucracy would look up from their feeding bowls and immediately recognize in me a loyal state servant who deserved a push upwards. I wanted to believe it. However, ringing in my ears were some derisive words from my girlfriend; Helena Justina reckoned my trust in Laeta would come unstuck. Luckily, serious eating in Rome is men's work so Helena had been left at home tonight with a cup of well-watered wine and a cheesy bread roll. I had to spot any frauds for myself.

One thing was completely genuine at the Baetican Society: adorning their borrowed Augustan serving platters and nestling amongst sumptuous garnishes in ex-Neronian gilt comports, the food was superb. Peppery cold collations were already smiling up at us from low tables; hot meats in double sauces were being kept warm on complex charcoal heaters. It was a large gathering. Groups of dining couches stood in several rooms, arranged around the low tables where this luxurious fare was to be served.

"Rather more than a classic set of nine dinner guests!" boasted Laeta proudly. This was clearly his pet club.

"Tell me about the Society."

"Well it was founded by one of the Pompeys—" He had bagged us two places where the selection of sliced Baetican ham looked particularly tempting. He nodded to the diners whose couches we had joined: other senior clerks. (They mass together like woodlice.) Like him they were impatiently signaling to the slaves to start serving, even though people had still to find places around other tables. Laeta introduced me. "Marcus Didius Falco—an interesting young man. Falco has been to various trouble spots abroad on behalf of our friends in intelligence." I sensed an atmosphere—not hostile, but significant. Internal jealousy, without doubt. There was no love lost between the correspondence secretariat and the spies' network. I felt myself being scrutinized with interest—an uneasy sensation.

Laeta mentioned his friends' names, which I did not bother to memorize. These were just scroll-shufflers. I wanted to meet men with the kind of status owned by the great imperial ministers of olden days—Narcissus or Pallas: holding the kind of position Laeta obviously craved himself.

Small talk resumed. Thanks to my ill-placed curiosity I had to endure a rambling discussion of whether the Society had been founded by Pompey the Great (whom the Senate had honored with control of *both* Spanish provinces) or Pompey the rival of Caesar (who had made Baetica his personal base).

"So who are your members?" I murmured, trying to rush this along. "You can't be supporting the Pompeys now?" Not since the Pompeys fell from grace with a resounding thud. "I gather then that we're here to promote trade with Spain?"

"Jove forbid!" shuddered one of the high-flown policy-formers. "We're here to enjoy ourselves amongst friends!"

"Ah!" Sorry I blundered. (Well, not *very* sorry; I enjoy prodding sore spots.)

"Disregard the name of the Society," smiled Laeta, at his most urbane. "That's a historical accident. Old contacts do enable us to draw on the best resources of the province for our menu—but the original aim was simply to provide a legitimate meeting ground in Rome for like-minded men."

I smiled too. I knew the scenario. He meant men with like-minded politics.

A *frisson* of danger attended this group. Dining in large numbers—or congregating in private for any purpose at all—was outlawed; Rome had always discouraged organized factions. Only guilds of particular merchants or craftsmen were permitted to escape their wives for regular feasting together. Even they had to make themselves sound serious by stressing that their main business was collecting contributions for their funeral club.

"So I need not really expect to meet any substantial exporters of Spanish olive oil?"

"Oh no!" Laeta pretended to look shocked. Someone muttered to him in an undertone; he winced, then said to me, "Well, sometimes a determined group of Baeticans manages to squeeze in; we do have some here tonight."

"So thoughtless!" another of the scroll-pushers sympathized dryly. "Somebody needs to explain to the social elite of Corduba and Gades that the Society of Baetican Olive Oil Producers can manage quite well without any members who actually hail from southern Spain!"

My query had been sheer wickedness. I knew that among the snobs of Rome—and freed slaves were of course the *most* snobbish people around—there was strong feeling about pushy provincials. In the Celtic faction, the Spanish had been at it far longer than the Gauls or British so they had honed their act. Since their first admission to Roman society sixty or seventy years ago, they had packed the Senate, plucked the plum salaried jobs in the equestrian ranks, conquered literary life with a galaxy of poets and rhetoricians, and now apparently their commercial tycoons were swarming everywhere too.

"Bloody Quinctius parading his retinue of clients again!" muttered one of the scribes, and lips were pursed in unison sympathetically.

I'm a polite lad. To lighten the atmosphere I commented, "Their oil does seem to be high quality." I collected a smear on one finger to lick, taking it from the watercress salad. The taste was full of warmth and sunshine.

"Liquid gold!" Laeta spoke with greater respect than I anticipated from a freedman discussing commerce. Perhaps this was a pointer to the new realism under Vespasian. (The Emperor came from a middle-class family, and he at least knew *exactly* why commodities were important to Rome.)

"Very fine—both on the food and in the lamps." Our evening was being lit with a wide variety of hanging and standard lights, all burning with steady clarity and of course, no smell. "Nice olives, too." I took one from a garnish dish, then went back for more.

"Didius Falco is famous for political analysis," commented Laeta to the others. News to me. If I was famous for anything it was cornering confidence tricksters and kicking the feet from under criminals. That, and stealing a senator's daughter from her lovely home and her caring relatives: an act which some would say had made me a criminal myself.

Wondering if I had stumbled on something to do with Laeta's motive for inviting me, I carried on being reverent about the liquid gold: "I do know your estimable society is not named after any old table condiment, but a staple of cultured life. Olive oil is any cook's master ingredient. It lights the best homes and public buildings. The military consume vast quantities. It's a base for perfumes and medicines. There's not a bathhouse or athletic gymnasium that could exist without oily body preparations—"

"And it makes a fail-safe contraceptive!" concluded one of the more jolly stylus-shovers.

I laughed and said I wished I had known that seven months ago.

Feeling thoughtful, I returned my attention to the food. Plainly this suited the others; they wanted outsiders to keep quiet while they showed off. The conversation became encoded with oblique references to their work.

The last speaker's remark had me grinning. I could not help thinking that if I passed on the stylus-shover's suggestion Helena would scoff that it sounded like making love to a well-marinaded radish. Still, olive oil would certainly be easier to obtain than the illegal alum ointment which we had intended to use to avoid starting a family. (Illegal because if you took a fancy to a young lady who was of the wrong status you were not supposed to speak to her, let alone bed her—while if your fancy was legal you had to marry and produce soldiers.) Olive oil was not cheap, though there was plenty available in Rome.

There was a suitably Hispanic theme throughout the meal. This made for a tasty selection, yet all with a similar presentation: cold artichokes smothered in fish-pickle sauce from the Baetican coast; hot eggs in fish-pickle sauce with capers; fowl forcemeats cooked with fish-pickle and rosemary. The endives came naked but for a chopped onion garnish—though there was a silver relish dish of you-guessed-it placed handily alongside. I made the mistake of commenting that my pregnant girlfriend had a craving for this all-pervasive *garum;* the gracious bureaucrats immediately ordered some slaves to present me with an unopened amphora. Those who keep frugal kitchens may not have noticed that fish-pickle is imported in huge pear-shaped vessels—one of which became my personal luggage for the rest of the night. Luckily my extravagant hosts lent me two slaves to carry the dead weight.

As well as the deliciously cured hams for which Baetica is

famous, the main dishes tended to be seafood: few of the sardines we all joke about, but oysters and huge mussels, and all the fish harvested from the Atlantic and Mediterranean coasts—dory, mackerel, tuna, conger eel, and sturgeon. If there was room to throw a handful of prawns into the cooking pot as well, the chef did so. There was meat, which I suspected might be dashing Spanish horse, and a wide range of vegetables. I soon felt crammed and exhausted—though I had not so far advanced my career an inch.

As it was a club, people were moving from table to table informally between courses. I waited until Laeta had turned away, then I too slipped off (ordering the slaves to bring my pickle jar), as if I wanted to circulate independently. Laeta glanced over with approval; he thought I was off to infiltrate some policy-molders' network.

I was really intending to sneak for an exit and go home. Then, when I dodged through a doorway ahead of my bearers and the *garum,* I crashed into someone coming in. The new arrival was female: the only one in sight. Naturally I stopped in my tracks, told the slaves to put down my pickle jar on its elongated point, then I straightened my festive garland and smiled at her.

TWO

She had been swathed in a full-length cloak. I like a woman well wrapped up. It's good to ponder what she's hiding and why she wants to keep the goodies to herself.

This one lost her mystery when she bumped into me. Her long cloak slithered floorwards, to reveal that she was dressed as Diana the Huntress. As definitions go, "dressed" was only just applicable. She wore an off-one-shoulder little gold pleated costume; one hand carried a large bag from which emerged a chink of tambourine clackers while under her spare armpit were a quiver and a silly toy hunting bow.

"A virgin huntress!" I greeted her happily. "You must be the entertainment."

"And you're just a big joke!" she sneered. I bent and retrieved her cloak for her, which allowed me to peruse a shapely pair of legs. "You're in the right place to get kicked somewhere painful!" she added pointedly; I straightened up fast.

There was still plenty to look at. She would have come up to my shoulder but was wearing cork heels on her natty hide hunting boots. Even her toenails were polished like alabaster.

Her smooth, extremely dark skin was a marvel of depilatory care; she must have been plucked and pumiced all over—just thinking about it made me wince. Equal attention had been lavished on her paintwork: cheeks heightened with the purple bloom of powdered wine lees; eyebrows given super-definition as perfect semicircles half a digit thick; lids glowing with saffron; lashes smothered in lampblack. She wore an ivory bangle on one forearm and a silver snake on the other. The effect was purely professional. She was nobody's expensive mistress (no gemstones or filigree) and since women were not invited tonight, she was nobody's guest.

She had to be a dancer. Her physique looked well fleshed but muscular. A shining swatch of hair, so black it had a deep blue sheen, was being held back from her brow in a simple twist which could be rapidly loosened for dramatic effect. She had both hands posed with a delicacy that spoke of practice with castanets.

"My mistake," I pretended to apologize. "I had been promised a Spanish dancer. I was hoping you were a bad girl from Gades."

"Well I'm a good girl from Hispalis," she countered, trying to sweep past me. Her accent was crisp and her Latin abrasive. But for the Baetican theme of the evening it might have been hard to place her origins.

Thanks to my trusty amphora I was keeping the doorway well blocked. If she squeezed through, we were going to be pleasantly intimate. I noted the look in her eye, suggesting that one wrong move in confined conditions and she was liable to bite my nose off.

"I'm Falco."

"Well get out of my way, Falco."

Either I had lost my charm, or she had sworn a vow to avoid handsome men with winsome smiles. Or could it be she was worried by my big jar of fermented fish entrails?

An oldish man with a cithara stepped from a room across

the corridor. His hair was grizzled and his handsome features had dark, Mauretanian coloring. He took no interest in me. The woman acknowledged his nod and turned after him. I decided to stop and watch their performance.

"Sorry; private room!" she smirked, and closed the door smack in my face.

"Absolute nonsense! The Baetican Society has never encouraged plotting in smoky corners. We don't allow private parties here—"

It was Laeta. I had dallied too long and he had followed me. Overhearing the girl turned him into the worst kind of clerk who knows it all. I had stepped back to avoid getting my elegant Etruscan nose broken, but he pushed right past me intent on barging after her. His overbearing attitude almost made me decide against going in, but he had drawn me back into his orbit once more. The patient slaves wedged my amphora on its point against the doorframe and we sailed into the salon where the rude girl was to do her dance.

As soon as my eyes wandered over the couches I realized that Laeta had lied to me. Instead of the high-class world governors he had led me to expect, this so-called select dining club admitted people I already knew—including two I would have crossed Rome on foot to avoid.

They were reclining on adjacent couches—which was worrying in itself. The first was my girlfriend's brother Camillus Aelianus, a bad-mannered, bad-tempered youth who hated me. The other was Anacrites, the Chief Spy. Anacrites loathed me too—mainly because he knew I was better than him at the work we both did. His jealousy had nearly had lethal results, and now if I ever had the chance I would take great delight in tying him to a spit on the top of a lighthouse, then building a very large signal fire under him and setting light to it.

Maybe I should have left. Out of sheer stubbornness I marched straight in after Laeta.

Anacrites looked sick. Since we were supposed to be colleagues in state service he must have felt obliged to appear polite, so beckoned me to an empty place beside him. Instead of reclining myself I signaled the slaves to put my amphora to bed there with its neck on the elbow-bolster. Anacrites hated eccentricity. So did Helena's brother. On the next couch, the illustrious Camillus Aelianus was now simmering with fury.

This was more like it. I grabbed a cup of wine from a helpful server, and cheered up dramatically. Then ignoring them both I crossed the room after Laeta who was calling me to be introduced to someone else.

THREE

As I caught up with Laeta, I had to make my way through an odd roomful. I had hoped I would have no reason to take a professional interest tonight, but my suspicions of the Chief Secretary's motives in inviting me had kept me on the alert. Besides, it was automatic to size up the company. Whereas Laeta had first led me among a hardcore group of regular eaters and drinkers, these men seemed almost like strangers who had reclined together just because they spotted empty couches and were now stuck with making a night of it. I sensed some awkwardness.

I could be wrong. Mistakes, in the world of informing, are a daily hazard.

This salon had always been designed as a dining room—the black and white mosaic was plain beneath nine formal, matching, heavyweight couches, but boasted a more complex geometric design in the center of the floor. Laeta and I were now crossing that square, where the low serving tables were currently set but the dancer would be performing in due course. We were approaching a man who occupied the pivotal position like some grand host. He looked as if he thought he was in charge of the whole room.

"Falco, meet one of our keenest members—Quinctius Attractus!"

I remembered the name. This was the man the others had complained about for bringing in a troupe of real Baeticans.

He grunted, looking annoyed with Laeta for bothering him. He was a solid senator in his sixties, with heavy arms and fat fingers—just the right side of debauchery, but he obviously lived well. What was left of his hair was black and curly and his skin was weathered, as if he clung to old-fashioned habits: prowling his thousand-acre vineyards in person when he wanted to convince himself he stayed close to the land.

Maybe his collateral lay in olive groves.

I was clearly not obliged to make conversation, for the senator showed no interest in who I was; Laeta himself took the lead: "Brought another of your little groups tonight?"

"Seems an appropriate venue for entertaining my visitors!" sneered Quinctius. I agreed with the man in principle, but his manner was off-putting.

"Let's hope they will benefit!" Laeta smiled, with the serene insolence of a bureaucrat making a nasty point.

Not understanding the sniping, I managed to find amusement of my own. When I first came in Anacrites had been enjoying himself. Now when I looked back in his direction I could see he was lying straight and very still on his couch. His strange light gray eyes were veiled; his expression unreadable. From being a cheerful party guest with slicked-back hair and a meticulous tunic, he had become as tense as a virgin sneaking out to meet her first shepherd in a grove. My presence had really tightened his screw. And from the way he was staring—while pretending not to notice—I didn't think he liked Laeta talking to Quinctius Attractus like this.

I quickly glanced around the three-sided group of couches. It was easy to spot the Baetican interlopers whose invasion had annoyed Laeta's colleagues. Several men here had a distinct Hispanic build, wide in the body and short in the leg. There were two each side of Quinctius, forming the central row in the most honored position, and two more on the side row to his right. They all wore similar braid on their tunics, and dinner sandals with tough esparto rope soles. It was unclear how well they knew one another. They were speaking in Latin, which fitted the prosperous weave of their garments, but if they had come to Rome to sell oil they seemed rather restrained, not displaying the relaxed confidence that might charm retailers.

"Why don't you introduce us to your Baetican friends?" Laeta was asking Quinctius. He looked as if he wanted to tell Laeta to take a one-way trip to the Underworld, but we were all supposed to be blood-brothers at this dinner, so he had to comply.

The two visitors on the right-hand row, introduced rapidly and rather dismissively as Cyzacus and Norbanus, had had their heads together in close conversation. Although they nodded to us, they were too far from us to start chatting. The nearer pair, those on the best-positioned couches beside Quinctius, had been silent while Laeta spoke to him; they overheard Laeta and the senator trying to outdo one another in urbane unpleasantness, although they hid their curiosity. An introduction to the Emperor's Chief Secretary seemed to impress them more than it had done the first two. Perhaps they thought Vespasian himself might now drop in to see if Laeta had tomorrow's public engagement list to hand.

"Annaeus Maximus and Licinius Rufius." Quinctius Attractus named them brusquely. He might be patron to this group, but his interest in them hardly took a paternal tone. However he did add more graciously, "Two of the most important oil producers from Corduba."

"Annaeus!" Laeta was in there at once. He was addressing the younger of the two, a wide-shouldered, competent-look-

ing man of around fifty. "—Would that make you a relative of Seneca?"

The Baetican assented with a head movement, but did not agree to the connection with enthusiasm. That could be because Seneca, Nero's influential tutor, had ended his famous career with an enforced suicide after Nero grew tired of being influenced. Adolescent ingratitude at its most extreme.

Laeta was too tactful to press the issue. Instead he turned to the other man. "And what brings you to Rome, sir?"

Not oil, apparently. "I am introducing my young grandson to public life," answered Licinius Rufius. He was a generation older than his companion, though still looked sharp as a military nail.

"A tour of the Golden City!" Laeta was at his most insincere now, feigning admiration for this cosmopolitan initiative. I wanted to crawl under a side table and guffaw. "What better start could he have? And is the lucky young man with us this evening?"

"No; he's out on the town with a friend." The Roman senator Quinctius interrupted with ill-concealed impatience. "You'd best find a perch, Laeta; the musicians are tuning up. Some of us have paid for them, and we want our money's worth!"

Laeta seemed satisfied that he had made his mark. He had certainly annoyed the senator. As we picked our way back across the room through the slaves who were lifting the food tables in order to clear a central space, Laeta muttered to me, "Unbearable man! He throws his weight about to a degree that has become quite unacceptable. I may ask you, Falco, to help me with my endeavors to deal with him. . . ."

He could ask as much as he liked. Keeping members of dining societies in order was not my work.

My host had not yet finished bopping upstarts on the nob.

"Anacrites! And who amongst our refined membership has deserved *your* attentions?"

"Yes, it's a working supper for me—" Anacrites had a light, cultured voice, about as unreliable as a dish of overripe figs. I felt bilious as soon as he spoke. "I'm here to watch you, Laeta!" To do him justice, he had no fear of upsetting the secretariats. He also knew when to thrust his knife in quickly.

Their warfare was pretty open: the legitimate administrator, who dealt in manipulation and guile, and the tyrant of the security forces, who used blackmail, bullying and secrecy. The same force drove them; both wanted to be the dunghill king. So far there was not much difference between the power of a well-honed damning report on first-quality papyrus from Laeta, and a snide denunciation whispered by the spy in the ear of the Emperor. But one day this conflict was bound to reach a head.

"I'm quaking!" Laeta insulted Anacrites by using nothing worse than sarcasm. "—Do you know Didius Falco?"

"Of course."

"He should do," I growled. Now it was my turn to attack the spy: "Anacrites may be disorganized, but even he rarely forgets occasions when he sends agents into hostile territory, then deliberately writes to let the local ruler know to look out for them. I owe this man a great deal, Laeta. But for my own ingenuity he might have had me tied out on a rock in the Nabataean desert for all the crows of Petra to pick clean my bones. And in the case of unwelcome visitors I don't believe the cruel Nabataeans bother to kill you first."

"Falco exaggerates," Anacrites smirked. "It was a regrettable accident."

"Or a tactical ploy," I returned coolly.

"If I was at fault, I apologize."

"Don't bother," I told him. "For one thing you're lying, and for another, it's a pleasure to continue hating your guts."

"Falco is a wonderful agent," Anacrites said to Laeta. "He

knows almost everything there is to know about tricky foreign missions—and he learned it all from me."

"That's right," I agreed mildly. "Campania, two years ago. You taught me all the mistakes and bungles. All the ways to upset local sensitivities, trample the evidence and fail to come home with the goods. You showed me that—then I went out and did the job properly. The Emperor still thanks me for learning to avoid your mistakes that summer!"

Laeta took a turn: "I'm sure we all profit from your mutual past relationship!" He was letting Anacrites know I was working for him now. "The entertainment is starting," Laeta smiled in my direction. The general noise in the room had dropped in response to signs of impending action from the dancer. Laeta patted me on the shoulder—a gesture I found highly annoying, though I made sure Anacrites did not see me react. "Stay and enjoy yourself, Falco; I'd like to hear your opinion in due course. . . ." It was obvious he was not talking about the musicians. He wanted Anacrites to think something was going on. Well, that suited me.

Only two vacant couches remained, at each end of the side rows on opposite sides of the room. I had decided my preference, but just at that moment someone beat me to it. It was a man I found hard to place—a fellow in a subdued oatmeal tunic, about my age. He dropped onto the couch as if it had been his place previously and was soon leaning on his elbows to watch the dancer, with his muscular legs sprawled behind him. He had an old scar down one forearm and bunioned feet that had done their share of tramping pavements. He spoke to no one but appeared sociable enough as he tossed grapes into his mouth and grinned at the girl who was about to perform.

I grabbed a wine refill to brace myself, then took the final couch—the one which was already partially occupied by my amphora of fish-pickle, alongside Anacrites.

FOUR

There were two musicians, both with that deep black North African skin. One played the cithara, fairly badly. The other was younger and with more menacing, slanted eyes; he had a hand drum. He pattered on it in a colorful manner while the girl from Hispalis prepared to thrill us with the traditional gypsy display. I gave Anacrites a pleasant smile that was bound to annoy him as we waited to marvel at the suppleness of her hips. "Diana looks hot stuff. Have you seen her before?"

"I don't believe so . . . What's our Falco been up to then?" I hated people who addressed me in that whimsical way.

"State secret." I had just spent a winter delivering subpoenas for the lowest class of barrister and helping out as an unpaid porter at my father's auction house. Still, it was fun pretending that the Palace harbored a rival spy network, one run by Claudius Laeta over which Anacrites had no control.

"Falco, if you're working for Laeta, my advice is watch your back!"

I let him see me chuckle then I turned back to the dancer. She was giving us a few teasing poses with her golden bow and arrow: standing tiptoe on one foot with the other kicked up behind her while she pretended to shoot at diners, so she could lean back and show off her half-bared chest. Since this was Rome, it was nothing to cause a riot. Well, not unless any respectable equestrian went home and described her little Greek costume too graphically to his suspicious wife.

"I've been talking to young Camillus." Anacrites had leaned across to whisper in my ear. I made a violent scratching movement as if I thought a beetle had landed on me. I just missed blinding him. He popped back onto his couch.

"Aelianus? That must have tried your patience," I said. Just the other side of Anacrites Helena's angry brother was making sure he avoided my eye.

"He seems a promising young character. It's clear that he doesn't care for you, Falco."

"He'll grow up." The spy should have learned by now there was no future in baiting me.

"Isn't he your brother-in-law or something?" It was casually offensive.

"Or something," I agreed calmly. "What's he doing here? Don't tell me he heard there would be top men from the bureaucracy, and he's trying to worm his way into a sinecure?"

"Well, he's just back from Baetica!" Anacrites loved being obscure.

I loathed the thought of Helena's hostile brat of a brother hobnobbing here with the spy. Maybe I was getting overexcited, but the scenario had a whiff of plots being hatched against me.

The girl from Hispalis was now well into her routine, so conversation ceased. She was showy, but not outstanding. Dancing girls are a thriving export from southern Spain; they all seem to train in the same terpsichoreal school, one where the movement-coach needs retiring. This wench could roll her eyes, and various other parts of her anatomy. She threw herself about the floor as if she wanted to polish the whole mosaic with her wildly swinging hair. Once you've seen one snappy lass bent over backwards with her clackers in a frazzle, the attention may start wandering.

I was looking around. The room contained a disparate group. The world-weary, middle-class-looking pair of Baeticans on the other row of couches were as unreceptive as me to the girl's efforts; they still muttered among themselves. Quinctius Attractus, who had claimed to be paying for this, leaned on his elbow looking full of himself for the benefit of the more patrician pair of visitors either side of him. They watched politely, though the elder in particular looked as if he would normally be too aesthetic to indulge in this kind of show. All the Baeticans looked so polite it had to be forced, and I wondered why *they* thought they had been favored here. Anacrites, the professional state meddler, appeared perfectly at home, though I could not believe Quinctius Attractus had intended him to join the group. Then there was Aelianus, too young to be a member of the dining club in his own right. Who had brought him? And who was the man in the oatmeal tunic at the end of the opposite row from me, who enjoyed himself in that seemingly sociable manner—yet actually spoke to nobody?

I nudged Anacrites. "Who's that fellow?"

He shrugged. "Probably a gate-crasher."

The dancer ended a set, twanging away an arrow for real. It hit young Aelianus, who squeaked as if it packed more force than her toy bow suggested. She then let off a shower, most of which found a mark, causing me to make a note that if anybody died later of a slow poison, I would know who to pull in for questioning. As she retired for a breather she indicated, with eyes full of sluttish promise, that Camillus Aelianus could keep his pretty arrow as a souvenir.

I slid upright, walked around Anacrites, and deliberately seated myself on Aelianus' couch, forcing the brat to salute me. "Oh you're here, Falco!" he said rudely. He was a thickset though physically undisciplined lad, with straight floppy hair and a permanent sneer. He had a younger brother who was both better looking and more likable. I wished it were Justinus here tonight.

I fingered the arrow as if Aelianus were a schoolboy with some illegal toy. "This is a dangerous memento. Better not let your parents find it in your bedroom; favors from performing artistes can be misconstrued." I liked to worry him with threats that I might blacken his name in the way he always tried to blacken mine. My reputation had never existed, but he would be standing for election to the Senate soon, and had something to lose.

He snapped the arrow in two: an impolite gesture, since the girl from Hispalis was still in the room, talking to her musicians. "She's nothing special." He sounded sober as well as bored. "She's relying on saucy eyes and a scanty outfit; her technique's very basic."

"That so?" I know a snake dancer who says people only watch for the dress—or lack of it. "So you're a connoisseur of Spanish choreography?"

"Anyone is, who has done a tour in the province." He shrugged offhandedly.

I smiled. He must have known his youthful experience in peaceful Baetica would not impress an imperial agent who had specialized in working at the Empire's trickiest boundaries. I had crossed them too, when a risk was needed. "So how did you enjoy Hispania?"

"Well enough." He did not want to have to talk to me.

"And now you're placing your expert knowledge at the disposal of the Society of Baetican Olive Oil Producers! Do you know the ones over there with Quinctius Attractus?"

"Slightly. I was friendly with the Annaeus lads in Corduba."

"What about the grandson of Licinius Rufius? He's here in Rome at the moment."

"I believe so." Aelianus was certainly not intending to discuss his friends. He could hardly wait to be rid of me.

"I gather he's out on the town tonight—I would have thought you would have been there."

"I'm here instead! Do you mind, Falco; I want to see the dancer."

"Nice girl," I lied. "I had a pleasant chat with her."

It misfired; "Of course; you must be going short," Aelianus suggested unpleasantly. "With my sister in her condition." How Helena and I lived was our own affair. I could have told him that sharing our bed with several months of unborn offspring had not impeded a healthy love life, but merely set greater challenges. "So now you're upsetting Helena by scurrying after entertainers. If anyone tells her maybe she will miscarry."

"She won't!" I snapped.

I had just spent six months trying to reassure Helena (who had in fact lost one child in pregnancy, though her brother may never have been told of it). Now it was hard work convincing her that she would give birth safely and survive the ordeal. She was terrified, and I was not much happier myself.

"Maybe she'll leave you!" he speculated eagerly. That had always been a possibility.

"I see you really have her interests at heart."

"Oh I'm happy to see her with you. I think when I stand for the Senate I'll make my election platform denouncing your relationship—I'll be a man of such traditional rectitude I even criticize my own sister—"

"You won't succeed," I told him. He might. Rome loves a pompous bastard.

Aelianus laughed. "No; you're probably right. My father would refuse to finance the election." Camillus Verus, father of my beloved and of this poisonous young ferret, always looked like an uncomplicated old buffer, but evidently Aelianus was sharp enough to realize that their parent loved Helena and understood that I did too; however much he regretted our relationship, the senator knew he was stuck with it. I had a sneaky idea he was quite looking forward to having a grandchild too.

"Jupiter, you must be really gloating, Falco!" Helena's brother's bitterness was even worse than I had realized. "You've jumped up from nowhere and seized the only daughter of a patrician house—"

"Cobnuts. Your sister was glad to fly off her perch. She needed rescuing. Helena Justina did her duty and married a senator, but what happened? Pertinax was a disaster, a traitor to the state, who neglected and mistreated her. She was so miserable she divorced him. Is that what you want? Now she's with me, and she's happy."

"It's illegal!"

"A technicality."

"You could both be accused of adultery."

"We regard ourselves as married."

"Try that in the Censor's court."

"I would. No one will take us there. Your father knows Helena made her own choice, and she's with a man who adores her. There is no moral objection the senator can make."

Across the room the dancing girl with the limited technique shook out her waist-length hair. She seemed to know how to do that. I realized she had been watching us quarreling. It gave me an uneasy qualm.

To end the fight I stood up, preparing to return to my own couch. "So, Camillus Aelianus, what does bring you among the revered Society of Baetican Olive Oil Producers?"

The angry young man calmed down enough to boast: "Friends in high places. How did you get in, Falco?"

"Much better friends, in even more select positions," I told him crushingly.

Settling back the other side of Anacrites came almost as a relief. Before he tried to have me killed we had been able to work together. He was devious, but like me he had lived. He enjoyed a good wine, he was in control of his barber, and he had been known to crack the occasional joke against the Establishment. With an emperor who liked cost-cutting and hated too much security, Anacrites must be feeling beleaguered. He wanted me, for one, well out of his way. He had tried to discredit me, and he had planned to get me executed by a tricky foreign potentate. But even now, I knew where I was with him. Well, I knew it as much as you ever could with a spy.

"What's this, Falco? Is my young friend from the noble family pursuing vindictive claims against you?"

I said his young friend was about to get his nose pulled off. Anacrites and I resumed our usual hostility.

Gazing up, I fixed my eyes on a lamp. Burning with the clear, odorless flame of fine Baetican oil, it was in gleaming bronze and the shape of a flying phallus. Either this rude vessel was swinging more than it should, or the whole room had begun to maneuver in some swooning routine . . . I decided I had reached my full capacity for Barcino red wine. At the same moment, as so often happens, a slave poured more into my cup. I sighed and settled down for a long night.

I must have had yet more drink later, though I cannot provide a catalogue. As a result, nothing of interest happened—not to me, anyway. Others no doubt threw themselves into risk and intrigue. Someone presumably made an assignation with the dancer from Hispalis. It seemed the kind of party where traditional customs would be observed.

I left when the atmosphere was still humming. Nobody had noticeably fallen out, and certainly at that stage there was nobody dead. All I recall of my final hour are some tricky moments trying to shoulder my amphora; it was half as high as me and immovable to a man in my condition. The young fellow in the oatmeal tunic from the other row of couches was also collecting his cloak; he seemed relatively sober, and helpfully suggested I roust out some more slaves to lug the cumbersome container home for me on a carrying pole. I suddenly saw the logic of this. We exchanged a laugh. I was too far gone to ask his name, but he seemed pleasant and intelligent. I was surprised he had been at the dinner all on his own.

Somehow my legs must have found their way from the Palatine to the Aventine. The apartment where I had lived for some years was six floors up in a dismal tenement; the slaves refused to come up. I left the amphora downstairs, tucked out of sight under a pile of dirty togas in Lenia's laundry on the ground floor. It was the kind of night where my left foot set off in one direction and met my right one coming back. I have no recollection of how I persuaded them to cooperate and find their way upstairs.

Eventually I awoke from troubled blackness to hear the distant cries of market stallholders and the occasional clonk of a harness bell. I realized the activity in the streets below had been disturbing me for some time. It was the first day of April and the outdoor street life was hectic. Watchdogs were barking at chickens. Cockerels were crowing for the fun of it. Day had dawned—quite a few hours ago. On the roof tiles outside a pigeon cooed annoyingly. Light, with a painful midday intensity, streamed in from the balcony.

The thought of breakfast marched into my brain automatically—then receded fast.

I felt terrible. When I squirmed upright on the saggy reading couch where I had flung myself last night, one look around the apartment made everything worse. There was no point calling out to Helena, not even to apologize. She was not here.

I was in the wrong place.

I could not believe I had done this—yet as my head throbbed it seemed all too plausible. This was our old apartment. We did not live here anymore.

Helena Justina would be in our new home, where she

would have waited for me all last night. That's assuming she had not already left me on the grounds that I had stayed out partying. A fact which any reasonable woman would interpret as meaning I had stayed out with another girl.

FIVE

There was a dark first-floor apartment on the shady side of Fountain Court. At first glance the shady side looked superior, but that was only because the sun failed to light the decay that encased all these buildings like a moldy crust. Shutters peeled. Doors sagged. People frequently lost heart and stopped paying their rent; before the landlord's muscle-bound assistants beat them up as a penalty, they quite often died in misery of their own accord.

Everyone who lived here was trying to leave: the basket weaver with the street-level lock-up wanted to retire to the Campagna, the upstairs tenants came and went with a rapidity that said much about the facilities (that is, that there were none), while Helena and I, the weaver's sub-tenants, dreamed of escaping to a plush villa with piped water, a boundary of pine trees, and airy colonnades where people could hold refined conversations on philosophical subjects . . . Anything, in fact, would be better than a three-room, small-dimensioned let, where the spitting and swearing totters who lived in the upper stories all had a right of way past our front door.

The front door had been stripped and planed down, ready

for new paint. Inside, I squeezed down a corridor full of stored items. The first room off it had bare walls and no furniture. The second was the same, apart from an unbelievably obscene fresco painted straight opposite the entrance. Helena was spending much time doggedly scratching off the lewd copulating couples and the coarse satyrs in garish hyacinth wreaths and panpipes who lurked behind laurel bushes while they ogled the scene. Obliterating them was slow work and today all the wet sponges and scrapers lay abandoned in a corner. I could guess why.

I walked further down the corridor. Here its newly nailed floorboards were firm beneath my feet. I had spent hours getting them level. On the walls hung a series of small Greek plaques with Olympic scenes, Helena's choice. A niche seemed to be awaiting a pair of household gods. Outside the final room lay a red and white striped rug which I didn't recognize; on it slept a scruffy dog who got up and stalked off in disgust when I approached.

"Hello, Nux."

Nux farted quietly, then turned round to survey her rear with mild surprise.

I tapped the lintel gently, and opened the door. Part of me hoped the usual occupant had gone out for a stroll.

There was no reprieve. She was there. I should have known. If she went out without me I had ordered her to take the guard dog. She was not in the habit of obeying my instructions, but she had become fond of the hound.

"Hello, brown eyes. Is this where Falco lives?"

"Apparently not."

"Don't tell me he's run off to become a gladiator? What a swine."

"The man is grown up. He can do as he likes." Not if he had any sense.

Routinely, Falco's new office had been furnished as a bedroom. Informing is a sordid job and clients expect to be shocked by their surroundings. Besides, everyone knows that an informer spends half his time giving his accountant instructions how to cheat his clients, and any spare moments seducing his secretary.

Falco's secretary was lying against the pleasant scallop-shell bedhead reading a Greek novel. She doubled as Falco's accountant, which might explain her disillusioned manner. I did not attempt to seduce her. A tall, talented young woman, her expression hit me like a sudden gulp of snow-chilled wine. She was draped in white, with fine dark hair, loosely pinned up with ivory side combs. On a small table beside her lay a manicure set, a bowl of figs, and a shorthand copy of yesterday's *Daily Gazette.* With these she occupied her time while awaiting the master's return. This had left her copious spare capacity for inventing whiplash retorts.

"How are you?" I inquired, tenderly checking up on her condition.

"Angry." She enjoyed being frank.

"That's bad for the baby."

"Leave the baby out of this. I hope to shield the baby from knowing it has a father who is a degenerate stop-out whose respect for his home life is as minimal as his courtesy to me."

"Nice talking, Demosthenes!—Helena, my heart, you *are* angry!"

"Yes, and it's bad for you."

"I do have an explanation."

"Don't make me tired, Falco."

"I've tried to produce something lucid and witty. Want to hear?"

"No. I'll be happy with your shrieks of grief as a posse of soldiers marches you away."

"I made a stupid mistake, fruit. I had too much to drink and went home to the wrong house."

"Lucid," she smiled weakly. "Though only witty in the

sense that it's ludicrous . . . Whose house?" Suspicion dies slowly.

"Ours. Over the road. Whose did you think?" I jerked my head in the direction of my old apartment.

Helena had always taken the line that she hated half the things I did—yet chose to believe that I told her the truth. In fact I did. She was too shrewd for deceit. In sudden relief she dropped her face in her hands and burst into tears. It was involuntary, but the worst punishment she could have chosen to whack me with.

I reflected sadly on the fact I was still half drunk and bound to have the ghastly breath to prove it. Rubbing one hand over my chin, I met relentless stubble. Then I crossed the room and gathered my poor cumbersome darling into my arms, taking the opportunity to slide my own body alongside her on the bed.

I had reached the point of comforting Helena just in time. I needed to get horizontal. The ravages of the night before would have had me keeling over otherwise.

We were still there, collapsed in a comfortable mound, about an hour later. Helena had been holding me and staring at the ceiling. I was not asleep, just slowly recovering.

"I love you," I gurgled eventually, to take her mind off whatever dark thoughts held her transfixed.

"You do know when to splash out on a romantic phrase!" She gripped me by the bristled chin and stared into my bleary eyes. A girl of great courage, even she went slightly pale. "Falco, your raffish good looks are the worse for wear."

"You're a charitable woman."

"I'm a fool!" She frowned. Helena Justina knew she had let herself be lured into caring for an unsatisfactory lowlife who would only bring her sorrow. She had convinced herself she enjoyed the challenge. Her influence had already refined me, though I managed to conceal the evidence. "Damn you, Marcus, I thought you had been carried away by the excitement of your orgy and were lying in the lap of a dancing girl."

I grinned. If Helena cared enough for me to be upset there was always hope. "There *was* a dancing girl at the party but I had nothing to do with her. She was got up as Diana in a fraction of a costume. Spent her time leaning backwards so you could look right down—"

"At your food bowl, if you were sensible!"

"Exactly," I assured my beloved.

She gave me a fierce hug; by accident I let out a revolting belch. "Then I thought you had been set upon and were bleeding in a gutter somewhere."

"Just as well it didn't happen. I was carrying a valuable quantity of top-quality liquamen, which I managed to pinch from the party as a gift for my lady love, whose pregnancy has given her insatiable cravings for the most expensive kind of sauce."

"My unerring good taste! As a bribe, it's virtually enough," she conceded. Always fair.

"It's a whole amphora."

"That's the way to show your remorse!"

"I had to borrow two slaves to drag it home."

"My hero. So is it from Baetica?"

"The label on the shoulder says Gades."

"Sure it's not just cheap old Muria?"

"Do I look like a second-class tunnyfish salesman? Entrails of prime mackerel, I promise you." I had not tested the *garum* but the boast seemed safe. Given the high standard of food at the dinner, the condiments were bound to be excellent. "Am I forgiven, then?"

"For not knowing where you live?" she jibed pointedly.

"Yes, I'm suitably embarrassed."

Helena Justina smiled. "I'm afraid you will have to face quite a lot more embarrassment. You see, Marcus my darling—I was so worried by your nonappearance that I rushed out at first light to see Petronius Longus." Petronius, my best friend, was not above sarcasm when it came to my escapades. He worked as an inquiry officer in the local watch. Helena gurgled prettily. "I was distraught, Marcus. I insisted he get the vigiles to look everywhere for you . . ."

Helena assumed the demure expression of a girl who intended to enjoy herself, knowing I was condemned to suffer in a very public manner. She did not need to continue. Everyone on the Aventine would have heard that I disappeared last night. And whatever lies about my drunken return I tried telling, the true story was bound to come out.

SIX

Luckily Petronius must have had enough to do chasing real villains. He had no time to come looking for me.

I spent my morning in modest domestic pursuits. Sleeping. Asking for headache remedies. Giving attention to the selfless woman who had chosen to spend her life with me.

Then a distraction turned up. We heard a man who was hot and fractious arriving on the outer stairs. We ignored the noise until he burst in on us. It was Claudius Laeta: he seemed to expect rather more ceremony than the quiet stare he received from both of us.

I had got myself bathed, shaved, massaged, combed, dressed in a clean tunic, revitalized with several pints of cold water, then further nourished with a simple meal of lightly cooked cucumber in eggs. I was sitting like a decent householder at my own table, talking to my own woman and politely allowing her to select whatever subject she liked. The chat was undemanding because Helena had her mouth full of mustcake. She had bought it for herself that morning, half suspecting I would turn up eventually with some disgraceful tale. There had been no suggestion of offering me any.

So we sat, decorous and peaceful after lunch, when a man with a commission I didn't want or care for burst into our home: for an informer, this was a normal event. I greeted him resignedly. Luckily we had our temporary table in the room without the obscene plasterwork. I took my time fetching another seat from a cubbyhole. I knew whatever Laeta had come to say would be burdensome.

Laeta sat down. Here, in a low street on the turbulent Aventine, the great man was well out of his fishpond. Like a grounded carp he was gasping, too. I never told anyone my new address, preferring to let trouble go to the old one. He must have stomped up the six flights to my room across the road, then stumbled down them all again before Lenia at the laundry (who had callously watched him going up) drawled out that I also leased an apartment over the basket shop opposite. He had vented his curses on the ox-wagon driver who had knocked him down as he was crossing Fountain Court.

"Perhaps Marcus Didius can advise you on suing the driver?" murmured Helena, with the refined patrician mockery which was the last thing he could cope with in his present indignant state.

I introduced her formally: "Helena Justina, daughter of Camillus Verus, the senator; he's a friend of Vespasian, as I expect you know."

"Your wife?" quavered Laeta, alarmed by the incongruity and trying not to sound surprised.

We smiled at him.

"What's the problem?" I asked gently. There had to be a problem, or a high-class official would not have dragged himself here, especially without an escort.

He cast a wild glance towards Helena, meaning I should get rid of her. Not easy. Not easy, even if I had wanted to. Quite impossible while she was two months away from giving birth and shamelessly exploiting it: groaning with restrained discomfort as she settled into her wicker armchair with her tired feet on her personal footstool. She folded her stole around herself and smiled at Laeta again—then continued with the remains of her cake. He was not worldly enough to suggest he and I go out to a wine bar, so Helena prepared to listen.

As she licked her long fingers I watched her wicked brown eyes survey the top clerk. He was sweating badly, partly from his hike up to my old aerie and partly from agonies of awkwardness here. I wondered what Helena made of him. In fact, I wondered what I really made of him myself.

"Did you enjoy the dinner, Falco?"

"Excellent." Years of encouraging difficult clients had taught me to lie smoothly. I seemed to have a prospective client here. Well I had already turned down people who were more important than him.

"Good; good . . . I need your help," he confessed.

I raised an eyebrow as if that sordid idea had never crossed my mind. "What can I do for you?"

This time Laeta turned to Helena directly. "Perhaps you have some weaving you want to attend to?" He was persistent, yet had the sense to make it sound like a joke in case she still refused to budge.

"Afraid not." She waved her arm around the empty room. "We're still waiting for the loom to be delivered."

I grinned. Helena Justina had never promised me the traditional attributes of a good Roman wife: reclusive social habits, a submissive demeanor, obedience to her male relatives, a big fat dowry—let alone home-woven tunics. All I got was bed and banter. Somehow I still ended up convinced that I had it better than the old republicans.

Laeta stopped fidgeting. He fixed his gaze on me as if to make my eccentric companion invisible. "I need assistance from someone who is totally reliable."

I had heard that before. "You're saying the job is dangerous!"

"This could bring you large rewards, Falco."

"That old song! This is work of an official nature?"

"Yes."

"And is it official as in 'just between friends,' official as in 'a highly placed person whose name I won't mention needs this,' or official as in 'the highly placed person must never know about it and if you get in trouble I'll deny I've ever heard of you'?"

"Are you always so cynical?"

"I've worked for the Palace before."

Helena cut in, "Marcus Didius has risked his life on public service. His reward has been slow payment, followed by a refusal of social promotion even though it had previously been promised him."

"Well I know nothing of your last employment terms, Marcus Didius." Laeta knew how to blame other departments. A natural. "My own secretariat has an unblemished record."

"Oh good!" I jeered. "Yet my enthusiasm for your bureau's clean habits doesn't mean I accept the job."

"I have not told you what it is," he twinkled.

"By Jove; no you haven't! My curiosity is bursting."

"You're being satirical."

"I'm being rude, Laeta."

"Well, I'm sorry you take this attitude, Falco—" There was an unspoken hint of regret that he had honored me with his invitation to the oil producers' party. I ignored it. "I had been told you were a good agent."

"Good means selective."

"But you refuse my work?"

"I'm waiting to hear about it."

"Ah!" He assumed an expression of huge relief. "I can promise I shall take personal responsibility for the payment of your fees. How much are we talking about, by the way?"

"I'll fix the terms when I accept the work—and I'll only accept if I know what it is."

There was no escape. He looked uncomfortable, then he came out with it: "Someone from our dinner last night has been found badly beaten in the street."

"Then you must call for a surgeon and inform the local cohort of the watch!"

I avoided looking at Helena, aware she was newly anxious on my own behalf. If I had known we had to talk about people being beaten up, I would have whipped Laeta out of doors as soon as he arrived.

He pinched his mouth. "This is not for the watch."

"What makes a late-night street mugging peculiar? Homegoing revelers are always being attacked."

"He lives at the Palace. So he wasn't going home."

"Is that significant? Who is this man?"

I should have worked out the answer, if only from the high status of my visitor and his unhealthy excitement. Yet it was quite unexpected when Laeta informed me with an air of panache: "Anacrites, the Chief of Intelligence!"

SEVEN

"Anacrites?" I laughed briefly, though not at the spy's misfortune. "Then the first question you should be asking is whether I did it!"

"I did consider that," Laeta shot back.

"Next, the attack may be connected to his work. Maybe, unknown to you, I'm already involved."

"I understood that after he landed you in trouble on your Eastern trip, the last thing you would ever do is work with him."

I let that pass. "How did he get himself beaten up?"

"He must have gone out for some reason."

"He wasn't going home? He actually lives at the Palace?"

"It's understandable, Falco. He's a free man, but he holds a sensitive senior position. There must be considerations of security." Laeta had clearly given much thought to the luxury Anacrites had fixed up for himself: interservice jealousies were seething again. "I believe he has invested in a large villa at Baiae, but it's for holidays—which he rarely takes—and no doubt his retirement eventually—"

Laeta's obsession with his rival's private life intrigued

me—as did the amazing thought that Anacrites could somehow afford a villa at ultrafashionable Baiae. "How badly is he hurt?" I butted in.

"The message said he might not live."

"Message?"

"Apparently he was discovered and rescued by a householder who sent a slave to the Palatine this morning."

"This man identified Anacrites how?"

"That I don't know."

"Who has checked Anacrites' condition? You have not seen him?"

"No!" Laeta seemed surprised.

I restrained myself. This was looking like a mess. "Is he still with the charitable private citizen?" Silence confirmed it. "So! You believe Anacrites has been knocked about, and possibly murdered, by somebody or some group he was investigating. Official panic ensues. You, as Chief of Correspondence—a quite separate bureau—become involved." Or he involved himself, more likely. "Yet the Chief Spy himself has been left all day, perhaps without medical attention, and in a place where either he or the helpful citizen may be attacked again. Meanwhile nobody from the official side has bothered to find out how badly Anacrites is hurt, or whether he can speak about what happened?"

Laeta made no attempt to excuse the stupidity. He linked the fingertips of both hands. "Put like that," he said, with all the reasonableness of an important official who had been caught on the hop, "it sounds as if you and I should go straight there now, Falco."

I glanced across at Helena. She shrugged, resigned to it. She knew I hated Anacrites; she also knew that any wounded man needs help from someone sensible. One day the body bleeding in the gutter might be mine.

I had a further question: "Anacrites runs a full complement of agents; why are they not being asked to see to this?" Laeta looked shifty; I dropped in the real point: "Does the Emperor know what has occurred?"

"He knows." I could not decide whether to believe the clerk or not.

At least Laeta had brought an address. It took us to a medium apartment on the south end of the Esquiline—a once notorious distinct, now prettied up. A famous graveyard which had once possessed a filthy reputation had been developed into five or six public gardens. These still provided a venue for fornication and robbery, so the streets were littered with broken wine jugs and the locals walked about with their heads down, avoiding eye contact. Near the aqueducts some pleasant private homes braved it out. On the first level of living quarters in a four-story block, up a cleanly swept stair which was guarded by standard bay trees, lived a fusspot bachelor architect called Calisthenus. He had been trapped at home all day, unwilling to leave a mugging victim who might suddenly revive and make off with his rescuer's collection of Campanian cameos.

Laeta, with unnecessary caution, refused to identify himself. I did the talking: "I'm Didius Falco." I knew how to imbue that with authority; there was no need to specify what post I held. "We've come to carry off the mugging victim you so kindly took in—assuming he is still alive."

"Just about, but unconscious still." Calisthenus looked as if he thought he deserved our official attention. I contained my distaste. He was a thin, pale weeping willow who spoke in a tired drawl. He implied he had great ideas preoccupying him, as if he were a grand temple designer; in reality he probably built rows of little cobblers' shops.

"How did you come across him?"

"Impossible to avoid: he was blocking my exit."

"Had you heard any disturbance last night?"

"Not specially. We get a lot of noise around here. You learn to sleep through it." And to ignore trouble until they could not step over it.

We reached a small closet where a slave normally dossed down. Anacrites was lying on the meager pallet, while the slave watched him from a stool, looking annoyed that his blanket was being bled on. The spy was indeed unconscious. He was so ill that for a second I found him unrecognizable.

I spoke his name: no response.

There was a cloth in a bowl of cold water; I wiped his face. His skin was completely drained of color and felt icily moist. The pulse in his neck took careful finding. He had gone somewhere very far away, probably on a journey that would have no return.

I lifted the cloak covering him, his own garment presumably. He still wore last night's reddish tunic held together along all its seams with padded braid in dark berry colors. Anacrites always swanked in good stuff, though he avoided garish shades; he knew how to mix comfort with unobtrusiveness.

There were no bloodstains on the tunic. I found no stabbing wounds nor general signs of beating, though he did have identical bad bruises on both his upper arms as if he had been fiercely grabbed. The side of one shin had a small cut, new and about a digit long, from which ran a dried trickle of blood, thin and straight as a dead worm. No serious wounds accounted for his desperate condition until I drew back another cloth. It had been placed at the top of his head, where it formed a wad pressed against his skull.

I peeled it off gently. This explained everything. Someone with unpleasant manners had used Anacrites as a pestle in a very rough mortar, half scalping him. Through the mess of blood and hair I could see to the bone. The spy's cranium had been crushed in a way that had probably damaged his brain.

Calisthenus, the droopy architect, had reappeared in the doorway. He was holding Anacrites' belt; I recognized it from last night. "He was not robbed. There is a purse here." I heard it clink. Laeta grabbed the belt and searched the purse, finding just small change in normal quantities. I didn't bother. If he hoped to discover clues there, Laeta had never dealt with spies. I knew Anacrites would carry no documents, not even a picture of his girlfriend if he had one. If he ever carried a note-tablet he would have been too close even to scratch out a shopping list.

"How did you know he belonged in the Palace, Calisthenus?"

Calisthenus handed me a bone tablet, the kind many officials wear to impress innkeepers when they want a free drink. It gave Anacrites a false name which I had heard him use, and claimed he was a palace secretary; I knew that disguise too, and presumably so did whoever at the Palace received the architect's message.

"Was anything else with him?"

"No."

I lifted the Chief Spy's lifeless left wrist, splaying the cold fingers on mine. "What about his seal ring?" I knew he wore one; he used it to stamp passes and other documents. It was a large chalcedony oval engraved with two elephants entwining trunks. Calisthenus again shook his head. "Sure?" He was growing indignant as only an architect can (all that practice bluffing out overspent estimates and expressing disbelief that clients expect a house that looks like what they asked for . . .). "No disrespect, Calisthenus, but you might have thought the ring would cover any costs you incurred in tending the victim?"

"I can assure you—"

"All right. Settle down. You have rescued an important state servant; if it does impose any financial burden, send your invoice to the Palace. If the ring turns up it should be returned straightaway. Now if your boy can run out for a litter, my colleague here will take this poor fellow away."

Laeta looked put out that I assigned him to babyminding, but as we watched Anacrites being loaded into a hired chair for what could be his last journey anywhere, I explained that if I was being asked to work on the problem I had best nip off and start. "So what is required, Laeta? You want me to arrest whoever bopped him?"

"Well, that would be interesting, Falco." In fact Laeta sounded as if apprehending the villain was his least concern. I began to wonder if it was wise to let him escort the wounded spy back to the Palatine. "But what investigation do you think Anacrites was working on?"

"Ask the Emperor," I instructed.

"Vespasian is unaware of any major exercise that could be relevant." Did that mean the Emperor was being kept in ignorance—or simply that the intelligence network had no work? No wonder Anacrites always gave the impression he feared compulsory retirement was lurking just around the corner.

"Have you tried Titus?" The Emperor's elder son shared the business of government. He happily involved himself in secrets.

"Titus Caesar had nothing to add. However, it was he who suggested bringing in your good self."

"Titus knows I won't want to tangle with this!" I growled. "I told you: interview Anacrites' staff. If he was on to something, he will have had agents out in the field."

Laeta was frowning. "I have been trying, Falco. I cannot identify any agent he was using. He was very secretive. His record-keeping was eccentric to say the least. All the named employees on his bureau's roll seem very low-grade runners and messengers."

I laughed. "No operative who worked for Anacrites would be high class!"

"You mean he couldn't choose good people?" Laeta seemed pleased to hear it.

Suddenly I felt angry on the damned spy's behalf. "No, I mean that he was never given any money to pay for quality!" It did raise the question of how his own villa at Baiae had been acquired, but Laeta failed to spot the discrepancy. I calmed down. "Look, he was bound to be secretive; it comes with the job. Olympus! We're talking about him as if he were dead, but that's not so, not yet—"

"Well no indeed!" Laeta muttered. The litter-bearers were maintaining their normal impassive stare straight ahead. We both knew they were listening in. "Titus Caesar suggests we ensure no news of this attack leaks out." Good old Titus. Famous for flair—especially, in my experience, when organizing cover-ups. I had helped him fix a few of those.

I looked Laeta firmly in the eye. "This could have something to do with the dinner last night."

Reluctantly he admitted, "I was wondering about that."

"Why was it you invited me? I had the feeling there was something you wanted to discuss?" He pursed his lips. "Why were you keen to have me meet that senator?"

"Only my own general impression that Quinctius Attractus is getting above himself."

"Might Anacrites have been investigating Attractus?"

"What reason could he have?" Laeta would not even admit that Anacrites might have noticed the man's behavior just as he did.

"Spies don't have to have legitimate reasons; that's why they are dangerous."

"Well somebody has made this one quite a lot less dangerous, Falco."

"Perhaps," I suggested nastily, "I should be asking whether *you* got on with him badly." Since I knew better than to expect a sensible answer, I turned my attention back to the spy himself.

I wondered whether it would have been better to leave Anacrites discreetly at the house of Calisthenus, paying the architect to have the sick man nursed and to keep quiet about it. But if someone really dangerous was about, the Palace would be safer. Well, it ought to be. Anacrites could be the victim of a straightforward palace plot. I was sending him home to be looked after—that nasty ambiguous phrase. Maybe I was sending him home to be finished off.

Suddenly I felt a surge of defiance. I could see when I was being set up as the booby. Laeta loathed the spy, and his motives towards me were ambiguous. I didn't trust Laeta any more than Anacrites, but whatever was going on, Anacrites was in deep trouble. I had never liked him, or what he represented, but I understood how he worked: knee deep in the same middenheap as me.

"Laeta, Titus is right. This needs to be kept quiet until we know what it's about. And you know how rumors fly at the Palace. The best solution is to put Anacrites somewhere else where he can die in peace when he decides to go; then we can choose whether or not to announce it in the *Daily Gazette*. Leave everything to me. I'll carry him to the Temple of Aesculapius on Tiber Island, swear them to secrecy, but give them your name to inform you of developments."

Laeta thought hard, but submitted himself to my plan. Telling him that I had a few ideas of my own to pursue, I waved him off.

I then examined the doorway where Anacrites had been found. It was easy to see where and how he had been hurt; I discovered an ugly clump of blood and hair on the house wall. It was below chest height; the spy must have been bent over for some reason, though he carried no marks of any blow that would have doubled him up. I looked around, covering some distance, but found nothing significant.

The wounded man had been propped in a chair long enough; I told the bearers to come along with him. I did walk them to Tiber Island where I unloaded Anacrites and dismissed the chair. Then, instead of depositing the sick man amongst the clapped-out abandoned slaves who were being cared for at the hospital, I hired another chair. I led this one further west along the riverbank in the shadow of the Aventine. Then I took the unconscious spy to a private apartment where I could be sure of his good treatment.

He might yet die of last night's wound, but no one would be allowed to help him into Hades by other means.

EIGHT

Though I was a man on a charitable mission, my greeting was not promising. I had dragged Anacrites up three flights of stairs. Even unconscious he made trouble, buckling me under his weight and tangling his lifeless hands in the handrail just when I had got a good rhythm going. By the time I arrived upstairs I had no breath to curse him. I used my shoulder to knock open the door, a worn item that had once been red, now a faded pink.

A furious old biddy accosted us. "Who's that? Don't drag him in here. This is a peaceful neighborhood!"

"Hello, Mother."

Her companion was less blunt and more witty. "Jove, it's Falco! The little lost boy who needs a tablet round his neck to tell people where he lives! A tablet he can consult himself too, when he's sober enough to read it—"

"Shut up, Petro. I'm giving myself a hernia. Help me lie him down somewhere."

"Don't tell me!" raged my mother. "One of your friends has got himself in trouble and you expect me to look after him.

It's time you grew up, Marcus. I'm an old woman. I deserve a rest."

"You're an old woman who needs an interest in life. This is just the thing. He's not a drunk who fell under a cart, Ma. He's an official who has been cruelly attacked and until we discover the reason he has to be kept out of sight. I'd take him home but people may look for him there."

"Take him home? That poor girl you live with doesn't want to be bothered with this!" I winked at the unconscious Anacrites; he had just found himself a refuge. The best in Rome.

Petronius Longus, my big grinning friend, had been lounging in my mother's kitchen with a handful of almonds while he regaled Ma with the now famous finish of my big night out. Seeing my burden his mood quietened, then when he helped me shove Anacrites on a bed and he glimpsed the damage to the spy's head, Petro's face set. I thought he was going to say something but he buttoned his lip.

Ma stood in the doorway, arms folded; a small, still energetic woman who had spent her life nurturing people who didn't deserve it. Olive black eyes flicked over the spy with flashes like signal torches announcing an international disaster. "Well, this one won't be a lot of trouble. He's not going to be here long!"

"Do your best for the poor fellow, Ma."

"Don't I know him?" Petronius mumbled in a low voice to me.

"Speak up!" snapped Ma. "I'm not deaf and I'm not an idiot."

Petronius was frightened of my mother. He replied meekly, "It's Anacrites, the Chief Spy."

"Well he looks like a nasty dumpling that should have been eaten up yesterday," she sneered.

I shook my head. "He's a spy; that's his natural attitude."

"Well, I hope I'm not expected to work some miracle and save him."

"Ma, spare us the quaint plebeian cheerfulness!"

"Who's going to pay for the funeral?"

"The Palace will. Just take him in while he's dying. Give him some peace from whoever is trying to get him."

"Well; I can do that," she conceded grumpily.

I come from a large feckless family, who rarely permit themselves to perform deeds of kindness. When they do, any sensible conscious man wants to run a fast marathon in the other direction. It gave me a grim pleasure to leave Anacrites there. I hoped he came round and got thoroughly lectured—and I hoped that when it happened I would be present to watch.

I had known Petronius Longus since we were both eighteen. I could tell he was holding back like a nervous bride. As soon as we could, we edged to the door, then bidding Ma a fast farewell we were out of the apartment like the naughty schoolboys she reckoned we both still were. Her derogatory cries followed us downstairs.

Petronius knew I realized there was something he was bursting to say. In his usual aggravating way he kept it to himself as long as possible. I clamped my teeth and pretended not to be wanting to knock him into the copper shop opposite for keeping me on tenterhooks.

"Falco, everyone's talking about a body the Second Cohort found this morning." Petro was in the Fourth Cohort of vigiles, lording it over the Aventine. The Second were his counterparts who covered the Esquiline district.

"Whose body's that?"

"Looked like a street attack; happened last night. Man had his head stove in, in a remarkably violent manner."

"Rammed against a wall, perhaps?"

Petro appraised my suggestion. "Sounds as if it could have been."

"Know anybody friendly in the Second?"

"I thought you'd ask that," Petro replied. We were already making headway on the long route back to the Esquiline.

The Second Cohort's guardhouse lies on the way out to the Tiburtina Gate, close to the old Embankment which carries the Julian Aqueduct. It is situated between the Gardens of Pallentian and the Gardens of Lamia and Maia. A bosky spot—much frequented by elderly grubby prostitutes and persons trying to sell love potions and fake spells. We burrowed in our cloaks, walked quickly, and discussed the races loudly to reassure ourselves.

The Second Cohort were in charge of the Third and Fifth regions: some routine squalor, but also several large mansions with tricky owners who thought that the vigiles existed solely to protect them while they annoyed everyone else. The Second patrolled steep hills, run-down gardens, a big chunk of palace (Nero's Golden House) and a prestigious public building site (Vespasian's huge new amphitheatre). They faced some headaches, but were bearing up like Stoics. Their inquiry team were a group of relaxed layabouts whom we found sitting on a bench working out their night-shift bonus pay. They had plenty of time to tell us about their interesting murder case, though perhaps less energy for actually solving it.

"Io! He took a knock all right!"

"Bang on the knob?" Petro was doing the talking.

"Cracked open like a nut."

"Know who he is?"

"Bit of a mystery man. Want a look at him?"

"Maybe." Petronius preferred not to be that kind of sightseer, until it was unavoidable. "Can you show us the scene of the mugging?"

"Sure! Come and see the happy fellow first . . ."

Neither of us wanted to. Blood is bad enough. Spilt brains we avoid.

Luckily the Second Cohort turned out to be an outfit with

caring methods. While they waited for someone to come forward and claim the victim, they had slung his body in a sheet between two laundry poles, in the shed where they normally kept their fire engine. The pumping machine had been dragged out to the street where it was being admired by a large group of elderly men and small boys. Indoors, the corpse lay in a dim light. He had been neatly arranged and had his head in a bucket to contain leakage. The scene was one of respectful privacy.

I did not enjoy looking at the body. I hate becoming introspective. Life's bad enough without upsetting yourself drawing filthy parallels.

I had seen him before. I had met him briefly. I had talked to him—*too* briefly, perhaps. He was the cheerful lad at the dinner last night, the one in the oatmeal tunic who kept his own council in a diffident manner while watching the dancer Attractus had hired. He and I had later shared a joke, one I could not even now remember, as he helped me round up some slaves to shoulder my amphora of fish-pickle.

The victim was about my own age, build and bodyweight. Before some thug split his skull apart he had been intelligent and pleasant; I had had the impression he lived in the same world as me. Although Anacrites had pretended not to know who he was, I wondered if that had been a lie. An uneasy feeling warned me the dead man's presence at the dinner would turn out to be relevant. He left the Palatine at the same time as me. He must have been killed very soon afterwards. Whoever attacked him may well have followed us both from the Palace. He went off alone; I had been escorted by two hefty slaves with my amphora.

A nagging premonition suggested that had I also been unaccompanied, the body in the firefighters' shed could well have been mine.

NINE

Petronius and I made a cursory survey of the corpse, trying to ignore the head damage. Once again we found no other significant wounds. But a stain on the sheet which was cradling the body made me lift his right leg. Behind the knee I discovered a torn flap of skin—little more than a scratch, though it had bled freely because of its location, and it must have stung when he acquired it.

"Petro, what do you make of that?"

"Snagged himself on something?"

"I don't know . . . Anacrites also had a cut leg for some reason."

"You're scavenging, Falco. It's nothing."

"You're the expert!" That always worried him.

The Second Cohort had ascertained that the dead man's name was Valentinus. It had only taken a few moments of asking around locally. He had rented lodgings on the Esquiline, just ten strides from where somebody had battered him to death.

The neighbor who identified the body had told the Second that Valentinus had lived alone. His occupation was unknown.

He had gone out and about at different hours and quite often received callers of various kinds. He went to the baths, but avoided temples. He had never been any trouble to his neighbors. He gave no signs of enjoying himself much, nor had he ever been arrested by the vigiles. Until the night he died, he had always taken care of himself.

The Second led us to his apartment, which they had previously searched. It was a two-room fourth-floor lease in a dark tenement. Its furnishings were sparse but neat. The inner room held his bed, a couple of tunics dumped on a bench, his spare boots, and a few unrevealing personal items. The outer room contained a table, his smart red gloss food bowl, his winecup with a jocular message, his stylus and string-bound note tablet (clean of useful information), and a hook with his cloak and hat. Each room was lit by one high window, too far away to see out.

Petronius and I took a somber look around while the Second Cohort members tried not to show that they resented us checking their work. We found nothing remarkable, nothing to identify the man or his occupation. Even so, to me the style of his living quarters was depressingly familiar.

Then, as we were all trooping out again, I stopped. Light from our lantern happened to fall on the doorpost outside the apartment. There, somebody some years ago had drawn a neat pictogram of a single human eye. I knew the faded symbol. It's a sign informers use.

Petro and I stared at each other. Looking more keenly for clues, I noticed that although the doorlock appeared innocuous its fine bronze lion-headed key, which the Second had taken from the body, showed that instead of the common pin-tumbler fastener that most people use, Valentinus had invested in a devious iron rotary lock, which would be difficult to pick or force without the proper key. Then, crouching near ground level, Petro spotted two tiny metal tacks, one knocked into the door itself, one in the frame. A classic tell-tale: tied between the tacks had been a human hair. It had been broken, presumably when the Second first entered.

"No offense, lads, but we'd better think about this again," said Petro, looking virtuous.

He and I went back inside. Quietly and carefully we searched the room afresh, as if Valentinus had been a pal of ours. This time the Second watched us in fascination while we took the place apart.

Under the bed, lashed to its frame, we found a sword capable of quick release by pulling one end of a knot. Although the windows looked out of reach, if you dragged the table to one, or climbed on the upended bench below the other, you could reach outside and discover that somebody had banged in a couple of useful hooks. One had an amphora of good Setinum red wine hung up to warm in the sunlight; the other, through which a lithe man might just wriggle, had a stout rope neatly rolled up but long enough to reach a balcony roof on the story below. Under most of the floorboards lurked nothing of interest, though we did find some letters from his family (parents and a cousin, who lived a few miles from Rome). We discovered no money. Like me, Valentinus probably kept a bankbox in the Forum, with its access number stored securely in his head.

One floorboard in the bedroom actually had nails with false heads. It came up quite smoothly when you pulled it up by way of a knot, waggled your fingers underneath the wood and released a specially constructed bar that pivoted aside. Built under the board was a small, locked wooden compartment. Eventually I located the key, concealed in a hollow carved under the seat of the stool in the outer room. In his secret box the dead man had kept spare, succinct notes about his work. He was a neat, regular record-keeper. We already knew that: Valentinus' hat had been double lined; inside it Petronius had found expense sheets of a type I knew all too well.

Some work that the dead man did, probably from necessity, was just the kind of dreary intrigue I often had to carry out myself for private clients. The rest was different. Valentinus had been more than an informer, he was a spy. He was claiming for many hours spent on surveillance. And although there were no names for the people he had been recently watching, the latest entries on his claim sheet were all code-named "Corduba." Corduba is the capital of Romanized Baetica.

We reckoned we knew who had commissioned this work. One of the expense claims from his hat had already been stamped and approved for payment. The stamp was a large oval, featuring two elephants with entwined trunks: Anacrites' chalcedony seal.

TEN

Petronius left me in the Forum. The task was mine now. Facing up to it with my usual compulsion and stamina, I went home to bed.

Next day, striking while some impetus was with me, I walked back to the Forum, up through the Cryptoporticus where the scoffing Praetorians knew me well enough to admit me after a few threats and jeers, then into the old Palace. I had no need of Claudius Laeta to advise me who to interview or to smooth the way. I possessed other contacts. Mine were probably no more reliable than the devious correspondence chief, but I was attached to them on the usual perverse grounds that make you trust men you have known for some time even when you suspect that they lie, cheat and steal.

Momus was a slave overseer. He looked as healthy as a side of condemned beef and as dangerous as an escaped gladiator on the run. His eyes were moist with some infection, his body was scarred, his face was a fascinating gray shade as if he had not been outside for the past decade. Being an overseer was something he no longer worked at very hard; he left the rituals of slave market, placement, whipping and bribe-taking to others.

Momus now held some nebulous position at the Palace; in effect, he was another spy. He did not work for Anacrites. He did not care for Anacrites either. But in a bureaucracy every employee has to have another officer who reports on him to his superiors. Anacrites was attached to the Praetorian Guard but worked directly for the Emperor, so he was judged by Vespasian himself when it came to matters of reprimand or reward. Both Anacrites and I believed Momus to be the nark who told the Emperor what he should think of the Chief Spy's work. That meant Anacrites despised and loathed him, but it made Momus a friend of mine.

I told him the Chief Spy had been seriously hurt. It was supposed to be a secret but Momus already knew. I guessed he had also heard that Anacrites was supposed to be hidden away at the Temple of Aesculapius on Tiber Island—but maybe he had not yet found out that the victim was really laid up on the Aventine with Ma.

"Something funny's going on, Momus."

"What's new, Falco?"

"This attack is supposed to relate to intelligence work. Nobody even knows what Anacrites was investigating. I'm trying to track down his agents, or records of what he's been involved with—"

"You'll have a job." Momus enjoyed disheartening me. "Anacrites is like an Athenian vote machine."

"That's a bit subtle for me."

"You know; it's a gadget to prevent nobbling. When they used open jars fistfuls of votes used to go astray. So now the voters put balls in the top of a closed box; they wiggle down inside and then the election results pop out at the bottom. No fraud—and no fun, either. Trust the bloody Greeks."

"What's this to do with Anacrites?"

"People pile information into his brain and if he's in the

right mood he farts out a report. In between, everything is locked up."

"Well it looks as if the next person he blows a report at could be Charon the ferryman."

"Oh dear, poor Charon!" sneered Momus, with the cheery expression of a man who was just thinking that if Anacrites had sailed away on the decrepit punt to Hades, he might immediately apply for Anacrites' job. Some state employees love to hear about a colleague's premature demise.

"Charon's going to be busy," I commented. "Villains have been cracking spies' heads all over the Esquiline. There was also a pleasant lad who used to do surveillance work."

"Do I know him, Falco?"

"Valentinus."

Momus let out a snarl of disgust. "Oh Jupiter! Dead? That's terrible. Valentinus who lived on the Esquiline? Oh no; he was class, Falco. He must have been the best snuffler Anacrites used."

"Well, he's not on the staff roll."

"Better sense. He stayed freelance. Self-employed. I used him myself sometimes."

"What for?"

"Oh . . . tracking down runaways." The alleged overseer looked vague. I reckoned whatever Momus used Valentinus for would give me a queasy stomach. I decided not to know.

"Was he good?"

"The best. Straight, fast, decent to deal with, and accurate."

I sighed. More and more this sounded like a man I would have liked to share a drink with. I could have made friends with Valentinus last night at the dinner, if I had only realized. Then maybe if we had rolled out of the Palace together like cronies, events might have turned out differently for the freelance. Together we might have fought off his attackers. It could have saved his life.

Momus was eyeing me up. He knew I had an interest. "You going to sort this out, Falco?"

"It looks like a murky fishpond. Reckon I stand a chance?"

"No. You're a clown."

"Thanks, Momus."

"My pleasure."

"Don't enjoy yourself too much with the hard-hitting insults; I may prove you wrong."

"Virgins might stay chaste!"

I sighed. "Heard anything about any dirty goings-on in Baetica?"

"No. Baetica's all sunshine and fish-sauce."

"Know anything about the Society of Olive Oil Producers, then?"

"Load of old belchers who meet in the basement and plot how they can straighten out the world?"

"They didn't seem to be plotting last evening, just stuffing their faces. Oh, and most were trying to ignore a group of genuine Baetican visitors."

"That's them!" grinned Momus. "They pretend to love anything Hispanic—but only if it can be served on a dish." I gathered that the Society was officially deemed innocuous. As usual, Momus knew more about it than a slave overseer should. "Anacrites got himself voted into the club so he could keep an eye on them."

"Was political scheming likely?"

"Piddle! He just liked feeding at their well-filled manger."

"Well as anarchists they didn't look very adventurous."

"Of course not," scoffed Momus. "I haven't noticed the world being straightened out, have you?"

There was not much else Momus could tell me about Anacrites or Valentinus—or at least nothing he was prepared to reveal. But with his knowledge of the unfree workforce he did know which usher had been running the dinner for the Society. While I was at the Palace I looked out this man and talked to him.

He was a lugubrious slave called Helva. Like most palace types he looked oriental in origin and gave the impression he misunderstood whatever was being said to him, probably on purpose. He had an official job, but was trying to improve himself by sucking up to men of status; the Baetican Society members obviously saw him as a soft touch to be sneered at and put upon.

"Helva, who did the organizing for this exclusive club?"

"An informal committee." Unhelpful: clearly he could see *my* status did not call for an ingratiating style.

"Who was on it?"

"Whoever bothered to turn up when I insisted someone tell me what was wanted."

"Some names would help," I suggested pleasantly.

"Oh, Laeta and his deputies, then Quinctius Attractus—"

"Is he an overweight senator who likes holding court?"

"He has interests in Baetica and he's the big mover in the Society."

"Is he Spanish by origin?"

"Not the slightest. Old patrician family."

"I should have known. I understood the Society's real links with Hispania are defunct and that members try to deter provincials from attending?"

"Most do. Attractus is more enlightened."

"You mean, he sees the Society as his personal platform for glory and he likes to suggest he can work wonders in Rome for any visitors from Spain? Is that why he hogs a private room?"

"Well unofficially. Other members annoy him by barging in."

"They think he's someone to annoy, do they?"

It looked to me as if Attractus, and possibly his Baetican friends, had been under observation—probably by both Anacrites and his agent. Was Anacrites suspicious of something they were up to? Did Attractus or the Baetican group want to wipe him out as a result? It looked all too obvious if they were the attackers. They surely must realize questions would be asked. Or was Attractus so arrogant he thought the attacks could be got away with?

Needing to think about that, I went back to my original question. "Who else organizes events?"

"Anacrites—"

"*Anacrites?* He never struck me as a dinner party planner! What was his role?"

"Be reasonable, Falco! He's a spy. What do you think his role is? On rare occasions when he exerts himself, he causes upsets. He really enjoys carping about the guests other members bring. *'If you knew what I know, you wouldn't mix with so-and-so . . .'* All hints, of course; he never says why."

"Master of the nonspecific insult!"

"Then if ever I upset him he'll query the accounts for the previous party and accuse me of diddling them. The rest of the time he does nothing, or as little as possible."

"Did he have anything special to say about yesterday?"

"No. Only that he wanted space for himself and his guest in the private room."

"Why?"

"Usual reason: it was bound to offend Attractus."

"And the spy's guest was Valentinus?"

"No, it was the senator's son," said Helva. "The one who just came back from Corduba."

"Aelianus?" Helena's brother! Well that explained how Aelianus had wheedled his way in—on the tunic tail of the Chief Spy. Unhealthy news.

"I know the family—I didn't realize Anacrites and Aelianus were on such good terms."

"I don't suppose they are," Helva remarked cynically. "I expect one of them thought the other would do him some good—and if you know Anacrites you can bet which way the benefit was supposed to flow!"

It left an unanswered question. "You knew who I meant when I mentioned Valentinus. Who brought him last night?"

"No one." Helva gave me a narrow look. He was trying to work out how much I knew. All I had to do now was work out what dubious situation I was reckoned to know *about,* and I could press him hard. Until then I was likely to miss something important.

"Look, was Valentinus an official member of the Society?" Helva must have known I could check up; he reluctantly shook his head. "So how much money did he slip you to let him in?"

"That's a disgusting suggestion; I'm a reputable state servant—"

I named the sum that I would have offered and Helva in his gloomy-faced way told me I was a mean bastard who gave bribery a bad name.

I decided to appeal to his better nature, if he had one. "I don't suppose you've heard—Anacrites has been badly hurt."

"Yes. I heard it's a big secret."

Then I told him that Valentinus was actually dead. This time his face fell. All slaves can spot serious trouble. "So this is bad, Helva. Time to cough, or it will be the Guards you have to talk to. Had Valentinus paid you to admit him to any previous dinners?"

"Once or twice. He knew how to behave himself. He could fit in. Besides, I had seen Anacrites wink at him so I assumed it was something I was supposed to allow."

"How did he wangle himself a place in the private room?"

"Pure skill," said Helva, frowning with admiration. "He picked up one of the Baeticans as they arrived in the lobby and sauntered in chattering to him." I knew the trick. A few minutes discussing the weather can admit you to many private parties. "Quinctius Attractus was not officially supposed to reserve that room for himself. If there were free places anyone could take them."

"So he didn't object to Valentinus?"

"He couldn't. Any more than he could complain about being landed with Anacrites. They took their couches among his party as if it were a coincidence, and he had to put up with it. Anyway, Attractus is not observant. He was probably so busy getting hot under the tunic about Anacrites, he never noticed Valentinus was there too."

I wondered if the blinkered senator had noticed me.

I asked Helva about the entertainment. "Who booked the musicians?"

"I did."

"Is that routine? Do you pick the performers yourself?"

"Quite often. The members are only really interested in food and wine."

"Is there always a Spanish dancer?"

"It seems appropriate. She's not really Spanish, incidentally." Just like most "Thracian" gladiators, "Egyptian" fortunetellers, and "Syrian" flute players. Come to that, most of the "Spanish hams" bought at food markets were previously seen skipping around pig farms in Latium.

"She? Is it always the same one?"

"She's not bad, Falco. The members feel reassured if they recognize the entertainment. They don't watch her much anyway; they only care about their food and drink."

"Attractus was boasting he paid for her. Is that usual?"

"He always does. It's supposed to be a generous gesture—well, it shows he's rich, and of course he gets to have the dancing performed first wherever he's dining himself. The other members are happy to let him contribute, and his guests are impressed."

He told me the girl's name was Perella. Half an hour later

I was bracing myself to square up to the immaculate body that I had last seen in hunting gear.

I had a slight surprise. I was expecting to meet the dashing Diana with the blue-black hair who had elected to be so rude to me. To my surprise Perella, who was supposed to be the dancer who performed regularly at the Society of Olive Oil Producers of Baetica, was a short, stout, surly blonde.

ELEVEN

Blonde" was putting it kindly. She had hair the texture of mule fodder and about the same shade. It looked as if she styled it once a month then just poked in more bone pins when ends worked loose. You could see why independent-minded pieces of the fantastic coiffure might want to make a break for freedom. The high-piled construction looked as if she was keeping three white mice and her dowry in it.

Lower down, the scenario improved somewhat. I won't say she was tasty, but her person was clean and tidy. As a chaste, ethereal moon goddess she would be a disaster, though as a companion in a wine bar she might be cracking good fun. She was of an age where you could rely on her having had a fair old amount of experience—in almost anything.

"Oh! Am I in the right place? I'm looking for Perella. Are you her friend?"

"I'm her!" So Perella was definitely the wrong dancer. She was putting out a smile that she meant to be winsome: wrong assumption, but I could cope with that. "What might you be looking for, centurion?"

"Chaste conversation, sweetheart." She knew better than to

believe it. Her outlook on society was mature. "The name's Falco." It meant nothing to her, apparently. Well, sometimes it was best if my reputation had not gone before me. Critics can be uncouth. "I expect you'd like my credentials. Do you know Thalia, the snake dancer at Nero's Circus?"

"Never heard of her." So much for my guaranteed entrée to the world of Terpsichore.

"Well if you knew her, she'd vouch for me."

"As what?" asked the dancer, pointedly.

"As an honest man on an important quest with a few simple queries to put to you."

"Such as?"

"Why wasn't a luscious piece like you dancing at the dinner for the Society of Baetican Oil Producers two nights ago?"

"Why do you ask?" leered Perella. "Were you there hoping to watch me—or were they only letting in the rich, handsome ones?"

"I was there."

"I always told them they had a slack door policy."

"Don't be cruel! Anyway, you're a regular. What happened to you that night?"

Getting tough actually softened her up. "Don't ask me," she confided in a cheerful tone. "The message just came that I was not wanted so I stayed in and put my feet up."

"Who sent you the message?"

"Helva presumably."

"No. Helva still thinks you did the act. He told me to ask you about it."

Perella squared up, looking angry. "Then somebody's messed me about!"

The thought crossed my mind that Helva himself might have decided to employ a higher-class dancer and that he had been scared of telling Perella—but then he would hardly have sent me along here to give him away. "Who was it came to warn you off, Perella? Can you give a description?"

"No idea. I never took any notice of him." I waited while she scanned her memory, a slow process apparently—though I did wonder if she was considering whether she wanted to tell me the truth. She looked older than a dancer should, with coarser skin and bonier limbs. Close to, these performers are never as refined as they appear when in costume. "Dark fellow," she said eventually. "Had a few years on him." Sounded like one of Diana's tame musicians.

"Seen him before?"

"Not to remember."

"And what exactly did he say?"

"That Helva apologized, but the bloody Baetican trough-nuzzlers had decided not to have music."

"Any reason?"

"None. I thought either the new Emperor had put his foot down about them using the rooms for enjoying themselves, or they had run out of money and couldn't find my fee."

"They looked a well-packed lot."

"Mean, though!" replied Perella, with feeling. "Most of them spend the whole time moaning how much the dinners cost them; they wouldn't have entertainers at all. There's a swank who pays—"

"Quinctius Attractus?"

"That's him. He usually pays up, but it takes several tries to get it and there's never a sniff of a tip!"

"So he could decide to hire his own girl, if he wanted to?"

"The bastard could," Perella agreed sourly.

"Would he bother to tell Helva?"

"No. He's a nob. He doesn't understand about organization. He wouldn't think of it."

"And would the girl be able to get in without Helva noticing that she wasn't you?"

"Helva's so shortsighted you have to get an inch from his nose before he can see who you are. Anyone who rattled a tambourine would sail straight in."

So there had been a set-up. It came as no surprise that the so-called "good girl from Hispalis" was not as good as she pretended. In my experience good girls never are.

Perella had nothing more to tell me. I was left with a loose end: unknown entertainers had deliberately muscled in and taken the usual dancer's place. They knew enough to use Helva's name in a convincing fake message. Knew it, or had been told what to say. Were they specifically booked by Attractus, or did he just accept that Helva had acquired them? And why? I would be asking the senator, but somehow I guessed in advance that tracing the lovely Diana and her two dark-skinned musicians would be next to impossible.

They could have been sent to the dinner by Anacrites. They could have been infiltrated by someone outside (a jealous would-be member of the dining club, perhaps?). Or they could have come of their own accord. They might have nothing at all to do with the attacks on Anacrites and Valentinus. Even though circumstances had made them look suspicious, they might simply be struggling performers who had failed to persuade Helva to give them an audition, and who then used their initiative.

But I told Perella she had been trounced by a very slick rival, and probably one who had had more than Spanish dancing in mind. Perella shoved a couple of new hairpins into her tumbling scarecrow coiffure, and gave me an unfathomable look. She threatened to "sort" the girl from Hispalis. She sounded as if she meant it too. I left her my address in case she had any success.

"By the way, Perella, if you do meet this girl be careful how you tangle with her. It looks as if she was involved in a killing that night—and in a nasty attack on the Chief Spy."

Perella went white. "Anacrites?"

As she stood staring I added, "You'd do best to avoid her. Finding this one is a job for an agent—and a good one at that."

"And you reckon you're up to it, Falco?" Perella asked dryly.

I gave her my best smile.

I was not yet ready for another conversation with Laeta, so I escaped from the Palace, ran some domestic errands, then went home to Helena for lunch. Fried anchovies in a plain wine sauce. Unassuming but tasty.

Helena told me I had received a message of my own that morning. It was from Petronius. He had found out something useful: I went straight out after eating, taking Helena with me for the exercise, and also Nux in the vain hope that while the scruffy hound was careering around in circles we might lose her somewhere. Petro was at home, off duty. Helena went off with his wife while Nux and I found my old crony in the yard at the back, doing woodwork.

"This is for you, Falco. I hope you're grateful."

"What is it—a small coffin or a large brooch box?"

"Stop playing the fool. It's going to be a cradle." Nux jumped in to try it. Petro turfed her out again.

"It's going to be a good one then," I smiled. That was true. Petro enjoyed carpentry and was skilled at it. Always methodical and practical, he had a decent respect for wood. He was making a bed where eventually the sturdy unborn one who was already kicking me in the ribs every night would be safe; it had half-moon rockers, a knob to hang a rattle on, and a canopy over the pillow end. I felt touched.

"Yes, well; it's for the baby, so if your lousy behavior makes Helena Justina leave you, this cradle will have to go with her."

"I doubt it," I scoffed. "If she flits she'll leave the baby behind." Petronius looked horrified, so I carried on appalling him: "Helena only likes children when they are old enough to hold adult conversations. The bargain is, she'll carry my offspring and give it birth but only on condition I'm there to defend her from the midwife and that afterwards I bring it up myself until it's old enough to pay its own tavern bills."

Petronius gave me a piercing stare; then he laughed weakly. "You maniac! I thought you were serious . . ." He lost interest, which saved me having to disillusion him with the news that I meant what I said—and so did Helena. "Listen, Falco, I've come up with some evidence for you: the Second must want to redeem their reputation after missing all that stuff in Valentinus' apartment. They went back to the crime scene this morning and did a hands and knees creep."

I joined him in chuckling at the thought of his luckless colleagues enduring stones in the kneecap and backache. "Anything turn up?"

"Could be. They want to know if we think this is relevant—"

Petronius Longus placed a small item on his sawing bench. I blew the road dust off it, then sighed quietly. This was relevant enough to identify the attackers: it was a small golden arrow, as neat as a toy but dangerously sharp. On its tip was a rusty stain that was probably blood. Remembering the small leg wounds carried by both Anacrites and Valentinus, I guessed that both victims had been surprised by being shot in the calf from behind. The toy arrow would sting enough to bother them, then when they stooped to investigate they were rushed, grabbed, and run hard against a nearby wall.

Helena Justina had come out behind us, unnoticed. "Oh dear!" she exclaimed, ever one with the unwelcome insight. "I suppose that belonged to your mysterious Spanish dancer. Don't tell me it's just been found in a compromising position at the scene of a crime?"

Gloomily we confirmed it.

"Ah never mind, Marcus," Helena then chivvied me kindly. "Cheer up, my love! You ought to have lots of fun with this—

it looks as though somebody is setting you up against a beautiful female spy!"

Naturally I retorted that I was not in the mood for clichés—though I have to admit my heart took an uneasy lurch.

TWELVE

There was no chance of interviewing the girl from Hispalis. I didn't even know her name—or her alias. If she was sharp she would have left Rome. Smirking, Petronius Longus promised to place her description on his list of wanted suspects. He offered to subject her to a personal interrogation. I knew what that meant.

I told him not to exert himself; I would probe her secrets myself. Petronius, who believed that men with pregnant wives were bound to be looking for extra-domestic exercise, twinkled wisely and promised to inform me the minute the beauteous Diana came his way. At this point Helena said coldly that she would take herself home.

I went to see Quinctius Attractus.

When a case involves a senator, I always start at the top. I don't mean this was a step towards clearing up uncertainties. Not at all. Interviewing a member of Rome's revered patrician order was likely to introduce pure chaos of the kind that is believed by some philosophers to comprise the outermost limits of the eternally whirling universe: a vortex of limitless and fathomless darkness. In short, political ignorance, commercial deceit, and blatant lies.

Even provincials among you will deduce that M. Didius Falco, the intrepid informer, had posed questions to senators before.

You'll spot this too: I went to see Quinctius Attractus to get any whirling vortex straight out of the way.

Once I had managed to impress the doorkeeper with my rank—well, once I had slipped him half a denarius—I was allowed to step inside away from a sharp April wind that was darting through the city streets. Attractus lived in an imposing house, groaning with art torn from more ancient and more refined civilizations than our own. Egyptian turquoise and enamel vied for space with Thracian gold and Etruscan bronze. Pentellic marble crowded his corridors. Forests of plinths bore up porphyries and alabasters. Racks bowed beneath uncatalogued rows of vases and craters, against which lolled unmounted wall plaques and fabulous old armor which must have been plundered from many famous battlefields.

Quinctius Attractus condescended to come to his public rooms to meet me. I remembered the heavy build and weathered country countenance from two nights ago; today I was being given the full urban look—the statesman putting an invisible peg on his nose so he could follow the old Roman tradition and be nobly at home to the unwashed.

Our interview was hardly private. In every archway lurked a toga-twitcher just itching to dart out and pluck straight a pleat. They kept him perfect. His boot-thongs were aligned. His sparse curls gleamed, rigid with pomade. If a finger-ring slipped sideways a lithe slave nipped forwards to straighten it. Every time he walked three paces his purple-striped garments all had to be realigned on his wide shoulders and fat arms.

If I hated this parade when he first came to receive me, I felt utter frustration once he started to talk. It was all condescension and empty guff. He was the type who liked to lean back slightly, gazing above his companion's head, while intoning nonsense. He reminded me of a barrister who had just lost a case, coming out into the Forum knowing he will have to face a tricky interview. I said I had come to discuss the Oil Producers' dinner—and he seemed to be expecting it.

"The Society—oh, it's just a meeting place for friends—"

"Some of the friends met very nasty accidents afterwards, senator."

"Really? Well, Anacrites will vouch for us all—"

"Afraid not, sir. Anacrites has been badly hurt."

"That so?" One of his flapping footmen found it necessary to rush up and straighten a thread of fringe on a heavily decorated tunic sleeve.

"He was attacked the night of the dinner. He may not survive."

"I'm shocked." Checking the fall of his toga, he looked as if he had just heard about a minor skirmish between locals in some remote area. Then he noticed me watching and his fleshy jowls set for a ritual senatorial platitude: "Terrible. A sound man."

I swallowed it whole, then tried to fix the slithery senator to a firm base: "Were you aware that Anacrites was the Chief Spy?"

"Oh certainly. Bound to. You can't have a man like that attending private functions unless everybody knows what his position is. Men would wonder. Men wouldn't know when it was safe to speak freely. Be a shambles."

"Oh? Does the Society of Baetican Olive Oil Producers often discuss sensitive issues, then?" He stared at my effrontery. I hadn't finished yet: "You're telling me the Chief of Intelligence was openly invited to join your group, in order to suborn him? I'm willing to bet you allowed Anacrites membership without the indignity of subscription fees!" A nice life, for a spy who was gregarious.

"How formal is this?" Attractus demanded suddenly. I knew the type. He had assumed that his rank gave him immunity from questioning. Now I was being nasty, and he couldn't believe it was happening. "You say you're from the Palace—do you have some kind of docket?"

"I don't need one. My commission is from the highest quarters. Responsible people will cooperate."

Just as suddenly he changed attitude again: "Ask away then!" he boomed—still not seriously expecting I would dare.

"Thank you." I controlled my temper. "Senator, at the last assembly of the Society for the Olive Oil Producers of Baetica you dined in a private room with a mixed group, including several Baeticans. I need to identify your visitors, sir." Our eyes met. "For elimination purposes."

The old lie proved sufficient, as it usually does. "Business acquaintances," he guffed with an offhand air. "See my secretary if you must have names."

"Thanks. I have the names; we were introduced," I reminded him. "I need to know more about them."

"I can vouch for them." More vouching! I was used to the fine notion that the slightest trade connection made for complete blood-brotherhood. I knew how much faith to place in it too.

"They were your guests that evening. Was there any special reason for entertaining those particular men that particular night?"

"Routine hospitality. It is appropriate," mouthed Quinctius sarcastically, "that when senior men from Baetica visit Rome they should be made welcome."

"You have strong personal connections with that province?"

"I own land there. I have a wide range of interests, in fact. My son has just been appointed quaestor to the province too."

"That's a fine honor, sir. You must be proud of him." I didn't mean the compliment, and he didn't bother acknowledging it. "So you take the lead in encouraging local business interests in Rome? You're a *proxenos*." The handy Greek term might impress some people, but not Attractus. I was referring to the useful arrangements all overseas traders make to have their interests represented on foreign soil by some local with influence—a local who, in the good old Greek tradition, expects them to grease his palm.

"I do what I can." I wondered what form *that* took. I also wondered what the Baeticans were expected to provide in return. Simple gifts like the rich produce of their country—or something more complex? Cash in hand, perhaps?

"That's commendable, sir. Going back to the dinner, Anacrites was also present. And a couple of others, including myself."

"That may be so. There were spare couches. I had intended to take my son and a friend of his, but that kind of occasion can be too stiff for the young so they were excused."

"One guest was Camillus Aelianus, the son of Vespasian's friend Verus."

"Oh yes. Back from Corduba. Straightforward lad; knows what he's doing." Quinctius was just the sort to approve of that pompous young bigot.

"Perhaps you remember one other man. I need to identify what he was doing there—reclining on the right-hand end couch, opposite Anacrites—quiet fellow; hardly spoke. Did you know him?"

"Never even noticed him." Thirty years in politics made it impossible for me to tell whether Quinctius Attractus was honest. (After thirty years in politics, almost certainly he was not.) "What's his significance?"

"Nothing anymore: the man is dead." If he had anything to do with killing Valentinus, he was good; he showed complete indifference. "And finally, may I ask if you knew the entertainers, sir? There was a girl who danced, with a pair of

Libyan-style accompanists—I believe you paid their fee. Did you know them personally?"

"Certainly not! I don't mingle with tarts and lyre-players."

I smiled. "I meant, did you book them for the dinner specially, sir?"

"No," he said, still contemptuous. "There are people to do that. I pay for the musicians; I don't need to know where they come from."

"Or know their names?"

He growled. I thanked him for his patience. Still playing the big man in Baetica, he asked me to report any developments. I promised to keep him informed, though I had no intention of it. Then, since he had mentioned that I might, I went to see his secretary.

Correspondence and record-keeping at the house of Quinctius Attractus was conducted by a typical Greek scribe in a tunic almost as neat as his master's. In a clean little office, he catalogued the senator's life in curious detail. A cynic might wonder whether this implied that the senator feared he might one day be called to account. If so, he must be very worried indeed. Any tribunal investigating Quinctius was going to expire under the weight of written evidence.

"The name's Falco." The scribe made no move to note me down but he looked as if he would later list me under *"Visitors: Uninvited, Category: Dubious."* "I'm inquiring about the senator's guests at the last dinner for the oily Baeticans?"

"You mean the Society of Olive Oil Producers?" he corrected humorlessly. "I have details, certainly."

"His honor says you will tell me."

"I shall have to confirm that."

"You do so then."

I sat on a stool among racks of locked scroll boxes while the slave disappeared to check. Don't ask me how I know that the boxes were locked.

When he came back his manner was even more pedantic, as if he had been told I was trouble. He unlocked a silver box and removed a document. I was not allowed to crane over his shoulder, but I could see the script. It was a perfect, neutral cursive hand that could not have changed since he first learned to copy by rote.

He read out five names: *"Annaeus Maximus, Licinius Rufius, Rufius Constans, Norbanus, Cyzacus."* Then he corrected himself: "No; Rufius Constans was not at the dinner. He is the grandson of Licinius. He had gone to the theater, I understand, with my master's son." That almost sounded as if he were reciting something somebody had drummed into him.

"How old are these two lads?"

"Quinctius Quadratus is twenty-five. The Baetican boy looks younger." Hardly adolescents then. The younger Quinctius would have just been elected to the Senate if he was to be a provincial quaestor as his father had boasted.

"Is the senator a stern father? Was he annoyed by them bunking off to a play?"

"Not at all. He encourages their friendship, and their independence. They are both promising young men."

I grinned. "That fine phrase can mean they are promising to cause trouble!" The secretary gazed at me coldly. He had never been trained to gossip. I felt like a slug spotted taking a stroll across a particularly elegant dish of dressed salad. "The Baetican visitors make an interesting list. We have an Annaeus—presumably from the same Corduban family as the famous Seneca's?" I had picked that up from Laeta at the dinner. "And who else? A couple of men from the provincial merchant class? What can you tell me?"

"I cannot give personal information!" he cried.

"I don't need to know who slept with a flute girl or the state of their impetigo! Why were they welcome guests of a Roman senator?"

Looking distasteful the slave squeezed out: "My master is

a very important figure in Baetica. The first of those I mentioned, Annaeus and Licinius, are large landholders in Corduba." Those would be the favored pair who had been dining either side of Attractus at the dinner. "The last two are businessmen from further south, involved with transportation, I believe."

"Norbanus and Cyzacus?" The two who kept their heads down, conversing among themselves. Lower-class—perhaps even ex-slaves. "They are shippers?"

"So I understand," agreed the secretary, as if I was making him swear an oath to undertake physical torments and huge financial expense on behalf of an extremely bad-tempered god.

"Thank you," I answered heavily.

"Is that all?"

"I need to interview these men. Are they staying here?"

"No."

"Can you give me the address of their lodging in Rome?"

"They *were* staying here," admitted the cautious Greek reluctantly. "All of them left Rome very early today."

I raised an eyebrow gently. "Really? How long had they been with you?"

"Just a few days." The secretary made an effort not to look uncomfortable.

"How many is a few?"

"About a week."

"*Only a week?* Wasn't their decision rather sudden?"

"I could not say." I would have to ask the house steward if I wanted precise details of the Baeticans' original booking—but private informers are not given access to the domestic staff in a senator's house.

"Is it possible to interview the senator's son?"

"Quinctius Quadratus left for Corduba as well."

"Was that planned?"

"Of course. He is taking up his new provincial post."

I could not fault the newly fledged quaestor—but how

many provincials, especially men of status, would make a long sea trip to Rome then skip for home almost immediately, without fully enjoying the sights, exploring the possibilities for social advancement, and making sure they stayed away long enough to make those at home believe they had conquered Roman society?

As tourists their behavior was highly suspicious. They might as well have left behind a wall plaque telling me these gadfly Corduban businessmen were up to no good.

THIRTEEN

That night I took Helena to the refined Capena Gate district to dine at the large, slightly faded villa which had been her family home. It was time her mother had another chance to rage at her about the poor arrangements we were making for the baby's birth and upbringing. (Julia Justa had a well-rehearsed script on this subject.) And I wanted to see her father. I like to keep my senators in sets.

As usual, before my official meeting I made sure that Helena's papa and I had conspired so our stories would match. I found Decimus Camillus Verus at the baths we both frequented. He was a tall, stooping figure with thinning, spiked hair, who already looked hunted even before I invited myself to dinner and explained that I now required him to play the heavy father to one of his rebellious sons.

"This is imperial business. I need to interview Aelianus. I'm telling you in advance so you can make sure he'll be there!"

"You overestimate my paternal authority, Marcus."

"You're a Stoic!" I grinned and explained the situation.

Then I gave Camillus a stiff bout of swordplay to make him feel even more despondent, and we parted friends.

His attitude to me, whom many in his place would have loathed, was open and amiable: "I have no objection to you providing me with grandchildren, Marcus. A new generation is my one hope of getting someone on my side!"

"Oh *I'm* with you, senator!" In fact we both knew his relationship with me (like mine with his daughter) was the main reason the illustrious Camillus had a hard time at home.

Neither of the young Camillus brothers, Aelianus and Justinus, were at dinner. They were bright fellows in their early twenties brought up to have moderate habits—so naturally they were out on the town. As a sober citizen of thirty-three, approaching the grave honor of Roman fatherhood, I tried not to look as if I wished I were out there with them.

"Is Justinus still keen on the theater?" Their youngest rascal had taken up leering after actresses.

"They both like to keep me worried!" Camillus senior reported dryly. He kept his troubles close to his chest. "Aelianus has promised to return in an hour." Immediately I noticed his wife working out that he and I must have discussed this subject previously.

"At least he knows *where* his home is!" Julia Justa had a tart version of Helena's sarcasm. She was a handsome, hard-done-by woman, like her daughter, with fierce intelligence and liquid brown eyes. Maybe Helena would end up like this. Helena herself stabbed at her bowl of shrimp dumplings, looking morose. She knew what was coming.

Her mother took a deep breath, in a way that was familiar to me. I had a mother too. The views of these two women from distinctly different backgrounds were tragically similar, especially in regard to me. "You look as if you are about to rush away with acute diarrhea, Marcus Didius," smiled the noble Julia through thin lips. She understood men. Well, she was married to one, and had produced two more.

"I wouldn't dream of insulting the wonderful banquet before us!" It was a workaday spread, in fact, for the Camilli were struggling against the dire financial troubles that afflict hereditary millionaires. Still, flattery seemed wise.

"Someone has to ensure that my daughter is fed." A certain kind of woman always goes for the self-righteous in insults.

"Cobnuts!" Helena contributed. It was perhaps injudicious to use a phrase she had clearly picked up from me. "With donkey bells on them!" she added—an embellishment of her own.

"I don't believe I know that expression, Helena."

"The nuts are mine," I admitted. "I take no credit for the bells." To Helena I said, "If word's going around that I starve you, I'll have to buy you a pork rissole on the way home and insist that you eat it in public."

"Cobnuts again. You never let me do anything scandalous."

"Please be serious!" her mother retorted. After a day hard at work, I felt too tired to respond politely and Julia Justa seemed to sense my weakness. On first hearing the news of our forthcoming child her reaction had been muted, but since then she had had six months to brood. Tonight she had opted for the full lecture. "I simply feel there are things we all ought to face up to, since it does look as if Helena will be carrying her child to term. This time," she added unnecessarily, as if to have had one miscarriage was somehow Helena's fault. "I had hoped to see you married before this, Helena."

"We *are* married," said Helena stubbornly.

"Be sensible."

"Marriage is an agreement between two people to live together. Marcus and I have clasped hands and agreed."

"It's plain you have done more than that—" Julia Justa tried appealing to me, pretending she thought I was more reasonable: "Marcus, help me out!"

"It is true," I mused, "that if I went before the Censor and was asked *'To the best of your knowledge and belief, and by your own intention, Didius Falco, are you living in a valid state of marriage?'* I should bravely answer *'Yes, sir!'* "

The senator smiled and engaged in a bit of private commentary. "I love that *'to the best of your knowledge and belief'*!" His own wife received this very coolly, as if she suspected some hidden jibe.

"Formalities are not required," growled Helena. "We don't need an augury because we know we are going to be happy—" It sounded more of a threat than a promise. "And we don't need a written contract to tell us how our affairs will be unwound if we part, because we won't ever separate." Actually we didn't need a contract because there was nothing financial to unwind. Helena possessed money but I refused to touch it. I had none, which saved a lot of fuss. "Just be grateful we are sparing Papa the expense of a ceremony and the burden of a dowry. Times will be hard if he is to put both of my brothers into the Senate—"

"I doubt that will occur," her mother replied bitterly. She decided not to specify why, though it was obviously our fault: bringing the family into disrepute.

"Let's be friends," I said quietly. "I'll do my best to acquire greater status, and when I'm a suave equestrian counting beans on my farm in Latium and fiddling my taxes like respectable people do, we'll all wonder what the fuss was about."

Helena's father was keeping quiet. He knew his daughter was not the problem nowadays. It was his sons he needed to watch. Without extremely careful treatment Justinus was likely to end up entangled with an actress (specifically illegal for the son of a senator) while my current inquiries were beginning to suggest that Aelianus was involved in an intrigue that could be both dangerous and politically disastrous. He had told his father nothing about it—a bad omen in itself.

Luckily at that point a slave brought a message that Aelianus had come home. His father and I were able to escape to the study to interview him. By the rules of convention Helena Justina would remain with her mama.

Well, she would do until she lost her temper. That might happen fairly soon. I overheard her mother asking, "How are your bowels, Helena?" I winced, and fled after her papa. He had already skipped out of it. For a senator, he was a wise man.

FOURTEEN

Three of us were seated together, like an intellectual symposium. Lack of space in the small, scroll-filled room made civilized reclining impossible. Letters, accounts and intriguing works of literature were piled all around us in teetering stacks. If challenged about his untidiness (as he regularly was by his wife) Decimus Camillus Verus would say that he knew exactly where everything was. One of his likable characteristics: in truth he could have had no idea.

The senator and I were both upright on his reading couch. Aelianus had squeezed onto a stool which his father's secretary occupied in the daytime. While he fiddled with a pot of pens, a bust of Vespasian stared down from a shelf above him, as if our eminent Emperor were checking that the young man's neck was clean.

This son and his father looked fairly alike. They had matching strong eyebrows, though the boy was more thickset. He was also surly where his father was mild-mannered. It was a phase of youth—unfortunately a phase which could lose him the chance of making useful friends. There was no point telling him that. Being critical of his social skills was the certain way to rush him into making life's fatal mistakes.

"I don't have to talk to you, Falco!"

"It's advisable," his father chastised him briefly.

I kept my voice quiet. "You can talk to me informally here—or you can be sent for a full grilling on the Palatine."

"Is that a threat?"

"Senators' sons don't get beaten up by the Praetorian Guard." I made it sound as if they could be, when someone with my clout requested it.

Aelianus glared. Maybe he thought that if he had been anybody else's son I would have taken him to a wine bar and enjoyed a much more easygoing chat without involving his family. Maybe he was right.

"What's this about?" he demanded.

"One man dead and another close to Hades. A strong Baetican connection, and an unhealthy whiff of conspiracy. Your presence at the last Olive Oil Producers' dinner in close company with one of the victims now needs accounting for."

He went pale. "If I have to explain myself I want to see someone more senior."

"Of course," I agreed. "I'll just point out that asking for special treatment makes you sound like a man in trouble. People with nothing to hide give their evidence to the regular official."

"And that's you?" He was being careful now.

"It's me. Orders from the top."

"You're trying to implicate me in something." Dear gods, he was truculent. And I hadn't even started yet.

"Actually I want to clear you."

"Just answer the questions," his father instructed patiently.

Hoping for filial obedience, I tried greater formality: "Camillus Aelianus, how did you come to know Anacrites, and why did he take you to that dinner as his guest?"

"Why don't you ask him?" Useless. Well, I was somebody's son. I should have known the odds on obtaining filial obedience were short.

"Anacrites has been attacked—and by thugs who killed one of his agents the same night. He's been taken to a place of safety, but he's likely to die. I need to find out very quickly what is going on." I remembered how long it had been since I dumped the spy on my mother. It was time to make dutiful inquiries—or to relieve her of the corpse.

The senator leaned towards me anxiously. "Are you saying *Aulus* may have been in danger that night?" Aulus must be his elder son's personal name. One which the young chap was unlikely to invite me to use.

Unless Aelianus had been dabbling in something far bigger than I gave him credit for, I could not believe professional killers would bother with him. "Don't worry, senator. Presumably your son is an innocent bystander." I thought the bystanding innocent looked leery, in fact. "Aelianus, did you realize your dinner host was the Emperor's Chief Spy?"

The young man seemed chastened. "I understood something of the sort."

"What was your connection with him?"

"Nothing really."

"Then how did you come to meet him?"

He did not want to tell me, but admitted, "I had been sent to him with a letter when I returned from Corduba."

His father looked surprised. Forestalling his interruption, I asked, "Who wrote the letter?"

"It's confidential, Falco."

"Not anymore!" his father snapped briskly. He wanted to know about this as much as I did. Though he appeared so easygoing, Camillus had old-fashioned views on a father's rights. The fact that none of his children agreed with him was just a father's usual hard luck.

"It was from the quaestor," Aelianus replied irritably.

"Quinctius Quadratus?"

He looked surprised at my knowledge. "No, his outgoing predecessor. Cornelius had just heard that his father is sending him on a trip to Greece before he has to come back to Rome. Since I *was* coming back, he gave the thing to me."

We were talking about the young finance officer in charge of collecting taxes for Rome. "A provincial quaestor would normally correspond with the Chief Secretary, Claudius Laeta." His letters would travel via the *cursus publicus,* the imperial post service. It was quick, secure, and reliable. "So why send something to Anacrites, and why entrust it to you? You were friendly with this Cornelius?"

"Yes."

"If he wanted it entrusted to safe hands, was this letter very sensitive?"

"Presumably. Don't ask me what was in it," Aelianus continued triumphantly, "because it was heavily sealed and I had strict instructions to deliver it unopened straight to the Palatine." Very convenient.

"Were you present when Anacrites read it?"

"He asked me to wait in another office."

"And then what was his reaction?"

"He came in and invited me to the Baetican dinner as if to thank me for its safe delivery."

I changed the subject: "If you knew the outgoing quaestor, do you know Quinctius Quadratus too?"

"What's that got to do with anything?"

"He had been meant to attend the dinner as well. His father had booked him a place—but he went to the theater instead."

"I leave the theater to my brother!" Aelianus sneered self-righteously.

"Do you know Quadratus?" I repeated.

"Slightly," he then admitted. "He was in Corduba last autumn—preparing himself to bid for the Baetican quaestorship I imagine, though he never came clean at the time. I had a disagreement with him about some work his people did on my father's estate. Now we don't particularly get on."

"And besides, you had cornered yourself an invitation from a mighty official? Being noticed by Anacrites would be something to brag about!"

Aelianus gave me a nasty look. "Have you finished, Falco?"

"No," I snapped back. "We need to discuss your time in Corduba. Your father sent you out there to gain experience, and you were working informally in the proconsul's office—"

"I was never privy to policy meetings," Aelianus took pleasure in telling me.

"No. It would be an unusual office if the governor's young staff actually noticed what was going on." While he was here, and under parental supervision, I determined to pick his brains. "There were some top Baeticans dining with Quinctius Attractus at the dinner. I presume you knew most of them?"

"Provincials?" Aelianus sounded hurt at being associated with foreigners.

"Given that men of Hispanic origin fill a third of the Senate that you yourself are trying to join, snobbery is short-sighted. I assume you know who they were! I'm interested in this group: Annaeus Maximus, Licinius Rufus, someone called Norbanus and another called Cyzacus."

"Annaeus and Rufus are leading citizens of Corduba."

"Big in olive oil production?"

"Annaeus has the largest estate. Licinius isn't far behind."

"Is there rivalry between the landowners?" his father put in.

"Only mild jostling." This was better. When he cooperated, Aelianus was a useful witness. The best kind: he liked showing off. He lacked the dry wit of other members of his family, but had grown up with their analytical attitude. He was, moreover, a great deal more intelligent than he wanted to allow himself to be. "The producers all compete to obtain the highest yield and quality, and to demand the best prices, but in general there is a good community spirit. Their main obsessions are getting rich, then demonstrating their wealth by way of luxurious houses, benefactions in the community, and holding local magistracies and priesthoods. Long term, they all want to buy positions in Rome if possible. They take pride in anyone from Corduba being successful, because that increases the status of all."

"Thanks," I said, rather surprised at his sudden fluency.

"What about the other two names Falco mentioned?" inquired the senator, who was taking a keen interest.

"Cyzacus is from Hispalis. He runs a fleet of barges; upriver at Corduba the Baetis is too narrow for big vessels, so bargees take the amphorae downstream. I knew him by sight, but that's all."

"Not a producer himself?"

"No, he just collects. And Norbanus is a negotiator."

"Negotiating what?" I asked.

Aelianus gave me a pitying look. "Negotiating anything, but mostly space on the ocean-going ships that pick up the amphorae of oil once they are assembled at Hispalis. He's a Gaul." The young man was dismissive.

"So everybody hates him!"

"Well, even provincials need someone else to despise, Marcus." The senator joked, while his son merely looked superior.

"I'm getting a picture of a happy flock of middlemen," I commented. "The estate owners produce the oil, then the bargemen take it downstream to an entrepôt—that's Hispalis—after which negotiators find it space in ships to take it abroad. So producers, bargemen, negotiators, and shipowners are all expecting their cut. This is before any retailers in the Emporium and the Roman markets get their sticky fingers on the amphorae. If all these chancers are creaming off profits, no wonder we pay nice prices."

"It's no worse than any other commodity." Camillus Verus was a fair man.

"Except that oil carries the highest premium. It's a commodity everybody needs, from the Emperor down." I turned back to Aelianus. "So what is your evaluation of the commercial situation?"

He shrugged. "Olive oil is increasingly important. Production in Baetica is rising steeply. It's rapidly overtaking the traditional sources in Greece or Italy. That's partly because from Spain it's easy to send it north to meet the huge demand in Gaul, Britain and Germany, as well as dispatching it direct to Rome. It's fine quality for emollient usages—and the taste is reckoned to be special too. The producers in Baetica are lucky men. There are fortunes to be made."

"A star product." I looked him in the eye. "And what's the scope for funny business?"

"I don't know what you mean, Falco."

"Price-fixing, for example," I specified crisply. Once I started considering how many amphorae of olive oil were being shipped around the Empire, I realized that millions of sesterces were involved. "Cornering the market and withholding supplies—the usual pretty tricks of commerce are what I mean!"

"I wouldn't know." Now he had shown us that his time in the governor's office had at least taught him to give a sensible briefing, I reckoned he was being disingenuous.

I had no more to ask. His father let Aelianus go. The young man said he was off out again; Decimus told him to stay indoors, though he did not make too much of giving the order, in case Aelianus disobeyed.

Just as he reached the doorway I called out, "One more thing!" He made the mistake of stopping. "You carried the mysterious letter to Anacrites with you. How did you travel to Rome? By sea or land?"

"By sea."

"That's a week's journey?" He nodded, and I gave him a pleasant grin. "So tell me, *Aulus*—" He finally noticed I was not being friendly. "What exactly did you read in the letter when your curiosity broke and you picked the seal?"

To his credit, Aulus Camillus Aelianus managed not to blush. He knew when he was rumbled. He sighed, thought about it, then slowly admitted the truth: "It was a reply to a request from Anacrites to the proconsul for a report on the stability of the oil market. The quaestor had assessed the situation, and answered on the lines of what I told you earlier: that olive oil is going to be very big business." Aelianus braced himself then added honestly, "He also confirmed what you suggested, Falco—that there might be some scheming locally in Corduba. A possible cartel to rig and control the price of oil. He felt it was at an early stage, and could be contained."

"Did he name names?"

"No," said the noble Aelianus, rather quietly. "But he said that the proconsul had asked him to mention that inquiries had not been welcome. He felt the situation could become dangerous for everyone involved."

FIFTEEN

Without speaking, the senator and I walked slowly through the house in search of our womenfolk. It was dusk, on one of the first fine nights of the year. Passing through a folding door that gave access to the garden we dabbled our fingers in a hiccuppy fountain then joined Julia Justa who was reclining under a portico, eating grapes. She regarded us in silence. She could certainly pluck fruit from its stem in a telling manner: she was a woman with burdens, and we two men were contributors to her grief.

The senator had learned how to live with reproach; he surveyed the roses on his sagging trelliswork, apparently oblivious. I stayed on my feet, close to a pillar, with my arms folded. On the other side of the colonnade, which was dimly lit by oil lamps, I could see Helena Justina. She had separated from her mother for some reason (one I could guess) and was picking dead leaves from a huge urn of neglected agapanthus. I watched, waiting for her to look across and notice me.

Lately she had become withdrawn, lost even to me in the concerns of her pregnancy. She moved carefully now, with her back slightly arched for balance. She spent a lot of time being busy on her own, engaged in tasks I never really knew about. We were still close; I had, for instance, been favored with full details of all the physical problems which her mother kept mentioning. I had myself scoured apothecaries for cures, and had my head bitten off for bringing them home.

Helena still told me her private thoughts. I knew she wanted the baby to be a girl (and I knew why). I also knew that if one more person asked if she was hoping for a boy, she was likely to knock them down and jump on their heads. She was heartily sick of being nagged. And the main reason she was starting to lose her temper was that she was afraid. I had promised to stay near and share everything with her, but she reckoned when it came to it I would find an excuse to escape. Everyone we knew believed I would let her down.

The senator sighed, still in contemplation of our conversation with his son. "Marcus, I would be happier if neither you nor Aelianus were in contact with the palace spy network."

"So would I," I agreed somberly. "Anacrites has given me plenty of aggravation. But he has given me work too—and I need that. Don't worry. Anacrites is in no condition to trouble Aelianus again. Even if he makes a miraculous recovery I reckon I can handle him." The gods knew, I had had enough practice. The senator must have heard details of my long enmity with the Chief Spy—and we both thought it was Anacrites who had intervened with the Emperor's son Domitian to ensure I was refused promotion socially. That had been a personal blow to the Camilli. They wanted me to make equestrian rank, in order to protect Helena's good name.

"In general, Marcus, how do you see the Chief Spy's role?"

"Interesting question. On a descending curve, I should say. Anacrites is devious, but he's not as efficient as he ought to be and he works with a historical disadvantage: his team has always been small, and his line of command is through the Praetorian Guard. So his theoretical task, like that of the Praetorians, is limited to acting as the Emperor's bodyguard." Of course that now included providing protection for Vespasian's two sons, Titus and Domitian.

"I think the whole show is due for a shakeout," the senator said.

"Be disbanded?"

"Maybe not. Both Vespasian and Titus hate the idea of being emperors who openly pay for trumped-up evidence to destroy their political enemies. Vespasian won't change, but Titus might want a tougher organization—and Titus is already commander of the Praetorians."

"Are you telling me you know something, sir?"

"No, but I can sense a mood among the palace staff that there will soon be scope for men who offer to help Titus achieve his ends. He's a dasher; he wants everything yesterday—"

I knew what that meant. "By the quickest means—legal or not! That's bad news. We don't want to go back to the old state-employed informers. The network that was so notorious under Tiberius and Nero—little more than torturers in basement prison cells."

Decimus was mulling this over gloomily. He was an old crony of Vespasian, and a shrewd judge of a situation. His advice mattered. "Marcus, it's your world. If there is a power struggle, I suppose you may want to involve yourself—"

"I'd prefer to run fast the other way!" I was thinking about the implications. "Rivalries already exist," I confirmed, thinking of the open antagonism between Anacrites and Laeta that I had witnessed at the dinner. "Anacrites has been tussling with just the kind of clever bureaucrat who might suggest to Titus that he should develop a new agency, one with a fuller remit, which could answer directly to Titus himself— In any case, Anacrites is seriously wounded. If he dies there will be a scuffle among people who want his old job."

"Who's the bureaucrat?"

"Laeta."

The senator, who naturally knew the correspondence chief, shuddered distastefully.

I felt I was myself already being used as a patball between Laeta and Anacrites. This was the kind of situation where the general good—for instance the smooth running of the Spanish olive oil trade—could be overturned in the pursuit of some disastrous administrators' feud. And it was a situation where Rome could, yet again, end up in the grip of sinister forces who ruled by torture and infamy.

It was at this point that Julia Justa, who had been sitting with us in silence as a respectable matron ought to when her male relatives debate world issues, decided she would exert her rights. She waved to Helena, signaling her to come over and join us.

"I would prefer to keep Aelianus right out of this," her father carried on. "I'm beginning to be sorry I ever sent him out to Spain. He seemed a bit raw; the governor was a friend; it looked like an ideal opportunity. My son could see administration working, and I had bought a new estate on the River Baetis which needed organizing." Helena Justina had condescended to notice her mother waving and was coming around the portico. Decimus continued, "Of course he's inexperienced—" I had realized what was coming. "I could still use a friend to look at the estate." Sensing that I preferred her not to overhear, Helena sped up and reached us. By that time her father was unstoppable: "The oil problem in that quaestor's letter sounds like something a man like you could clear up in a matter of weeks if you were out there on the spot, Marcus!"

Julia Justa removed a grape pip from her elegant lip fastidiously. Her voice was dry. "Well it's not as if he's needed here. Having babies is women's work!"

I didn't stop to look at Helena's expression: "Baetica is off-limits. I promised Helena I would be here when the child is born. It's more than a promise; it's what I want."

"I'm only surprised you don't suggest taking her with you!" her mother sniffed.

This was unfair when I had already taken the decent line. Helena Justina's smile was dangerously quiet. "Oh taking me away to Baetica is out of the question!" she said.

That was when I knew for sure that Baetica was where I would be when I let Helena down.

SIXTEEN

I kept him alive," snarled my mother. "You never said I was expected to make him sensible as well. If I know men, he never was." She glanced at Helena, whose eyes gleamed warmly in agreement.

Apparently Anacrites was now lurching in and out of consciousness. He could yet lurch the wrong way and die. Once I would have been glad. Now the bastard had made me feel responsible. Meanwhile, whenever he opened his eyes, Ma pulled his mouth open too and spooned in chicken broth.

"Does he know where he is?"

"Not even *who* he is. He doesn't know anything."

"Has he spoken?"

"Just mumbles like a hopeless drunk."

There could be a reason for that. "Are you giving him your brothers' wine?"

"Only a dribble." No wonder he wasn't lucid. Uncles Fabius and Junius, who shared a farm when they were not trying to tear each other's throats out, produced a harsh red Campagnan rot-gut with a kick that blew the wax out of your ears.

A goatskin or two was enough to lay out a whole cohort of hard-living Praetorians.

"If he can survive that, you must have saved him!"

"I never knew what you've got against your uncles," grumbled Ma.

I loathed their awful wine, for one thing. I also thought the pair of them were illogical, moody clowns.

Helena and I inspected the invalid. Anacrites looked unpleasantly pale, and already much thinner. I could not tell whether this was one of his conscious phases or not. His eyes were nearly closed, but not quite. He made no attempt to speak or move. Calling his name caused no reaction.

"Ma, I've found out more about what's been going on and I've decided it's too dangerous keeping him. He's part of the Praetorian Guard; I reckon they can be trusted to look after one of their own. I've spoken to a centurion I know, and Anacrites is going to be taken into the safety of the Praetorian Camp. A man called Frontinus will turn up and whisk him away secretly. Then don't mention to anybody that you had him here."

"Oh I see!" complained Ma, highly affronted. "Now I'm not good enough!"

"You're wonderful," Helena soothed her. "But if his attackers find out where he is, you're not strong enough to fend them off." Actually, if I knew my mother she would have a damned good try.

Helena and I sat with Anacrites for a while, so Ma could have a rest. My mother's idea of having a rest was to gather five shopping baskets and rush out to the market, pausing only to shower Helena with rude comments on her appearance and dark advice on managing her pregnancy. I watched Helena bite her tongue. Ma scuttled off. If she met any of her witchy cronies, which was quite likely, she would be away for hours. This made a mockery of us coming to visit her, but was typical in my family. At least it prevented quarrels. I knew we had just narrowly avoided yet another one.

Anacrites, Helena and I now had the apartment to ourselves. Without Ma whirling to and fro it felt unnaturally quiet. She had stashed the invalid in a bed that had belonged at various times to my elder brother and me. Sometimes when we were boys we had shared it, so this had been the scene of much lewd talk and a multitude of ludicrous plans—plans that were now doomed to be forever unfulfilled. I left home, and ended up as an informer. My brother was dead. Before he was killed in Judaea Festus had dossed here on trips home from the army. The gods only know what scenes of surreptitious debauchery our little room had seen then.

It seemed odd to be here with Helena. Odder still that the familiar old bed, with its rickety pine frame and twisted webbing, now possessed a brown checkered cover that I did not recognize and a spanking new pillow. Before long my eyes were sending messages that had Anacrites not been inconveniently in possession I would have grabbed Helena and renewed my own acquaintance with the bed . . .

"Don't push your luck," murmured Helena, with what I hoped was shared regret.

Since there was no hope of persuading Anacrites to contribute usefully, the choice of conversation was ours. It was the morning after our dinner at the Camillus house. I had reported the latest facts to Helena, but we were still chewing over the story.

"Someone's been stupid," I said. "There may be a commercial conspiracy in Corduba. Presumably Anacrites and his man were attacked in a feeble attempt to deter investigation. The way that group of Baeticans left Rome immediately afterwards certainly makes it look as if they knew something about it. But our officials are aware of whatever's going on; Claudius Laeta can take whatever steps he thinks necessary from this end. He's made himself acting Chief Spy, apparently. It's his decision. I'm certainly not going out there."

"I see," replied my beloved, ever queen of the unexpected. "There is nothing to discuss then." Her brown eyes were thoughtful; that tended to precede trouble. "Marcus, you do realize that you may have had a lucky escape the night of the dinner and the attacks?"

"How would that be?" I made an attempt to act the innocent.

"You're known as an imperial agent, and you had been talking to Anacrites. I expect you also found a reason to meet the beautiful dancing girl—" I pished. Helena carried on regardless. "And you spoke to Valentinus. You were probably seen doing that, then when you both left the dinner at the same time, it must have looked like more than coincidence. But unlike Anacrites and Valentinus you didn't leave the Palatine alone. You came home to Fountain Court with two palace slaves, carrying your *garum* jar. Perhaps if it hadn't been for them you would have been set upon too."

"I had thought of that," I admitted. "I didn't want to worry you."

"I *was* worried."

"Well don't brood on it. This must be the first recorded incidence of a man having his life saved by an amphora of fish-pickle."

Helena was not laughing. "Marcus, you're involved whether you want to be or not."

We were silent for a while. Anacrites seemed to be fading right before my eyes. I felt a surge of anger again. "I'd like to get whoever murdered Valentinus."

"Of course you would, Marcus."

"Fellow feeling."

"I know."

Helena Justina always spoke her mind and let me know exactly where I stood. If there was any chance of an argument she set about it briskly. Sounding meek was worrying. It meant she might be planning some big surprise.

"Helena, I'm not going to let these killers get away with it. If they are still in Rome—"

"They won't be," said Helena.

She was right. I had to swallow it. "Then I'll be wasting my time as usual."

"Laeta will ask you to be the man who goes to Baetica."

"Laeta can go red in the face and burst a blood vessel."

"Laeta will make the Emperor or Titus order it."

"They'll be ordering trouble then."

She gazed at me somberly. "I think you ought to be prepared to go to Spain."

Helena's offer seemed out of the question—and yet straight away I began to wonder if it might be feasible.

We believed we had nearly two months before the baby would be born. I did a rapid calculation: a week lost on the journey out, plus several days to travel inland to Corduba. Ten more days for returning home. In between, another week should be ample to identify and assess the personnel involved and tackle a solution . . . Oh yes. Easy to go, do the job, and come home just in time to put down my luggage on the doormat and receive the newborn baby into my arms from a smiling midwife who had just finished tidying its proud and happy mama . . .

A fool could convince himself that it would work, provided nothing went wrong. But I knew better. Traveling always takes longer than you hope. And things always go wrong.

It was far too tight. And what if the baby came early anyway? Apart from outfacing the oil cartel conspirators—something which hardly interested me, though that was what would make the state provide my fare—where in this ludicrous timetable was there any allowance for tracing Diana and her murderous musicians?

"Helena, thanks for the offer, but be sensible. Just because everyone else assumes I'm planning to bunk off and abandon you, doesn't mean they are right!"

"I'm coming with you," she told me. I knew that tone of voice. This was no mere suggestion. Being bossed and bullied by relatives was irritating her too much. Helena had decided to abscond from Rome.

It was at that moment Anacrites opened his eyes and stared at me vaguely. By the looks of him his body was giving up and his black soul was on the ferryboat to Hades. His mind was just about still here, however.

I told him bitterly, "I've just been informed I have to sail to Baetica on this dead-end job of yours!"

"Falco . . ." he croaked. What a compliment. He might not have known who *he* was, but he recognized me. I still refused to spoon-feed the bastard with broth. "Dangerous woman!" he moaned. Maybe it was apropos of nothing, though it sounded like fair comment on my chosen partner in life.

He faded out again. Well, enigmas are what you expect from spies.

Helena Justina ignored him. "Don't mention to your mother that we're going," she instructed me.

"And don't you tell yours either!" I retorted nervously.

PART TWO:

BAETICAN SPAIN: CORDUBA

A.D. 73: mid-April

The trader I consider to be an energetic man, and one bent on making money; but it is a dangerous career and one subject to disaster. On the other hand it is from the farming class that the bravest men and the sturdiest soldiers come, their calling is most highly respected, their livelihood is most assured and is looked on with the least hostility, and those who are engaged in that pursuit are least likely to be disaffected.

Cato the Elder

SEVENTEEN

You pay me by the mile," said the carriage-hire man.

I didn't believe it. That would mean at the end of our hiring period I just had to lie to him about how far I had driven. He was an ex-legionary. How could he be so innocent?

"What's the catch?" I asked.

He grinned, appreciating that I had at least had the courtesy to query the system, instead of jumping in with intent to cheat. "No catch."

The hireman was a wide-shouldered former footslogger whose name was Stertius. I was unsure what to make of him; my mission was making me distrust everyone. This man owned a commercial transport business in the southern Baetican port of Malaca—mainly ox-wagons collecting amphorae of fish-pickle from all along the coast to bring them to port, but also gigs, carts and carriages for travelers. It would be an ideal cover if he engaged in espionage; he would see everyone who came and went. He had been in the Roman army; he could easily have been recruited by the legions to work for Anacrites; even Laeta could have coerced him somewhere along the line. Equally, local loyalty could put him firmly in league with the men I had come to investigate— or the dancing girl.

Helena sat down on our mound of baggage in the quiet, unobtrusive manner of a woman who was making a point. We had been sailing for a week, then landed in the wrong place so we now had a lengthy trip by road ahead of us. She was very tired. She was sitting in the hot sun. She did not need me dragging out what ought to have been a straightforward commercial transaction. She stroked Nux as if the dog were her only friend.

I still felt queasy from the ocean. It was possible to travel the entire way from Rome to Gades overland if you had the time to spare. Someone like Julius Caesar who wanted to show up well in his memoirs took pride in reaching Hispania without crossing water. Most people with interesting lives to lead preferred the quicker sea trip, and Helena and I were not in a good state for forced marches anyway. So I had agreed to take a boat. Getting this far was torture for anyone like me who could be seasick just looking at a sail. I had been groaning all the way, and my stomach was still not sure it had returned to land. "I'm dazed. Explain your system."

"You pay me what I freely admit is a hefty deposit." Stertius had the typical sardonic air of an old soldier. He had retired from the army after decades in North Africa, then crossed the Straits to Spain to start his business. Up to a point I trusted him commercially, though I was beginning to fear he was the type who enjoys himself inflicting arcane mysteries on helpless customers. "If you don't use up your allocation, I'll give you a rebate. If you overrun of course, I'll have to charge you more."

"I'm taking the equipage to Corduba."

"As you wish. I'll be giving you Marmarides as your driver—"

"Is that optional?" I was facing enough unknowns. The last thing I wanted was to be saddled with someone else's employee.

"It's voluntary," grinned the hireman. "—In the legionary

sense!" It was compulsory. "You'll get on with him fine. He's one of my freedmen. I've trained him well, he's a natural with horseflesh and he has a good temperament." In my experience that meant he would be a maniacal driver who let the mules get the staggers and tried to knife his customers. "Marmarides will bring the carriage home when you've finished. He'll tell you the mileage price at the end."

"He'll just tell us? Excuse me!" Baetican commercial practice seemed to have its extraordinary side. "I'm sure the amiable Marmarides has your absolute trust, but I like the right to query costs."

I was not the first suspicious Roman to land in Malaca. Stertius had a well-worked-out routine for technical quibbles: he crooked one finger knowingly, then led me to the rear of the sturdy two-wheeled, two-mule carriage which I was attempting to lease. Its iron-bound wheels would bounce painfully on the track to Corduba, but the passenger compartment had a leather cover which would protect Helena from rough weather, including hot sun. Nux would enjoy trying to bite the wheels.

Stertius bent over one axle hub. "I bet you've never seen one of these before," he claimed proudly. "Look, centurion: this commodious vehicle that I'm letting you have at negligible rates is fitted with an Archimedes hodometer!"

Dear gods, he was a mechanical enthusiast. A flywheel and twisted rope man. The kind of helpful character who asks for a drink of water then insists on mending your well-tackle that has been out of use for three generations. He was almost certainly building himself a complete siege warfare catapulta in the garden of his house.

The wheel hub over which we were crouched in the dust had been fitted with a single-tooth gear. Every rotation of the carriage wheel caused this gear to engage with a flat disc set vertically at right angles above it, which was cut into numerous triangular teeth. Each wheel rotation moved the disc on by a notch, eventually operating a second gear which in turn moved on a second disc. That one, which was horizontal, had been drilled with small holes, upon each of which was balanced a smooth pebble. Every operation of the top disc moved up a new hole, allowing a pebble to drop through into a box below, which Stertius had secured with a fierce padlock.

"The top disc rotates one hole for every four hundred revolutions of the carriage wheel—which takes one Roman mile!"

"Amazing!" I managed to utter. "What beautiful workmanship! Did you construct this yourself?"

"I do a bit of metalwork," Stertius admitted shyly. "I can't think why these are not fitted as standard on all hired vehicles."

I could. "Wherever did you get the idea, Stertius?"

"Road-building with the Third Augusta in bloody Numidia and Mauretania. We used something like it for measuring accurate positions for the mileposts."

"Amazing!" I repeated feebly. "Helena Justina, come and look at this; it's an Archimedes hodometer!"

I wondered how many more colorful eccentrics I was doomed to meet in Baetica.

"There's just one thing that has to be understood," Stertius warned me as Helena dutifully dragged herself over to inspect his mileage measurer. "You'll find Marmarides can turn his hand to most things, but he won't deliver babies!"

"That's all right," Helena assured him, as if we were a couple who had plans for all contingencies. "Didius Falco is a Roman of the traditional, hardy type. He can plough his fields with his left hand, while his right delivers twins. At the same time he can spout a finely phrased republican oration to a group of senatorial delegates, and invent an ode in praise of the simple country life."

Stertius gave me an approving look. "Handy, eh?"

"Oh I do my best," I answered, with traditional Roman modesty.

EIGHTEEN

It took nearly a week's driving to Corduba. Stertius had charged us a deposit based on a main journey of a hundred and twenty-five Roman miles. I reckon he was accurate. He must have checked it already with his miraculous hodometer. I guessed that crazy man had measured every road in Baetica, and he owned marked-up itineraries to prove it.

Nobody of status ever went the way we did. I had not planned it myself. Once we had chosen the sea trip there were further options available. One sailing route went north of Corsica then came south hugging the coast of Gaul and Tarraconensis; it was famous for shipwrecks. The alternative nipped between Corsica and Sardinia; provided we didn't run aground on either island and fall into bandits' eager hands it had appeared a better bet. It probably was for most people, though not those prone to emptying their stomach at the first ripple of a wave.

What most folk did then was to sail right past Malaca to Gades, and take a boat up the grand River Baetis. I had decided against that for excellent reasons: I wanted to disembark as soon as possible. I also planned to arrive in Corduba in an unexpected manner that would bamboozle my Baetican suspects. So I had pored over route-charts and picked out my landfall on the eastern coast at Carthago Nova, proposing then to drive along the Via Augusta, the main inland highway through southern Hispania. This formed the final link of the great Via Herculana; it was supposedly the immortal hero's route across Europe to the Gardens of the Hesperides, imbued with romantic associations as the pathway to the ends of the earth. Better than that, it would be a fast paved road with well-equipped mansios.

Another reason for my choice was Carthago Nova itself—the center of esparto grass production. My mother, to whom I owed a belated bribe for nursing Anacrites, had supplied me with a more than usually detailed list of presents to bring home, including baskets, mats and even sandals for her numerous grandchildren. A decent Roman lad respects his ma.

Mine would be unsurprised to discover that I had failed her. She would have to make do with a few jars of *garum* from Malaca, for the captain of our vessel had unexpectedly decided the winds were wrong for the landing he had previously promised.

"He's an idiot! I should have found out earlier—"

"How could you?" asked Helena. "He would never have admitted *'Yes, your honor; I'm an idiot.'* "

By the time I realized, he had sailed right past Carthago Nova and was halfway to Gades. He seemed pretty pleased with himself. I forced him to put in at Malaca. From here a road to Corduba did exist, though not a good one. It would be shorter than coming all the way west from Carthago, but the grim quality of the road would probably use up the extra time. Time was just what I could not afford.

Once in the carriage we started well enough, but the level plain with a few dry, pointy little hills quickly gave way to barren gray slopes speckled with sparse vegetation and creased by dry watercourses. Soon we met a range of hills with almost vertical crags; although we traversed them without incident, I had some bad moments riding on top with Marmarides as we passed slowly through the landscape of deep ravines and precipitous rocks. Further inland, the unpopulated countryside changed again to gently rolling ground. We came to the first olive trees, their gnarled trunks rising from low sprigs of greenery, set out with good spaces between them in the stony soil. In the richer, redder ground that came later the olives were interspersed with blocks of fruit trees, grain, or vegetable fields.

Settlements, or even farms, were few. There were mansios, of a meager kind, where the innkeepers all looked astonished to have their bare little rooms inspected by a senator's daughter in an advanced state of pregnancy. Most expected Romans to be traveling with an entourage. Most Romans would indeed ensure they took a bustle of friends, freedmen and slaves. We found it easiest to pretend we had lost our escort temporarily.

There was no point trying to bluff Marmarides, of course. He knew we were without companions, and it afforded him much amusement. "You come to Baetica for a nice summer holiday, lord?"

"That's right. I'm hoping for a sun-drenched spell in an esparto rope hammock. As soon as I can, I'll be stretched out under an olive tree with the dog at my feet and a jug of wine."

Stertius must have picked him up in North Africa; he was as black as the Baetican olives. I tried to forget I was distrusting everyone I met and accept him as a welcome addition, though I wished he had been as broad as his master (Stertius was built like a bacon pig). Marmarides had a neat slim build, whereas I wanted a type who went into a fight smiling, and came out of it five minutes later having wrung the oppositions' necks.

Our driver's face creased into satirical wrinkles and he

laughed at us breathily. "Stertius reckons you're a government agent, and your lady's been sent abroad to have her baby in disgrace!"

'I see you're frank talkers in Baetica."

"You want any help with your agenting?" he offered hopefully.

"Forget it. I'm just a loafer on holiday."

Marmarides burst out laughing again. Well, I like a man who is happy in his work. That's more than I was.

Some of the mansio landlords seemed to believe we were carrying out a trick accommodation survey on behalf of the provincial quaestor. I let them think it, hoping to improve the quality of supper. Hoping in vain.

The landlords' fears derived from their resentment of bureaucracy. Maybe this meant they thought the quaestor made an efficient job of checking their returns. I could not tell whether it implied that Roman financial management worked well here generally, or whether it was a specific comment on Cornelius, the young friend of Aelianus who had just left his post. Presumably Quinctius Quadratus, the new boy, had yet to make his mark.

"Helena, tell me about your father's estate." I had seized the advantage of a smooth patch of road on one of the occasions when I was riding inside the carriage with her.

"It's quite small, just a farm he bought when he thought of sending Aelianus to Baetica." Camillus senior owned the statutory million's worth of land in Italy which was his qualification for the Senate, but with two sons to equip for the high life he was trying to create a bigger investment portfolio. Like most wealthy men he aimed to distribute his spare holdings among the provinces in order to avoid suffering too much in times of drought or tribal revolt.

"Aelianus lived on the estate?"

"Yes, though I expect he enjoyed the high life in Corduba

whenever possible. There's a villa rustica where he was supposed to spend his spare time quietly—if you believe that." Helena had of course been brought up to respect her male relatives—a fine Roman tradition which all Roman women ignored. "Aelianus found a tenant who now occupies part of the house, but there will be room for us. The farm is a little way inland of the river, in olive-growing country, though I'm afraid it's typical of my dear papa, that he bought through an agent who palmed him off with very few olive trees."

"It's a dud?"

"Well there are almonds and grain." Nuts and feed were not going to turn the Camilli into tycoons.

I tried not to let any insult to her noble father's acumen show; Helena was deeply fond of him. "Well, Spanish grain is the best in the Empire apart from African or Italian. And what else is wrong with this agricultural gem your father acquired? He said you would tell me about some problems he wants me to look into."

"Papa was being cheated over the olive oil pressing. That was why Aelianus took on a tenant. Using an overseer of our own wasn't working. This way Papa receives a fixed rent, while the man with the lease is responsible for whether he makes a profit or not."

"I hope we're not having to share accommodation with one of your brother's friends!"

"No, no. The man had fallen on hard times somehow and needed a new farm. Aelianus decided he was honest. I don't suppose he knew him personally; can you imagine my brother sharing a drink with a farmer?"

"He may have had to lower his snooty standards in the provinces."

Helena looked skeptical about that. "Well what I do know is that this man—whose name is Marius Optatus—volunteered to point out that Papa was being cheated in some way. It sounds as if Aelianus brushed his advice aside—but then had the sense to check, and found it was right. Remember my father had entrusted him with seeing that the estate was running properly. It was the first time Aelianus had such a responsibility, and whatever you think of him he did want to do well."

"I'm still surprised he listened."

"Maybe he surprised himself."

An honest tenant sounded unlikely, but I wanted to believe it. If I could report back to Camillus Verus that his son had at least put in a good man to work the estate, that suited me. Whereas if the tenant proved a bad one, I had agreed to sort things out—one more claim on my hard-pressed time.

I'm no expert on big villa economy, though I had been partly brought up on a market garden so I should be able to spot gross bad practice. That was all Helena's father required. Absentee landlords don't expect to make vast profits from remote holdings. It is their estates on the Italian mainland, which they can tour in person every year, that keep the rich in luxury.

Something was on Helena's mind. "Marcus, do you trust what Aelianus told you?"

"About the farm?"

"No. About the letter he brought home."

"It looked as though he was coming clean. When I told him what had happened to the Chief Spy and his agent your brother seemed to realize he was in deep trouble." Back in Rome I had tried to find the letter, but Anacrites' papers were in too much disarray. Sight of it would have reassured me, and even if Aelianus had told me the truth I might have learned further details. Laeta had had his own staff search for it, without success. That could just mean Anacrites had devised a complicated filing system—though whenever I had visited his office his scheme seemed to consist of merely throwing scrolls all over the floor.

The road had become rough again. Helena said nothing

while the carriage lurched over the uneven pavings. The northward cross-country road to Corduba was not exactly a marvel of engineering, precision built by the legions in some mighty politician's name, and intended to last for millennia. The regional council must have charge of this one. Public slaves occasionally patched it up well enough to last through the current season. We seemed to be traveling when the work gang were overdue.

"Aelianus must also have realized," I added when the carriage stopped jolting, "the first thing I would do—whether I had to correspond from Rome or whether I came here myself—was to ask the proconsul's office for their side of the correspondence. In fact I'm hoping to discuss the whole business with the proconsul himself."

"I had a go at him," Helena said. She still meant Aelianus. I felt sorry for her brother. Helena Justina could have been a cracking investigator had it not been impossible for respectable women to converse freely with people outside their family, or to knock on strangers' doors with nosy requests. But I always felt a mild pang of resentment when she took the initiative. She knew that, of course. "Don't fret. I was careful. He's my brother; he wasn't surprised I cornered him."

If he had told her anything worthwhile I would have heard about it before now. So I just grinned at her; Helena grabbed at the carriage frame as we were flung forward by a violent bounce. I braced my arm across in front of her for protection.

Just because Aelianus was her brother did not mean I intended to trust him.

Helena squeezed my hand. "Justinus is going to keep prodding him."

That cheered me up. I had shared time abroad with her younger brother. Justinus looked immature, but when he stopped mooning after unsuitable women he was shrewd and tenacious. I had great faith in his judgment too (except of women). In fact there was only one problem: if Justinus discovered anything, sending correspondence to Spain was highly unreliable. Helena and I would probably be home again before any letter could arrive. I was out here on my own. Not even Laeta would be able to contact me.

Changing the subject Helena Justina joked, "I hope this won't be like our trip to the East. It's bad enough finding corpses face down in water cisterns; I don't care for the idea of plucking a preserved one from a vat of olive oil."

"Messy!" I grinned.

"And slippery too."

"Don't worry; it won't happen."

"You were always overconfident!"

"I know what I'm talking about. It's the wrong time of year. Harvest starts in September with the green olives, and is over in January with the black. In April and May the presses stand still and everyone is chipping away at weeds with hoes, spreading manure made from last year's squelched olive pulp, and pruning. All we'll see will be pretty trees with jolly spring flowers hiding tiny fruit buds."

"Oh you've been reading up!" Helena scoffed. Her teasing eyes were bright. "Trust us to come at the wrong time of year."

I laughed too—though it was exactly the right time for some things: In spring the labor-intensive work of tending the olive trees was at its least demanding. That could be when the olive owners found the time to scheme and plot.

The closer we got to the great oil-producing estates south of the River Baetis, the more my unease grew.

NINETEEN

There is a fine tradition that when landowners arrive unexpectedly on their lush estates they find the floors unswept for the past six months, the goats roaming free in the vineyard eating the new young fruits, and grooms asleep with unwashed women in the master's bed. Some senators stop in the next village for a week, sending messages of their imminent arrival so the cobwebs can be sponged down, the floozies persuaded to go home to their aunties, and the livestock rounded up. Others are less polite. On the premise that having their names on a five percent mortgage from the Syrian lender in the Forum gives them right of possession, they turn up at dinnertime expecting hot baths, a full banquet and clean apartments with the coverlets already folded down for their accompanying forty friends. They at least get to publish fine literary letters full of satirical complaints about country life.

We had no one to send ahead as a messenger and we were sick of inns, so we pressed on and turned up unannounced, quite late in the day. Our appearance caused no visible panic. The new tenant had passed the first test of his efficiency. Marius Optatus didn't exactly welcome us with fresh roses in blue glass bud vases, but he found us seats in the garden and summoned a passable julep jug, while he ordered curious servants to prepare our rooms. Nux scampered off after them to choose a good bed to sleep on.

"The name's Falco. You may have heard Aelianus railing about me."

"How do you do," he answered, omitting to confirm whether or not he had been told I was a reprobate.

I introduced Helena, then we all sat around being polite and trying not to show that we were people with nothing in common who had been thrown together unavoidably.

Helena's father had bought himself a traditionally built Baetican farmhouse almost alongside the nearest road. It had mud-brick foundations below wooden panels; the arrangement was one long corridor with reception rooms at the front and more private accommodation behind them. The tenant lived in rooms along one side of the corridor, with views over the estate. The other rooms, which flanked a private garden, were supposed to be set aside for the Camilli if ever any of them visited. This part had been left unused. Either the tenant was scrupulous—or he had been warned to expect visitors.

"You're being extremely gracious!" I was cheering up now I had been told that the amenities included a small but functioning bath suite, slightly separate from the house. "With young Aelianus barely off the premises you must have imagined you were safe from further inspection for at least twenty years."

Optatus smiled. For a Spaniard he was tall, very thin, rather pale, with a foxy face and bright eyes. Among the Balearic mix of curly Iberians and even more shaggy Celts, all of whom were stocky and short, he stood out like a thistle spike in a cornfield. He looked a few years older than me, mature enough to run a workforce yet young enough to have some hopes in life. A man of few words. Silent men can be simply bad news at a party—or dangerous characters. Before we even fetched the baggage in I felt there was something about him I needed to investigate.

Supper was a simple affair of salt tuna and vegetables, shared with the house slaves and our driver Marmarides, in the old family tradition. We all ate in a long, low kitchen at the back of the house. There was local wine, which seemed good enough if you were tired, and if you added enough water to make the old woman who prepared meals and the lamp boy (who were staring fixedly) think you vaguely respectable. But afterwards Helena suggested I invite Optatus to share a glass of a more refined Campanian I had brought with me. She declined the wine, but sat with us. Then while I, with my fine sense of masculine decorum, tried to keep the conversation neutral, Helena recovered from her weariness enough to start interviewing her father's tenant.

"My brother Aelianus says we had great good fortune in finding you to take on the estate." Marius Optatus gave us one of his reserved smiles. "He mentioned something about you having had some bad luck—I hope you don't mind me asking?" she added innocently.

Optatus had presumably met people of senatorial rank (not including Helena's brother, who was too juvenile to count), but he would rarely have dealt with the women. "I had been rather ill," he hedged reluctantly.

"Oh that I didn't know! I'm so sorry—was that why you had to find a new estate? You were farming hereabouts before, weren't you?"

"Don't be grilled if you don't want to be," I grinned, helping the man to a modest top-up of wine.

He saluted me with his cup and said nothing.

"I'm just making polite conversation, Marcus," Helena protested mildly. Optatus wouldn't know she had never been the kind of girl who bothered with idle chat. "I'm a long way from home, and in my condition I need to make friends as quickly as possible!"

"Are you intending to have the baby here?" Optatus asked, rather warily. He was probably wondering whether we had been dispatched abroad to have it in secret and hide our disgrace.

"Certainly not," I retorted. "There is a battery of antique nursemaids at the Camillus house all anxiously awaiting our return to Rome—not to mention the crabby but very cheap old witch who once delivered me, the highly exclusive midwife Helena's mother places her faith in, my younger sister, Helena's second cousin the Vestal Virgin, and phalanxes of interfering neighbors on all sides. It will cause a social scandal if we fail to use the birthing chair which helped Helena's noble mama produce Helena and her brothers, and which has been purposely sent to Rome from the Camillus country estate—"

"But you'll gather most of Rome disapproves of us," Helena quietly inserted into my satire.

"How true," I said. "But then I find myself increasingly disapproving of most of Rome . . . Optatus, in case you're wondering, you should treat Helena Justina as the noble daughter of your illustrious landlord, though you may pray to the gods that I whisk her away before her lying-in. You can treat me how you like. I'm here on some urgent official business, and Helena was too spirited to be left behind."

"Official business!" Optatus had found a sense of humor. "You mean my new landlord Camillus Verus has not sent you out in a hurry to see whether his youthful son has unwisely signed a lease with me? I was intending to rush out at dawn to make sure the cabbage rows are straight."

"Aelianus was satisfied you know how to farm," said Helena.

I backed her up: "He said you had informed him his father was being cheated."

A shadow briefly crossed the tenant's face. "Camillus Verus was losing a lot of the profits from his olive trees."

"How was that?"

Optatus' face darkened even more. "Several ways. The muleteers who take the skins of oil to the Baetis were stealing from him outright; they needed to be supervised. The bargemen on the river were also somehow miscounting when they stowed his amphorae—though they try to do that to everyone. Worst was the lie he was being told about how much oil his trees were yielding."

"Who was lying?"

"The men who pressed his olives."

"How can you be sure?"

"I knew them. They are from my ex-landlord's personal estate. Camillus Verus does not own his own press here. Millstones are very expensive and the number of trees does not justify it. Better if a neighbor contracts to do the work. My exlandlord's family used to do it, on an amicable basis—but when your father bought his estate the good relationship was abandoned."

I sucked my teeth. "And how would Camillus, thousands of miles away in Rome, ever have known he was being misled? Even when he sent Aelianus, the boy would have been too inexperienced to realize."

Optatus nodded. "But I found out. My father and I had always lent workers to help our landlord at harvest, then his workers used to come to help us in turn. So my own people were present when the Camillus fruit was crushed. They told me of the fraud."

"Does this have anything to do with why you lost your own farm?" Helena put in suddenly.

Marius Optatus placed his winecup on a stool, as if refusing to be lulled into any confidence by the drink—or by our offer of friendship either, if I was any judge. "There were two reasons why I was asked to leave. Firstly, I was a tenant, as my family had been there for many years."

"It was hard to lose?" Helena murmured.

"It was home." He was terse. "I lost my mother some years ago. Then my father died. That gave my landlord an excuse to alter our arrangement. He wanted the land back for himself. He declined to sign a new tenancy with me." He was only just managing to remain calm. "The second reason of course was my disloyalty."

"When you told Aelianus that my father was being cheated?" That would not have made him popular with anyone. Optatus had chosen the outsider, not the local community. Fatal, wherever you live.

"People had been hoping to make money from Camillus."

"Deceiving a foreigner is always a good game," I said.

"And how did your ex-landlord maneuver you out?" Helena inquired.

"Unluckily that was when I fell ill. I had a fever on the brain. I should have died." There was deep unhappiness behind this story. I rather thought the worst of it would never be told. "There was a long period while I was too weak to do anything. Then I was ousted from my land on the pretext that it had been badly neglected; I was a bad tenant."

"Harsh!"

"I had certainly not expected it. I stand by what I did—and had I not been ill, I would have argued the issue. But it's too late now."

"Did nobody defend you?" Helena demanded indignantly.

"None of my neighbors wanted to become involved. In their eyes I had become a troublemaker."

Helena was furious. "Surely once you had recovered everyone could see you would run things properly again?"

"Everyone who *wanted* to know the truth," I said. "Not a landlord who was keen to end the tenancy. And besides, in that situation it's sometimes best to accept that goodwill has broken down." Optatus agreed with me; I could see he wanted to end the discussion.

Helena was still too angry. "No, it's monstrous! Even at this late stage you should take your landlord before the regional council and argue for reinstatement."

"My ex-landlord," Optatus replied slowly, "is an extremely powerful man."

"But disputes can be heard before the provincial governor." With her deep hatred of injustice, Helena refused to give in.

"Or the quaestor if he is sent to the regional court as the proconsul's deputy," Optatus added. His voice was tight. "In Corduba that usually happens. The quaestor spares his proconsul the business of hearing pleas."

Remembering that the new quaestor was to be Quinctius Quadratus, the son of the senator I had met and disliked in Rome, I was losing my confidence in the regional rule of law. "The quaestor may be young, but he is a senator-elect," I argued, nevertheless. Not that I had ever felt any awe for senators-elect. Still, I was a Roman abroad and I knew how to defend the system. "When he stands in for his governor he ought to do the job properly."

"Oh I'm sure he would!" Optatus scoffed. "Perhaps I should mention, however, that my previous landlord is called Quinctius Attractus. I should be making my petition to his son."

Now even Helena Justina had to see his point.

TWENTY

I wanted to know Optatus better before I discussed anything with political overtones, so I yawned heavily and we went to bed. He had described some lively local disputes and crookedness. Still, that happens everywhere. Big men stamp on little men. Honest brokers stir up their neighbors' antagonism. Incomers are resented and regarded as fair game. Urban life seems to be noisy and violent, but in the country it's worse. Poisonous feuds fester behind every bush.

Next day I persuaded Optatus to tour the estate with me. We set off to inspect the olive trees that all the fuss was about, while Nux gamboled wildly around us, convinced that our walk was for her sole benefit. She had only ever known the streets of Rome. She tore about with her eyes mere slits in the wind, barking at the clouds.

Optatus told me that along the Baetis, especially running west towards Hispalis, were holdings of all sizes—huge estates run by powerful and wealthy families, and also a variety of smaller farms which were either owned or leased. Some of the big holdings belonged to local tycoons, others to Roman investors. Camillus Verus, who was perennially short of cash, had bought himself a pretty modest one.

Though small, the place had potential. The low hills south of the Baetis were as productive in agriculture as the mountains to the north of the river were rich in copper and silver. Camillus had managed to obtain a good position, and it was already clear his new tenant was putting the farm to rights.

Optatus first showed me the huge silo where grain was stored underground on straw in conditions that would keep it usable for fifty years. "The wheat is excellent, and the land will support other cereal crops." We walked past a bed of asparagus; I cut some spears with my knife. If my guide noticed that I knew how to select the best, how to burrow down into the dry earth before making my cut, and that I should leave a proportion for growing on, he made no comment. "There are a few vines, though they need attention. We have damsons and nuts—"

"Almonds?"

"Yes. Then we have the olive trees—suffering badly."

"What's wrong with them?" We stood under the close rows, running in an east-west direction to allow breezes to waft through. To me an olive grove was just an olive grove, unless it had a chorus of nymphs tripping about in windblown drapery.

"Too tall." Some were twice as high as me; some more. "In cultivation they will grow to forty feet, but who wants that? As a guide, they should be kept to the height of the tallest ox, to allow for picking the fruit."

"I thought olives were shaken down by banging the trees with sticks? Then caught in nets?"

"Not good." Optatus disagreed impatiently. "Sticks can damage the tender branches that bear the fruit. Falling can bruise the olives. Hand-picking is best. It means visiting every tree several times in each harvest, to catch all the fruit when it is exactly ripe."

"Green or black? Which do you favor for pressing?"

"Depends on the variety. Pausian gives the best oil, but only while the fruit is green. Regia gives best from the black."

He showed me where he was himself stripping back the soil to expose the roots, then removing young suckers. Meanwhile the upper branches were being severely pruned to reduce the trees to a manageable height.

"Will this harsh treatment set them back?"

"Olives are tough, Falco. An uprooted tree will sprout again if the smallest shred of root remains in contact with the soil."

"Is that how they can live so long?"

"Five hundred years, they say."

"It's a long-term business. Hard for a tenant to start afresh," I sympathized, watching him.

His manner did not alter—but it was pretty restrained to start with. "The new cuttings I have planted this month in the nursery will not bear fruit for five years; it will take at least twenty for them to reach their best. Yes; the olive business is long term."

I wanted to ask him about his old landlord Attractus, but I was not sure how to tackle it. Last night, with supper and wine inside him he had shown his feelings more freely, but this morning he had clammed up. I am the first to respect a man's privacy—except when I need to extract what he knows.

In fact he saved me the trouble of opening the discussion.

"You want me to tell you about the Quinctii!" he announced grimly.

"I'm not harassing you."

"Oh no!" He was working himself up well. "You want me to tell you how the father did me down, how I suffered, and how the son gloated!"

"Is that how it was?"

Optatus took a deep breath. My quiet attitude had relaxed him too. "Of course not."

"I didn't think so," I remarked. "If we had been talking about an obviously corrupt action you wouldn't have stood for it, and other people would have come out on your side. Whatever pressure the Quinctii applied to make you leave, you must have felt that technically at least, they had the law on their side."

"I'm not the man to judge what happened," Marius Optatus said. "I only know I was helpless. It was all achieved very subtly. I felt, and still feel, a deep sense of injustice—but I cannot prove any wrongdoing."

"The Quinctii had definitely decided that they wanted you out?"

"They wanted to expand their own estate. The easiest way, and the cheapest of course, was to kick me off the land that my family had been improving for several generations and take it over themselves. It saved them buying more ground. It saved them clearing and planting. I couldn't complain. I was a tenant; if I gave them cause, ending the contract was their right."

"But it was harsh, and it was done badly?"

"The father was in Rome. His son dealt with me. He doesn't know," Optatus shrugged, still almost with disbelief. "Young Quinctius Quadratus watched me leave with my bed, and my tools, and my saltbox—and he really did not understand what he had done to me."

"You call him young," I rasped. "He has been given charge of all the financial affairs of this province. He's not a child."

"He is twenty-five," Optatus said tersely.

"Oh yes! In his year." Quadratus had achieved the quaestorship at the earliest possible date. "We're in circles where golden youths don't expect to hang about. They want their honors now—so they can go on to grab more!"

"He's a shooting star, Falco!"

"Maybe somebody somewhere has a sharp arrow and a long enough reach to bring him down."

Optatus did not waste effort on such dreams. "My family were tenants," he repeated, "but that had been our choice. We were people of standing. I was not destitute when I left the farm. In fact," he added, becoming quite animated, "it could have been worse. My grandfather and father had always understood what the situation was, so every last wooden hayfork that belonged to us was inventoried on a list. Every yoke, millstone and plough. Every basket for straining cheese. That gave me some satisfaction."

"Did Quadratus try to haggle about what you could take with you?"

"He wanted to. I wanted him to try it—"

"That would be theft. It would have destroyed his public face."

"Yes, Falco. He was too clever for that."

"He is intelligent?"

"Of course."

They always are, those golden boys who spend their lives destroying other people.

We strolled to the nursery where I inspected the tiny sprouts, each standing in a hollow to conserve moisture and with a windbreak made from an esparto sack for protection. Optatus was carrying out this task himself, though of course he had workers on the estate including slaves of his own. While we were there he puddled in his precious nurselings with water from a barrel, stroking their leaves and tutting over any that looked limp. Seeing him fuss, I gained some sense of his grief at losing the farm where he grew up. It did not improve my opinion of the Quinctius family.

I could tell he wanted to be rid of me. He had been polite, but I had had my ration. He walked me back to the house formally, as if ensuring I was off the scene.

We stopped on the way to look into some outbuildings, including one where olives that were stored for domestic consumption were kept in amphorae, packed in various preparations to preserve them through winter. While we were engrossed, disaster struck. We arrived at the small garden area in front of the main building, just as Helena was trying to catch Nux. The dog rushed towards us ecstatically, with what appeared to be a twig in her mouth.

Optatus and I both immediately knew what it really was. I cursed. Optatus let out a wild cry. He seized a broom and began trying to smash it down on the dog. Helena squealed and stepped back. Loosing off a smothered protest, I managed to grab the culprit, picking up Nux by the scruff of her neck. We jumped out of reach of Optatus. With a hard tap on the nose I prised the trophy from Nux, who compounded her crime by scrabbling free again and leaping about yapping and pleading with me to throw the thing for her. No chance!

Optatus was white. His thin frame went rigid. He could hardly speak for anger—but he forced the words out: "Falco! Your dog has torn up the cuttings in my nursery bed!"

Just my luck.

Helena captured Nux and carried her off to be scolded, well out of sight. I strode back to the churned-up plant nursery, with Optatus stalking at my heels. Nux had torn up only one tree, in fact, and knocked a few others over. "I'm sorry; the dog likes chasing things, big things mainly. At home she's been known to frighten vintners delivering wine amphorae. She has simply never been trained to be loose on a farm . . ."

Scuffing earth flat quickly with the side of my boot, I found the damage much less than it could have been. Nux had been digging, but most of the holes had missed the little trees. Without asking, I found where the rescued cutting belonged and replaced it myself. Optatus stood by in fury. Part of me expected him to snatch the twiglet from me; part knew he was shrinking from it as if the dog had contaminated his treasure.

I picked off the damaged leaves, checked the stem for

bruising, redug the planting hole, found the support stake, and firmed in the little tree in the way my grandfather and great-uncle had taught me when I was a small boy. If Optatus was surprised that a street-pounding Roman knew how to do this, he showed nothing. His silence was as bleak as his expression. Still ignoring him, I walked quietly to the water barrel and fetched the jug I had seen him use earlier. Carefully I soaked the plant back into its old position.

"It's gone limp, but I think it's just sulking." I arranged its sackcloth windbreak then I stood up and looked straight at him. "I apologize for the accident. Let's look on the bright side. Last night we were strangers. Now everything's changed. You can think me an inconsiderate, wantonly destructive townee. I can call you an oversensitive, agitated foreigner who is, moreover, cruel to dogs." His chin came up, but I wasn't having it. "So now we can stop sidestepping: I'll tell you the unpleasant political nature of the work I'm really sent here to do. And you," I said clearly, "can give me a true assessment of what's wrong in the local community."

He started to tell me which plot in Hades I could go and sink my roots in. "Perhaps first of all," I continued pleasantly, "I should warn you that I came to Corduba to investigate two matters: one involves a scandal in the oil market—and the other is murder."

TWENTY-ONE

I had managed to strike Optatus dumb, which was no mean feat. When normally silent types do decide they are bursting with indignant exclamations, they tend to be unstoppable. But on a quiet sunlit slope among the timeless dignity of olive trees, murder sounds a powerful word.

"Falco, what are you talking about?"

"One man dead, possibly two of them, in Rome. And it looks as if somebody from Baetica arranged it." That night I had dinner at the Palace seemed a long way off, yet the thought of Anacrites lying pallid and still and almost a stranger to himself came clearly to mind. Even more vivid was Valentinus' corpse: that young man so like myself, lying in the dim light of the Second Cohort's engine house.

Marius Optatus looked disgusted. "I know nothing of this."

"No? Then do you know two big landowners called Licinius Rufius and Annaeus Maximus? When I was introduced to them they set themselves up as honest men of high renown—but they were in doubtful company that night, and after the attacks they behaved very oddly themselves. Then what about a *scapharius* called Cyzacus? Well, when was a bargee to be trusted? A *navicularius* called Norbanus? He's a Gaul, I believe, and a shipping negotiator into the bargain, so you don't have to pretend to like him. When I met them all these fellows were dining with someone you certainly do know—a certain Roman senator called Quinctius Attractus! In Rome he's regarded as a big bean in Baetica, though in Baetica you may prefer your legumes homegrown. He's regarded by *me* as a very suspicious character."

"Attractus has for some time been inviting groups of people to visit him in Rome," Optatus agreed, blinking with amazement at my angry speech.

"Do *you* think he's up to no good?"

"After my experience of him as a landlord, I'm bound to think that—but I'm prejudiced, Falco."

"I'll ask you something different then. You're a bachelor, I gather; I don't suppose you have any lithe girlfriends in Hispalis who might just have returned abruptly from a trip to Rome?"

Optatus looked po-faced. "I know nobody from Hispalis."

"You'd know this one again if you saw her; she's a dancer—just bursting with talent of one kind or another."

"There must be thousands of girls who dance, but most of them have gone to Rome—"

"With their fee paid by Attractus? And a habit of leaving their props behind at the scenes of bloody crimes?"

I had been going too fast for a countryman. "Who are you?" Optatus demanded in apparent bewilderment. "What are these people from Baetica to you? What harm are you bringing them?"

"The harm has been done," I retorted. "I saw the corpse, and the dying man too. Now I'm looking for the killers, at the request of Titus Caesar—so if you're honest, Marius Optatus, you will help me with my task."

The tall, pale figure beside me began to recover his equanimity. Crouching down on one knee he firmed in the disturbed cutting to his own satisfaction. There was nothing wrong with the way I had replanted it, but I stood unmoved while he left his own scent on the damned thing.

He stood up. He had become more serious than ever. Brushing soil from his long hands he stared at me. Enduring the fascinated gaze was routine work for an informer and I remained relaxed. I could stand hostile scrutiny. "So what do you see?"

"You know what you are, Falco."

"Do I?"

"You arrive like a naive tourist." Optatus had assumed a critical voice to which I was no stranger. He had stopped regarding me just as a rather raffish Roman in a patched tunic. He had realized he hated what I did. "You seem inoffensive, a mere joker, a lightweight. Then people notice that you are a watcher. You have a stillness which is dangerous. You carry a sharp knife, hidden in your boot; you cut asparagus like a man who has used that knife for many unpleasant tasks."

My knife had certainly hacked some bad meats, but he wouldn't want to know about that. "I'm just a joker."

"You tell jokes, while unknown to your listener you are measuring the quality of his conscience."

I smiled at him. "I am the Emperor's agent."

"I have no desire to know of this, Falco."

"Well that's not the first time a prude told me my presence tainted his air."

He stiffened, then accepted the rebuke: "You will say that your work is necessary, I realize that."

I clapped him gently on the shoulder, to reassure him if possible. He himself seemed like an innocent abroad. According to my famous worldly experience, that probably meant he was a devious swine, and setting me up.

We began walking towards the house again, along a dry track where even so early in the year the soil smelt hot and dusty. The red Baetican earth had already stained my boot-leather. It was pleasant weather. Just the kind of day when the men who were plotting the olive oil cartel were probably riding out on fine Spanish horses to each other's estates, refining their plans.

"Optatus, I mentioned some names. Tell me about them. I need to know how the men I saw in Rome relate to each other and to their fine friend Attractus."

I watched him struggle with fastidious dislike of the topic. Some people are eager to gossip, but a few unusual souls do find discussing their neighbors distasteful. These are the ones who are best value to an informer. They are offended by offers of payment, and better still they tell the truth.

"Come on, Marius! You *must* know the Corduban oil tycoons. The Annaei are one of the most prominent families in Corduba. Annaeus Maximus ought to carry top weight in Baetica. He's from the family of the Senecas; we're talking about extraordinary wealth."

"This is true, Falco."

"Since it's public knowledge, there is no need to be coy. So what about Licinius Rufius?"

"Not so grand a family."

"Any senators?"

"No, but their time must come. Licinius himself is elderly but he has worked to become important in Corduba and he intends to build a dynasty. He is extremely ambitious for his two grandchildren, whom he brought up when their parents died. The young man should do well—"

"Local priesthoods and magistracies?"

"Rufius Constans is bound for Rome, Falco: it is a distinct and separate career." I gathered Optatus slightly disapproved.

"Doesn't the one lead to the other?"

"That is not how it works. In the provinces you have to make a choice. Think of the Annaei whom you mentioned: the elder Seneca was a leading citizen and famous author and bibliographer, yet he remained socially obscure. Of his three sons, the first went straight into a senatorial career in Rome and achieved prominence, the next became an equestrian first, also in Rome, and only entered the Senate when he showed the promise that was to make him a major figure. The youngest son remained all his life in Corduba."

"As the Annaei nowadays all choose to do?"

"There is no disgrace in provincial life, Falco."

"Rome has its moments too," I commented. "So going back to the other man's grandson, Rufius Constans— This young man, a jewel of Baetican high society, is in his early twenties and to promote him his grandfather took him off to Rome recently?"

"I heard so."

"He enjoys the theater, I'm told!"

"Is that significant?"

"I didn't think so when I heard it—but he went with your new provincial quaestor. If the younger generation are so friendly, their elders may be nuzzling up to each other too."

"People here tend to keep Roman landowners like Attractus at arm's length. He has hardly ever been here."

"But they go to Rome at his invitation? Maybe he helps them with the fare. Then they arrive, eager to see the Golden City, flattered by the attention of a man with influence. Clearly he *does* have influence—he's the type who can get the Senate to vote a particular provincial post to his son."

"You think his visitors become open to persuasion?"

"He may be offering just what they want: for instance patronage for the Rufius grandson—and did you say there's a girl in that family?"

"Claudia Rufina is expected to marry my ex-landlord's son." Optatus never mentioned his dispossessor by name if he could avoid it. Nor the quaestorly son. "I trust Licinius, Falco. For instance, I shall be sending the olives from this estate to his presses next autumn, so we don't get cheated elsewhere.

Of the others you mentioned," he went on crisply, trying to blot out mention of his own troubles, "Norbanus is a shipping negotiator, as you said. He buys and sells space in the ocean-going craft that come upriver as far as Hispalis. I have met him, but I don't know him well. My family used someone else."

"Any reason for not using him?"

For once Optatus smiled. "Ours was a remote cousin."

"Ah!"

"Norbanus, however, is the most well known. He is chief of the guild of negotiators at Hispalis. He also has his own office at Ostia, in the port of Rome."

"He's well-to-do, then. And Cyzacus must be top man among the Baetis bargees?"

"You have heard of Cyzacus?"

"You mean, how do I know he's the tribal chief? I worked it out. Attractus appears to go for the most prominent men. So how do they all get on together? Norbanus and Cyzacus seemed to be deep in gossip. Are the two estate owners close drinking cronies too?"

"Shippers and landowners exist in mutual contempt, Falco. Cyzacus and Norbanus would have been lucky to get anybody else to speak to them. They and the producers spend most of their lives trying to mislead each other about prices or complaining about late deliveries, or how the oil has been handled . . . As for Annaeus and Licinius, they are in the same business as each other, so they are rivals in earnest." That was good news. Wedges might be inserted here. This is how conspiracies are toppled by agents who know how. We find a cozy clique, which has internal rivalries, and we nimbly cause dissent. "One difference is, the Annaeii came from Italian stock many years ago, the very first Roman settlers here. The Rufii are of pure Spanish origin and have ground to make up."

"I see you have plenty of local snobberies!"

"Yes, people who have vital interests in common do love to despise one another for grand reasons."

"Tell me what makes the two olive growers hate each other? Is it purely commercial jostling?"

"Oh I think so. There is no deadly quarrel," Optatus told me rather wryly, as if he assumed I thought provincial towns were hotbeds of family feuds and intriguing sexual jealousy. Well no doubt they had their fun, but making money took precedence. On the other hand, in my work when people denied the existence of strong emotions, it was usually a prelude to finding corpses with knives in their backs.

We had reached the villa rustica. I could hear Nux barking, probably in protest because Helena had locked her up. I made my retreat before Optatus could remember his heartache over the torn-up tree.

TWENTY-TWO

Corduba sits on the north bank of the River Baetis, overlooking a fertile agricultural plain. Marmarides drove Helena and me there the next day. Where the navigable water petered out into spongy pools and channels we crossed a bridge, made of stone, which everyone claimed replaced one that Julius Caesar had built. Even in April the river was virtually fordable at this point.

Corduba has an old local history, but had been founded as a Roman city by Marcellus, the first Roman governor of Spain. Then both Caesar and Augustus had made it a colony for veteran soldiers, so Latin was the language everyone now spoke, and from that staged beginning must have come some of the social snobberies Optatus had described for me. There were people with all sorts of pedigrees.

Even while it was being colonized the district had a turbulent history. The Iberian landmass had been invaded by Rome three hundred years ago—yet it had taken us two hundred and fifty to make it convincingly ours. The numerous conflicting tribes created trouble enough, but Spain had also been the entry route for the Carthaginians. Later it made a fine feuding ground for rivals every time prominent men in Rome plunged us into civil war. Corduba had repeatedly featured in sieges. Still, unlike most large provincial centers I had visited, mainly on the frontiers of the Empire, there was no permanent military fort.

Baetica, which possessed the most natural resources, had yearned for peace—and the chance to exploit its riches—long before the wild interior. At home in the Forum of the Romans was a golden statue of Augustus set up by wealthy Baeticans in gratitude for his bringing them a quiet life at last. How quiet it really was, I would have to test.

We passed a small guardhouse and crossed the bridge. Beyond lay stout town walls, a monumental gate and houses built in the distinctive local style of mud walls topped with wood; I discovered later the town had a prominent fire brigade to cope with the accidents that endanger timber buildings in close-packed urban centers where lamp oil is very cheap. They also boasted an amphitheater, doing well according to a rash of advertising placards; various bloodthirsty-sounding gladiators were popular. Aqueducts brought water from the hills to the north.

Corduba had a mixed, cosmopolitan population, though as we forced a passage through the twisting streets to the civic center we found the mixture was kept strictly separate—Roman and Hispanic areas were neatly divided by a wall running west to east. Notices carved on wall plaques emphasized the divide. I stood in the forum, labeled as Roman, and thought how odd this strict local schism would seem in Rome itself, where people of every class and background are thrust up against each other. The rich may try to keep apart in their mansions, but if they want to go anywhere—and to be anyone in Rome you must be a *public* man—they have to accept being buffeted by the garlic-eating hordes.

I had a good idea that in Corduba both the elegant Roman administrators and the aloof, inward-looking Baeticans would soon find themselves in a close pact on one subject: disapproval of me.

Like all decent tourists we had made our way first to the forum. It was in the northern sector. As soon as we inquired for directions I learned that the governor's palace was back down by the river; distracted by talking to Helena, I had let myself be driven past it. Helena and Marmarides, who were keen to see the sights, went off to explore. Helena had brought a town plan left behind by her brother. She would show me any decent landmarks later.

I was obliged to register my presence with the proconsul of Baetica. There were four judicial regions in this sun-drenched province—Corduba, Hispalis, Astigi and Gades. I knew therefore that there was only a one in four chance of finding the governor at home. Since the Fates regard showering me with disappointment as a good game of dice, I expected the worst. But when I presented myself at the proconsular palace, he was there. Things were looking up. That didn't mean I could get the mighty man to meet me.

I set myself a pleasant wager: seeing how soon I could wangle an official interview. I tried to make my approach subtle, since there was an obvious need for secrecy. A simple request fell flat. Producing a tablet with the dignified seal of Claudius Laeta, Chief of Correspondence to the Emperor, obtained mild interest among the flunkies, who must have written Laeta's name on a few thousand dreary communiqués. One neatly cropped fellow said he would see what he could do then ducked out into a corridor to discuss his last night's wine consumption with a friend. I put on the bleak expression auditors wear when tasked to eliminate excessive staff numbers. Two other relaxed lads put their heads together and worked out their order for lunch.

There was only one thing for it. Dirty tactics.

I leaned against a side table and whittled my nails with my

knife. "Don't hurry," I smiled. "It's not going to be easy informing the proconsul his great-grandfather has finally died. I wouldn't have minded the job, but I'm supposed to explain about the old blighter changing his will, and I just don't see how I can do that without mentioning a certain little Illyrian manicurist. If I'm not careful we'll be getting into the business of why his honor's wife didn't go to the country as instructed, and then the ding-dong with the charioteer will slip out. Jove knows they should have kept it quiet but of course her doctor talked, and who can blame him when you hear where the proconsul's spare epaulettes were sewn—" Both the flunky in the corridor and his friend stuck their heads slowly round the door to join the others staring at me goggle-eyed. I beamed at them. "Better not say any more, even though it is all over the Senate. But you heard it from me first! Remember that when the drinks are being got in . . ."

I was lying of course. I never socialize with clerks.

The first young person dashed off, zipped back rather breathless, then shunted me into the presence. The proconsul was looking surprised, but he didn't know he had become a celebrity. His loyal scroll-pushers would be clustered outside the door, applying winecups to the lacquered panels in the hope of overhearing more. Since the personage in charge sat on his dais under some purple curtains at the far end of a room which seemed the length of a running stadium, our mundane discussion of trade issues would be out of earshot of the gossips with their ears on fire. There were still a few scribes and cup-bearers attending the mighty man, though; I wondered how to get rid of them.

The proconsul of Baetica was a typical Vespasian appointee: he looked like a pig farmer. His tanned face and ugly legs would not have counted against him when he was chosen to sit here on an ivory seat between the dusty set of ceremonial rods and axes, below the rather tarnished and tired gold eagle. Instead Vespasian would have noted his illustrious career—bound to include commanding a legion and a stint in a consulship—and would also have marked the shrewdness behind the man's intent hooded eyes. Those eyes watched me approach down the lengthy audience chamber, while a brain as sharp as a Pict's hatchet was summing me up just as fast as I was evaluating him.

His was a post that needed a strong grip. It was only three years since two Hispanic provinces played their part in the legendary Year of the Four Emperors: Tarraconensis in backing Galba, then Lusitania in supporting Otto. Galba had actually stood for emperor while still a provincial governor, using the legions of his official command to uphold his claim. This caught on, as bad ideas do: Vespasian eventually used the same ploy from Judaea. Afterwards he had to take firm action in Hispania. He reduced the Spanish legions from four to one—a fresh one—and even before I met this man I was sure the proconsul had been chosen for his allegiance to Vespasian and all that the new Flavian emperors stood for. (Those of you in the provinces may have heard that your new Roman governors are selected by a lottery. Well, that just shows how magically lotteries work. They always seem to pick out the men the Emperor wants.)

Hispania had lost its chance of glory when Galba slipped off the throne after only seven months and Otto barely lasted three; they were past history in Rome. But the rich estate- and mine-owners of Corduba had been among Galba's allies. Here there could still be dangerous tingles of resentment. Needless to say, outside the massive walls of the administrative palace, the town had appeared to be going about its business on this bright southern morning, as if setting up emperors carried no more world importance than a small scandal to do with amphitheater ticket sales. Yet maybe among the olive groves ambitions still seethed.

"What's the news on the Palatine?" The proconsul was blunt. He had been working in informal dress—a bonus of life in the provinces—but seeing me in my toga he slid into his surreptitiously.

"I bring you cordial greetings from the Emperor, Titus Caesar, and the Chief of Correspondence." I handed over a scroll from Laeta, introducing me.

He didn't bother to unseal it. He was not a man for etiquette. "You work for Laeta?" He managed to restrain a humph. Secretariat employees would be rare visitors—and unwelcome ones.

"I was sent here by Laeta—well, he signed a docket for my fare. There's an interesting situation at home, sir. The Chief Spy has been nastily knocked on the head, and Laeta has assumed some of his responsibilities. I was chosen to come out because I have what we'll call diplomatic experience." Calling myself an informer tended to explode ex-generals and ex-consuls into unsavory bouts of flatulence.

The proconsul absorbed my story and sat up slightly. "Why send you?"

"Expediency."

"Good word, Falco. Covers a wealth of donkey dung." I started to like the man.

"More like pulped olive manure," I said.

He got rid of his staff.

Achieving an interview was one thing. In the lustrous halls of power I often ended up dissatisfied. Like eating a meal in a bad mansio in Gaul.

We quickly established that I had an official mission, for which the proconsul did not wish to be responsible. He had an official mission too. Since he represented the Senate and I represented the Emperor, our interests did not necessarily collide. It was his province; his role took precedence. That was preserving good relations with the local community.

I described the attacks on Anacrites and Valentinus. The proconsul looked politely regretful about the Chief Spy and merely dismissive of the fate of an unknown underling. He denied knowing any dancers from Hispalis too, and looked annoyed that I had asked. However, he did suggest that the local aediles in her hometown might have the murderous Diana on their lists of licensed entertainers; to find out I would have to go to Hispalis.

He told me I could count on him for full support—although due to the Emperor's wish to reduce provincial expenditure, no resources could be allocated to assist me. That was not unexpected. Luckily I pay for my own boot-leather, and I could charge Laeta for necessary bribes.

I requested comments on the local personnel. The proconsul said I was the expert: he would leave judgments to me. I deduced that he was a frequent dinner guest in at least the more upper-class suspects' homes.

"Obviously the export of olive oil is a major trade which Rome intends to safeguard." And obviously it was the proconsul's place to sum up. I was only the expert; I bit my tongue. "If there *were* to be an attempt to influence prices unfavorably, Falco, we would have to stamp on it severely. The consequences for the home market, the army, and the provincial outlets would be appalling. However I don't want to upset sensitivities here. You must do what you have to, but any complaints and you'll be bumped out of my province faster than you can breathe."

"Thank you, sir."

"Is that all?"

"Just a minor point, sir." I usually manage to call them "sir" a few times. The shrewd ones are never fooled. "You had some correspondence with Anacrites recently, but it's lost in his coded filing library. I'd like permission to see the documents at your end."

"Financial subject. My quaestor was the official point of contact."

"That would be Cornelius? I gather it was time for him to move on—had he discussed the issue with you?"

"In general terms." I gained the subtle impression this was

only one of a myriad of topics on meeting agendas, and that the proconsul could not bring to mind the salient facts. But then he seemed to change his mind. "Are you the agent Anacrites warned us he was sending?" That was a development I had not known about.

"No; Laeta took me on, after Anacrites was put out of action. Valentinus, the man who was killed in Rome, looks the likeliest person to have been sent by the Chief Spy. I assume no one else has turned up?"

"No one has made contact."

"Then we can assume I'm doing the job now."

The proconsul decided to be frank with me. "Well to clear your passage: Anacrites wrote to query whether the olive oil market was stable. I've been in the business long enough to assume that meant he suspected it was not; he would not have expressed an interest otherwise. I had Cornelius review the situation urgently."

"He could be trusted?"

"Cornelius was reliable." He seemed about to add something on that topic, but instead went on, "There did appear to be restiveness, the kind of mood in the business community that is hard to define and harder still to tackle. I was unhappy, certainly. We sent a report. The response was that an agent would be coming out at once." I wondered if the reason Anacrites had left the Palace after the dinner I attended was to meet Valentinus and order him to make a trip to Corduba.

"Thank you; that's clear, sir. From all I've heard, you'll be missing Cornelius. He sounds a useful deputy. And now you've had an unknown quantity wished on you, I hear— Will the new quaestor now be taking over the oil cartel issue, sir?"

I had kept my expression neutral, but I let the proconsul see me watching him. Since the new lad in charge of financial matters was the son of a man who appeared to be piping the tune for the oil producers, this could become delicate.

"My new officer is unfamiliar with the subject," stated the

proconsul. It sounded as if he was warning me not to alert young Quinctius. I felt reassured.

"I believe he's in Corduba already?"

"He came in and had a look around the office." Something sounded peculiar. The proconsul looked me straight in the eye. "He's not here at the moment. I gave him some hunting leave. Best to let them get it out of their system," he told me dryly, like a man who had had to train a long procession of administrative illiterates.

I thought his real meaning was different. The proconsul would have had little choice about his new officer. The appointment of Quinctius Quadratus would have been lobbied by his influential father and fixed up by the Senate. The Emperor had the right of veto but to use it would be a mark of disfavor, one which the Quinctius family had not openly deserved. "I met his father in Rome," I said.

"Then you will know Quinctius Quadratus comes to us with fine recommendations." There was not a flicker of irony.

"Certainly his father carries weight, sir."

I was hardly expecting a proconsul to damn a fellow senator. It didn't happen either. "Tipped for a consulship," he commented gravely. "Would probably have got it by now if there hadn't been a long queue for rewards." After coming to power Vespasian had been obliged to offer honors to his own friends who had supported him; he had also two sons to be ritually made magistrates every few years. That meant men who had thought they were certainties for honors were now having to wait.

"If Attractus does get his consulship he'll be in line for a province afterwards," I grinned. "He could yet take over from you, sir!" The great man did not find it a joke. "Meanwhile the son is expected to go far?"

"At least as far as hunting leave," the proconsul agreed more jovially. I felt he quite enjoyed having kicked out the young Quinctius, even though it could only be temporary. "Luckily, the office runs itself."

I had seen offices that allegedly ran themselves. Usually that meant they were kept steady by one wizened Thracian slave who knew everything that had happened for the past fifty years. Fine—until the day he had his fatal heart attack.

Hunting leave is an ambiguous concept. Young officers in the provinces expect a certain amount of free time for slaying wild animals. This is normally granted as a reward for hard work. But it is also a well-known method for a pernickety governor to rid himself of a dud until such time as Rome sends out some other dewy-eyed hopeful—or until he himself is recalled.

"Where can we contact you?" asked the great man. He was already shedding his toga again.

"I'm staying on the Camillus Verus estate. I expect you remember his son Aelianus?" The proconsul signaled assent, while avoiding comment. "The senator's daughter is here at present too."

"With her husband?"

"Helena Justina is divorced—widowed too." I could see him noting that he would have to meet her socially, so to avoid the agony I added, "The noble Helena is expecting a child shortly."

He gave me a sharp look; I made no response. Sometimes I tell them the situation and stare them out. Sometimes I say nothing and let someone else gossip.

I knew, since I had picked it open and read it, that my letter of introduction from Laeta—as yet unopened on the proconsul's side table—gave a succinct description of our relationship. He described the senator's daughter as a quiet, unassuming girl (a lie which diplomatically acknowledged that her papa was a friend of the Emperor). I won't say what he called me, but had I not been an informer it would have been libelous.

TWENTY-THREE

The flock of scribes scattered like sparrows as I emerged. I winked. They blushed. I screwed out of them directions to the quaestor's office, noting that my request seemed to cause a slight atmosphere.

I was greeted by the inevitable ancient slave who organized documents in the quaestor's den. He was a black scribe from Hadrumetum. His will to subvert was as determined as that of the smoothest oriental secretary in Rome. He looked hostile when I asked to see the report Cornelius sent to Anacrites.

"You'll remember inscribing it." I made it clear I understood how delicate the subject matter had been. "There will have been a lot of fuss and redrafting; it was going to Rome, and also the material was sensitive locally."

The inscrutable look on the African's face faded slightly. "I can't release documents without asking the quaestor."

"Well, I know Cornelius was the authority on this. I expect the new fellow has had a handover, but the governor told me he hasn't been granted his full authority yet." The scribe said nothing. "He came in to meet the proconsul, didn't he? How do you find him?" I risked.

"Very pleasant."

"You're lucky then! A baby-faced brand-new senator, working abroad, and virtually unsupervised? You could easily get one who was arrogant and boorish—"

The slave still did not take the bait. "You must ask the quaestor."

"But he's not available, is he? The proconsul explained about your new policy in Baetica of screwing poll tax out of wild boars! His honor said if you had taken a copy of the letter you should show me that."

"Oh I took a copy! I always do."

Relieved of responsibility by the proconsul's authority (invented by me, as he may well have guessed), the quaestor's scribe at once started to hunt for the right scroll.

"Tell me, what's the word locally on why Anacrites first took an interest?" The scribe paused in his search. "He's the Chief Spy," I acknowledged frankly. "I work with him from time to time." I did not reveal that he was now lying insensible in the Praetorian Camp. Or already ashes in a cinerary urn.

My dour companion accepted that he was talking to a fellow professional. "Anacrites had had a tip from somebody in the province. He did not tell us who. It could have been malicious."

"It was anonymous?" He inclined his head slightly. "While you're finding the report Cornelius wrote I'd be grateful for sight of the original inquiry from Anacrites too."

"I was getting it. They should be linked together . . ." Now the scribe was sounding abstracted. He was already looking worried, and I felt apprehensive. I watched him once more search the round containers of scrolls. I believed he knew his way around the documents. And when he found that the correspondence was missing, his distress seemed genuine.

I was starting to worry. When documents go missing there can be three causes: simple inefficiency; security measures taken without a secretariat's knowledge; or theft. Inefficiency is rife, but rarer when the document is highly confidential. Security measures are never as good as anyone pretends; any secretary worth his position will tell you where the scroll is really stowed. Theft meant that somebody with access to officialdom knew that I was coming out here, knew why, and was removing evidence.

I could not believe it was the new quaestor. That seemed too obvious. "When Quinctius Quadratus was here, did you leave him alone in the office?"

"He just looked around from the doorway then rushed off to be introduced to the governor."

"Does anyone else have access?"

"There's a guard. When I go out I lock the door." A determined thief could find a way in. It might not even take a professional; palaces are always rife with people who look as if they have the right of entry, whether they do or not.

When I calmed the scribe down I said quietly, "The answers I want are known by your previous quaestor, Cornelius. Can I contact him? Has he left Baetica?"

"His term ended; he's going back to Rome—but first he's traveling. He's gone east on a tour. A benefactor offered him a chance to see the world before he settles down."

"That could take some time! Well if the junketer's unavailable, what can you remember from the scrolls that are lost?"

"The inquiry from Anacrites said hardly anything. The messenger who brought it probably talked to the proconsul and the quaestor." He was a scribe. He disapproved. He liked things safely written down.

"Tell me about Cornelius."

The scribe looked prim. "The proconsul had every confidence in him."

"Lots of hunting leave, eh?"

Now he looked puzzled. "He was a hardworking young man."

"Ah!"

"Cornelius was very worried," the scribe continued doggedly. "He discussed things with the proconsul, though not with me."

"Was that usual?"

"It was all so sensitive."

"He dictated the report to you though. What did it say?"

"Cornelius had concluded that people might want to inflate the price of olive oil."

"More than general overcharging?"

"Much more."

"Systematic fixing?"

"Yes."

"Did he name names?"

"No."

"Still, he thought that if action was taken quickly the cartel could be nipped in the bud?"

"Did he?" asked the scribe.

"It is a customary phrase. I was told that was his verdict."

"People are always repeating wrong statements that are supposed to be in reports," said the scribe, as if the very untidiness of the habit upset him. Something else was annoying me: Camillus Aelianus had apparently lied to me about this point.

"So Cornelius felt the situation was serious? Who was supposed to act on it?"

"Rome. Or Rome would order action by us—but they preferred to send their own investigator. Isn't what why you are here?"

I smiled—though the fact was, with Anacrites out of it and Laeta so untrustworthy, I had no idea.

TWENTY-FOUR

There was no hope of further help: today was a public holiday. Informers work loose hours and try to ignore such things, but everyone else in the Empire realized that this was eleven days before the Kalends of May—the big spring festival. The governor's palace had been working for a couple of hours, following the fine tradition of pretending that state business is too important to stop. But now even the palace was closing down, and I had to leave.

After walking uphill again, I found Marmarides in a tavern; I left him there. Helena was moping in the basilica entrance in the forum, looking at plans for a spanking new Temple of the Imperial Cult; she was clearly bored and it was time to remove her before she tried chalking faces on the Corinthian columns in the elegant design elevations. Ceremonies were about to start in any case.

I slipped my hand around hers and we walked slowly down the flight of steps among increasing crowds, Helena being careful to keep her balance. Reaching street level we dodged acolytes with incense-sprinklers as they gathered for a sacrifice.

"That looked a zippy new hexastyle portico they're going to build for the Imperial Cult!"

"When you start spouting architecture, I know you're in trouble," she said.

"I'm not in trouble—but somebody soon will be."

She gave me a skeptical look, then made some dry comment about the crisp modeling of the proposed temple's capitals. I said I wondered who would pay for this fine community monument. The citizens of Rome, perhaps, through exorbitantly priced olive oil.

I told Helena today's events as we found a space in the piazza, to view whatever was about to happen. Corduba is set on rising ground, the older part with a maze of narrow streets which come up from the river, its houses close set to keep out the hot sun. These byways lead uphill to the public buildings where we now were. Helena must have surveyed the small forum pretty well while she was waiting for me, but the festival pageantry revived her. "So the proconsul has given you permission to operate in his territory. You're looking, without much hope, for a dancing girl who kills people—"

"Yes, but I imagine somebody hired her to do it."

"For which your group of suspects are the Baeticans you saw at the dinner: Annaeus, Licinius, Cyzacus and Norbanus. Optatus told us Quinctius Attractus has been making overtures to other people too—"

"He would have to. Price-rigging only works if all the producers band together."

"But the ones who were in Rome when Valentinus was killed have made themselves suspects you have to concentrate on."

"It could be just their hard luck that they got themselves tangled up in a killing. But yes; it's those I'm after."

Helena always considered every possibility: "I suppose you don't think the dancing girl and her accomplices could be ordinary thieves whose method is to size up guests at parties then rob the rich ones as they stagger home drunk?"

"They didn't pick the rich ones, sweetheart; they jumped the Chief Spy and his agent."

"So you definitely think the attacks are linked to what's going on in Baetica?"

"Yes, and showing that the Baetican visitors were involved in the attacks will not only do right by Valentinus, but ought to discredit the whole conspiracy."

Helena grinned. "It's a pity you can't talk to the much-admired Cornelius. Who do you think has paid for his 'chance to see the world before he settles down'?"

"A gold-laden grandpa I expect. Types in those posts always have them."

"The proconsul sounds very suspicious of the new incumbent. Surely that's unusual? The lad hasn't even started yet."

"It confirms that his father is regarded as a bad influence in Baetica."

"The proconsul would be too tactful to libel Attractus of course . . ."

"He was! I could tell he dislikes the man, though—or at least he dislikes the kind of pushiness Attractus represents."

"Marcus, since Attractus himself isn't here you may be forced to have a look at his son. Have you brought your hunting spears?"

"Jupiter, no!" I had brought a sword for protection, though. "Given the chance to pursue wolves around a wild peninsula with my old friend Petronius I'd jump—but the quaestor will have gone on a rich idiots' trip. If there's one thing I can't stand it's a week of camping in a forest with a group of braying bastards whose idea of fun is sticking javelins into beasts that thirty slaves and a pack of vicious hounds have conveniently driven into nets."

"And no women," Helena nodded, apparently sympathetically.

I ignored the jibe. "Too much drink; too much noise; half-cooked, half-warm greasy meat; and listening to boasts and filthy jokes."

"Oh dear! And you the refined, sensitive type who just wants to sit under a thorn bush all day in a clean tunic with a scroll of epic poetry!"

"That's me. An olive tree on your father's farm will do."

"Just Virgil and a sliver of goat's cheese?"

"Seeing we're here, I'd better say Lucan; he's a Corduban poet. Plus your sweet head upon my knee, of course."

Helena smiled. I was pleased to see it. She had been looking tense when I found her at the basilica but a mixture of banter and flattery had softened her.

We watched a pontifex or flamen, one of the priests of the imperial cult, make a sacrifice at an altar set up in the open forum. A middle-aged, portly Baetican with a jolly expression, he wore a purple robe and a pointed, conical hat. He was attended by assistants who were probably freed slaves, but he himself flashed the equestrian ring and was a citizen of social solidity. He had probably held a senior military post in the legions, and maybe a local magistracy, but he looked a decent jolly soul as he rapidly cut a few animals' throats, then led out a fitful procession to celebrate the Feast of the Parilia, the lustration of the flocks.

We stood respectfully in the colonnade while the troop of civic dignitaries squashed by, on their way to the theater where a day of fun would take place. The procession was accompanied by some worried sheep and a skipping calf who clearly had not been told he was to form the next sacrifice. Persons who were pretending to be shepherds came past with brooms, supposedly for sweeping out stables; they also carried implements to light fumigatory fires. A couple of public slaves, clearly fire watchers, followed them with a water bucket, looking hopeful. Since the Parilia is not just any old rustic festival but the birthday of Rome, I bit back a surge of patriotic emotion (that's my story). A personification of Roma armed with shield and spear and a crescent moon on her helmet, swayed dangerously on a litter midway down the line. Helena half turned and muttered sarcastically, "Roma Resurgans is rather perilous on her palanquin!"

"Show some respect, bright eyes."

An official statue of the Emperor teetered before us and nearly toppled over. This time Helena obediently said nothing, though she glanced at me with such a riotous expression that while the wobbly image of Vespasian was being steadied by its bearers I had to pretend a coughing fit. Helena Justina had never been a model for perfect sculptural beauty; but in a happy mood she had life in every flicker of her eyelashes (which were in my opinion as fine as any in the Empire). Her sense of humor was wicked. Seeing a noble matron mock the Establishment always had a bad effect on me. I mouthed a kiss, looking moody. Helena ignored me and found another tableau to giggle at.

Then, following her line of sight, I spotted a familiar face. One of the broad burghers of Corduba was sidestepping the shepherds as they wrestled with a willful sheep. I recognized him at once, but a quick check with someone in the crowd confirmed his name: Annaeus Maximus. One of the two major oil producers at the dinner on the Palatine.

"One of those puffed-up dignitaries is on my list. This seems a good opportunity to talk to a suspect . . ."

I tried to persuade Helena to wait for me at a streetside foodshop. She fell silent in a way that told me I had two choices: either to abandon her, and see her walk away from me forever (except perhaps for a brief return visit to dump the baby on me)—or else I had to take her along.

I attempted the old trick of holding her face between my hands, and gazing into her eyes with an adoring expression.

"You're wasting time," Helena told me quietly. The bluff

had failed. I made one more attempt, squashing the tip of her nose with the end of my finger while smiling at her beseechingly. Helena bit my playful digit.

"Ow!" I sighed. "What's wrong, my love?"

"I'm starting to feel too much alone." She knew this was not the moment for a domestic heart-to-heart. Still, it never is the right time. It was better for her to be abruptly honest, standing beside a flower stall in a narrow Corduban street, than to bottle up her feelings and end up badly quarreling later. Better—but extremely inconvenient while a man I wanted to interview was scuttling away amongst the ceremonial throng.

"I do understand." It sounded glib.

"Oh do you?" I noticed the same frowning and withdrawn expression Helena had been wearing when I found her outside the basilica.

"Why not? You're stuck with having the baby—and obviously I can never know what that's like. But maybe I have troubles too. Maybe I'm starting to feel overwhelmed by the responsibility of being the one who has to look after all of us—"

"Oh I expect you'll cope!" she complained, almost to herself. "And I'll be poked out of the way!" She was perfectly aware it was her own fault she was stuck on her feet in a hot noisy street in Baetica.

I managed a grin, then followed it with a compromise: "I need you! You've been summing up my job for me pretty accurately. How about being poked onto a seat at the theater next to me?" I gave her my hand again, and we hurried together the way the procession had gone. Fortunately I possessed skills which most urban informers lack. I am an expert tracker. Even in a completely strange city I know how to trace a Parilia procession by following the newly deposited animal dung.

My experiences in Baetica already warned me that when I

caught up with the priest and magistrates I might detect an equally pungent smell.

I hate festivals. I hate the noise, and the wafts of lukewarm pies, and the queues at the public lavatories—if you can even find one open. Still, coming to Corduba on the Parilia could prove useful as a study of town life.

As we hurried through the streets, people went about their business in a pleasant mood. They were short and stocky, vivid evidence of why Spanish soldiers were the Empire's best. Their temperament seemed level too. Acquaintances greeted each other with a relaxed style. Women were not accosted. Men argued over curbside space for tying up wagons in a lively, but nonviolent way. Waiters in wine bars were friendly. Dogs yapped, then soon lost interest. All this seemed everyday behavior, not some holiday truce.

When we reached the theater, we found events were unticketed because the religious stuff was public and the dramatic scenes had all been paid for by the decurions, members of the town council; they, the Hundred Men, had the best seats, of course. Among them we picked out Annaeus Maximus again, and from his position he was a duovir, one of the two chief magistrates. If Corduba was typical, the Hundred Men controlled the town—and the duovirs controlled the Hundred Men. For conspirators, that could be very convenient.

Annaeus was the younger of the two landowners I had met in Rome, a square-faced Spaniard with a wide girth, giving me maybe fifteen or twenty years. Coughing slightly in the wafts of incense as the pontifex prepared to slaughter the calf and a couple of lambs, Annaeus was the first to rush forward to greet the governor. The proconsul had arrived direct from his palace, escorted by lictors. He was wearing the toga I had seen him in, not a military breastplate and cloak; ruling the senatorial provinces was a purely civic office.

In fact his role, we soon saw, was as a figurehead on somebody else's ship. The cream of Corduba had welcomed him as an honorary member of their own tightly knit top-notch Baetican club. He sat on his throne in the center of the front rows of seats around the orchestra, flanked by well-dressed families who gossiped and called out to each other—even shouting to the pontifex in mid-sacrifice—as if the entire festival was their own private picnic.

"It's sickening!" I muttered. "The Roman proconsul has been swallowed up by the ruling families, and he's become so much a part of the local clique it must be hard for him to remember that the Roman treasury pays his salary."

"You can see how it is," Helena agreed, only a little more mildly. "At every public occasion the same few men are in charge. The same faces cluster in the best positions. They're terribly rich. They're completely organized. Their families are linked intimately by marriage. Their ambitions may clash sometimes, but politically they are all one. Those people in the front-row seats run Corduba as their hereditary right."

"And in Gades, Astigi and Hispalis it's going to be the same—some of the faces will match too, because some of the men will be powerful in more than one place. Some must own land in several areas. Some will have taken rich wives from other towns."

We fell silent for the sacrifice. In acquiring foreign provinces, the plan was to assimilate local gods into the Roman pantheon, or simply add them to it if people liked to keep lots of options. So today at the Parilia ceremony two Celtic deities with unintelligible names received a lavish sacrifice, then Jupiter was allowed a slightly weedy lamb. But the Baeticans had been wearing Roman dress and speaking Latin for decades. They were as Romanized as provincials could be. And like the patricians of Rome, keeping a rigid grip on local politics through a small group of powerful families came as naturally as spitting.

"You can see it all," I muttered to Helena. "I bet the governor goes to all their private dinner parties, then when he holds a reception, this same crowd fills out the guest list. These folk will be at the Palace every week, munching dainties and sipping free wine. No one else gets a look in."

"If you live here, and belong to the charmed circle, you have to hobnob with the same suffocating group continually." That tedium was never going to afflict a dusty pleb like me—and Helena would have lost her own invitation the minute the proconsul read Laeta's letter about me.

"I'm just surprised the old man was as frank as he was!" I muttered.

Helena looked worried. "Do you regret making yourself known to him?"

"No; I represent Laeta; I had to report in. It's safe; the proconsul is one of Vespasian's men. But now I've seen what social obligations he has, I'll hold back from contact again."

The dramatic performances began. These consisted of brief scenes or tableaux which had been decreed suitable for public show on an occasion of organized celebration. There was little content, and less humor. I had seen more exciting theater; I had even written a better play myself. No one was going to wet themselves with outrage here.

We watched dutifully for some time. I had been in the army; I knew how to endure misery. Eventually Helena wilted and said she wanted to go home. "I can't see any point in waiting. Annaeus will never talk to you in the middle of all this."

"No; but since he's a duovir he has to keep a house within a mile of the town. He's bound to be there this evening. I could visit him then."

Helena looked depressed and I was not pleased at the thought of hanging around town all afternoon until my man made himself available. Still, I needed to tackle him about the cartel and see if I could establish a link between him and the dancing girl.

Helena and I left the theater, amazing the doorkeeper who thought we should have been engrossed in the drama. We rousted out Marmarides, who still seemed fairly sober, and I told him to drive Helena home. I would find my own transport back tonight or tomorrow—another prospect that made me glum. Riding home on a hired mule after dark through unknown roads can be disastrous.

I went with them as far as the bridge over the Baetis. "I'll make a bargain," Helena declared. "If I go home quietly and let you stay on your own to investigate Annaeus, then I'm going to go over to the Licinius Rufius estate tomorrow and make friends with his granddaughter."

"Find out if she can dance!" I chortled, knowing that the wealthy family she came from would be scandalized if she did.

The bridge at Corduba is three hundred and sixty-five paces long, one for every day of the year. I know, because I counted as I marched miserably back.

To fill in time I went to investigate the shipping offices of the bargees, in the vague hope of interviewing my other suspect, Cyzacus. All the wharfside huts were locked. A bleary-eyed man fishing off a jetty said the offices were closed for the festival, and that they would be for the next three days.

TWENTY-FIVE

Later that day, after a few inquiries, I left by the northwestern gate. Annaeus Maximus owned a lovely home outside the town walls, where he could plot the next elections with his cronies and his wife could run her salon for other elegant socially prominent women, while their children all went to the bad. Beyond the cemetery lining the route out of town lay a small group of large houses. An enclave of peace for the rich—disturbed only by the yapping of their hunting dogs, the snorting of their horses, the rioting of their children, the quarreling of their slaves and the carousing of their visitors. As town houses go, the Annaeus spread was more of a pavilion in a park. I found it easy to identify—lit throughout, including the long carriage drive and surrounding garden terraces. Fair enough. If a man happens to be an olive oil tycoon, he can afford a lot of lamps.

The clique we had seen at the theater were now assembling for a dinner party at this well-lit house with garlanded porticoes and smoking torches in every acanthus bed. Men on splendid horses were turning up every few minutes, alongside gilded carriages which contained their overindulged wives. I recognized many of the faces from the front rows at the theater. Amidst the coming and going I also met the shepherds from the Parilia parade; they may indeed have been here for ritual purification rites in the stables, though I thought it more likely they were actors who had come to be paid for their day's work in town. There were a few shepherdesses among them, including one with hugely knowing dark brown eyes. Once I would have tried to put a light of my own into eyes like that. But I was a responsible father-to-be now. Besides, I could never take to women with straw in their hair.

I made myself known to an usher. Baetican hospitality is legendary. He asked me to wait while he informed his master I was here, and as the whole house was pervaded by delicious cooking smells I promised myself I might be offered a piquant dish or two. There was bound to be plenty. Excess breathed off the frescoed walls. However, I soon learned that the Cordubans were as sophisticated as Romans. They knew how to treat an informer—even when he described himself as a "state official and associate of your neighbor Camillus." "Associates" received short commons in Corduba—not so much as a drink of water. What's more, I had to wait a damned long time before I got noticed at all.

It was evening. I had set out from town in the light, but the first stars were winking over the distant Mariana mountains when I was led outside to meet Annaeus Maximus. He had been mingling with his guests on one of the terraces, where they were soon to hold an outdoor feast, as is traditional at the Parilia. The supposed shepherds had really been setting fire to sulfur, rosemary, firwood and incense in at least one of the many stables so the smoke would purify the rafters. Now heaps of hay and straw were being burned on the well-scythed lawns, so that a few by now extremely tired sheep could be compelled to run through the fires. It's hard work being a ceremonial flock. The poor beasts had been on their trotters all day, and now they had to endure being ritually lustrated while humans stood around being sprinkled with scented water and sipping bowls of milk. Most of the men had one eye out for the wine amphorae, while the women kept flapping their hands about, in the vain hope of preventing their fabulous gowns being imbued with lustral smoke.

I was kept well back in a colonnade, and it wasn't to protect me from the sparks. The invited guests began to seat themselves for the feast out amongst the regimented topiary, then Annaeus stomped up to deal with me. He looked annoyed. Somehow I have that effect.

"What's this about?"

"My name is Didius Falco. I have been sent from Rome."

"You say you're a relative of Camillus?"

"I have a connection—" Among snobs, and in a foreign country, I had no qualms about acquiring a respectable patina by shameless usage of my girlfriend's family. In Rome I would have been more circumspect.

"I don't know the man," Annaeus snapped. "He's never ventured out to Baetica. But we met the son, of course. Knew my three boys."

The reference to Aelianus sounded gruff, though that could be the man's normal manner. I said I hoped Helena's brother had not made himself a nuisance—though I wished he had, and that I was about to hear details I could use against him later. But Annaeus Maximus merely growled, "High spirits! There's a daughter who's got herself in trouble, I heard?" News flies round!

"The noble Helena Justina," I said calmly, "should be described as high-minded rather than high-spirited."

He stared at me closely. "Are you the man involved?"

I folded my arms. I was still wearing my toga, as I had been all day. Nobody else here was bothering with such formality; provincial life has some benefits. Instead of feeling civilized, being overdressed made me hot and slightly seedy. The fact that my toga had an indelible stain on its long edge and several moth-holes did not help.

Annaeus Maximus was viewing me like a tradesman who had called with a reckoning at an inconvenient time. "I have guests waiting. Tell me what you want."

"You and I have met, sir." I pretended to stare at the bats swooping into the torchlight above the laughing diners' heads. I was really watching him. Maybe he realized. He appeared to be intelligent. He ought to be. The Annaei were not country bumpkins.

"Yes?"

"In view of your reputation and your position I'll talk straight. I saw you recently in Rome, at the Palace of the Caesars, where you were a guest of a private club who call themselves the Society of Olive Oil Producers of Baetica. Most neither own olives nor produce oil. Few come from this province. However, it is believed that among your own group the oil industry in Hispania was the topic under discussion, and that the reason is an unhealthy one."

"That is an atrocious suggestion!"

"It's realistic. Every province has its own cartel. That doesn't mean rigging the price of olive oil is something Rome can tolerate. You know how it would affect the Empire's economy."

"Disastrous," he agreed. "It will not happen."

"You are a prominent man, Annaeus. Your family produced both Senecas and the poet Lucan. Then Nero left you with two enforced suicides because Seneca had been too outspoken and Lucan allegedly dabbled in plots— Tell me, sir, as a result of what happened to your relatives, do you hate Rome?"

"There is more to Rome than Nero," he said, not disputing my assessment of his family's reduced position.

"You could be in the Senate; your financial position entitles you."

"I prefer not to move to Rome."

"Some would say it was your civic duty."

"My family have never shirked our duty. Corduba is our home."

"But Rome's the place!"

"I prefer to live modestly in my own city, applying myself to business." If Seneca, Nero's tutor, was renowned for his dry Stoicism and wit, his descendant had failed to inherit this. Maximus became merely pompous: "The oil producers of Baetica have always done business fairly. Suggesting otherwise is scandalous."

I laughed quietly, unmoved by the feeble threat. "If there is a cartel, I'm here to expose the perpetrators. As a duovir—and a legitimate trader—I assume I can count on your support?"

"Obviously," stated the host of the feast, making it plain he was now returning to the singed meats at his open-air barbecue.

"One more thing—there was a dancer at that dinner; she came from this area. Do you know her?"

"I do not." He did look surprised at the question, though of course he would deny a connection if he knew what she had done.

"I'm glad to hear it," I said coldly. "She's wanted for murder now. And tell me, why did you leave Rome so abruptly?"

"Family troubles." He shrugged.

I gave up, without obvious results, but feeling I had been touching nerves. He had remained too calm. If he was innocent I had insulted him more than he had shown. If he was truly ignorant of any conspiracy, he ought to have been excited to discover that one existed. He ought to be shocked. He ought to be outraged that maybe some of the well-clad guests at his own table tonight had betrayed the high standards he had just proclaimed for Baetican commerce. He ought to be afraid that they had offended Rome.

Without doubt, he knew a cartel was being brokered. If Annaeus did not himself belong to it, then he knew who did.

As I was leaving I saw what his family troubles must be. While their elders were only just sitting down to their banquet, the younger generation were rushing off to places unknown and habits unseemly. If the three Annaeus sons had been friends of Aelianus, he must have enjoyed a jolly time in Baetica. They were various ages, but of a similar mentality: as they set off riding out from the stables when I began my own slow walk to the front of the house they galloped either side of me, coming closer than I found comfortable, while they whooped and whistled and chided each other loudly for not flattening me properly.

A young woman who might be their sister was also leaving the house as they raced off down the drive. She was a self-assured piece in her mid-twenties, wrapped in a furred stole. She was wearing more pearls and sapphires than I had ever seen layered on a single bosom—too many, in fact, to let you see what kind of bosom it was (though it looked promising). She was waiting to enter a carriage from which emerged the head of a man about the same age as her. He was indecently handsome. He was cheering a younger male, very drunk already, who had rushed out from the carriage to be violently ill on the mansio's immaculate steps. Corduba at festival time was the place to be.

I might have asked for a lift in the carriage, but I did not fancy being thrown up on. To her credit, as I passed her the daughter did warn me to watch where I stepped.

Unfed, unwatered, and unlustrated, I turned away and set off wearily back towards Corduba. There was no chance of returning to the Camillus estate tonight. I needed to find myself a lodging where the owner was still sober and had a bed to offer despite the festival crowds. Before that I would have to flog through the dark countryside that lay beyond the Annaeus property, back to the even darker streets of the town, passing the cemetery on the way. I am not afraid of ghosts—but I don't care for the hideous real-life characters who lurk among the tombs of a necropolis at night.

I walked steadily. I folded my toga, as well as you can fold a cumbersome ellipse, then slung it over one shoulder. I had gone beyond the reach of the torches, though I had pulled one up and stolen it. I was finding my way along the track back to town, concentrating on my thoughts about the day. I did not hear anyone following, even though I stayed alert to the possibility. But I certainly felt the sharp stone that flew out of nowhere and smacked into the back of my neck.

TWENTY-SIX

Instinct wanted me to slap my hand on the pain, and to bow my head. Damn instinct. I wanted to stay alive.

I spun around. I drew my sword. In Rome carrying a weapon is illegal—but here that did not apply. All Romans know the provinces are hotbeds of banditry. All Romans on holiday or foreign service go armed.

Ironically my sword, an unofficial relic of my five years in the army, was a short stabbing blade made from the finest Spanish steel.

I listened. If there was more than one assailant out there I could be in deep trouble. Was this how Anacrites and Valentinus had felt when the arrows stopped them in their tracks?

Nobody rushed me. There was only silence, however hard I listened.

Had I imagined it? No; there was blood on my neck. At my feet lay the culprit stone, large and pointed like a flint. There was no mistake. I picked it up; it also had my blood on it. I tucked it into the pouch at my belt. Well, I was enjoying myself in a foreign province; I was bound to want a souvenir.

Sometimes in the country yokels let fly with missiles.

Sometimes in the city idiots hurl tiles and bricks. It is a territorial gesture, an act of defiance when strangers pass. I did not believe that was what had just occurred.

I rammed my torch into soft ground at the edge of the track and moved away from it. Letting the toga slide down to my elbow, I wound the cloth around my forearm so it could act as a shield. With the torch alight I was still providing a target, but I preferred to risk that than to douse the flame and plunge myself into darkness in the middle of strange countryside. I strained my ears, shifting position continually.

Eventually, when nothing happened, I pulled up the torch again and searched around in circles. On either side of the track lay olive groves. In the dark they were full of hazards, though these were purely natural. Weeding hoes lay waiting to be stepped on, their handles all set to spring up and break my nose. Low branches were ready to crack my brow. For all I knew the groves contained courting couples who might turn nasty in a wild provincial manner if I interrupted them in mid-fumble. I was about to give up when I stumbled into a disoriented sheep.

The animal was very tired. It must belong to the lustral flock. Then I remembered the shepherdess with the interesting eyes. I had seen her before. She had looked very different in her sophisticated little gold costume as Diana, but even smothered in sheepskin I ought to have recognized the girl.

Keeping my sword out, I walked back grimly to the Annaeus house. Nobody attacked me again—which was odd. Why hadn't the dancer tried to kill me out there on the track?

Fired up by annoyance at myself as much as anything, I made a formal complaint. This time, with blood trickling down my neck, I was given a better welcome. I kept making a fuss until Annaeus Maximus reluctantly ordered a search for the girl. The chief shepherd, who was still there with most of his accomplices, was summoned to respond to my accusations.

Annaeus seemed taken aback by my story. According to him,

most of the group were well known to everyone, actors from the local theater. They routinely earned extra money by providing assistance with civic rituals. This was better than allowing real shepherds to get big ideas, I could see that. Naturally the man then claimed this particular girl was a stranger to him.

The leader of the actors turned up, still dressed as the chief shepherd and emitting a belch after his supper. He confessed he had employed a few extras to pad out the parade today. This included the shepherdess with the big brown eyes (whom he rather clearly remembered). She had presented herself when he was auditioning; he had no idea where she came from, though her name was supposed to be Selia. He said she wasn't local, though by that he merely meant she did not come from the immediate confines of Corduba; Hispalis would still be a possibility. I had just let the killer of Valentinus slip right through my fingers. And needless to say, all the slaves Annaeus had sent out to look for her came back empty-handed.

"I'm sorry." The actor appeared pretty genuine. "Next time I'll ask for references."

"Why?" I scoffed bitterly. "Do you think she'd admit she was up to no good? Anyway—are you constantly being offered the services of undulating women?"

He looked shamefaced. "No," he mumbled. "Though that was the second one this week."

"And what was the first one like?"

"Older, though she could dance better."

"Why didn't she get the job instead of Selia, then?"

"She wasn't from around here." Trust a local to take precedence. He looked even more ashamed, then rallied with his big excuse: "Well, Selia was thoroughly professional; she even brought her own sheep!"

"She's abandoned it now!" I retorted. She was a professional killer—and if she could claim a whole sheep, whoever was paying her expenses must be allowing her a substantial daily rate.

TWENTY-SEVEN

I spent the night at the Annaeus house. The notables let me feed at their table (well, their tenants' table). They loaned me an empty cell in their slaves' barracks. It was near the well, so I even managed to get something to wash my wounded neck—and there was all I could wish for to drink. What civilized people. Next morning their steward sent me away on a very slow horse which he said I could borrow indefinitely since its useful life had run out. I said I would report my gracious treatment by the Annaei to the Emperor. The steward smiled, openly showing his contempt.

The three sons had come home at dawn. I met them thundering in as I rode away. On principle they left me in a cloud of dust again, though the initiative had gone out of them to some extent and they were all looking faintly tired. As far as I knew the daughter was still out. Women have more stamina.

The Camillus estate lay bathed in sunlight when I finally rode back. As I expected, Helena had already followed up her promise to go over to the Licinius Rufius spread and pursue the next suspect for me. Marmarides, looking annoyed at having his nose put out of joint, told me Marius Optatus had driven her.

It gave me time to bathe and change my tunic, then to hang around the kitchen until the cook found me the kind of nourishing breakfast certain old women like to lay before an honest young man who is known to have fathered an almost-born baby and who clearly needs his strength built up. As I enjoyed the food, she cleaned my cut neck with a thyme wash and stuck on some sort of salve. Needless to say, its main ingredient was olive oil.

Helena returned to find me still being pampered. She grabbed me by the scruff of the neck and inspected the damage. "You'll live."

"Thanks for the loving concern."

"Who did it?" I winked; she took the point. We walked outside to the shady area of garden near the house, where a bench was placed under a fig tree on a wall. There, safe from being overheard, I told her about the shepherdess. Helena winced. "You think this pageant queen all bundled up in smelly wool is the 'dancer from Hispalis'?"

I did not want to say I had definitely recognized her, since that gave a false impression of me gawking too keenly at women. "Striking down men from behind certainly seems to be her trademark. But Anacrites and Valentinus were then rammed against walls. Apart from the fact that there were none available last night, if it *was* Selia, she made no attempt to follow up."

"Maybe she relies on her two musicians to do the dirty work, and didn't have them with her."

"Then what was the point of the stone? It seemed random—more like a warning than anything."

"Marcus, if the stone had hit you on the head, would you have been killed?" Sparing Helena's feelings, I said no. It certainly could have done more damage. But stone-throwing takes a good aim.

"Don't worry. What it's done is put me on my guard."

Helena frowned. "I do worry."

So did I. I had been struck by a recollection of Anacrites mumbling "dangerous woman" when I said I was coming to Baetica. I now realized it was not Helena he had meant. He too must have been warning me—about his assailant.

To lighten the atmosphere I related my experience with Annaeus Maximus. "I gained some insight into his attitude. His family is in a political trough. He is socially crippled by what happened to Seneca. Undeserved or not, the taint has lingered. Wealth alone might recapture the family's old luster, but they've clearly lost heart too. Maximus certainly does not want a career in Rome, though he doesn't seem to mind being the big boy around here. Still, the Annaei are yesterday's heroes, and now it all depends whether running Corduba will be enough for them."

"Will it?"

"They are not stupid."

"What about the younger generation?" Helena asked.

"Running wild with great panache." I described what I had seen of the sons and the jewel-clad daughter.

Helena smiled. "I can tell you about the daughter—including where she stayed last night!"

I pricked up my ears. "Scandal?"

"Nothing like it. Her name is Aelia Annaea. She was at the Licinius Rufius house. Despite the alleged feud between their families Aelia Annaea and Claudia Rufina, the other fellow's granddaughter, are good friends."

"How sensible you women are! And so you met both of them today?"

"Yes. Claudia Rufina is quite young. She seems genuinely good-natured. Aelia Annaea is more of a character; the bad girl enjoys knowing that her papa would hate her to accept hospitality from Licinius when the two men aren't speaking."

"What does Licinius feel about it?"

"I didn't meet him."

"Aelia sounds a bundle of trouble. And if Licinius encourages her to upset her father, he sounds a wicked old man."

"Don't be a prig. I liked Aelia."

"You always like rebels! What about her little friend?"

"Much more serious. Claudia Rufina yearns to endow public buildings and earn a statue in her honor."

"Let me guess: the Annaea babe is pretty—"

"Oh you thought so?" Helena asked quickly; she had not forgotten me saying that I had seen Aelia Annaea at her home last night.

"Well, she's rich enough to get herself admired for her necklaces, and she's polite," I corrected myself. "Honestly I hardly noticed the girl . . . Nice sapphires!"

"Not your type!" Helena sneered.

"I'll decide my type, thank you! Anyway, she was being picked up by someone last night; I bet she's betrothed to the handsome god I saw in the carriage when she went off. I suppose the Rufius poppet with the commendable social ambitions will be very plain—"

Helena's eyes were bright. "You're so predictable! How can you ever judge human nature when you're so bound up in prejudice?"

"I get by. Human nature makes people fall into distinct pigeonholes."

"Wrong!" Helena said crisply. "Claudia is just rather serious." I still reckoned Claudia Rufina would turn out to be plain. "The three of us had a civilized chat over a refreshing tisane. And you're wrong about Aelia Annaea too."

"How's that?"

"She was happy and lighthearted. Nobody has burdened her with a future husband of any kind, least of all a good-looking untrustworthy one." Helena Justina had never liked handsome men. So she claimed, anyway. There must have been some reason why she chose to fall for me. "She was overdressed in jewelry, but wore nothing like a betrothal ring. She is very direct. If the situation called for it, she would have asked for one."

"The arrangement may not be public knowledge yet."

"Trust me; she's not spoken for! Claudia Rufina, on the other hand, was sporting a heavy bracelet of garnets, which cannot be to her taste (she told me she collects ivory miniatures). The awful bracelet looked just the thing a man would grab at a goldsmith's for a girl he feels obliged to present with a formal gift. Expensive and horrible. If she does ever marry the man who gave it to her, she will be obliged to treasure it for a lifetime, poor soul."

I found myself smiling. Helena herself was dressed simply, in white, with hardly any extra decoration; while pregnant she found wearing jewelry uncomfortable. She unconsciously fingered a silver ring which I had given her. It was a plain design with its love message hidden inside. It represented the time I had suffered as a slave in a silver mine in Britain. I hoped any comparison she was making with Claudia Rufina's gift was favorable.

I cleared my throat. "Well, did you meet any male hangers-on today?"

"No, but there was talk of 'Tiberius,' who was thought to be at the gymnasium. He sounds like the man you saw. If he's good-looking enough to irritate you, he's also bound to be crazed on sports."

"Because he's handsome?" I chortled. In fact having seen him I agreed he must be a handball lout. The man I saw had a thick neck and probably a brain to match. When he chose a wife he would be looking at the size of her bust and wondering how readily she would let him run off to exercise or hunt.

The thought of hunting made me wonder if his formal name was Quinctius.

"The youth you saw being sick on the steps was probably Claudia's brother."

"The lad who was taken to Rome with the Baetican group?"

"He never appeared this morning. He was still in bed. I heard distant groans that were supposed to be him with a wine-headache."

"If the handsome dog is after Claudia I bet there's a scheme to marry her brother to her best friend Aelia." I was always a romantic.

Helena was scathing: "Aelia Annaea would eat a young lad for lunch!" She seemed well disposed towards both girls, but I could tell Aelia Annaea was the one who really appealed to her.

I scowled. "There's not much to gain from courting the young people. It's the old men who run Corduba. From what I saw last night that's wise; their heirs look thoroughly overindulged: bored girls and bad young men."

"Oh they're just rich and silly," Helena demurred.

Her trip to the Licinius house had cheered her up since yesterday. Her mother's highly expensive midwife had advised me to keep her mind occupied for these last few weeks—though the woman probably did not expect Helena to be gallivanting about Baetica.

"So what's your verdict, my darling? Have we decided these young creatures just have too much spending cash and too little parental supervision—or are the brats up to no good?"

"I don't know yet, Marcus. But I'll find out."

I stretched lazily. "You should enjoy yourself more. A good long bathe is what I recommend. If you whistle loudly while you're steaming, Optatus and I will keep out of the way."

Helena Justina patted her bulge and told the child-in-waiting that if she had as many baths as its father suggested the baby would be washed away. Sometimes I wondered if Helena saw through my schemes. It would be like her to have found out exactly what the midwife had told me—and to disobey deliberately.

"So I've seen the gem-encrusted Aelia. What's Claudia Rufina like?"

"Neat, smart, and rather shy," said Helena. "She has a rather big nose which she unfortunately accentuates by tilting back her head then looking at people over it. She needs a *tall* husband—which is interesting, Marcus, because from the way Marius Optatus insisted on driving me today instead of Marmarides, I'd say he has a yen for Claudia! When we got there he vanished to discuss farming with the old man, but I swear he only wanted to go so he could offer greetings to the girl."

I raised my eyebrows. Naturally I disapproved of unions that broke barriers. "Unless I've misunderstood the rules of Baetican etiquette I reckon Optatus is risking it!"

"He's a free man," Helena reminded me snootily. "Anyway, when did the fact that a girl was unsuitable ever stop a man taking a chance?"

I grinned at her.

At that point we shelved the discussion because Optatus himself came out into the garden. He was splitting his sides over the decrepit horse I had brought home, and said he hoped I had not paid out money for it; I assured him it was a virtual gift from the gracious Annaei. Marius Optatus gravely replied that the Annaei had always been renowned for their generosity.

I noticed a whiff of smoke and burnt rosemary hanging around his work clothes. It would not surprise me if he was the serious sort who quietly cleansed his stables each Parilia with a private lustration made in genuine reverence. The sober tenant seemed like a dedicated farmer with no space in his life for frivolity. But once I had started to see him as a ladies' man, eyeing up the handsome dowry of a neighbor's rather big-nosed granddaughter, anything could be possible.

TWENTY-EIGHT

Helena had invited Claudia Rufina to return her call, but the social rules dictated there should be a short lapse of time first. Our young neighbor was probably dying to inspect Helena's paramour, but the poor thing would have to wait to see my friendly face. Meanwhile I decided to see her grandfather; now I had met Annaeus I needed to compare the rivals soon before I ended prejudiced either for or against the one just because I met him first. Since the Rufius family had had one visit from us today, Helena told me I should wait until tomorrow. It gave me an afternoon loafing about. That suited me.

"You'll like their house," Helena giggled, for reasons she refused to divulge.

I rode over the next morning on my borrowed horse. His name was allegedly Prancer. It must have been given to him a long time ago. I think he wanted to be a botanist. His notion of a canter was a decorous sidle, slow enough to inspect every dockleaf on the way.

The Licinius Rufius estate lay comparatively close, though (given my mount) not as near as I would have liked. This was mainly because of a large number of intervening olive groves which belonged to someone else. Marius Optatus had warned who it was: his ex-landlord, Quinctius Attractus. I surveyed the senator's holding with great interest. He was happily ostentatious. After the olive groves I had to pass his fields of flax, his market gardens, his vineyards, his pig farm and his wheat.

When I did reach the Rufius villa, I saw what Helena Justina had meant: the family had embarked on a truly brave improvement program. It was easy to see where the money for it came from: once I had entered a gateway with their name on a column I had ridden through at least a couple of miles of well-aged olive trees, grand monsters with several trunks growing from stocks with huge circumferences; these were clearly only a fraction of the whole estate. I had passed a working area where they had not one but two oil-presses. Even more significant was the fact that they actually owned their own kilns for making amphorae. This estate, which ran on until it bordered the river, was obviously near enough to water transport at Corduba not to need to use mules for carrying the oil down for shipment. (The estate roads were in fact immaculate.) The kilns were five in number; alongside them were rows of bricks drying in the sun awaiting their turn to be home-fired too.

In an area the builders were using as their yard, I spotted the youth I had last seen being ill at the Annaeus house. He must be the grandson, as we had guessed. He was wearing a brilliant tunic in broad stripes of red and murex purple, a garment that shouted loudly that his family could afford the best. He was helping a bailiff decide something with a carpenter who had a new window frame on a trestle. Young Rufius looked barely into his twenties, awake though perhaps not yet fully alert. Still, he was the one holding the building plan, his relations with the workmen sounded pleasant, and he did appear quite confident discussing the chart. I went past without making myself known and left Prancer under an oak tree; it did not seem worthwhile tethering him.

The house made me gulp.

It had once been a modest Baetican country villa, like the one on the Camillus estate—a short axial design based on a single corridor, with a very basic suite of reception rooms and small cubicles for private use on either side. But this was no longer enough for people who clearly thought themselves the rising stars in Corduba.

The whole building was scaffolded. The roof was off. A second story was being raised on top. Some of the walls were being torn down so their traditional construction could be replaced with Roman concrete faced with the type of bricks I had seen being made in the yard. A massive entrance portico had been stuck on the front, complete with marble steps and columns the full height of the new roof. The Corinthian order had arrived in Baetica in a big way. These capitals were fabulously carved riots of acanthus leaves—though one had unfortunately been dropped. It lay where it had fallen, split in two. Work on the entrance had come to a standstill, presumably while the masons went into a corner to think up a good story to explain the accident. Meanwhile the entire ground plan of the house was being expanded to twice or three times its original area. To my astonishment, the family were still living in the old core of the house while the work went on.

When I asked for Licinius Rufius, the first person who came to greet me was his wife. She found me in the new vestibule, gawking at some gigantic paintings of Alexander the Great's campaigns. I was wondering whether I dared explore the huge internal peristyle garden which had been expanded from an original courtyard into a wonder of imported marble colonnades and topiary lions, beyond which I could just see a monumental dining room still under construction.

An elderly, upright woman, Claudia Adorata's centrally parted gray hair was held in a low bun in the nape of her neck with a circle of crystal pins. She was swathed in saffron linen and wore a fine necklace of twisted gold wires, with agate, emerald and rock crystal stones in a complex setting that resembled a butterfly. "Excuse the mess!" she apologized, reminding me of Ma. Maids had decorously followed her into the echoing atrium, but when she saw I looked fairly tame she clapped her hands and sent them scurrying back to their looms. Their work must have been well impregnated with building dust.

"Madam, I salute your courage and initiative!" I grinned candidly.

It appeared the old lady had no notion of why I had come. We mentioned Helena, and the Camillus family, which seemed enough to gain me admittance. She said her husband was out on the estate but had been summoned to meet me. While we waited, she offered a tour of the renovations. Since I try to be polite to ancient dames, I said obligingly that I was always glad of a chance to pick up ideas. The crude apartment that Helena and I were renting in Rome would have been beyond this lady's comprehension. I was not even sure she realized that I was the father of the noble Helena's child.

By the time Licinius Rufius appeared his wife and I were sitting beside the new fishpond (the length of the house), exchanging gardening notes on the new Campanian roses and Bithynian snowflake bulbs, and taking warmed wine from bronze goblets like a pair of old friends. I had admired the five-room bathhouse with its complicated heating system, special dry heat box, and exercise area; praised the half-finished but pleasing black and white mosaics; envied the new kitchen suite; taken the name of the fresco painter who ornamented the summer and winter dining rooms; cooed over the space where the library was to be; and expressed suitable disappointment that I could not view the suite of upstairs bedrooms because the stairs had not been built.

Now we were seated on an expensive set of folding chairs,

placing our drinks on a matching collapsible table, covered with a fine Spanish linen tablecloth. These had been set out for us on a small paved patio which had an astounding vista of a fashionable apsidal grotto at the end of the pool, where a twinkling glass mosaic of Neptune enthroned amidst a lot of writhing sea creatures was surrounded by a heavy border of seashells. No doubt the Baetican murex industry had helped provide the shells.

Delicate probing had ascertained that Claudia Adorata described her family's financial position as "comfortable."

There was a reason for the sudden renovation campaign. She and her husband were creating a glorious backdrop for the anticipated achievements of their much-loved grandchildren, the youth in particular. His handle was Gaius Licinius Claudius Rufius Constans, which would make a long and ornamental honorific inscription when his fabulous deeds came to be celebrated in his native town one day. Clearly the Senate in Rome must be keeping a chair warm for him, and it was hoped he would eventually rate a consulship. I tried to look impressed.

Claudia told me she and her husband had brought up the two grandchildren since they were orphaned at an early age. Their mother had died a few weeks after producing the young male prodigy; their father, himself the only son and heir, had lasted another three years then caught a fever. The two tots had become their grandparents' consolation and hope for the future—as dangerous a situation as young people could ever find themselves in. At least they had money in indecent quantities to help them through it. On the other hand, having so much money so young could make their situation even more dangerous.

Licinius Rufius strode out through the fug of dust, washing his hands in a silver bowl held by a slave who had to scamper after him. He was wide-set but not overweight, with a heavy face and a shock of crinkled hair that shot off to one side. Of an older generation than Annaeus Maximus, he remained firm on his feet and dynamic. He greeted me with a knuckle-crushing handshake, then took one of the chairs, flattening its cushion and causing the delicate legs to bow. He helped himself to black olives from a fancies dish, but I noticed he did not take wine. Perhaps he felt more cautious than his wife about my motives. Claudia Adorata herself smiled, as if she felt reassured now he was in charge, then she slipped away.

I too picked up some of the olives. (They were superb quality, almost as lush as the finest from Greece.) Eating allowed us both a short pause to do some sizing up. Licinius would have been viewing a thoughtful character in a plain green tunic and a graded Roman haircut, clearly displaying the traditional virtues of honesty, uprightness, and personal modesty. I saw an elderly man with an inscrutable expression, whom I decided I would not trust one jot.

TWENTY-NINE

From the beginning I felt that, unlike his wife, Licinius Rufius knew *exactly* why I had come to Baetica. He let me pass some idle remarks about the mad scale of his home improvements, but soon the conversation shifted to agricultural matters, which would lead to the real subject of my interview. We never mentioned the magic word "cartel," though it was always our point of reference. I began frankly: "I could say I'm checking over the family estate for Decimus Camillus—but actually my trip out here has an official purpose—"

"There was a rumor of an inspector from Rome," Rufius answered readily. Oh yes. Well, why pretend? News that Anacrites had planned to send an agent, and that I for one was actually here, would have been leaked from the proconsul's office—and possibly confirmed to all his Baetican friends by the proconsul himself.

"I am hoping to talk to you about oil production, sir."

"Obviously Baetica is the place for that!" Licinius made it sound as though I was just on a mild fact-finding survey, instead of investigating a vicious conspiracy where agents had had their heads smashed in. I could feel the old man taking over. He was used to sounding off with his opinions. Thinking they know it all is a habit of rich men who build up large outfits of any kind.

"I've been discussing some figures with Marius Optatus at the Camillus estate," I interrupted as quickly as I could. "He reckons there may be as many as five million olive trees and a thousand oil presses in the River Baetis hinterland. An owner of standing like yourself could possess maybe three thousand *acti quadrati*—say eight or ten centuries of land?"

He nodded but made no comment, which almost certainly meant he owned more. That was a massive area. There used to be an old system of measurement which we all learned at school, where two *acti* equaled a "yoke," and two yokes were a "hereditary area"—that's the amount of land that was supposed to suffice for one person in the frugal republican days. By that reckoning the average oil magnate in Baetica could support seven hundred and fifty people—except that the old method of measurement would have been when farming merely consisted of barley, beans and cabbages for domestic consumption, not a luxury export crop like olive oil.

"What's an average yield per century?"

Licinius Rufius was offhand. "Depending on the soil, and the weather that year, between five and six hundred amphorae." So the typical plot we had been talking about would produce between four and five thousand amphorae per year. That would buy a whole forest of Corinthian columns, plus a fine public forum for their owner to endow.

"And how is my young friend Optatus?" Rufius smoothly changed the subject.

"Bearing up. He told me a little about his misfortunes."

"I was delighted when he took his new tenancy," the old man said in a tone of voice I found irritating, as if Marius Optatus were his pet marmoset. From what I had seen of Optatus, he would not accept being patronized.

"The way he lost the old one sounds hard. Do you think he had bad luck, or was he sabotaged?"

"Oh it must have been an accident," Licinius Rufius exclaimed—as if he knew damn well it had not been. He was not going to support accusations against a fellow landowner. Quarreling with colleagues is a bad business move. Encouraging victims never brings in cash.

Licinius had sounded fairly sympathetic, but I remembered Optatus' bitterness when he told me the locals had refused to become involved in his quarrel with his ex-landlord. I took a chance. "I gather Quinctius Attractus conducts business in a pretty ruthless manner?"

"He likes to be firm. I cannot argue with that."

"It's a long way from the benevolent paternal style that we Romans like to consider traditional. What's your opinion of him personally, sir?"

"I hardly know the man."

"I don't expect you to criticize a fellow producer. But I would suppose someone as shrewd as you would have firmed up *some* conclusions after being the man's guest in Rome and staying at his house!" Licinius was still refusing to be drawn so I added coldly, "Do you mind if I ask who paid your fare?"

He pursed his lips. He was a tough old bastard. "Many people in Baetica have been invited to Rome by Attractus, Falco. It's a courtesy he extends regularly."

"And does he regularly invite his guests to help him corner the oil market and drive up prices?"

"That is a serious accusation."

Rufius was sounding as prim as Annaeus when I interviewed him. Unlike Annaeus he did not have the excuse of guests to drag him away so I was able to press him harder: "I make no accusations. I'm speculating—from my own, maybe rather cynical standpoint."

"Do you have no faith in human ethics, Didius Falco?" For once, the old man seemed genuinely interested in my reply.

He was now staring at me so closely he might have been a sculptor trying to decide if my left ear was a fraction higher than my right.

"Oh all business has to be based on trust. All contracts depend on good faith."

"That is correct," he declared autocratically.

I grinned. "Licinius Rufius, I believe all men in business want to be richer than their colleagues. All would happily cheat a foreigner. All would like the running of their own sphere of commerce to be sewn up as tight as a handball, with no uncontrollable forces."

"There will always be risk!" he protested, perhaps rather dryly.

"The weather," I conceded. "The health of the businessman, the loyalty of his workers. War. Volcanoes. Litigation. And unforeseen policies imposed by the government."

"I was thinking more of the fickleness of consumers' taste," he smiled.

I shook my head, tutting gently. "I forgot that one! I don't know why you stay in the business."

"Community spirit," he laughed.

Talking to Licinius Rufius resembled the overblown jollity of a military dining club the night the pay-chest came—when everyone knew the sesterces were safely in camp, but the distribution would happen tomorrow so nobody was drunk yet. Maybe we two soon would be, for Rufius seemed to feel he had led me astray from my purpose so successfully he could now afford to clap his hands for a slave to pour him wine. I was offered more, but declined, making it plain I was only waiting for the nervous waiter to remove himself before I continued the interview. Rufius drank slowly, surveying me over the rim of his cup with a confidence that was meant to beat me down.

I dropped my voice abruptly. "So I met you in Rome, sir. We both dined on the Palatine. I then called on you at the

Quinctius house, but you had gone. Tell me, why did you leave our splendid city so suddenly?"

"Family ties," he replied, without pausing.

"Indeed? I gather your colleague Annaeus Maximus suddenly developed pressing family ties too! And the bargeman, I suppose—and the negotiator from Hispalis! Forgive me, but for men of affairs you all seem to have made that long journey without enough forward planning."

I thought I saw him check, but the reaction was slight. "We had traveled to Rome together. We traveled home in one group too. Safety, you know." For the first time I detected a slight impatience with my questions. He was trying to make me feel like a lout who had abused his hospitality.

"I'm sorry, but your departure looks suspiciously hurried, sir."

"None of us ever intended a long stay in Rome. We all wanted to return home for the Parilia." Very rustic! And he had dodged a direct answer with the glibness of a politician.

"And of course this had nothing to do with Quinctius Attractus trying to promote a cartel?"

Licinius Rufius stopped answering me so smoothly.

We stared at each other for a few beats of time.

"There is no hoarding or price-fixing in Corduba!" His voice rasped so harshly it startled me. He sounded extremely angry. His protest could be genuine. He knew why I had come here though, so he had had time to prepare a convincing show of outrage. "There is no need for it. There is plenty for everyone. The olive oil trade is now flowering in Baetica as never before—"

"So once the trees are planted you can all just sit back and watch the fortunes flowing in! Tell me this then, sir: Why did that group of you really decide to visit Rome?"

I saw him regain control of himself. "It was a normal business voyage. We were renewing ties with our agents in Ostia and exchanging goodwill with our contacts in Rome. This happens all the time, Falco."

"Oh yes. Nothing unusual at all—except that the night your main contact entertained you all in the Palace of the Caesars, two men who had been in the same dining room were later brutally attacked!"

I could see he was forcing himself not to react. He chose to try and bluff it out: "Yes, we heard about that just before we left."

Twitching an eyebrow, I asked gently, "Oh? And who told you this, sir?"

Rufius belatedly realized he had walked into trouble. "Quinctius Attractus." A neat dodge, since Quinctius had enough importance in Rome to be well informed about everything.

"Really? Did he tell you who told him?"

"He heard it at the Senate."

"He could well have done," I smiled, "only the dinner for the Society of Olive Oil Producers of Baetica was held on the last night of March. The Senate goes into recess from the beginning of April to the middle of May!"

Licinius almost gave away the fact that he was struggling now: "Well, I cannot say where he heard it. He is, after all, a senator and hears all the important news before most of Rome—"

"It was never news," I corrected him. "An order had been given on the highest authority that the attacks should not be made public. You people left the very day afterwards. At that time only a handful of people on the Palatine—a very small group in the intelligence service and Titus Caesar himself—knew that killers had been at work."

"I think you underestimate the importance of Quinctius Attractus," answered Licinius.

There was another short silence. I sensed a worrying force

behind his words. Ambitious men like Attractus always do carry more weight than they deserve.

Licinius felt a gloss was necessary: "The fact that we had dined with two men who died was, Falco, as you are suggesting, one of the other reasons my colleagues and I took our leave. The incident sounded a little too close for comfort. We decided Rome was a dangerous city, and I confess we fled."

He struck me as a man who would not normally run away from a spot of civic disorder.

Natural curiosity about the tragedy gripped him. He leaned forwards and murmured in a confidential tone, "Did *you* know these two men?"

"I know the one who is not dead."

I spoke it very gently, leaving Rufius to wonder which one had survived; how well I knew him; and what he had managed to say to me before I left Rome.

I might have taken things further, though I doubt I would have been any more successful. In any case, it was my turn to be called away unexpectedly. An uproar disturbed us, then almost immediately a slave came running to tell me I had better come quick because my borrowed horse Prancer had wandered through the new entrance portico, and into the gracious peristyle garden with the beautiful topiary. Prancer's yearning for foliage was insatiable, and he had lost all discretion. By the time he was spotted many of the clipped trees had ceased to look so elegant.

The Rufii coped with this accident in a terribly good-natured manner and assured me the lions would grow again. They just scoffed when I offered to pay for the damage. We all joked merrily that it was an act of revenge from their rivals the Annaei who had lent me the horse.

They could afford to replace the boxtrees and I couldn't, so I thanked them quietly for their generous attitude—then Prancer and I left, as fast as I could make him trot.

THIRTY

Helena Justina had very few clothes on. Any ideas this might have given me were soon banished by the fact that she smelled like a salad.

"I see you're marinading the child!"

Calmly she continued to massage neat olive oil into her stomach. "Apparently this will ease my stretched skin—and if there's any over I can pour it on our lunch."

"Wonderful stuff. Want any help rubbing it in?"

Helena waved a Baetican redware jug at me. "No."

"Well, it should do you good."

"I'm sure! Like using oil in dough; perhaps I'll be more flexible, and with a moist crust . . ." Helena loved to collect interesting lore, but often had a hard time taking it seriously.

I threw myself on a couch and settled down to watch. Stricken with an odd quirk of modesty, Helena turned her back. "Was there ever a more useful substance?" I mused. "Olive oil prevents burns from blistering and it's good for your liver, it stops rust in iron pots, and preserves food; the wood makes bowls and it flames well in a fire—"

"In this country the children are weaned on a porridge

made from olive oil and wheat," Helena joined in, turning back to me. "I've been talking to the cook. Baetican midwives smother a new mother with oil to help slide the baby out."

I chortled. "And then they present the happy father with a little dressed onion to name!"

"I'm giving Nux a spoonful a day to try to improve her coat."

Hearing her name, Nux looked up from a rug where she had been sleeping and thumped her tail enthusiastically. She had fur like rough turf; around her unpleasant extremities it stuck together in impenetrable clumps. "Nothing will improve Nux's coat," I said regretfully. "She really needs a complete shave. It's time you broke the news to her that she'll never be a pampered lapdog. She's a smelly street scruff, and that's it."

"Give Marcus a nice lick for loving you so much!" Helena cooed at the dog, who immediately roused herself and jumped straight on the middle of my chest. If this was a clue to what kind of subversive mother Helena Justina intended to be, I was heading for more trouble than I'd thought. As I fended off a long, frenzied tongue, Helena disarmed me by suddenly saying, "I like it here. It's peaceful in the countryside and nobody harangues us about our situation. I like being on my own with you, Marcus."

"I like it here too," I grunted. It was true. Were it not for the baby and my fixed intention to return Helena to our mothers' care in time for them both to supervise the birth, I could have stayed here for months. "Maybe we should emigrate to some far province away from everyone."

"You belong in the city, Marcus."

"Perhaps. Or perhaps one day I'll set up home with you in some villa in a river valley—choose your spot."

"Britain!" she quipped wickedly. I returned to my original dream of a town house above the Tiber with a garden on a terrace with a view across to Rome.

Helena watched me as my thoughts idled romantically. She must know my situation was so disappointing all hope seemed pointless and all plans looked doomed. Her eyes sparkled in a way that made me push the dog aside. "Marcus, another thing the cook told me is that a diet rich in oil makes women passionate and men softer."

I held out my arms to her. "We can easily test that!"

THIRTY-ONE

Helena was asleep. Off guard and helpless, she looked more tired than when she knew I was checking up on her. I told myself some of her present exhaustion reflected my rampant skills as a lover, but her drawn face was starting to worry me.

I should never have let her travel so far. Bringing her to Baetica was stupid. I had no real hope of finishing my task before the baby arrived. The past two days had convinced me of what I should have known from the first: none of the suave local dignitaries was likely to admit what was going on. Exposing the conspiracy would take halfway to forever—and finding "Selia," the dancing girl who liked attacking agents, might be impossible.

I had to allot more time to Helena, though I had to balance this carefully with letting her help in my work; it tired her nowadays more than she wanted to admit. Another man with a different woman might have kept work and home separate. For us there was no choice. Helena became distant and unhappy if I left her out of a problem. If I encouraged her to help me, she tore in wholeheartedly—but was it wise? If not, how could I dissuade her? This was how we had first come to know one another and her interest was unlikely ever to diminish. Besides, now I was used to it I relied on her help.

As if she sensed my thoughts, she awoke. I watched the relaxed expression on her face alter to suspicion that I was up to no good.

"Don't squash the baby," she murmured, since I was lolling all over her.

I roused myself and prepared to get up. "I'm taking advantage while I still can. You know Roman children expect to start barging their parents aside from the moment they're born."

"Oh it will bully you all right," Helena laughed. "You'll spoil this baby so much it will know it can do as it likes with you . . ." Behind the banter she was looking concerned. I was probably frowning, thinking yet again that somehow we had to get it born first. Alive.

"Maybe we ought to investigate a midwife in Corduba, fruit. Just in case anything starts happening early—"

"If you will feel happier." For once she seemed prepared to accept advice. Maybe that was because it was me talking. I liked to think I could handle her—though from the first hour I met her I had realized that with Helena Justina there was no hope of issuing instructions. She was a true Roman matron. Her father had tried to create in her a meek, modest partner to some all-knowing male. But her mother's example of quiet contempt for the opposite species was just as traditional, so Helena had grown up forthright, and doing just as she liked. "How did you progress with Licinius Rufius?" she asked sweetly.

I started pulling on tunics. "We were gossiping like foster-brothers until Prancer took to munching his clipped trees."

"Any results?"

"Oh yes, he cut them down to size—" Helena threw a boot at me. "All right, seriously: Rufius takes the line that hoarding oil and fixing prices would be unnecessary. He says there is plenty for all. Like Annaeus he feigns shock at the suggestion that any upright Corduban businessman would be so greedy as to plot a cartel."

Helena slid onto the edge of the bed beside me so she too could dress. "Well you're used to being considered a crude slanderer of men with crystal consciences—and you're also used to proving them villains in the end."

"Whether these two have actually joined the conspiracy I wouldn't like to say—but someone has definitely asked them about it. I'm convinced the issue was discussed when they went to Rome."

"Would Annaeus and Rufius be particularly important in setting up a price ring?" Helena wondered, slowly combing her hair.

While she was trying to wind up a chignon, I tickled her neck. Being a rascal always helped me to think. "I bet they would. Annaeus is a duovir, for one thing; he carries clout in Corduba. Consider him first: from a great Hispanic family with extraordinary wealth. He could perhaps feel he's above corrupt business ideas. He might even feel too much loyalty to Rome."

"Or too much to lose!" Helena commented.

"Exactly. But still he's tinged with disgrace that was not of his making; he now belongs to a family of enforced outsiders—and he has his sons to think about. He looks a disaffected rebel in the making. Add to that his huge influence on the local political scene, and if I was recruiting for a cartel, I'd certainly be after him."

"He may just prefer to opt out," Helena argued. "His family have seen what happens to schemers. He may want the quiet life." I conceded the point as she pouted thoughtfully. "What about Rufius?"

"Different: a new man. Driven by ambition for his grandchildren," I said. "If he joins in, it will be because he wants a short route to power and popularity. If a price ring is set up, it would suit him to be known as the man who started it; other members would more readily support him in pushing his grandson. So I shall have to decide: Is he honest or crooked?"

"What do you think?"

"He looks honest." I grinned at her. "That probably means he's a complete crook!"

At last Helena managed to lean away from me long enough to skewer her hair with an ivory pin. She lurched upright and went to our bedroom door to let in Nux; I had shut out the dog earlier because she was jealous if we showed each other affection. Nux scampered in and shot under the bed defiantly. Helena and I smiled and sneaked out, leaving Nux behind.

"So what now, Marcus?"

"Lunch." An informer has to honor the priorities. "Then I'm going back to Corduba to see if I can roust out Cyzacus, the bargee. He's not a damned shepherd; he can't have a load of flocks to fumigate. I don't believe his office is really closed up for three days on account of the Parilia."

I rode in on the horse, slowly. So slowly I started dozing and nearly fell off.

The bargee's office *was* still closed. I failed to find anyone who knew where his private house was. Another afternoon of my precious time was wasted, and I could see there was little point returning here for at least another day.

While I was in Corduba, I seized advantage of Helena's agreement and sought out a midwife. For a stranger in town, this was fraught with difficulties. My sisters back in Rome, who were keen on sensational stories, had already scared me with wild tales of crazy practitioners who tried shaking out babies using physical force on the mother, or their hopeless assistants who tied the poor woman in labor to the top of the bed, then lifted the foot in the air and dropped it suddenly. . . . My eldest sister had once had a dead baby dismembered in the womb; none of the rest of us had ever quite recovered from hearing the details over nuts and mulled wine at our Saturnalia gathering.

I walked to the forum and asked various respectable-looking types for advice, then I double-checked with a priestess at the temple who laughed dryly and told me to see somebody quite different. I suspect it was her mother; certainly the dame I eventually visited looked seventy-five. She lived down a lane so narrow a man with decent shoulders could hardly squeeze through it, but her house was tidy and quiet.

I sniffed at her to see if she had been drinking and I squinted at her fingernails to make sure she kept her hands clean. Without actually seeing her in action, that was all I could do; by the time I did test her methods, it would be too late.

She asked me a few questions about Helena, and told me dourly that as she sounded a bonny girl she would probably have a large baby, which of course might be difficult. I hate professionals who cover themselves so obviously. I asked to see the equipment she used, and was readily shown a birth-stool, jars of oil and other unguents, and (very quickly) a bagful of instruments. I recognized traction hooks, which I supposed could be used gently to pull out living children; but then there was also a set of metal forceps with two hideous rows of jagged teeth along its jaws, which I guessed from my sister's old story must be for crushing skulls to remove them in pieces when all else had failed and a stillbirth became inevitable. The woman saw me looking sick.

"If a child dies, I save the mother if I can."

"Let's hope it won't come to that."

"No; why should it?" she replied calmly. There was a small sharp knife for cutting birth-cords, so maybe the old dame did manage to produce infants intact occasionally.

Somehow I escaped on terms which left us free to send for the midwife if we needed her, though I had omitted to tell the woman where we stayed. Helena could decide.

I was so disturbed I lost my way and left by the wrong city gate. White pigeons fluttered as I passed. Needing to think, I led Prancer along the track outside the town walls which would bring me to the river. The bright day mocked my gloomy mood. Poppies, borage and daisies raised their heads beside the way, while pink oleanders crowded against the ramparts and plunged down towards the river which I eventually reached. I was on the upstream, totally unnavigable side, where the low marshy ground looked as if it never flooded. Meandering streams dawdled among tracts of firmer land which supported wild tangles of undergrowth and even large trees where birds that looked like herons or cranes nested. Other significant winged creatures—maybe falcons, or hoopoes—occasionally swooped fast among the foliage, too far away to identify properly.

Nearer to me midges swarmed, and above them were swallows. Less idyllically, a dead rat lay in a cart rut, complete with its phalanx of flies. Further on I came to a group of public slaves; I won't call them workmen. One was dancing, two took their ease on stools, and four more leaned against the wall while they all waited for the stonecutter to carve the sign that said they had completed a repair today. Not long afterwards I came to the bridge.

The afternoon was a waste of time, and my visit to the midwife had failed to reassure me. Feeling more tense than ever, I rode back to the estate. Evening was falling on the distant Mariana mountains, and I wanted to be with my girl.

THIRTY-TWO

The next day turned out to be slightly more productive, though I began it gloomily.

Tormented by my thoughts about Helena and the baby, I tried clearing my mind by helping Marius Optatus on the estate. He was spreading manure that morning, which I found appropriate. I reckon he could see the mood I had worked myself into, but in his usual way he said nothing, just handed me a rake and let me work up a sweat among his slaves.

I could not ask his advice. In the first place he was a bachelor. Besides, if any of his slaves overheard us they were bound to join in the conversation with colorful country lore. The last thing an expectant Roman father needs is a bunch of rural types cackling at his anxieties and telling him to sacrifice expensive animals to invisible woodland deities at some Celtic shrine in a grove guarded by a stone lion.

I would have paid for a kid and for a priest of the Imperial Cult to deal with it too, if I had thought it would do Helena any good. But the only gods I ever had faith in are the faceless kind who come in dark hoods with sinister downturned torches, looking for new clients to introduce to the Underworld.

I was close to madness. I admit it. Anyone in my position who had paid attention to the high rate of mother and infant mortality would be just as bad.

About the time the slaves were starting to hint that Optatus should signal a break for a cup of posca and an apple—in fact while they were making loud jokes about what a dour-faced overseer he was—the boy from the house came out to inform him visitors had called. Optatus merely nodded to show he had received the information. I leaned on my rake and questioned the lamp-boy, who said we had been favored by Claudia Rufina and her friend Aelia Annaea.

Optatus still doggedly carried on working as long as he could. His attitude intrigued me. He would not stop work for women—even if Helena was right and he hankered after one of them. He was the first man I had ever met who appeared to have perfectly normal inclinations yet who would rather spread manure.

Eventually, when the slaves' mutters of rebellion did force a halt, he and I handed over to a foreman and walked back to the house. We then had to wash rather thoroughly, but the young women seemed determined to wait until we both appeared; they were still talking to Helena in the garden when we finally emerged.

As Optatus and I walked outside to the sun-drenched garden we heard giggling: the result of allowing three women to gossip together for an hour with a jug of what passed for herbal tea. All three would have described themselves as quiet creatures with serious outlooks. Optatus may have believed it. I knew better.

Claudia Rufina, the girl I hadn't seen before, must have been older than her brother. She looked just over twenty—

easily marriageable, especially since she had a huge dowry and was part-heiress to a man of some age. The girl should have been snapped up by now. Her head lifted, and she stared at me with solemn gray eyes over the big nose Helena had previously described. She was a sturdy young lady with a worried expression. Perhaps it was caused by constantly seeing the world at an angle.

Her friend had mastered the feminine trick of appearing serene. I recognized Aelia Annaea from seeing her at her father's house, though today she was not quite so plastered in gems. At close quarters she was a little older than I had first thought, and several years older than Claudia; she looked much more of a challenge too. She had a fine-featured, very delicate face with clear skin and hazel eyes which missed absolutely nothing that went on.

This trio looked like an exposition of the architectural orders. If Helena was Ionian with her smooth wings of hair pinned aloft with sidecombs, then Aelia Annaea inclined to the Doric severity of a neat pediment of brown hair fixed dead square upon her small head; young Claudia, in Corduban modernist fashion, had allowed a maid to inflict on her a Corinthian flourish of ringlets. Our two visitors were the kind of close friends who went out together in same-color dresses—blue, today; Claudia in lighthearted aquamarine and Aelia more subdued in a deep squid-ink shade. Helena wore white. All three women were enjoying themselves making constant small gestures: adjusting their stoles, preening their hair, and rattling their bracelets (of which there were enough to stock a market stall).

I sat down with Marius Optatus. Though we had washed, we retained a close memory of the smell of manure so we tried to keep still and limit how much we exuded. I picked up the jug, and found it empty. I was not surprised. I had already noticed a plate which must once have been piled high with sesame cakes; it too had been thoroughly cleaned up, except for a few seeds. When the talk is of fashion tips, the munching gets serious.

Optatus greeted everyone with a silent nod. Helena introduced me.

"Have you come to Baetica on business, Marcus Didius?" inquired Aelia Annaea disingenuously. I reckoned she had overheard enough from her grumbling relatives at home to know just what my position was. This was a young lady who picked up all the news.

"It's no secret," I answered. "I'm the hated agent who has been sent from Rome to poke his nose into the olive oil business."

"Oh what's the reason for this?" she responded lightly.

I just smiled, trying to look like a dumb cluck who would be satisfied with any tale her untrustworthy papa wished to hand me.

"We had heard there was somebody coming from Rome." Claudia was the serious one, utterly straightforward: the type who had never realized that when a delicate question had been posed it was perfectly permissible to keep quiet. Especially if your grandpapa might have something to hide. "My grandfather thought it was somebody else."

"Someone else in particular?" I asked, smiling again.

"Oh a strange old woman who had approached him asking questions when he was out in the fields one day. He actually wrote to your father about it, Aelia!"

"Did he?" Aelia Annaea was too clever to tell Claudia to shut up; it would only draw attention to her tactlessness.

"Well that was a surprise!" Catching my curious expression Claudia explained, "Everyone was amazed to find them corresponding. Grandpapa and Annaeus Maximus usually avoid each other if they can."

"An old feud?"

"Just professional rivalry."

"That's sad!" I grinned. "I was hoping for a hot tale of

seething envy and passion. Was there no stolen land? No favorite slavegirls raped on riverbanks? No runaway young wives?"

"You read the wrong poetry," said Helena.

"No, love; I read the law reports!"

Marius Optatus said nothing, but chuckled to himself. He was not much help with repartee. I was perfectly prepared to handle three women at once, but an occasional respite would have been useful; in fact, this situation called for my rascally friend Petronius.

"What happened to the old biddy?" I inquired of Claudia.

"She was shooed away."

Aelia Annaea had been watching me. She was thinking herself a match for any undercover agent—especially one investigating openly. I winked at her. She was no match for that.

Apropros of nothing Helena asked, "So were you both acquainted with my brother?"

Oh of course, squeaked both wenches, in enthusiastic tones. Past acquaintance with Aelianus would be their public reason for making much of Helena, a new face (with a Roman hairstyle, and perhaps bringing a scroll of Roman recipes). Apparently Aelianus had been a jewel of Corduban society (these were very polite young women). At least, he had been a close friend of Claudia's brother, Rufius Constans, and of Aelia's three brothers, who must all have owned impressive formal names in the Roman style, but whom she called Spunky, Dotty and Ferret.

What all the male juveniles had in common, it emerged, was that they were close cronies of Tiberius.

"Tiberius?" asked I, like a wide-eyed novice.

"Oh you must know Tiberius!"

"I'm afraid I don't have that honor. Tiberius who?"

"Tiberius Quinctius Quadratus," stated Marius Optatus suddenly. "In my house he has one or two less polite names."

"Your ex-landlord's son?"

"Our admired new quaestor, Falco."

His intervention had darkened the tone of the conversation. He looked as if he wanted to cause trouble. Aelia Annaea tried to soften the atmosphere: "Well, what can one say about Tiberius, except that he is charming?"

Helena said quietly, "Don't you just hate charming men? I always think charm is a certain clue to a man you shouldn't trust."

"This one is also extremely good-looking," I supplied. "If he's the hero I saw the other night collecting you from your father's house, Aelia Annaea?" She acknowledged it.

"Oh he has everything!" muttered Optatus jealously. "A distinguished father in a prominent position, a winning way, political promise, and the good opinion of everyone he comes into contact with." I saw young Claudia compress her lips slightly. She was embarrassed by his anger; her friend merely looked resigned.

I pretended to know nothing about him. "Is this paragon new to the area?"

"The family's Roman of course," Optatus answered bitterly. "But we know him well already. The Quinctii have large tracts of land. Quadratus has spent time in the district before, and we'll be seeing even more of him now he holds his official post."

I beamed at the two young ladies. "I take it he's related to Quinctius Attractus, the senator your father and grandfather stayed with in Rome just recently?" This time even Claudia had the sense merely to answer with a vague nod and smile. If they knew the visit to Rome was significant, somebody seemed to have told them not to discuss it with me. "I met Attractus myself. What a coincidence."

"You'll meet his son too," growled Optatus. "Don't worry about missing that treat, Marcus Didius. He's everywhere, is Tiberius." The two young ladies had fallen silent; fending off difficulties with Optatus had now gone beyond their control.

"I heard he was off hunting," I said.

"He's hanging around Corduba enjoying himself," replied Marius. "I heard the proconsul told him he wasn't to show his face in the office any more than strictly necessary."

He was wanting to argue with somebody, so I gave him his money's worth: "I reckon you're being hard on the new quaestor. From the glimpse I had, he seemed a gifted lad."

"Oh he's wonderful," breathed Claudia.

"Young lady, do I detect a blush?" I quipped. She obliged me, though it earned me a black look from Helena, who had already decided to support a romance for Optatus with Claudia. I refused to take the hint from my beloved, and carried on, "Claudia Rufina, your grandparents were telling me their plans for your brother's career—Rome, and so forth. They must have high hopes for you too. Does that include a handsome dowry to share with some promising star?"

This time Helena actually kicked me. Too late. While she squinted a reminder about Marius Optatus harboring a tenderness for Claudia, his expression remained decidedly neutral. But a sudden frosty tension told me three different women were cursing me and wondering how to be kind to him.

Claudia, the least adept, answered my question in her usual serious and strictly accurate way: "My grandfather has not discussed anything with me—" It sounded as though Licinius Rufius had actually told her it was too soon for public comment.

Helena Justina leaned forward and tapped my wrist with the herbal tea strainer. "Marriage isn't everything, Marcus!" She turned to Aelia Annaea. "I remember when my former husband first asked for me. I was young; I thought it was my duty to accept him. But I can recall feeling very angry that he had placed me in the position where I felt obliged to have him just because he was the one who had asked."

"I think I understand that," Aelia Annaea responded. Then,

somewhat to the surprise of both Helena and me, she mentioned that she had been married herself, then after three years and no children she had been very recently widowed. Something in her tone implied she had no plans to repeat the experience.

"Was your marriage happy?" Helena asked in her forthright way.

"I had nothing to complain about."

"That sounds rather qualified."

"Well I could never in conscience have requested a divorce."

"And yet?" asked Helena, smiling.

"And yet, Helena!" Aelia Annaea had probably not talked like this before. We watched the young widow surprising herself: "To be honest, when my husband died I felt I had been given another chance in life." Her eyes sparkled wickedly. "I do enjoy myself now. A widow has a different status. For a year at least, I shall have a certain independence—" She stopped, as if we might disapprove of what she was saying.

"Why only a year?" Helena growled.

Aelia looked rueful. "That's about as long as a woman with a fortune can expect to hold out against the hordes of people who want to suggest ways she can invest it with them!"

Claudia Rufina certainly looked shocked now. Helena turned to her kindly: "Don't listen to us crabby things! You should just try to feel sure that you share common bonds with your husband."

"Love?" asked Claudia, rather defiantly.

Helena laughed. "Well, that might be stretching it."

"Love is a luxury!" I joined in the teasing. "But you don't need to demand anything excessive—a shared fondness for chariot races, or a keen interest in sheep-breeding can be a wonderful basis for at least four or five years together."

Torn between Helena's advice and my flippancy, Claudia looked puzzled. I noticed Marius Optatus had been listening to all this and apparently watching both girls with curious interest. Apart from his one brief outburst he had said hardly anything, yet seemed quite content to sit here as one of the party.

I said gently to our two visitors, "Your friend Tiberius sounds fascinating. I think I'd like to meet this young man!"

They agreed that I must do so, then with one accord they jumped up from their seats and decided that they really had to leave.

I stayed behind alone while they were being seen off. I wanted to think about the "strange incident" when an old biddy (or a young dancer, well disguised?) had tried to talk to Claudia's grandfather.

THIRTY-THREE

Optatus tried to vanish for the rest of the afternoon. I had obviously upset him somehow, but he was useless as a sulker: he had the kind of stubborn nature that refused to let him miss his meals. At dinner he was there again, a silent presence. Helena and I talked to Marmarides our driver about going into Corduba next day. We let Optatus work his way through half a loaf of farm-baked bread, a bowl of preserved olive salad and some smoked sausage from the hanging rack above the hearth. Then he drank a whole jug of water from the dolium, and sat and picked his teeth.

Helena moved away from the bench at the table, needing space for two. With a slight sigh she eased herself into a chair near the hot water cauldron on the cooking bench. I put one leg up on the bench, twisting to look at our friend. I was still eating; I had more appetite than him.

"Something struck me today," Helena put in from her chair beside the cooking bench. "Those two young women called the Quinctius son charming. They were not just saying it because he had flirted with them prettily; they meant that everybody thinks he is wonderful."

"Everyone except you," I suggested to Marius Optatus. I would be the second exception, if I came up with my usual reaction to jumped-up lads in administrative posts.

"Don't answer if you don't want to, Marius," Helena said. "We are all living in the same house, and there are rules of good manners."

She had sensed what was the matter, and he finally broke his silence in reply. "What you do is horrible, Falco."

I pulled through my teeth a piece of sausage skin that was too tough to eat. "How have I offended you?"

"I think you must offend everyone."

"Close!" I took a spill from a vase that stood with the salt-box on the table. Everyone in Rome has been fed that myth about Hispanians cleaning their teeth with their own urine, so I was glad to find that in this villa rustica they had heard of using a sharp bit of stick. Never believe what you read. Half the time it has just been copied by a pig-ignorant hack from some previous author's bogus scroll.

Optatus pushed away his bowl and swung out from the table. In the measured pace of life in the country he took a small pottery lamp, carried it to to an amphora, filled a jug from the larger container, filled the lamp from the jug, brought it back to the hearth, lit his toothpick from the embers, lit the lamp wick, placed the light on the table and stood there thoughtfully. His actions alerted the lamp-boy to go about his task of lighting the rest of the house, and the cook to collect crockery to wash. Marmarides caught my eye, then went out to feed the carriage mules. People were now moving about freely in the kitchen, and our discussion took on a more informal tone.

"The Annaei and Licinii Rufii are my friends," he complained. "I grew up with them."

"Would that be with the boys—or the girls?" I asked pointedly. "Which am I not allowed to approach in my work, Marius?" He made no answer, so I added quietly, "Aelia Annaea *certainly* knew exactly what our conversation was about—and I really don't believe I took advantage of Claudia." Optatus resumed his place at the table at last, his tall shadow wavering on the kitchen wall as he sat down. "They both know my role; I told them quite freely. If those two young ladies have made a pet of Quinctius Quadratus, they are both mature enough to take the consequences."

"I don't see what this has to do—"

"His father is heavily implicated in a probable conspiracy. I think we can guess that deliberate influence was used to get the son his posting as quaestor. The Quinctii are building themselves a dangerous powerbase in Baetica. If I end up nailing Attractus, his son is almost certain to be disgraced at the same time. The son *may* be an innocent tool of a devious father, but that quaestorship makes him look a willing participant in the master plan. Even if he's as pure as snow, he's stuck with how it looks—though from what you told me about the way he kicked you out of your tenancy, 'pure' is not the word to use."

Optatus was brooding on his personal problems. "They will not succeed in their ambitions." At least he was talking again. "People here don't welcome their interference. People will resist them; I will do so myself. When I have money, I will buy land of my own. If I cannot achieve it myself, at least my descendants will be equal to the Quinctii."

"You've already been saving!" Helena guessed acutely. "You're mulling over a plan!"

"You could marry into an estate," I suggested. "That would help." He looked at me, affronted. "Marius Optatus, you are well respected in the local community. All sorts of people regard you kindly. Set your sights high."

"You are advising me from experience?" He sounded barbed.

I said, "A man should go for the girl he wants, my friend."

Helena was looking worried. "She might not always be available!"

"She might be," I retorted. I pretended to be unaware of any feelings Optatus had. "Take Claudia Rufina, for example—you could say the signs are all there that she's earmarked for the fabulous quaestor 'Tiberius.' But will it ever happen? I suggest it's unlikely. He comes from an old Italian family. The Quinctii are certain to look for a bride from the same patrician *Roman* background. Making money from the provinces is one thing. Making an alliance is another."

On reflection, Helena backed me up: "It's true. If you took a census of the men in the Senate, you'd find the Spaniards are married to Spanish women, the Gauls to Gauls—and the Romans to their own kind. So, Marcus, that's why nothing is being said openly about Claudia and the quaestor?"

"Nothing ever will be. The Quinctii aren't buying. Having met Claudia's grandfather, I'd call him shrewd enough to see it."

"The girl could be hurt by this," Helena frowned.

"Only if she's daft enough to fall in love with the charmer. I dare say she may be, but it need not be irretrievable. Well there you are!" I exclaimed to Optatus. "A nice rich girl who may soon have a heartache, and be going spare in the marriage market!"

He took it well. "Thanks, Falco!" He managed a grin and I knew we were friends again. "But maybe Claudia Rufina isn't nice enough or rich enough!"

Helena and I both beamed at him. We do like to manipulate a man who stands up for himself.

Optatus was still niggling about the way I had to work. "I was taking you to task, Falco."

"About what I do?"

"For all I know, when we converse in this friendly fashion, you are laying traps even for me!"

I sighed. "Rest assured. If there is a conspiracy, by the time the Quinctii started trying to arrange their cartel, you were on very bad terms with them. Only men who look amenable are invited on their friendly trips to Rome. Let's be fair to the Quinctii though; they may be honest as daisies."

"So you like to be fair!" he observed dryly.

"I've been caught out too many times! But I don't believe you were ever invited to join any price-fixing; you disapprove too strongly of corrupt practices."

Maybe I was being stupid. Maybe Marius Optatus was so utterly disgruntled by what had happened to him, that *he* was the moving spirit behind the plot Anacrites had wanted to investigate. He had just told us he was saving hard and harboring ambition. Perhaps I had been underestimating his importance here.

"I'm flattered," said Optatus. "So you will concentrate your efforts on the young ladies' handsome friend, Falco?"

"The charming Tiberius does pose one fascinating puzzle. If the Quinctii are villains, they appear to have everything well sewn up. But even so, the proconsul has sent Quinctius Quadratus on hunting leave."

"So what, Falco? He is a sporting type. He loves hunting; in a young man of promise that goes down well."

I smiled wisely. "In a young man who has just started a major public role, this phrase has other connotations. He's not hunting at present, is he?"

"He's enjoying himself in every way."

"Quite. Flirting with Aelia Annaea and Claudia. What a bastard."

"And he is influencing their brothers," Optatus told me. "Particularly young Rufius Constans; Quadratus has made himself the boy's mentor."

"That sounds unfortunate! But listen: I was telling you about hunting leave; you have to be aware of the subtleties here. In the army it's called 'being sent up country.' In civic life it's a different term, but same result: your quaestor is not actually expected to hunt. He can loaf on his father's estate, attend the gymnasium, entertain women—whatever he likes, just so long as he doesn't show his face. The fact is, at least temporarily, the proconsul has shoved this twinkling star out of the way."

Optatus looked pleased. He immediately saw that for the Quinctii and their ambitious plans this could be a disaster. The Senate might have been bought and the Emperor bamboozled, but here the proconsul had a mind of his own. Against all the odds, not everything was going right for Quinctius Attractus and his son. Apparently there was a black mark on a list somewhere, against the name of Tiberius Quinctius Quadratus.

Maybe Laeta had sent me to Baetica to be the man who turned the mark into a line drawn right through the name.

"What happens now, Falco?"

"That's easy," chortled Helena sleepily from her place beside the fire. "Marcus has the kind of job he likes: he has to find a girl."

"In order to disgrace one or both of the Quinctii," I explained quietly, "I have to link them to Selia, the dancing girl from Hispalis I mentioned to you before. She helped get a man killed in Rome—and someone almost certainly hired her."

For once it was Optatus who laughed. "I told you before! You won't find many of those girls in Baetica; they all sail off to make their fortunes in Rome!"

Well that was good. It should be easier to identify the one who had sneaked back to Spain.

"Mind you . . ." mused Optatus, as if he had had a thought he rather liked, "I ought to be able to introduce you to someone else—Quinctius Quadratus." I raised an eyebrow at the suggestion. He smiled. "Falco, you need to meet people and sample some entertainment in Corduba. I know where to find it."

"One of the boys, eh?" I tried hard to believe it, though it was difficult to see him as a ringleader at a bachelors' night out.

"In there with the best of them," he claimed.

"So what disreputable scheme do you have in store for us?"

"I've heard that Annaeus Maximus is going to visit his Gades estate. The last time he left Corduba—when he went to Rome to see Quinctius Attractus—his sons held a party where so much damage was caused they were forbidden to invite their friends home again."

"I saw them in passing the other night. Nice lads!"

Optatus grinned. "I've also heard that the minute Maximus leaves for Gades, Spunky, Dotty and Ferret will be defying their parents and holding open house again!"

Every parent's nightmare. Once I would have been delighted. Now I found myself wondering whether poor Annaeus Maximus could somehow be warned to take his cellar keys to Gades. I knew why I felt so dispirited: one day there would be out-of-control young persons throwing up in my own Attic vase collection. One day it would be my polished sandalwood table that some little drunken idiot decided to dance upon while wearing her sharpest-heeled shoes.

Then as I glanced at Helena (who was regarding me rather quizzically) I felt able to view coming events at the Annaeus house with greater complacency: after all, my own children would be brought up well. With model parents, they would love us and be loyal. They would heed our prohibitions and follow our advice. My children would be different.

THIRTY-FOUR

This job was taking longer than I wanted—like most of my work. At least it was civilized. I was more accustomed to being compelled to get drunk during long waits in seedy wine bars, and joining in the occasional fight with a bunch of roughs in the kind of location you don't let your mother know about.

Next day it was back to Corduba, determined this time to force a meeting with Cyzacus, the bargee I had seen being dined out by Quinctius Attractus back in Rome. Helena Justina came with me. She pretended my constant trips had made her suspect I was keeping a light woman somewhere, but it turned out that when we had driven in together on the Parilia Helena had discovered a manufacturer of purple dye, the expensive juice extracted from murex shells that is used for top-rank uniforms. While I had been chatting to the pro-consul she had ordered a quantity of cloth. Now she said she wanted my company—though it was also a chance to pick up her bargain.

"Sweetheart, I hate to be pedantic but nobody in either of our families is an army commander, let alone a candidate for emperor!" I wondered if she was making wild plans for our baby. Political ambition in Helena was a terrifying prospect. Helena Justina was the kind of girl whose wild plans came into effect.

"Bought here, the stuff is so reasonable, Marcus. And I know just who wants it!" I would never match her in deviousness: Helena intended to offer the purple material at cost to the Emperor's mistress when we went home. She reckoned that if all the stories of frugality (otherwise called meanness) in Vespasian's household were true, the lady Caenis would leap at this chance to kit out Vespasian, Titus Caesar, and the sprog Domitian in really cheap imperial uniforms. In return, there might be a chance that Vespasian's darling, strongly encouraged by *my* darling, would put in a good word for me to him. "It's more likely to work than smarming around your friend Laeta," Helena sneered.

She was probably right. The wheels of empire turn on barter. After all, that was why I was spending the end of April flogging around Corduba.

I had managed to persuade Helena to meet the midwife I had interviewed. She screwed out of me what had happened during my own introduction. "So that's what upset you!" she muttered darkly, grabbing my hand in a rather fierce manner. She must have noticed I came back from town yesterday in a bad mood. Her promise to have a look at the woman herself lacked conviction, I thought.

I was now very familiar with the sluggish River Baetis, its sudden petering out at the sixteen-arch bridge, and the lazy wheeling of marsh birds above the wooden wharf with its collection of rough and ready sheds. At last there were signs of activity, though the riverside was not exactly heaving with life.

Marmarides parked our carriage in a tree-shaded area where stakes had been set up for tethering wagons and mules.

It was a beautiful morning. We all walked slowly to the water's edge. Nux trotted happily alongside, thinking she was in charge of the party. We passed a large character who was crouching down talking quietly to a clutch of choice African fowl as he put together a new henhouse. Far out, a man was crouched in a small raft with a fishing line, with the air of having found a good excuse to sleep in the sun.

A barge which had been motionless at the wharf for three days to my knowledge now had its covers off; looking down into it we could see rows of the distinctive globular amphorae in which oil was transported long distances. They were packed several deep, each balanced between the necks of the previous layer, with reeds stuffed among them to prevent movement. The weight must have been enormous, and the sturdy barge had sagged low in the water.

Cyzacus' office—a shed with a stool set outside it—was open today. Not much else had improved.

Presumably once harvest time started in September the action here would be hectic. In spring, nothing much happened for days on end, unless a convoy of copper, gold or silver happened to come down from the mines in the Mariana mountains. Left in charge during this dead period was a run-down, rasping runt with one leg shorter than the other and a wine jug clamped under his arm. Nux barked at him once loudly, then when he turned and stared at her she lost interest and confined herself to blinking at clouds of midges.

"Cyzacus here?"

"No chance, legate!"

"When's he due?"

"You tell me."

"Does he ever show his face?"

"Hardly ever."

"Who runs the business?"

"I reckon it runs itself."

He was well trained. Most useless lags who pretend to be

watchmen feel compelled to tell you at length how pitiful the management is and how draconian are their own employment terms. Life was one long holiday for this reprobate, and he didn't intend to complain.

"When was the last time you saw Cyzacus down on the wharf?"

"Couldn't tell you, legate."

"So if I wanted to ask someone to arrange to ship a large load down to Hispalis, say, I wouldn't ask for him?"

"You could ask. It wouldn't do you any good."

I could tell Helena was losing her temper. Marmarides, who nursed the fond idea that what he called agenting was tough work with interesting highlights, was beginning to look openly bored. Being an informer is hard enough, without subordinates who expect thrills and quaking suspects.

"Who runs the business?" I repeated.

The lag sucked his teeth. "Well not Cyzacus. Cyzacus has pretty well retired nowadays. Cyzacus is more what you'd call a figurehead."

"Somebody must sign the invoices. Does Cyzacus have a son?" I demanded, thinking of all the other men involved in the conspiracy.

The man with the wine jug burst out laughing, then felt the need to take a hefty swig. He was already obstinate and awkward. Soon he would be obstinate, awkward, and drunk.

When he stopped chortling he told me the story: Cyzacus and his son had fallen out. I should have known, really. I fell out with my own father, after all. This son had run away from home—the only oddity was what he had run off to do: Spain produced the Empire's best gladiators. In most towns boys dream of upsetting their parents by fighting in the arena, but maybe in Spain that's the sensible career that they rebel against. At any rate, when Cyzacus junior had his blazing row with Papa and left home forever with just a clean tunic and his mother's hoarded housekeeping, *he* ran off to be a poet.

"Well, Hispania has produced a lot of poets," said Helena quietly.

"It's just a different way of messing me about," I snarled at the watchman. "Now look here, you great poppy: I don't want a tragic ode, I want the man in charge."

He knew the game was up. "Fair enough. No hard feelings—" My feelings should have been obvious. Then he told me that when Cyzacus senior was disappointed by his boy's flight to literature, he adopted someone more suitable: someone who had been a gladiator, so he had nothing to prove. "Now he has Gorax."

"Then I'll speak to Gorax."

"Ooh I don't advise it, legate!"

I asked what the problem was and he pointed towards the large man we had seen earlier engaged in building a henhouse: Gorax had no time for visitors because of his chickens.

Helena Justina gave up on my investigation and said she would go into town for her purple cloth. Marmarides escorted her back to the carriage, reluctantly because he knew the name Gorax: Gorax had once been famous even as far as Malaca, though now he was retired.

Never one to shrink from challenges, I said chickens or no chickens, he would have to speak to me.

I approached quietly, already having second thoughts. He was covered in scars. What he lacked in height he made up in width and bodyweight. His movements were gentle and he showed no wariness of strangers: if any stranger looked at him the wrong way Gorax could just wrap him around a tree. Gorax must have been a gladiator who had known what he was doing. That was why, after twenty bouts in the arena, he was still alive.

I could see the big fellow was really enjoying himself, building his chickens a house. I had been told by the watchman that Gorax had a girlfriend who lived downstream near

Hispalis; she had given him the poultry, to provide a safe hobby while he was away from her. It seemed to have worked; he was clearly entranced by the birds. The great soft-hearted lunk looked completely absorbed by his pretty cockerel and three hens as they pecked up maize.

They were finer than common barnyard poultry, special guinea-fowl so delicate they begged to be fussily hand-reared. Neat, dark-feathered birds, with bare heads and bony helmet crests, all speckled like fritillaries.

As I tentatively approached him, he stood up to stare at me. He might have been willing to allow a polite interruption, especially if I admired his pets. But that was before he glanced around his little flock and noticed that only two of the precious hens were there. The third had wandered off along the wharf towards the tethered barge—where she was about to be spotted by Nux.

THIRTY-FIVE

The dog let out quite a tentative yip when she first noticed the hen. For a single drumbeat, Nux pondered in an amiable fashion whether to make friends with the bird. Then the hen saw Nux and fluttered up onto a bollard with a frantic cluck. Delighted, Nux sprang into the chase.

As the dog began to rush towards the little hen, the huge gladiator dropped the hammer with which he had been nailing up a perch. He pounded off to save his pet, holding another bird under his arm. I sprinted after him. He naturally had the turn of speed a fighter needs to surprise an unwary opponent with a death-thrust. Oblivious, Nux sat down on her tail and had a meditative scratch.

Marmarides had been lurking by the carriage, unwilling to leave with Helena while I was talking to the famous Gorax. He saw the fun start. I glimpsed his slight figure running our way. Three of us were converging on the dog and the hen—though it was doubtful whether any of us would reach them in time.

Then the stunted watchman, still clutching his wine, began dancing about on the wharf. Nux thought it was a game; she remembered the hen and decided to fetch it for him. Marmarides whooped. I gulped. Gorax shrieked. The hen squawked hysterically. So did the other one, squashed against the mighty chest of Gorax. Nux barked again ecstatically and jumped at the hen on the bollard.

Flapping its wings (and losing feathers) the endangered fowl flew off the bollard, and scooted along the wharf just ahead of Nux's eager nose. Then the stupid thing took off and flapped down into the barge. Gorax rushed at Nux. She had been up on the edge of the planking having a bark at the hen but with a heavyweight bearing down on her, yelling obvious murder, the dog leapt straight after the hen. The hen tried to flutter up off the barge again but was terrified of the watchman peering down and calling obscene endearments. Nux floundered amongst the necks of the amphorae, paws flailing.

I jumped off the quayside onto the barge. It was basic—no features to grab. I had no time to judge my footing, so one end of the boat swung out suddenly into the stream as I landed. Gorax, who had been about to step aboard himself, slipped on the thwart as the tethered end bumped the quay unexpectedly; he crashed to the deck with one leg overboard. Landing on his chest, he crushed the hen he had been carrying. From his expression, he knew he had killed it. I teetered wildly, trying hard to keep my balance since I could not swim.

Marmarides skidded up the quay and chose a target. He gave the watchman a shove, so the befuddled fool tipped straight into the river. He started screaming, then gurgling. Marmarides had a change of heart and plunged in after him.

Gorax had let out a whine as he cradled the dead bird, but he dropped it as Nux scrabbled closer to the one that was still flapping. Gorax went for the dog, so I aimed at the fowl. We collided, lost our footing on the amphorae, and caused a nasty crack of pottery underfoot. The ex-gladiator had gone through one and was ankle-deep in broken pot. As he struggled to extricate his leg the container broke again, so he was up to his knee, with oil sloshing everywhere. To regain his balance he grabbed at me.

"Ooh be gentle!"

Unlikely! I had a swift glimpse of his gullet as he let out a wild cry. Even his tonsils were terrifying. I thought he was going to bite off my nose, but just then a refined voice cut through the racket saying, "Leave it out, Gorax! You're frightening the fish away!"

Gorax, all obedience, dragged his leg out of the smashed amphora, trailing blood and golden oil. Then he sat down on the edge of the barge and held the dead fowl on his massive knee, while tears streamed down his face.

"Thanks!" I said quietly to the newcomer. I grabbed Nux with one hand, and made my way carefully to the river side of the barge, where a thin man who was propelling a raft with a pole had stuck his head above the deckline to see what was going on. I crouched and offered a handshake. "The name's Falco."

"Cyzacus," he said.

I managed to keep my temper. "You're not the man I was introduced to by that name in Rome!"

"You must mean Father."

"Apollo! You're the poet?"

"I am!" he responded, rather tetchily.

"Sorry; I thought you had left home."

"I did," said Cyzacus junior, punting his raft around to the wharfside with some competence.

"You wield a mean oar, for a man of literature." Clamping the dog under my arm, I had regained the wharf. After Cyzacus tied up his raft I reached down and helped him spring up onto the jetty.

He had a slight body and a few whiffs of hair, amongst which was actually a stylus shoved behind his ear. Maybe the fishing was a cover for writing a ten-volume magisterial epic to glorify Rome. (Or maybe like my Uncle Fabius he was the crazy type who liked to note down descriptions of every fish he caught—date, weight, coloring, time of day, weather, and bait used on the hook . . .) He did look like a poet, saturnine and vague, probably with no sense about money and hopeless with women. He was about forty—probably the same as his adopted brother Gorax. There appeared to be no animosity between them, for Cyzacus went to console the big hulk, who eventually shrugged, tossed the dead hen into the river, and came back onto the wharf cooing over the live one fondly while it tried to fly away. He had simple emotions and a short attention span; perfect in the arena, and probably just as useful sorting out wholesalers who wanted to hire space on the barge.

"He organizes the loads," Cyzacus told me. "I keep the records."

"Of course, a poet can write!"

"There's no need for cheek."

"I'm just fascinated. You went to Rome?"

"And I came back," he said shortly. "I failed to find a patron. Nobody came to my public readings; my scrolls failed to sell." He spoke with much bitterness. It had never entered his head that wanting to be famous for writing was not enough. Maybe he was a bad poet.

I wasn't going to be the man who pointed this out, not with Gorax standing beside him looking immensely proud of his creative business partner. An ex-gladiator's brother is entitled to respect. The two were about the same height, though the big one filled about three times the space of the other. They looked totally different, but I already sensed there were closer bonds between them than between most real brothers who have grown up squabbling.

"Never mind," I said. "The world has far too many tragedies and almost enough satires. And at least while you're dreaming on a raft on the River Baetis you'll be spared too many crass interruptions to your thoughts." The failed poet suspected I was ragging him, so I went on quickly, "I was just explaining to Gorax when the fracas blew up, your father and I met at a very pleasant dinner in Rome."

"Father does the trips abroad," Cyzacus junior confirmed.

"What was it? Making contacts?"

Cyzacus and Gorax exchanged looks. One thought himself intellectual and one was a beaten-up punchbag—but neither was dumb.

"You're the man from Rome!" Cyzacus told me in a sour voice.

Gorax snarled. "We were expecting you."

"I should hope you were. I've been here three times!" I bluffed it out. "The office has been closed."

They exchanged looks again. Whatever they told me, I could see it would be a concocted story. Somebody had already primed them to be difficult.

"All right," I confided in a friendly fashion. "Corduba seems a town that has no secrets. I don't know how closely you work with your old man, but I need to ask him about the oil business."

"Father stays in Hispalis," the true son said. "That's where the guild of bargees have their headquarters. He's a big man in the guild." He looked pleased with himself for this unhelpfulness.

"I'd better go down to Hispalis, then," I retorted, undeterred. Once more I noticed the two brothers shifting nervously. "Is this load on the barge going downriver soon? Can I hitch a ride?"

They did tell me when the barge would be leaving; they were probably relieved to let their father deal with me. From what I remembered, he had looked a tougher proposition. Gorax even offered to let me go to Hispalis on the barge for free. This was one of the perks of informing. People I interviewed often seemed glad to pay my fare to send me on to the next person, especially if the next person lived a hundred miles away.

"It must be slightly inconvenient for the bargees," I suggested, "having so much trade from Corduba, when your guild is set up at Hispalis?"

The poet smiled. "It works. At Cyzacus et Filii we see ourselves as go-betweens in every sense."

I smiled back at the pair of them. "Many people have told me that Cyzacus et Filii are the most influential bargemen on the Baetis."

"That's right," said Gorax.

"So if the oil producers were banding together to further their trade, your firm would be in there too, representing the guild of bargees?"

The younger Cyzacus knew full well I was referring to the proposed cartel. "The bargees and the oil producers tend to stick firmly to their separate interests."

"Oh, I must have got it wrong then; I understood your father went to Rome to be part of some negotiations for a new system of price banding?"

"No, he went to Rome as part of a visit to the guild's offices at Ostia."

"I see! Tell me, does your father have any connections with dancing girls these days?"

They both laughed. It was perfectly genuine. They told me their parent had not looked at a girl for fifty years, and with the innocence of loyal sons they really believed it, I could tell.

Then we all had to stop sidestepping as our attention was claimed by a desperate cry. Still down in the river, my driver Marmarides was floating on his back in an approved Roman legionary manner (which he must have learned in the service of his master Stertius) gripping the watchman under the chin to keep his head above water, while the watchman clutched his wine jug and they both waited patiently for somebody to throw them down a rope.

THIRTY-SIX

My social life was looking up. I was acquiring a full calendar, what with Optatus promising me japes among the bachelors of Corduba, and my free ticket down the Baetis.

Had the elder Cyzacus been the sole reason for visiting Hispalis I might have dropped him as a suspect to interview, but there was also the negotiator Norbanus, who arranged ocean-going shipping from the downstream port. I might even trace the elusive and murderous "Selia"—assuming that the fake shepherdess who chucked the stone at me had used her real name. Hispalis posed a problem, however. On my map-skin it looked a good ninety Roman miles away—as the raven flies. The River Baetis appeared to meander atrociously. That could mean anything from a week to a fortnight floating down to do interviews that might add absolutely nothing to my knowledge. I could not afford to waste so much time. Every day when I looked at Helena Justina I was struck by anxiety.

Cyzacus and Gorax had almost certainly wanted to make me waste time for no good reason. If those two managed to put a government agent out of action for a fortnight by trapping him on a very slow barge miles away from anywhere, they would feel proud of themselves. They were protecting their father, not realizing how urgently I wanted to trace the dancer and that if I did go to Hispalis she would be my main quarry. I felt sure their father must have reported full details of the dinner, though whether he had told them anything about the attacks afterwards would depend on how much he trusted them. Clearly the poet's time in Rome, while it failed to make him a famous man of letters, had taught him to be a thoroughgoing Celtiberian pain in the backside.

I had now interviewed two suspects, Annaeus Maximus and Licinius Rufius. There were two more in Hispalis, assuming I ever made it there. Yet another pair could well be implicated, even though they had ducked out of the dinner on the Palatine: young Rufius Constans and the Quinctius son. They had both been in Rome at the right time. Optatus reckoned Quinctius Quadratus exerted a bad influence on Constans—though until I met Quadratus and judged him for myself I had to allow for some prejudice in his ex-tenant. Yet the wary Greek secretary at the house of Quinctius Attractus who first told me that the two young men had bunked off to the theater had been very reluctant to give me details. Neither the youngsters themselves nor their whereabouts had seemed important to the inquiry then. Now I was not so sure.

This was one avenue I would be able to pursue immediately, for Optatus had established that the three Annaei were holding their party only a couple of evenings later. Through old channels of communication he had obtained a ready invitation for the pair of us. Young Rufius was trying not to offend his grandfather by openly fraternizing with rivals, so he was pretending to visit us that evening and we were taking him. Marmarides would drive us, and later bring home any who had managed to remain sober. Helena seemed to be remembering the last time I went off without her, when I could not even find the right way home afterwards. She saw us off with an intense sniff of disapproval. Apparently Claudia Rufina was taking the same attitude; she stayed at home with their grandparents, though she seemed very fond of her brother and had sportingly agreed not to give him away.

I myself took a conscious decision that evening not to wear anything that might show stains. Optatus had dressed up; he was in a suavely styled outfit that made excellent use of the famous Baetican cinnabar dye, a rich vermilion pigment, complemented by heavily formal black braid on the neck and shoulder seams. With this came an incongruous set of antique finger-rings and a faint waft of balsam around his carefully shaved jowls. It all gave him an air of being up to no good. Even so, he was outshone by the youth.

This was my first real encounter with Rufius Constans. We were all just in tunics—no ceremony in the provinces—and his was the finest quality. I was barely neat; Optatus had on his best. Rufius Constans could well look down on both of us. In his casually worn white linen, his gleaming niello belt, his shaped calfskin boots and even a torque (Jove!), he was far more comfortable in his clothes; he had coffers full at home. So here was a rich lad with high aspirations, setting off for a night among friends, beautifully turned out—yet he was jumpy as a flea.

Constans was pleasant-looking, nothing more. His nose, set in a young, unformed face, was a weak shadow of his sister's but there was something of her in the way he peered shyly at the world. At twenty or so, I felt he had not yet decided his ethical position. He seemed unfinished, and lacking the weight he would need for the elite public career his proud grandfather had charted for him. Maybe I was feeling old.

"I've been meaning to ask you," I tackled the young man casually, "how did you enjoy the theater?"

"What?" He had a light voice and restless eyes. It may be that any lad of twenty who finds himself knee to knee in a jolting carriage with an older man who has a lively reputation may automatically look shifty. Or perhaps he had something to hide.

"I nearly met you during your trip to Rome with your grandfather. But you and Quinctius Quadratus decided to go to the theater instead." Was it my imagination or did the playgoer look hunted? "See anything good?"

"Can't remember. A mime, I think. Tiberius took me drinking afterwards; it's all a blur."

It was too early in the night to turn nasty on him. I smiled and let the lie go past. I felt convinced it *was* a lie. "You want to be careful if you go out on the town in Rome. You could get mugged. People are getting beaten up on the streets all the time. You didn't see any of that, I suppose?"

"Oh no."

"That's good."

"I'm sorry I missed the chance of meeting you," Rufius added. He had been brought up to be polite.

"You missed some excitement too," I said.

I did not say what, and he displayed no curiosity. An exceptional young fellow, apparently.

I felt sour. I was still thinking about the dead Valentinus, and even about Anacrites, when the carriage pulled up at the smart out-of-town Annaeus residence.

Lucius Annaeus Maximus Primus, Lucius Annaeus Aelius Maximus, and Lucius Annaeus Maximus Novatus (to honor Spunky, Dotty and Ferret officially) knew how to throw a bash. Money was no object, and neither was taste. They had the household slaves scampering about with great vigor. It was all much more exciting than the stultified jollifications I had seen here at the Parilia festival. Released from parental authority, our hosts were being themselves, and a hilarious trio they were. I was glad they weren't my boys.

They had bought up every garland of flowers in Corduba. Their father's frescoed house smelt like all the gardens of ancient Tartessos, its air thick with pollen, a nightmare for sensitive noses. To add to the lamp smoke, the floral scents and the all-pervading aromatic odors of young bodies given unaccustomed hours of grooming, the lads had devised an Egyptian theme for the evening. It involved a few homemade dog-headed gods, some wicker snakes, two ostrich-feather fans, and cones of scented wax which new arrivals were instructed to wear on their heads: as the heat of the party rose so the cones would melt, giving everyone a bitter aura of Pharaonic myrrh and impossibly matted hair. I made sure I lost mine.

Word had gone around all the baths and gymnasiums in town that the three great lads were holding a party. The news had spread like foot fungus. The seediest youths of the city had suddenly muttered to their parents that they were going over to a friend's house, being careful not to specify which friend. All over Corduba parents were now vaguely wondering where their pallid offspring had scuttled off to, and why there was such a reek of breath-freshening pastilles. Inadequate teenage owners of large personal allowances, mostly with skinny shoulders and pustular skin, had been waiting weeks for this night. They were hoping it would make men of them; the only certainty was that it would make them bilious.

Girls had come too. Some were nice, though their reputations might not last the evening. Some were slightly soiled to begin with and would be horrendous by the time they had swallowed several jugs of unwatered wine and had their frocks pulled off behind laurel bushes. Some were clearly professionals.

"It's worse than I expected, Falco," Optatus confessed.

"You're getting too old to take it?"

"I feel like a bad-tempered grandfather."

"You're not entering into the spirit."

"Are you?" he huffed defiantly.

"I'm here to work." That made me wonder: What was Marius Optatus here for? He had some ulterior motive, I was sure of it.

Optatus and I were the eldest men there. At least ten years separated the Annaeus sons. Primus, the eldest, might be almost our age, but his youngest brother was not yet twenty, and Fortune had arranged it that he was the one with the most friends. This largest group coalesced first, though all they did was to mill around trying to find food, drink or sinful women; they were stuck with the stuff in cups and bowls because they did not know how to recognize the other. We worried them. (They worried me.) We belonged to a wholly different generation. They all slipped by us, avoiding contact, because they thought we were somebody's parental police.

A second party had developed in the cellar, to which friends of Dotty, the middle son, zoomed with a sense of purpose which would quickly leave them. They despised food, and had probably tried women, but were all betrothed to sweet, virginal girls (who were currently behind bushes with other young men). Suspicions that they were being deceived, and that life would only bring them more of the same, made the middle son's cronies a brooding, cynical group. Optatus and I exchanged a few witty thoughts with them, before we moved on.

Spunky, who would be known to posterity and the Censor as the honorable Lucius Annaeus Maximus Primus, was pretending to be grown up. He had retreated from the noise and debauchery to his father's elegant library. It was a quiet upper room with a splendid balcony which gave views across the ornate gardens. There he and a few jaded companions were pulling scrolls from their pigeonholes, examining them satirically, then tossing them into a heap on the floor. An amphora had made a vicious ring on a marble side table. Another had been knocked over after uncorking, so some spirited soul had pulled down a curtain to mop up the mess. How thoughtful. I was pleased to see they were not all bad.

Optatus told me this Annaeus, unlike his two younger brothers, was actually married, though to a girl so young she remained with her parents while he simply enjoyed the income from her dowry and pretended he was still safe from responsibility. He was a plump-faced, solidly built young Baetican, whose amiable nature made him instantly forgive me for being the man he and his brothers had shoved about (twice) the last time I visited their palatial home. He greeted Optatus like a lost lamb. Optatus seemed genuinely friendly towards him.

Rufius Constans, though rather young for this group, had already made his way here. I thought he colored up when I first walked through the door, and after I found myself a place to squat he seemed to edge away as far as possible. Wine was being splashed around at that point, so maybe he just wanted to avoid the spillage. Slaves were serving, but they looked extremely anxious. When the guests wanted more, they bawled for it loudly; if nobody came soon enough they grabbed the jugs for themselves, deliberately missing their cups when they poured.

I had been among this type before. It was a long time since I had found them amusing. I knew what to expect. They would sit around for hours, getting pointlessly drunk. Their conversation would consist of bloody-minded politics, coarse abuse of women, boasting about their chariots, then making exaggerated assessments of their wealth and the sizes of their pricks. Their brains were no bigger than chickpeas, that's for sure. I won't speculate on the rest.

Several scions from other families were among this group. They were introduced to me at the time, though I reckoned there was no real need to remember them. These would be the chubby heirs to all the fine folk Helena and I had seen at the Parilia, the tight little section of snobs who ran everything in Corduba. One day these would be the snobs themselves. There would come a time for most of them when a father would die, or they married, or a close friend was killed very young; then they would move silently from being crass young idiots to being the spitting image of their staid fathers.

"Bollocks!" muttered a voice beside me in the chaos.

I had thought I was next to Optatus, but when I turned it was another who had joined us without introductions. I knew who he was. I had seen him here before, collecting Aelia Annaea, and since then I had learned that he was Quinctius Quadratus.

At close quarters familial resemblance to his father was clear. He had a thick thatch of black crinkled hair, muscular arms, and a lordly expression. He was tanned, hirsute and strong-featured. Sporting and popular. Possessed of ease and happy arrogance. He wore a white tunic with broad purple stripes and had even put on his scarlet boots, things I had rarely seen in Rome: he was a senator-elect, and new enough to want to be seen in every detail of the historic uniform. I was looking at the recently appointed financial controller of Baetica. Even though the proconsul was unhappy with his assignment here, Quadratus himself was flaunting it. So I already knew one thing: he had no official tact.

The cause of his exclamation was not a spot of mind-reading, but an uncouth response to a scroll which he had plucked from the library columbarium. I couldn't read the title. He sneered, rolled it up very tightly, then stuffed it into the neck of an empty wine vessel like a plug.

"Well, well," I said. "They told me you were charming and gifted, but not that your talents extended to instant crits of literature."

"I can read," he answered lazily. "I say, I don't believe we've met?"

I viewed him benignly. "The name's Falco. And of course I know who you are, quaestor."

"There's no need to be formal," he assured me in his charming way.

"Thanks," I said.

"Have you come out from Rome?"

"That's right," I replied for the second time that night. "We nearly bumped into each other there recently, but I hear you were at the theater instead. The last dinner for the Society of Baetican Olive Oil Producers?"

"Oh them!" he replied offhandedly.

"What was the play? Any good?"

"A farce, I think." Rufius Constans had pretended it was a mime. "So-so." Or not. He paused. He knew what I was doing here. "Is this an interview?"

"Great gods no," I laughed, reaching for more wine. "I'm bloody well off duty tonight, if you don't mind!"

"That's good," smiled Tiberius Quinctius Quadratus, quaestor of Baetica. He was off duty too, of course. The proconsul had arranged that.

THIRTY-SEVEN

The room was squashed, and noisy with brash young idiots' chatter. What was more, they were about to amuse themselves playing the ancient Greek game of *kottabos*. Spunky, who would have made a good crony for the Athenian reprobate Alcibiades, had been given the apparatus for his birthday—an aptly chosen gift from his younger brothers. Clearly nobody had told him that *kottabos* explains why the Greeks no longer rule the world.

For refined readers of this memoir who will certainly never encounter it, *kottabos* was invented by a group of uproarious drunks. You have a tall stand, with a large bronze disc suspended horizontally halfway up. A small metal target is balanced on the top of the stand. The players drink their wine, then flick their cups to expel the dregs. They aim to make the flying lees hit the target so it falls off and hits the lower disc with a noise like a bell. All the wine they flick splatters the room and themselves.

That's it: A little gem from the wise, wonderful people who invented the classic proportions of sculpture and the tenets of moral philosophy.

* * *

By mutual consent Quadratus and I took wine and cups to drink it from, then we moved out smartly to the balcony. We were the mature ones here. We were men of the world. Well, he was a Roman official, and *I* was a man of the world. So we drew apart to give ourselves space to spread a bit. (It's hard to fulfill your potential as a man of the world when your knees are jammed under a reading couch and a murex-merchant's nephew has just belched in your ear.) Optatus, who was talking earnestly to young Constans, raised his winecup wryly as I stepped over him, following my smart new pal.

We *were* going to be pals, that was obvious. Quadratus was accustomed to being friendly with everyone, apparently. Or maybe his father had warned him I was dangerous and should be disarmed if possible.

The night air was cool and perfect, barely touched by the scent of the torches that flickered on the terraces below. Occasional shrieks reached us from crude horseplay among the adolescents. We sat on the marble balustrade, leaning against pillars, and drank Baetican white and the fresh air in equal measure.

"So, Falco—Baetica must be a change from Rome?"

"I wish I had more time to enjoy it." There is nothing like a fake polite chat to bring on my apoplectic tic. "My wife's expecting. I promised to take her home for the birth."

"Your wife? She's the sister of Camillus Aelianus, isn't she? I didn't know you were actually married."

"There's a theory that marriage consists of the decision by two people to live as man and wife."

"Oh is there?" His reaction was innocent. As I expected, he had been educated by the best tutors—and he knew nothing. He'd be a magistrate one day, laying down laws he had never heard of to people whose lives in the real world he would never understand. That's Rome. City of glorious tradition—

including the one that if the landed elite can bugger up the little man, they will.

"Ask any barrister." I could be pleasant too. I grinned at him. "Helena and I are conducting an experiment to see how long it takes the rest of Rome to admit the fine theory holds good."

"You're very courageous! So will your child be illegitimate?" He wasn't carping, just curious.

"I had assumed so—until it struck me that if we regard ourselves as married, how can it be? I'm a free citizen and I'll register it proudly."

Quinctius Quadratus whistled quietly. After a while he said, "Aelianus is a good lad. One of our set. The best."

"Bit of a lively character?"

Quadratus chuckled. "He lost his rag over you!"

"I know."

"He'll be all right when he finds his feet."

"Good to hear." Young men with weak spots are always keen to assess others. The quaestor's patronizing tone almost made me defend Aelianus. "Lad about town?" I suggested, hoping for dirt.

"Not as much as he liked to think."

"A bit immature?"

"Cock shy."

"That won't last!"

We poured more wine.

"The trouble with Aelianus," the quaestor confided dismissively, "is he can't judge his length. The family's poor as Hades. He's aiming for the Senate with absolutely no collateral. He needs to make a rich alliance. We tried to set him up with Claudia Rufina."

"No good?" I prompted neutrally.

"He wanted more. His idea was Aelia Annaea. I ask you!"

"Too old for him, presumably?"

"Too old, too sharp, too aware of what she's got."

"And what's that?"

"A quarter of her papa's estate when he passes on—plus the whole of her husband's property."

"I knew she was widowed."

"Better than that. She had the good taste to be widowed by a man with no close family. There were no children and no coheirs. He left her everything."

"Wonderful! How much was 'everything'?"

"A whopping tract of land—and a small gold mine at Hispalis."

"She seems a nice girl!" I commented, and we laughed.

"The Annaeus lads look like a boisterous bunch."

"Just the job," cackled Quadratus. He libeled his friends without a second thought: "Thick as curd cheese, and just as rich!"

That seemed to sum up Spunky, Dotty and Ferret well enough for my purposes.

"What's your reaction to young Rufius?" I asked, hoping that his protégé at least would attract some approval.

"Oh Jupiter, what a waste!"

"How's that?"

"Haven't you noticed? All that energy being squandered on making him something, but he's just not up to it. There's some decent cash in the family, but Constans is never going to use it properly." He defined everything in monetary terms. It grew wearisome for a man like me, with virtually nothing in the bank.

"You don't think he will be the success his grandfather wants? Won't he make it to Rome?"

"Oh he can be bumped into the posts, of course. Licinius Rufius can afford to get him whatever he wants. But Constans will never enjoy it. He doesn't command much attention here, and the sharks in Rome will swallow him. He can't take Grandpa along to give him authority."

"He's young. He could grow into it."

"He's just a raw Spanish ham that's not been smoked enough. I try," Quadratus declared. "I show him a thing or two when I can."

"I expect he looks up to you."

A sudden grin split the handsome face. I had disturbed the smooth, bland, utterly plausible exterior and the result was a shock. "Now you're pissing yourself laughing at me!" He said it without malice. His candor in discussing his friends had had a tone I didn't care for, but he knew how and when to turn the conversation. He seemed modest now. People were right to compliment his charm.

"Someone told me, Quadratus, you were about to exchange contracts with the Rufius girl yourself?"

He gave me a level stare. "I couldn't comment. My father will make any marriage announcement in due course."

"Not ready yet?"

"You have to get it right."

"Oh yes; it's an important decision for anyone."

"There are personal issues—and I must think of my career."

I had guessed correctly. He would never be paired off in Baetica.

"Tell me about yourself, Falco."

"Oh I'm nobody."

"Bull's testicles!" he said crudely. "That's not what I heard."

"Why, what have you heard?"

"You're a political drain-cleaner. You do missions for the Emperor. There's some rumor about you sorting a problem in the British silver mines." I said nothing. My work in Britain was known only to a very close circle. It was highly sensitive. Records of the mission had been burned, and however important the quaestor's father thought himself in Rome, Attractus ought not to have known about it. If he really did, that would alarm the Emperor.

My experience in the mines at Vebiodunum, disguised as a slave, was one I never talked about. Dirt, vermin, beatings, starvation, exhaustion, the filthy overseer whose kindest punishment was to strangle the culprit while his only notion of reward was an hour of enforced buggery . . . My face must have changed. Quadratus was unobservant, however.

My silence did not make him stop to think. It merely offered another opportunity to show off what somebody had told him. "Don't you specialize in mineral rights, Falco? I thought you looked keen when I mentioned Aelia Annaea's legacy. You're in the right province. There's iron, silver, copper and gold in huge quantities. A lot of it's at Corduba—I have to know all this stuff for my work," he explained.

"The *aes Marianum*," I answered steadily. "That's the famous copper mine at Corduba that produces the fine ore for all Roman bronze coins. Tiberius wanted to bring it under state control. He had the millionaire who owned it, Sextus Marius, thrown off the Tarpeian Rock on the Capitol."

"How come?"

"Accused of incest."

"That's disgusting."

"It was a trumped-up charge." I smiled. I nearly added that nothing changes—but the dumb optimist in me hoped with Vespasian's arrival it might have done.

"You amaze me, knowing all that, Falco!"

"I collect information."

"For professional reasons?"

"I'm an informer. Stories are the material of my trade."

"I'll have to be careful, then," Quadratus grinned. "My father's on the Senate committee that runs the mint mines."

That gave me an unpleasant feeling: Quinctius Attractus trying to dabble one more sticky finger in Baetica. Fortunately there was an imperial procurator actually in charge of the *aes Marianum* mine. He would be an equestrian, a career official whose only concern would be doing the job right for his own sake. The other side of government: and not even the Quinctii could interfere with that.

"The Senate committee, eh?" It fitted the pattern. Attractus wanted influence in every sphere of this province. Getting a place on the committee would have been easy, given his strong local interests. "I'm surprised your family aren't involved in mineral production."

"Oh we are," laughed young Quadratus. "There's a silver mine that's run by a society at Castulo. My father shares the franchise; he's a leading member of the Society. I'm standing in for him while I'm out here. We have our own copper mine too."

I should have known.

"I'm surprised you have the time for personal work," I cut in coolly. I had let him run until I felt I knew him, but his time was up. "A quaestorship is not an easy ride."

"I'm not really worked in yet."

"So I gather."

His face did not alter. He had no idea what those in the know would think of him being given hunting leave before he had even started. How could he? He was a raw egg in bureaucracy. He probably thought the proconsul had done him some kind of favor. Favors are what people like him expect. Duties don't come into it.

"Of course there's a lot of responsibility," he declared. I put on my sympathetic face and let him talk. "I reckon I can handle it."

"The Senate and the Emperor must believe you can, quaestor."

"Of course there are well-established routines."

"And permanent employees who are used to doing the work."

"There will still be some tricky decisions to take. They'll need me for those."

The po-faced scribe from Hadrumetum whom I had met at the proconsular palace would be able to cope with any decisions the quaestor was supposed to put his name to.

I served Quadratus more wine. My own cup still sat brimful on the balustrade. "What's in your remit?" He shrugged vaguely. These lads are never sent to their provinces with a proper brief; I summarized the quaestor's role for him: "Apart from deputizing for the proconsul in the law courts, there's collection of property taxes, provincial poll tax, port taxes, inheritance tax, and the state percentage on manumission of slaves. Hispania's huge. Baetica may not be the biggest province, but it's the richest and most populous. The sums you oversee must be significant."

"It's not real money, though."

I disagreed. "It's real enough to the merchants and heads of household who have to cough up!"

"Oh it all comes out of their budget . . . From my point of view it's just figures. I'm not obliged to get my hands dirty counting coins."

I refrained from saying I was surprised he could even count. "You may never touch the dosh, but you've been entrusted with a full range of headaches: '*the collecting, disbursing, safeguarding, managing and controlling of public funds.*' "

Quadratus was taking the flippant line. "I suppose the records will come to me and I'll approve them—or I'll alter them if they don't fit," he giggled. He showed no sense of responsibility. I was struck by the horrific possibilities for embezzlement. "Let's face it, Falco—I have a title and a seal, but in reality I'm impotent. I can't alter the way things are run. Rome is fully aware of that."

"You mean because your stint in the post is only a year?"

He looked surprised. "No, because that's just how things are."

This was the rotten side of government. Enormous power was placed at the disposal of an untried, overconfident young man. His only superior here was the hard-pressed governor who had a full complement of legislative and diplomatic work himself. If the salaried officials who really ran the provinces were corrupt, or if they simply lost heart, here was an outpost of the Empire which could fall apart. With a brash and completely unprepared master placed over them, who could blame them if they did lose heart?

Something like that had happened in Britain over a decade earlier. I was there. I knew. The Icenian Revolt was brought about by a combination of indifferent politicians, overbearing armed forces and ill-judged financial control. This had alienated the local populace, with results that were sheer murder. Ironically, a major catalyst for trouble had been the sudden withdrawal of loans by Seneca—the big name from Corduba.

"I see what they mean about you," Quadratus said suddenly. I wondered who "they" were, who had been briefing him about me. He wanted to know how good I really was at my job—and how dangerous.

I quirked up an eyebrow, enjoying his unease as he went on, "You sit drinking your wine just as pleasantly as anyone. But somehow I don't reckon you're thinking 'This is a palatable vintage, if a little sweet.' You're in another world, Falco."

"The wine has its moments. Baetica suffers from too much wind from the south; it troubles the grapes."

"Jove, you know everything! I do admire that. I really do—" He really did. "You're a complete professional. That's something I'd like to emulate." He might—but not if it meant he had to work on my pay, eating gritty bread and paying too much rent for a hovel in a lousy tenement.

"You just have to be thorough." I couldn't be bothered with his sham flattery, or his ignorance of conditions in the real world.

"So what's on your mind, Falco?"

"Nothing changes," I said. "Lessons are constantly put before us—and are never learned."

Quadratus was still game, though his speech was becoming slow. I had drunk much less. I had no taste for it. I had lost my taste for philosophy too.

Below in the garden dim figures rushed about, engaged in some dubious form of hide-and-seek. It required neither skill in the chase nor subtlety in claiming the prize. I watched for a moment, feeling my age, then turned back to the quaestor. "So what, Tiberius Quinctius Quadratus, are you intending to do as quaestor to prevent the formation of an oil cartel in Baetica?"

"Is there one?" he asked me, suddenly as wide-eyed as the second-rate virgins who were squealing among the clipped myrtles on the terraces below.

THIRTY-EIGHT

I stood up to leave. I clapped his shoulder, and handed him the jug of wine. "Enjoy your evening."

"What cartel?" he slurred, much too solemnly.

"The one that can't possibly exist in this respectable province where the businessmen are so ethical and the officials perform their duties to the highest standards of probity!"

I stepped back into the heated room indoors. There was wine everywhere. The illustrious Spunky and his cronies were roaring with laughter, looking shiny and much redder in the face. They had reached the happy stage of dying with mirth at their own silliness. Marius Optatus had disappeared somewhere. I didn't blame him, though since we were sharing a carriage it was somewhat inconvenient. He had probably found a bailiff and was discussing the fine details of making chestnut withy baskets. His interests were so practical.

"Grand party!" I applauded my host. He looked pleased. "Is your sister here?"

"Locked in her bedroom pretending not to know it's going on!"

Maybe Aelia Annaea would welcome some refined masculine company. It had to be worth a try.

When I clambered over the revelers and out into the corridor, I left behind whoops of determined foolishness. I had noticed one poor soul already lying prone beside a cabinet of curios with his eyes tightly closed in misery. His capacity must be no bigger than a gnat's. By my reckoning they were all less than an hour from being sick over the balcony. There would be one or two who could not crawl that far. It boded ill for my host's father's porphyry vases and his silk-covered ivory-ended reading couch. His collected works of Greek men of letters had already been well trampled by flailing boots and his Egyptian carpet was being rolled up to make a swat in a game of "Human Fly."

Sticking my thumbs in my belt I moved carefully through the groups of rich children dangerously rollicking. This was not an occasion to reassure a father whose first offspring was only weeks from birth. Annaeus Maximus could have picked a better month to visit his Gades farms.

As I rather expected I learned nothing else that helped my mission, only that the town house of the Annaei covered two floors, was exquisite though slightly old-fashioned in decor, and possessed every amenity. I found a large number of beautifully appointed bedrooms, some occupied, though not by people who wanted my staid company. Becoming morose, I wandered down a staircase, stepping over various young ladies without partners who were sitting on the marble treads getting piles while they bemoaned the stupidity of Corduban boys. I concurred with their view, though perhaps not for the same reasons; what's more I had my doubts about some of the girls.

The ground floor comprised the normal public rooms and peristyles of a large, showy home. The rude huts of their forefathers had been transformed by the modern Annaei into high temples where they could act as patrons to the less well-off. It was meant to impress; I allowed it a few astonished gasps.

There was a full bathhouse suite, where some luckier young ladies were being repeatedly thrown by young men into the heated swimming pool; they squealed a lot then struggled out and ran back to be thrown in again. No one had drowned yet. In the attached ball-park a lively group thought it good fun to dress up a nannygoat in a garland of flowers and the robes which the important householder wore when he officiated as a priest. I greeted them serenely, then passed on into the covered arcade which led to the garden area.

This was more peaceful, apart from occasional troops of youths who galloped through it in a jiggling human daisy chain. Turning away from the main terrace, where the merry-making among the topiary looked more lewd than I could contemplate, I was heading for an ivy-covered gazebo, lit by torches. There were two figures conversing; they looked rather like Optatus and the gracious Aelia, sister of our three jolly hosts. Before I could reach them I was stopped by a pair who were stock-still on the gravel path, locked in a desperate, motionless embrace. They were about sixteen; she thought she might be losing him, whereas he held her with the calm reassuring air of a faithless swain who knew it had already happened.

Touched, I started doubling back to avoid disturbing their poignant and ultimately pointless idyll. Then I bumped into Marmarides. He was coming to find me to ask permission to borrow the carriage; he had become embroiled with a group of young creatures who were fascinated by his African appearance. Just by asking him the question, I had embroiled myself too: "I suppose they want to know about your Aethiopian potency!" He looked embarrassed but did not deny that his female admirers had the usual curiosity about his personal equipment. "Does this happen to you often?"

"Oh all the time, Falco! My master Stertius lives in terror

he'll be called to account when some citizen complains that I'm responsible for his lady having a dark child. The only reason I was allowed to come with you is that he reckoned yours was long past the dangerous stage!"

"Oh thanks! I wish I was back home with her now."

"I can take you, easy."

"We'd better deal with your supporters' club first. At least we may save a couple of young women from debauchery tonight!"

That was debatable, but I wanted an excuse to escape. Marmarides could have just dumped his admirers—but decent men don't, do we? He had promised to drive two of them home to Corduba before they got into trouble with their parents (or some such tale). I said I would leave at the same time. There would be no room for Optatus or Constans, but I could protect Marmarides from assault on the journey into Corduba, we could ditch the dames safely, then he could leave me in a tavern where I could have a quiet bite to eat while he went back to collect our comrades. Providing food lacked glamour for our hosts; they had omitted it.

We shoved a couple of the shrieking women inside the carriage; they were probably demure little things when sober, though drink had robbed them of all taste. I climbed up on top with Marmarides and we set off fast before our passengers could thrill themselves by swarming out to join us. When our mules reached the gate at the end of the long entry drive, we had to swerve madly; we passed a much larger piece of coachwork, drawn by two fiery horses and driven by a set-faced groom in livery. As we went out it was coming in.

"Keep going!" I grinned. "Marmarides, I rather think that Annaeus Maximus has remembered what happened the last time he left his boys at home unsupervised."

THIRTY-NINE

We found where the girls lived and persuaded them to go in quietly; we used the shameless trick of mentioning the return of Annaeus Maximus and warning them that that angry father would soon be talking to their own parents.

"Spunky, Dotty and Ferret are in big trouble! Best to nip indoors looking innocent and pretend you never went anywhere." I could just hear some pert little minx in the distant future trying this one out on me. I could just see me too, willing myself to believe the lie . . .

My plan to have supper alone seemed churlish now; we went back together to try to extricate Optatus and young Constans, if possible before they were publicly linked with the row. Approaching the town house we met a string of chastened youngsters being marched home in the custody of Annaeus' slaves. These were the walking wounded. Up at the house others who could not stagger had been collected up and laid out neatly in a colonnade. We gathered that parents had been sent for. We also sensed that it had not been done out of malice—but as a sensible precaution in case any of these stupid children had actually poisoned themselves with too much wine.

Of Spunky, Dotty and Ferret I saw no sign. Nor were their father and mother visible, though the slaves mopping up the battlefield were doing it very quickly and efficiently, with downcast eyes. The master's physician, overseeing the row of unconscious young bodies, was fiercely purse-lipped. There was no longer an amphora in sight.

We could find neither Optatus nor Constans. In the end we went home, before the oil in the carriage lamp ran out.

Helena Justina was still up, quietly writing letters to Rome. I sat on the floor at her feet and hugged her. "Dear gods, I'm sick of other men's sons! I hope mine's a daughter!"

As if to confirm it, the baby kicked me soundly in the face. "She's got huge hooves!" Helena muttered, after crying ouch herself.

"She'll be a darling . . . Listen, I'm establishing the rules now—boy or girl, it doesn't go out to visit friends without permission, without an escort of extremely prissy slaves, and without me personally going to fetch it home not more than an hour after it departs our house."

"Very wise, Marcus. I'm sure this will work wonderfully."

Helena laid down her pen on a side table and closed the inkwell gently. She ran her fingers through my curls. I pretended not to notice, while I let myself relax. Too large now to be flexible, instead of bending down to me as she once would have done, she kissed the tip of her finger and touched my brow consolingly. "What's the matter, you poor tired, miserable soul? Didn't you enjoy the party, then? What went wrong with your boys' night out?"

"They were too rough for me. I had a depressing experience talking to the fabled quaestor, who is the last word in moral toughness—if you think fluff is tough. Then the hosts' parents came home unexpectedly—a scheme I shall follow myself when our limb gets old enough. I scarpered. I couldn't find the other two—"

"Constans came back," she told me.

"The night is full of surprises. How did he find his way?"

"The quaestor brought him."

"That's commendable!"

"Charming," she agreed.

"You don't like him?"

"I deeply distrust charm. Even so, I let him share the guest room where he had deposited the snoring Constans."

"So Quadratus is not beyond redemption?"

"He seemed appalling. He apologized in a well-spoken voice. He introduced himself politely, then praised my brother Aelianus. I loathed him instinctively. But it was very late."

"Are they in the same bed?" I asked, wondering.

"No."

"It's not like that then!"

"He seems to treat young Constans as an immature lad who needs an older friend."

"*Really* charming!"

"So we are supposed to believe," said Helena.

It was then that Marius Optatus reappeared. He had walked much of the way, apparently. "I was looking for you, Falco!" he stormed tetchily.

"I looked for you too—honestly! I'd seen you hobnobbing with Aelia Annaea so I thought that since she owns her own gold mine you were in there doing yourself some good!"

"Was Claudia Rufina at the party, Marius?" asked Helena sympathetically.

"No," he said. Presumably that was one reason for his short temper.

"He was too wrapped up with Aelia," I teased. "The man has no loyalty."

"Probably talking about Claudia," retorted Helena.

Optatus had no sense of humor this evening. He was white

with tiredness, and irritation too. "I did my best for you, Falco, and in return you stole the transport and stranded me!"

"Why, what did you do?"

"I found out that Dotty and his merry selection of friends were—"

"In the cellar?"

"Yes."

"Soaking up all Papa's choice imported Falernian?"

"Yes."

"Putting the world to rights like depressed witches when half the coven's failed to show—yes?"

"—And watching a dancing girl," said Marius.

Helena Justina gripped me by the shoulders and removed me from my cozy position. I sat up with my arms around my knees. Helena demanded, "Marius Optatus, would this be a dancing girl Marcus has seen before?"

"How should I know?" He was still angry, though being polite to Helena. "I could not find Falco to compare points of similarity! I had decided to accost the girl myself, but then Attractus Maximus came home and the row started. In the chaos the dancer slipped away somewhere; that was understandable. Clearly you had done the same," he sneered at me. "I wanted to leave myself, but I thought I should try and find out about the girl for you—"

"You've taken to undercover work! What was she like?" I inserted quickly. "Loose-limbed, gorgeous and with luxurious black hair?"

"She was nothing of a looker—but she could certainly dance."

That was a surprise. I must have been even more drunk than I remembered at the dinner for the Society of Olive Oil Producers of Baetica. I had thought Diana was fairly personable but her repertoire lacked skill. Aelianus had also said she had her limitations. Maybe we were right; maybe Optatus took the uncritical view. For some men, if a woman has very few clothes on and is signaling that the rest might come off with modest encouragement, that's enough. "Marius, Baetica is full of women wielding tambourines to make a quick denarius. Why did you decide this one was significant?"

"Dotty told me she had been asking curious questions. She wanted to know where his father was. He reckoned she was making sure there was no chance of parental displeasure—wrong, as it turned out."

"She's a decent dancer, yet she was tantalizing teenagers?"

"Most dancers are short of money," he corrected me frostily.

"Was she dancing in a costume?"

"She was dancing in an immodest shift, Falco. That is what young men expect." The stern Marius had reached the sarcastic stage.

"I wonder how they found her? Is some sort of directory of dubious entertainers kept at the Temple of the Capitoline Triad, perhaps? I don't suppose the young Annaei were able to consult the aedile's list; the aedile would have gone straight to their papa."

"Please don't be facetious, Falco. Dotty was taking the credit for hiring her."

"My good Marius, you've been working hard."

"Don't bother to thank me! Dotty said that she had heard about the party and presented herself, offering to perform. He did not know where she came from." She must be hanging around Corduba—and she must have her ear to the ground.

"Rich young men have all the luck."

"I expect she charged a gigantic fee," chided Helena.

"Rich young men don't feel the pain."

"Anyway—" Optatus deflated and confessed with a sigh, "I know this is not the girl you want, Falco. Dotty was perfectly frank. He knew of Selia—she is familiar to all those young men, apparently. They don't care that she is not the most perfect dancer—she has other attractions that compensate. Dotty hadn't been able to hire her this evening because she is supposed to have returned to Hispalis. He did say the older one, the one they did have there, had been trying to find out what other dancers he knew."

"Did he own up to her that he had wanted Selia instead?"

"He's an oil producer's son, Falco! He's much too cute to do that."

While I was wondering whether the appearance of a second dancer was just coincidence, Helena decided to confess about the two young disasters who were asleep in a guest bedroom. Optatus was furious.

However, he calmed down next day, thanks to a jape we two devised. The quaestor and Constans had arrived at our house the night before riding together on a highly bred horse which they had stolen from the Annaeus stable. We solemnly promised to return it for them before there was a hue and cry. Then I sent them off back to their own homes on a special horse of my own.

"His name's Prancer. You have to check him or he dashes away. Hold on tight in case he bolts."

"Thanks, Falco." Quadratus had already realized he was the butt of a joke. "But this leaves you without a mount—"

"I will find Marcus Didius a horse," grinned Optatus pleasantly. "You keep that one—with our compliments!"

FORTY

Where next?

I was glad Optatus had offered me a decent mount. I had run out of options in Corduba, and badly needed to visit Hispalis. According to the youngest Annaeus, that was where Selia would be found. She had always been my prime target.

Had events been different, Helena and I would have enjoyed a slow boat ride together as offered by Cyzacus and Gorax. We had first come to know one another well on a trip across Europe which had included journeys by river. Ever since those long weeks falling in love we had adored water transport; we were nostalgic types. This time though, time was against us.

There was a good road all along the Baetis—the Via Augusta which traveled to Gades. If dispatch-riders of the imperial post with urgent missives could gallop fifty miles a day, I could certainly try to match them. I would use the horse our friend produced for me and ride into Corduba, then I would call at the governor's palace and demand that he give me authority to use the stables and lodges of the *cursus publicus*. Two days there; two days back; plus however long it took me to interview Cyzacus senior and Norbanus, then to search for the dancing girl.

While I executed this fantastic feat of logistics, Helena could wait on the estate, sleeping mostly. That was what she needed now.

Helena Justina pointed out quietly that I hate horses. I said I was a professional. I thought she hid a smile.

I had been up at dawn so I was at the Palace waiting when the clerks first strolled into their offices discussing last night's drinking bout. They had barely got on to how many stairs they had fallen down when they found me, looking brisk. My previous visit had left me a hero. There was no need to see the proconsul; these lads were mine to command. My scandalous stories about their master, invented or not, had worked: clerks are always longing for somebody to brighten up their lives.

Permits to use the *cursus publicus* are not readily available. They have to bear the Emperor's personal signature; that's their validation. Governors of provinces are supplied with a finite number, which they are supposed to use only in the proper circumstances. Prissy ones actually write home to check whether they are following the rules. But the clerks of the proconsul of Baetica decided that their man would approve one for me, without being put to the trouble of knowing he had done it. Nice lads.

I usually go on foreign missions already equipped with my own pass. I had not thought about it this time—and neither had Laeta—assuming he possessed the authority to give me one. I had been trying not to think about Laeta. But when I did, I asked the clerks whether he had become the official point of contact for intelligence issues.

"No, it's still supposed to be Anacrites, Falco."

"Isn't that typical! I left Anacrites on his deathbed. He must have been formally replaced by now."

"Well nobody tells us—unless Rome's decided to leave a corpse in charge!"

"Believe me, lads, you won't notice any difference if they replace the Chief Spy with a stiff."

"Suits us!" they giggled. "We hate getting letters from him. The old man always goes on the rampage because he can't understand what Anacrites is on about. Then if we send for clarification we get the same message back, only not just in cypher; all the references are changed to code names as well."

"How about Laeta? Have you noticed an increase in the volume of messages from him? More urgent signals, perhaps?"

"No more than usual. He can't use signals."

"Why? No entitlement?"

"He writes too much. The beacon flares can only send one letter at a time; it's too slow for long documents." Too inaccurate as well; you need nighttime, with exactly the right visibility, and even then every time a message is transmitted between watchtowers there is a risk that the signalers may misread the lights and pass along gobbledegook. "Laeta sends scrolls, always via the dispatch-riders."

"No sign of him having new responsibilities, then?"

"No."

"I don't suppose he's bothering to inquire after me?"

"No, Falco."

There was something I wanted to check up on. I gazed at them in a frank and friendly manner. "I'm asking because if Anacrites is laid up or dead, there may be changes on the Palatine . . . Listen, you know how I came out to Baetica with a letter for the proconsul saying I was a man on a secret mission?" They were bound to know; there was no harm in sharing the confidence. "The old man told me you had already been asked to note the presence of another person nobody talks about?" They glanced at each other. "I'm getting worried," I told them, lying well. "I think an agent might have gone missing. With Anacrites lying prone we can't find out who he had in the field."

More obvious looks were now being exchanged. I waited. "Letters of introduction from the Chief Spy's office carry the top security mark, Falco."

"I know. I use it myself."

"We are not allowed to read them."

"But I bet you do!"

Like lambkins they agreed: "Just before you came Anacrites sent one of his coded notes. It was his normal nutter's charter: the agent would not be making contact officially—yet we were to afford full facilities."

"I bet you thought that was about me."

"Oh no."

"Why not?"

"The agent was a woman, Falco."

"Well you'll enjoy facilitating her!" I had grinned, but I was groaning inside.

Anacrites *ought* to have been planning to send out Valentinus. He was definitely working on the case and Momus, my crony at the Palace, had told me Valentinus had been the best agent Anacrites used. Why send a female? Well Valentinus was a freelance, his own master. Perhaps he had refused to work abroad. That surprised me though. All I knew of him—not much, admittedly—had suggested he was a calm, efficient type who would not balk at anything. Most people welcome the offer of a free long-distance trip.

Surely even Anacrites hadn't fallen for the old belief that respectable businessmen like the oil producers of Baetica were likely to be seduceable? The ones I had met might possibly be so—but they were too long in the tooth to be blackmailed about it afterwards.

Maybe I had been living with Helena Justina for too long. I had grown soft. My natural cynicism had been squeezed out. I had forgotten that there will always be men who can be lured into pillow confessions by a determined dancing girl.

Just as I left I asked another question: "What do you think about the new quaestor? What are your views on Quadratus?"

"A bastard," my allies assured me.

"Oh go on. A quaestor is always a bastard; that's how they're defined. Surely he's no worse than the rest of them? He's young and jumped-up—but you've seen it all before. A few months with you showing him how the world works and he'll be all right, surely?"

"A double bastard," the lads reiterated solemnly.

One thing I always reckon in the marbled halls of bureaucracy is that the best assessments of personalities come from the clerks they kick.

I went back and sat down. I laced my fingers and leaned my chin on them. First the proconsul had taken the initiative to show he entertained doubts about Quadratus, and now these characters openly despised him without giving him a trial. "*Tell me!*" I said. So being obliging friends of mine, they did.

Quinctius Quadratus was not entirely clean. His personal record had preceded him to Baetica, and although it was confidential (*because* it was), it had been pored over by the secretariat: there was a bad story, one that Quadratus would find hard to shake off in his future career. On his route to the Senate in his late teens he had served as a military tribune. Posted to Dalmatia he had been involved in a messy incident where some soldiers attempting to reinstate a bridge on a flood-swollen river had lost their lives. They could have waited until the torrent abated, but Quadratus ordered them to tackle the job despite the obvious risk. An official inquiry had deemed the affair a tragic accident—but it was the kind of accident whose details his old commanding officer had bothered to pass on personally to the proconsul who was just inheriting Quadratus in a new civil post.

So there really was a black mark against his name.

Shortly afterwards, I had finally reached the corridor when I noticed some early arrivals queuing for an interview with the proconsul. A scribe who must be senior to the other men—because he had sauntered in even later and with an even worse air of being weighed down by a wine headache—had been waylaid by two figures I recognized. One was the elderly oil magnate, Licinius Rufius, the other his grandson Rufius Constans. The youth was looking sullen; when he spotted me he seemed almost afraid.

I overheard the senior clerk say the proconsul would not be available that day. He gave them some good reason; it was not just a brush-off. The old man looked irritated, but was accepting it reluctantly.

I nodded a courteous greeting to Licinius, but with a long hard ride ahead of me I had no time to stop. I took the road to Hispalis with problems cluttering my mind.

Most puzzling was the female agent Anacrites had intended to send to Baetica. Was she the "dangerous woman" he had been muttering about? Then *where* was she? Had he ever actually given her orders? When Anacrites was attacked, had she stayed in Rome without further instructions? Or was she here? Here perhaps even on her own initiative? (Impossible; Anacrites had never employed anyone with that much gumption.)

The female agent had to be identified. Otherwise *she* might be the dancer I was pursuing. I might have drawn all the wrong conclusions about Selia. She could have been at the dinner as backup for Anacrites and Valentinus; she could be innocent of the attacks; she could have dropped her arrow in the street during a meeting with them; the wounds on the two men could have had some other cause. If so, what was she up to now in Corduba? Had she been dressed as a shepherdess at the Parilia parade in order to follow up the cartel? Had she then disguised herself as an old woman to try and interview Licinius Rufius? Were she and I all along working for the same ends?—Well then, who was the real attacker of Valentinus and Anacrites?

The other possibility was that Selia was as dangerous as I had always thought—and that some other woman was in Baetica on the Chief Spy's behalf. One I had not encountered yet. Very likely the dancer Dotty had hired for the party. Some lousy fleabag Anacrites used, who was dogging my steps and liable to get in my way. That was the most likely. And it made me livid. Because maybe somebody at the Palace *knew* we were both out here—in which case why in Hades was it necessary? Why, when Helena Justina needed me, was I wasting my own time and duplicating effort?

I dismissed the idea. The Palace might well be capable of keeping agents in the dark, but under Vespasian double payment was never sanctioned where a single fee would do. So that meant there were two different offices actively involved. Laeta had sent me out, unaware that Anacrites had someone else in the field. Our objectives might be similar—or absolutely different. As I homed in on Selia, somebody else with conflicting orders could be doing the same. And in the long run, as I had suspected right from the night of the dinner on the Palatine, I myself would probably end up suffering: the hapless victim of a palace feud.

There was nothing I could do. Communications with Rome took too long to query this. I had to set off for Hispalis and do my best. But all the time I had to watch my back. I risked finding out that another agent had got there first and all my efforts were redundant. Somebody else might take the credit. Somebody else might earn the reward.

I could find no answers. Even when I had puzzled over the questions until I was sick of them there was still one more which might or might not be related, a new question that I had just left behind in Corduba. Why had Licinius Rufius wanted an interview with the proconsul? What had brought an elderly gentleman into the city so early in the morning, with his grandson morosely in tow?

PART THREE:

HISPALIS: CORDUBA: MONTES MARIANA

A.D. 73: May

What difference does it make how much is laid away in a man's safe or in his barns, how many head of stock he grazes or how much capital he puts out at interest, if he is always after what is another's and only counts what he has yet to get, never what he has already? You ask what is the proper limit to a person's wealth? First, having what is essential, and second, having what is enough.

Seneca

FORTY-ONE

Three mornings later I was sitting in a foodshop in Hispalis. Every muscle ached. I had blisters in obnoxious places. My brain was exhausted too.

Hispalis was growing hot. By midsummer this would be one of the most fiercely baked little towns in the Empire. Midsummer was closer than I dared contemplate. Weeks before then the child I had rashly fathered would be born. It could be happening while I was here. I could be breaking all my heartfelt assurances to Helena. The baby might have been born already without me. I could be a condemned man.

I felt like one, as I positioned my backside with extreme caution on the bench of this quiet place near the southwestern gate, within smell of the quays. The silence suited me. Eating bad food in an empty bar felt like home. For a moment I could imagine I was giving myself bellyache with a limp salad, somewhere on the crest of the Aventine. I was still enjoying the memory when the tambourinists arrived. Spotting a stranger they sidled up to try their luck with a noisy serenade. I would have left, but my stiffened limbs did not want to be disturbed.

Anybody who has lived in Rome has learned to ignore even the most vigorously orchestrated pleas from beggars. I had already set myself with my back to the wall, to avoid having my purse lifted from behind. I became resolutely deaf. Eventually someone who lived in a house next door threw open a shutter and screamed at the minstrels to lose themselves. They moved a few doorways up and stood there muttering. The shutter slammed. I kept chewing on rather tough lettuce.

This was supposed to be the third town in Baetica, after Corduba and Gades. My route had brought me in from the east, along with the aqueduct. Staggering under the town gate on the Corduba road last night, exhausted, I had ridden straight down the main street and discovered a modern civic forum complete with meeting-house, courts and baths: all people needed to dabble in the mire of local politics and justice, then wash off the stench afterwards. This morning I crawled out from the mansio, bleary-eyed and bilious, and soon found the original republican forum, with elderly temples and a more serene atmosphere, now too small for this thriving town. Further on towards the river was a third, extremely large piazza, the most busy of all, where commercial life hummed. Here the baths were bigger than in the forum, since there was more cash to build them, and the porticoes were more packed. Moneychangers had their stalls set out soon after dawn. Not long after that the throngs of distributors, merchants, shippers and other speculators started to appear. I had soaked in the atmosphere until I felt at home. Then I found this backstreet bar. I had been overconfident in my choice.

When more street musicians hove in sight, I paid the bill (pleasingly cheap). I took the last of my bread and smoked ham, and ate as I walked. I headed out of town to the river. Here the Baetis was broad and tidal. Its banks were crowded with jetties made from hewn stone blocks, and noisy with boatmen and porters. Everywhere were negotiators' offices. Everywhere cargoes were being transferred from barges to deep-sea vessels, or vice versa. Substantial fortunes were being made from commodities which nobody here would be using and nobody here had produced. Oil, wine, cloth, minerals from the interior mines, and cinnabar were being shipped in quantities. It was a middleman's dream.

Returning from the waterside hubbub, I discovered the clubhouse of the guild of bargees near the commercial square. A few permanent fixtures were already there; they probably lived in the clubroom—and they were certainly the bargees who did the least work. I learned that the elder Cyzacus was not there today. They spoke with a note of jealousy, and said he lived out at Italica.

"He's in demand a lot lately! What's making him so popular?"

"I can't answer that. I have never really met the man—who else wants him?"

"Someone we'd prefer to you! Someone a lot prettier."

"A woman?" It came as no surprise. And it irritated me intensely. Trust Anacrites to lumber me. Trust one of his minions to spoil the show before I had the chance to survey the ground. But I was working for Laeta (much as I distrusted him) and I felt determined not to stand back and give Anacrites a free run. The only time Anacrites had employed me direct, he dumped me and tried to kill me. I would never forget that. "So does Cyzacus come into Hispalis for meetings with lissom girls?"

"Not him. The old bastard comes into Hispalis to tell the rest of us what's what!" I gathered they viewed him as a leisured degenerate who thought himself above them.

I knew what that meant. Cyzacus really was the best. He had worked hard all his life. He had sons who still ran his business for him successfully. He won all the contracts because people could rely on him. He devoted effort to the affairs of the guild. Meanwhile these grumpy layabouts who liked to start lunching immediately after they finished breakfast sat about here playing Soldiers and drinking posca, and steadfastly complained.

"*Was* his girlfriend lissom—or long in the tooth?"

They cackled with grainy laughter, and I could get no sense out of them.

I had a good idea why Cyzacus might prefer the quiet life in Italica. I found out how to get there, then moved on to my next task.

Norbanus, the Gallic negotiator who arranged shipping space, occupied a majestic office right on the commercial square. People from whom I asked directions told me where it was, sneering openly. Nobody likes foreigners who demonstrate how successful they are. It was clear from his wide portals, carpeting of polychrome mosaic, statuettes on marble tripods, and neatly dressed office staff that Norbanus knew all there was to know about making money from other people's goods.

The staff were neat, but just as sleepy as subordinates anywhere once the master goes out. Because he was a Gaul, many of his menials were family. Their response was pretty Gallic. They excitedly discussed my question concerning his whereabouts amongst themselves for a long time, then one admitted with extremely formal wording that he wasn't here. They could have told me in a few words right at the start, but Gauls like the embroidery of debate. Urbanity for them means an impression of superior breeding—coupled with a barbarian yearning to swipe off your head with a very long sword.

I asked when Norbanus might be returning. They gave me a time that I felt was just a put-off. We all shook hands. They were smooth; I stayed polite. I ground my teeth in private. Then, having no option, I left.

It was death to my blisters, but I walked back to the mansio, claimed a new horse, and set off across the river to ride the five miles to Italica.

FORTY-TWO

Founded by Scipio as a colony of veterans, Italica boasted itself the oldest Roman town in Hispania. Before that the happy Phoenicians had known it, and the ancient tribes of Tartessos had made it a playground when the shepherds who had already exploited wool as far as possible, learned that their land possessed great mineral wealth and eagerly took to mining. Set on slightly hilly ground, with an open aspect, it was a very hot, dusty cluster—relieved by the presence of a grandiose complex of baths. Those who lived to be old men would know this dot in the provinces as the birthplace of an emperor. Even when I was there the rich used it as a hideaway, separated from Hispalis by just sufficient distance to make Italicans feel snooty.

There was a theater, and a good amphitheater too. Everywhere was spattered with plinths, fountains, pediments and statuary. If there was a bare space on a wall, someone erected an inscription. The wording was lofty. Italica was not the kind of place where you find a poster from the guild of prostitutes pledging their votes to some deadbeat in the local elections.

In the strict grid of well-swept streets near the forum I

found mansios that would not disgrace the finest areas of Rome. One of them belonged to Cyzacus. I was not allowed in, but I could see from the doorstep with its matched pair of standard bay trees that the entrance corridor was painted richly in black, red and gold, and that it led to a sumptuous atrium with a pool and gorgeous fresco-paneled walls. This was elegant public space for the patron's reception of his clients—but informers did not qualify.

Cyzacus was out. His steward told me quite agreeably. Cyzacus had been driven into Hispalis to meet a friend at the bargees' guild.

I was running around to no purpose here. The day was slipping away. This was the kind of work every informer dreads. The gods know it was appallingly familiar to me.

I went to the baths, felt too fretful to enjoy them, spurned the gymnasium, had a bowl of almond soup with enough garlic to ensure nobody spoke to me again for a week, then I returned to Hispalis myself.

FORTY-THREE

The bargees' clubhouse was a large bare room, with tables where the layabouts I had seen that morning were still dicing. With midday more members had come from the wharves to eat. Food was brought in from a thermopolium next door. It was probably bought at special rates, and looked good value; I reckon they got their wine for free. The atmosphere of comradeship was of the quiet kind. Men entering nodded to those present, and some sat down together; others preferred to eat alone. Nobody challenged me when I started looking around.

This time I found them: Cyzacus and Norbanus, two familiar faces from a month ago at the Baetican dinner on the Palatine. Sitting at a table in a corner, looking as deep in gossip as the last time I saw both of them. It seemed like their regular venue, and they looked like customary daytime debauchers. They had already finished their lunch. From the piles of empty bowls and platters it had been substantial and I guessed the wine jug would have been replenished several times.

My arrival was timely. They had reached the point of slowing down in their heavy meal. Where diners at a formal feast might now welcome a Spanish dancer to whistle at while they toyed with the fresh fruit, these two pillars of Hispalis commerce had their own diversion: me.

Cyzacus was a dapper, slightly shrunken old featherweight, in a slimline gray tunic over a long-sleeved black one. He was the quiet, better-mannered partner in what seemed an unlikely pair. He had a hollow, lined face with an unhealthy pallor, and closely clipped white hair. His bosom pal Norbanus was much heavier and more untidy, pressing folds of belly up against the table edge. His fat fingers were forced apart by immense jeweled rings. He too was a mature vintage, his hair still dark, though with wings of gray. Several layers of chin sported dark stubble. He had all the physical attributes that pass for a jolly companion—including a painfully raucous personality.

I slumped on a bench and came to the point: "The last time we met, gentlemen, I was at home and you were the visitors. We were dining, though." I cast my eyes over the empties, with their debris of fish skeletons, chewed olive stones, stripped chicken wings, oyster shells, bay leaves and rosemary twigs. "You know how to produce an impressive discard dish!"

"You have the advantage," Norbanus said. He sounded completely sober. Feasting was a way of life for these men. He had already buried his snout in his cup again, making no attempt to offer a drink to me.

"The name's Falco."

They did not bother to make eye contact, either with one another or with me: they had known who I was. Either they really remembered being introduced on the Palatine, or they had worked out that I was the none-too-secret agent investigating the cartel.

"So! You're the respected master bargeman Cyzacus, and you're the notable negotiator Norbanus. Both men with sufficient standing to be entertained in Rome by the eminent Quinctius Attractus?"

"The eminent crawler!" Norbanus scoffed, not bothering to

keep his voice down. Cyzacus gave him an indulgent glance. The negotiator's contempt was intended not just for the senator; it embraced all things Roman—including me.

"The eminent manipulator," I agreed frankly. "Myself, I'm a republican—and one of the plebs. I'd like to hope the senator and his son might have overstretched themselves." This time they both stilled. I had to look closely to spot it, though.

"I've been talking with *your* sons," I told the bargee. There was no way young Cyzacus and Gorax could have communicated with their papa in the three days since I saw them; I was hoping to make him worry what they might have said.

"Nice for you." He did not disconcert so easily. "How are my boys?"

"Working well."

"That makes a change!" I was in a world of rough opinions and plain speaking, apparently. Even so I felt this wary old man would not leave his boys in charge of business upstream at Corduba unless he really trusted them. He had taught them the job, and despite the ruck they must have had when the natural son went off to dabble with poetry, nowadays the three of them worked closely together. The two sons had struck me as loyal both to each other and to their father.

"Cyzacus junior was telling me about his literary career; and Gorax had his mind on some chickens. They explained to me how when I saw you in Rome you were there to talk tough about exports."

"I was there as a guest!" Cyzacus had the manner of a meek old chap whose mind was wandering. But he was defying me. He knew I could prove nothing. "Attractus invited me and paid for it."

"Generous!"

"Bottomless purse," cackled Norbanus, indicating that he thought the man a fool. I gained the welcome impression that these two had cynically accepted the free trip without ever intending to be coerced. After all, they were both in transport;

they could certainly go to Rome whenever they wanted, for virtually nothing.

"It strikes me that much as Attractus may admire your wit and conversation, to pay out fares and offer hospitality in his own fine home—all of which I gather he has done on more than one occasion for different groups of Baeticans—might suggest that the illustrious codger wants something?"

"Excellent business sense." Norbanus grinned.

"And a sharp eye for a deal?"

"He thinks so!" Another insult tripped lightly off the Gallic tongue.

"Maybe he wants to be the uncrowned king of Baetica."

Norbanus was still sneering: "Isn't he that already? Patron of Corduba, Castulo and Hispalis, representative of the oil producers in the Senate, linchpin of the copper mines—"

Talking about mines depressed me. "What part of Gaul are you from?"

"Narbo." This was close to Tarraconensis though outside Hispania. It was a major entrepôt in southern Gaul.

"You specialize in shipping olive oil? Is that just to Rome?"

He snorted. "You can't have much idea about the market! A lot of my contracts are bound for Rome, yes; but we're shipping thousands of amphorae. We cover the whole of Italy—and everywhere else. The stuff goes in all directions—up the Rhodanus in Gallia Narbonensis, to Gaul, Britain and Germany; I've done shipments straight across the Pillars of Hercules to Africa; I've sent it as far as Egypt; I've supplied Dalmatia, Pannonia, Crete, mainland Greece and Syria—"

"*Greece?* I thought the Greeks grew their own olives? Weren't they doing it for centuries before you had them here in Baetica?"

"Not got the taste. Not so mellow."

I whistled quietly. Turning again to Cyzacus I said, "Expensive business, exporting oil. I gather the price starts going up as soon as they funnel it into the amphorae?"

He shrugged. "The on-costs are terrible. It's not our fault. For instance, on the journey down from Corduba we have to pay port taxes every single time we stop. It all gets added to the bill."

"That's after your own profits have been taken out. Then Norbanus here wants his percentage, and the shipper too. All long before the retailer in Rome even has a smell of it."

"It's a luxury item," Cyzacus replied defensively.

"Luckily for all of you in Baetica it's an item in universal use."

"It's a very wonderful product," Norbanus put in dryly, in a holy voice.

"Wonderfully profitable!" I said. I had to change the subject. "You're a Gaul. How do you get on with the producers?"

"They hate my guts," Norbanus admitted proudly. "And it's mutual! At least they know I'm not some bloody interloper from Italy."

"Speculators!" I sympathized. "Coming out to the provinces from Rome solely because they can get away with low cash inputs, then drain off huge profits. Bringing their alien work practices. If they ever come out here in person, clinging together in tight little cliques—always planning to go home again once their fortunes are made . . . Attractus is a prime example, though he seems to want more from it than most. I know about his olive estate and his mineral mine—what interests does he have in Hispalis?"

"None," Cyzacus said, disapprovingly.

"He built the baths near the wool market," Norbanus reminded him. Cyzacus sniffed.

"Didn't it go down well?" I asked.

"The people of Baetica," Cyzacus informed me, sucking in his thin cheeks, "prefer to be honored with benefactions from men who were born here. Not outsiders who want to impress for their personal glory."

"Where does that leave you as a Gaul?" I demanded of Norbanus.

"Stowing my money in a bankchest!" He grinned.

I looked at them both: "But you two are friends?"

"We dine together," Cyzacus told me. I knew what he meant. These were two dedicated men of commerce. They could exchange public hospitality on a regular basis for years on end, yet I doubted if they had ever been to each other's houses, and once they retired from business they might never meet again. They were on the same side—cheating the oil producers and forcing up prices for the eventual customers. But they were not friends.

This was good news. On the face of it the men Quinctius Attractus had invited to Rome last month shared a common interest. Yet several kinds of prejudice divided them—and they all loathed Attractus himself. The bargees and negotiators tolerated each other, but they hated the olive producers—and those snobs on their grand estates shared no common feeling with the transport side.

Was this antagonism strong enough to prevent them all forming a price ring? Would their shared distrust of a Roman interloper dissuade them from joining him? Had Attractus miscalculated the lure of money? Might these hard-nosed operators reject him as a leader? Might they reckon there was sufficient profit to be made from oil, and that they were perfectly capable of squeezing out the maximum gain without any help from him—and without any obligation to him afterwards?

"You know why I'm here," I suggested. Both men laughed. After the size of meal they had eaten all this hilarity could not be good for them. "There are two reasons. Attractus has drawn attention to himself; he is thought to be a dangerous fixer—and I'm looking into ways of fixing him." The two men glanced at each other, openly pleased he was in trouble. "Of course," I said gravely, "neither of you has been approached to take part in anything so crooked as a cartel?"

"Certainly not," they agreed solemnly.

I smiled like a pleasant fellow. "Reputable businessmen would want nothing to do with such villainy?"

"Of course not," they assured me.

"And you would immediately report such an approach to the authorities?" I dropped the pose: "Don't bother to insult me by answering that!"

Old Cyzacus was picking his teeth, but behind the ensuing grimace he may have looked offended that I had just accused them of lying. Liars are always very sensitive.

Norbanus continued to be as unhelpful as possible. "Is there a cartel, Falco? If so, good luck to it!" he declared. Then he spat on the floor. "Tcha! They'll never do it—the bloody producers couldn't organize themselves!"

I leaned my elbows on the table, linking my fingers and surveying the reprobates over my hands. I tried ingratiating myself: "I think you're right. I've seen them in Corduba. They spend so much time making sure they don't get missed off the guest list for the next soirée with the proconsul, they can't manage much else."

"All they care about," Norbanus growled, "is taking a turn as duovir and sending their sons to ponce about in Rome spending money—wasting their capital!" he added, as if failure to thrive as an investor was an unforgivable offense.

"So don't you think Attractus managed to lean on them?"

Cyzacus took an interest: "He could lean until he fell over. The producers would never do anything risky."

"And what about you two?" I challenged. This only produced contemptuous smiles. "All right. You've been frank with me, so I'll return the compliment. I have to report to the Emperor. I'm going to tell Vespasian that I am convinced there is a cartel being mooted. That Attractus is the prime mover. And that all the men who were seen dining with him at the Society of Olive Oil Producers' dinner at the end of March have assured me they were horrified and that they spurned the idea. Well, you wouldn't want to be indicted with him before the court of conspiracy, would you?"

"Let us know if you get him there," Norbanus said dryly. "We'll all come and cheer."

"Perhaps you'd like to help me form a case? Perhaps you'd like to give evidence?"

Neither even bothered to reply. And I didn't bother offering another free fare to Rome on the strength of future assistance. They would not appear in court. Rome has its own snobberies anyway. A couple of foreigners engaged in transportation—however flourishing their business—would be despised. I needed to subpoena the estate owners at least. Land counts. Land is respectable. But to indite a senator with a long Roman pedigree even Annaeus and Rufius would not be enough. The Quinctii would walk, unless I could produce witnesses of their own social weight. And where were they?

I was glad I had spoken to these two in person, despite the long trip. I did feel their story carried weight. Their assessment of the producers matched my own. Norbanus and Cyzacus seemed too self-reliant to follow the lead of an entrepreneur from the political world—and too capable of making money on their own account. Not that I could ever rely on this: if the men Attractus had summoned to Rome had leapt at his suggestion, they were hardly likely to tell me. Price-fixing works on subtlety. Nobody ever admits it is happening.

I was leaving. "I said there were two reasons why I came to Baetica."

Cyzacus stopped wielding his toothpick. "What is the other one?" For a vague old man, he responded well.

"It's not pleasant. The night you dined on the Palatine a man was killed."

"Nothing to do with us."

"I think it was. Another man, a high official, was seriously wounded. He may be dead too. Both victims were at the dinner.

Both were in fact dining with Attractus—which means he's implicated, and as his guests so are you. Somebody slipped up that night—and it won't go away." This was a long shot. I was hoping that if the Baeticans were unconnected with the attacks, they would turn in the real perpetrator to absolve themselves.

"We can't help you," said Norbanus. So much for that pious hope.

"Oh? Then why did you leave Rome so fast the next day?"

"Our business was concluded. Since we turned down his offer, we all thought it would be presuming on the senator's hospitality to remain."

"You've just admitted that an offer *was* made," I pointed out. Norbanus grinned evilly.

The excuse for leaving could be true. Staying at the Quinctius house after refusing to play the Attractus game could have been embarrassing. Besides, if they hated the plan, they might want to escape before Attractus tried putting on more pressure. And if they had said so, then they heard about the murder and suspected it was connected with the cartel scheme, they were bound to flee.

"It looks bad," I returned somberly. "A sudden departure straight after a killing tends to appear significant in court. Part of my work includes finding evidence for barristers, and I can assure you that's the sort of tale that makes them gloat and think of massive fees."

"You're making wild accusations," Norbanus told me coolly.

"No."

My simple reply for once caused silence.

Cyzacus recovered himself. "We offer our sympathy to the victims."

"Then perhaps you would like to help. I need to find a girl who comes from Hispalis. In delicate official parlance: we think she may have important information relating to the deaths."

"She did it?" Norbanus sneered crudely.

I smiled. "She was at the dinner, dancing for Attractus; he claims he doesn't know her though he paid her fee. You may have recognized her; her name's Selia—probably."

To my surprise they made no quibble about it: they knew Selia. It was her real name. She was a local girl of moderate talent, struggling to make a career where all the demand was for dancers from Gades. (Gades dancers had organized a closed shop on the entertainment circuit . . . it had a familiar ring.) Cyzacus and Norbanus remembered seeing Selia at the dinner on the Palatine; they had been surprised, but assumed she had finally made the big breakthrough in Rome. Recently they had heard she was back in Hispalis, so they assumed it came to nothing.

I stared Cyzacus in the eye. "Just how well do you know her? Would Selia be the lovely who came here looking for you recently?"

"Girls like Selia are not welcome at the bargees' club-room," he maintained.

"So she never found you?"

"That's right," he answered with a cool glare that suggested he was lying again, but that I would extract no more.

Patiently I explained why I was asking: "There's another woman going around asking questions about this business. They're both trouble. I need to know which is up to what. Your fellow members implied that the girl who came here was a looker—but their standards may be more flexible than mine." The daytime skivers playing dice looked as if anything in a dress would make them salivate. "So was it Selia or not?"

"Since I never saw her," sneered Cyzacus, "I can't say."

He and Norbanus were closing up on me, but when I asked the most important question they did know the answer and they told me straightaway: they gave me directions to where Selia lived.

FORTY-FOUR

I walked back to the quays, needing to rid my mind of other men enjoying a long convivial lunch—which they called doing business. I hated my work. I was tired of working alone, unable to trust even the people who had commissioned me. This was a worse case than usual. I was sick of being a plaything in the pointless bureaucratic feud between Laeta and Anacrites.

If Helena had been here, she would have made me feel ludicrous by appearing to sympathize—then suggesting that what I wanted was a new job as a cut-out-fringe sewer in the suede-purse market, with a stall on the Via Ostiana. Just thinking about it made me grin. I needed her.

I found myself staring at the shipping. More boats than I would have expected had plied their way through the straits of Hercules and into the broad gulf at the start of the Atlantic Ocean, past Gades, past the lighthouse at Turris Caepionis, and up the wide estuary of the Baetica to reach Hispalis. Huge merchantmen from all around the Inner Sea were here, and even deep-sea ships that ventured around the outer edge of Lusitania to make landfall in North Gaul and Britain by the hard route. They lined the wharves; they jostled in the channel. Some were anchored out in the river, for lack of space on the quays. There was a queuing system for the barges that came down from Corduba. And this was April, not even the olive harvesting season.

It wasn't April. May had arrived. Some time this month, unavoidably, Helena would produce our child. While I stood here dreaming she might even be having it . . .

Now I had Selia's address. Even so, I was in no hurry to go chasing there. I was thinking about this just as carefully as a man who has finally made a successful move on a girl who had been playing hard to get—and with the same mixture of excitement and nerves. I would be lucky if the worst that happened was acquiring a slapped face.

Before I could tackle the dancer, I had to prepare myself. Brace myself. She was a woman; I could handle her. Well, I was a man so I assumed I could; plenty of us have been caught out like that. She might even be on my side—if I had a side. The evidence in Rome said Selia was a killer. It might be wrong. She might work for Anacrites. If she did, someone else must have attacked Valentinus and him—unless the Chief Spy was even more behind with approving expenses for his agents than usual. That would be typical, though not many of his deadbeats responded by trying to crack his skull.

If Selia was in the clear I still had to identify the real killer. That was a very big unknown.

Whatever the truth—and being realistic, I thought she *was* the killer—this woman knew I had come to Baetica; she would be waiting for me. I even considered approaching the local watch and asking for an escort, an option I rejected out of sheer Roman prejudice. I would rather go alone. But I had no intention of just strolling up to her door and asking for a drink of water like an innocent passerby. One wrong move and the dangerous lady might kill me.

* * *

I must have been looking grim. For once the Fates decided that I was so pessimistic I might give up this job altogether and deprive them of a lot of fun. So for the first time ever they decided to offer me a helping hand.

The hand was ink-stained and nail-bitten, attached to a weedy arm which protruded from a shrunken long-sleeved tunic with extremely ragged cuffs. The arm hung from a shoulder over which was slung a worn satchel; its flap was folded back for easy access and I could see note-tablets inside. The shoulder served as a bony hanger for the rest of the tunic, which came down below the knees of a short, sad-looking man with pouchy eyes and uncombed hair. Every dry old thong of his sandals had curled back on itself at the edges. He had the air of being much rebuffed and cursed. He was clearly ill-paid. I deduced, even before he confirmed the tragedy, that he worked for the government.

"Is your name Falco?" I shook the inky hand cautiously as a sign that it might be. I wondered how he knew. "I'm Gnaeus Drusillus Placidus."

"Pleased to meet you," I said. I wasn't. I had been half-enjoying myself remembering Selia as I prepared myself to visit her house. The interruption hurt.

"I thought you would be coming downriver to speak to me."

"You knew I was here?" I ventured cautiously.

"The quaestor's clerk told me to look out for you." The old black slave from Hadrumetum; the one who had lost the correspondence with Anacrites—or had it lifted from him.

"He didn't tell me about you!"

The man looked surprised. "I'm the procurator," he cried importantly. "I supervise the port taxes and export tax." My enthusiasm still failed to match his. In desperation he lowered his voice and hissed, "It was me who started this!"

I nearly let myself down completely by asking "Started

what?" But his urgency and the way he looked over his shoulder for eavesdroppers explained everything.

"It was you!" I murmured discreetly, but with the note of applause the man deserved. "You were the sharp-eyed fellow who first wrote to Anacrites, sounding the alarm!"

FORTY-FIVE

I was looking at him keenly now. Still an unimpressive experience. I would like to complain that he behaved officiously, but he was just perfectly straight. Nobody likes a government official they cannot moan about.

We walked nearer to the water, deliberately looking casual. As a procurator he would have an office, but it would be stuffed with staff from the cache of public slaves. They would probably look honest—until the day when it counted. What he and I had to discuss could be the big secret they were all waiting to sell.

"What's your history?" I asked. "You're not from Baetica? You sound Roman to me; you have the Palatine twang."

He was not offended at the question. He was proud of his life, with reason. "I am an imperial freedman. From Nero's time," he felt obliged to add. He knew I would have asked. Palace freedmen are always judged by the régime when their career took off. "But that does not affect my loyalty."

"Anyone who struggled to serve the state under Nero will welcome Vespasian with a huge sigh of relief. Vespasian knows that."

"I do my job." It was a statement I believed.

"So how did you reach this position?"

"I bought my freedom, worked in commerce, earned enough to be granted equestrian rank, and offered myself for useful posts. They sent me here." He had the kind of record I ought to pursue myself; maybe if I had been born a slave I might have managed it. Instead pride and obstinacy got firmly in my way.

"And now you've stirred up quite a controversy. What's the smell that you don't like?"

He did not answer immediately. "Hard to say. I nearly did not make a report at all."

"Did you discuss it with anyone?"

"The quaestor."

"Cornelius?"

He looked shocked. "Who else?" Clearly the *new* quaestor was not an alternative.

"Decent?"

"I liked him. No side. Did the job—you can't often say that!"

"How did Cornelius get along with the proconsul?"

"He was the chosen deputy, in the old-fashioned way. They had worked together before. He was the senior tribune when the old man had a legion. They came out as a pair. But now Cornelius needs a career move. He wants to show his face in the Senate. The old man agreed to release him."

"After which he had to take whatever he was sent as a replacement! But I heard Cornelius hasn't gone back to Rome? He's traveling."

An angry expression passed over Placidus' face. "Cornelius going on his travels is all part of the nasty smell!" That was intriguing. "Rome would have been too convenient, wouldn't it? He could have made the report on our problem himself."

"What are you telling me, Placidus?"

"Cornelius *was* going back. He *wanted* to go back."

"Keen?"

"Highly excited." One of those. A careerist. I kept my face neutral. On the lower rung of the public service ladder, Placidus was a careerist himself. "He was ready for politics. He wanted to get married too."

"A fatalist! So where exactly is he?" I demanded, with a sinking feeling. For some reason I felt he was about to say the young man was dead.

"In Athens."

Once I recovered from the unexpected answer I asked, "What's the attraction in Athens?"

"You mean apart from art, history, language and philosophy?" asked Placidus rather dryly. I had an idea he was the type of cultural dreamer who would adore a trip to Greece. "Well Cornelius didn't care much for those, in fact; he wasn't the type. Someone in Rome just happened to have an unused ticket on a ship from Gades to Piraeus; he spoke to Cornelius' father and offered free use of it."

"Generous! Cornelius senior was delighted?"

"What father would turn down the chance of getting his son to the University like that?"

Well, mine, for one. But mine had long ago realized the more I learned—about anything—the less control he had over me. He never lavished art, history, language or philosophy upon me. That way he never had to face me faking gratitude.

But I could sympathize with Cornelius; he would have been trapped. No senatorial career comes cheap. Nor does marriage. To preserve good relations at home he had to go along with whatever embarrassment his parent well-meaningly bestowed on him—just because some acquaintance at the Curia had smiled and offered it. My own father was an auctioneer. He could recognize a bribe coming five miles away. Not all men are so adept.

"So poor Cornelius only wanted to rush home to govern people, but he's stuck with a present that he would far rather dump—and he has his papa happily telling him it's a chance in a lifetime and he should be a grateful boy? Placidus, can I guess the name of his benefactor? Someone Cornelius did not want to write a nice thank-you letter to? Can the name of Quinctius Attractus be dropped into this conversation without causing a misfit?"

"You've thrown a six, Falco."

"I've thrown a double, I think."

"You know how to play this game."

"I've played before."

We stared at the river gloomily. "Cornelius is a very sharp young man," said Placidus. "He knows that a free trip always costs something."

"And what do you think this one will cost?"

"A great deal to consumers of olive oil!"

"Through Cornelius not mentioning his disquiet about the upcoming situation in Baetica? I suppose he couldn't argue with his father who was far away in Rome. He couldn't risk writing a letter explaining, because the subject was too sensitive. So he's forced to take the ticket—and once he goes, he's obligated to the Quinctii."

"I can see you have done your research," said Placidus, thoroughly miserable.

"Can I get the timing straight? You and Cornelius became anxious about the influence of the Quinctii when?"

"Last year when his son came out to Baetica. We knew there must be a reason and Cornelius guessed Quadratus was aiming to replace him in the quaestorship. At the same time Attractus was first starting to invite groups to Rome."

"So Quadratus may have warned his father that Cornelius might make adverse comments when he was debriefed by the Palace at the end of his tour? The Quinctii decided to delay him, while they consolidated their position. And when the unwanted cultural holiday arose, Cornelius gave in but you decided to take action?"

"I wrote a note."

"Anonymously?"

"Official channels were too dangerous. Besides, I did not want to land Cornelius with an enemy in Rome. He had always supported me."

"Was this why you approached Anacrites and not Laeta?"

"It seemed appropriate to involve the intelligence group."

Involving Anacrites was never appropriate, but one had to work with him to see it. "What happened next? Anacrites wrote back formally and asked the proconsul to investigate—so he handed the job straight to Cornelius? Won't that turn out awkward for him anyway?"

"He could say he had no choice. Once there was an instruction from Rome, Cornelius was bound to follow up. Still, we made sure his answering report was conveyed discreetly."

I laughed briefly. "I know! Whoever decided to send that report with Camillus Aelianus?"

"He was friendly with Cornelius."

I shook my head. "And with another young man too! Aelianus read the report and I have a nasty feeling he passed on the contents to exactly the wrong person."

Placidus paled. "Quinctius Quadratus?"

I nodded. Placidus hit his palm against his head. "I never thought!"

"It's not your fault. Young Quadratus is everywhere. Clearly it runs in the family."

We considered the situation like men of affairs. We looked grave; our talk was measured; we stared hard at the water, pretending to count fish.

"Being involved in many spheres of provincial life is not a crime, of course," Placidus commented.

"No, but at some point being over-busy speaks for itself. A

good Roman only flaunts himself if he's trying to get the populace to support him in a ballot—and even then he tries to look as if he hates putting himself forward."

"You picture a man I could vote for, Falco!" he cried admiringly. He was being ironic. So was I, come to that.

"And I'm *not* picturing Attractus. Everything he does has the smack of personal ambition and family gain."

"But the situation is not being ignored," Placidus tried to console himself.

"That's no guarantee of action. You learned your job on the Palatine. You know how things work. It's a difficult one."

"You are asking me to provide evidence?"

"And you're going to tell me there is none?"

He shrugged wearily. "How do you prove these things, Falco? Businessmen talk among themselves. If they are plotting to force up prices, only they know. They are hardly likely to tell me or you. Half of the small talk will be innuendo anyway. And if challenged, they will deny it all, and look outraged at the suggestion."

"You sound as if you had done ten years as an informer," I told him sadly.

His tone became more embittered. "Obtaining information is easy, Falco! A bit of cheap charm and a few bribes will do the trick for you. You want to try a job where you're taking money from people. That's the hard life!"

I grinned. I was starting to like him. Well, I had the same rule for state officials as I had always had with women: once the situation started getting friendly it was time to leave.

"Just one more thing, Placidus—I had no luck when I tried to see the original correspondence. There seem to be two versions. Am I right that in his report Cornelius told Anacrites you suspected a cartel was being set up, but it was at an early stage and could be contained?"

Placidus frowned slightly. "I didn't see the actual letter."

"But?"

"But that's not quite what he and I agreed."

"Which was?"

"Plans for price-rigging seemed to be at an early stage, certainly—but we were extremely concerned that because of the key personnel and their influence in Baetica, containment would be *very difficult!*"

FORTY-SIX

The procurator was seriously upset. "You just can't tell, can you? Cornelius and I had agreed the exact opposite of what you say was reported in! I would have sworn Cornelius was absolutely straight. And I would have banked on the proconsul to back him—"

"Calm down—"

"No, I won't! It's too bad, Falco. Some of us really try to do a decent job, but we're thwarted at every turn!"

"You're jumping to conclusions, friend. The wrong ones, I think."

"How can that be?"

"Two reasons, Placidus. First, I never saw any of the letters, so this is just hearsay. And second, while the report from Cornelius was in the custody of Camillus Aelianus, maybe he let it be tampered with."

"*Tampered with?* You mean, forgery?"

"I realize such words are odious to a conscientious man."

"And Aelianus, you say?"

"Don't be misled by his sweet smile."

"He's just a lad."

"He's twenty-four. A careless age."

"I heard he was some relative of yours?"

"He'll be my first child's uncle in a matter of weeks. That does not mean I shall trust him to rock the cradle unsupervised. He may have been a friend of the upright Cornelius, but he was also thick with the young Annaei—a disreputable crowd. Until they quarreled over a situation on their fathers' estates, he rode with Quinctius Quadratus too. You know this group?"

"Young fellows, some away from home, loose in a provincial capital and looking for a riot. Too much drinking; a lot of athletics and hunting. They're just wanting thrills—particularly if they think their elders won't approve. Quadratus had them dabbling with the cult of Cybele—"

"That's an Eastern religion!"

"Brought here by the Carthaginians. There is a temple in Corduba. At one stage they were all going there, then Annaeus Maximus stopped his sons, the proconsul made some sour remarks to Cornelius, and it tailed off."

"I expect they had second thoughts," I said gravely, "when they heard about the castration rites!"

Placidus laughed.

"Tell me more about Quadratus—he was out here last year?"

"His father sent him, allegedly to supervise their estate."

"Including the eviction of tenants whose faces didn't fit!"

At my sharp retort, Placidus looked purse-lipped. "There was some trouble, I gather." He was being cautious. I signaled that I had heard the full story. He then said, with a bluntness that seemed uncharacteristic, "Quinctius Quadratus is the worst kind, Falco. We've had them all. We've had them rude and overconfident. We've had debauched young tyrants who live in the brothels. We've had fools who can't count, or spell, or compose a sentence in any language, let alone in correspondence-Greek. But when we heard that Quadratus had been wished on us as quaestor, those of us in the know nearly packed up and left."

"What makes him so bad?"

"You can't pin him down. He looks as if he knows what he is doing. He has success written all over him, so it's pointless to complain. He is the sort the world loves—until he comes unstuck."

"Which he may never do!"

"You understand the problem."

"I've worked with a few golden boys."

"High-flyers. Most have broken wings."

"I like your style, Placidus. It's good to find a man who doesn't mind sticking his head over the rampart when everyone else is cowering. Or should I say, everyone except the proconsul? Despite everything, Quadratus is on hunting leave, you know."

"I didn't! Well that's one bright spot. His father's influence made the appointment look staged: the proconsul hates anything that looks off-color."

"Quadratus may have a black smudge against his name," I hinted, remembering what the proconsul's clerks had told me about the dead soldiers in Dalmatia. "Then a query about the family's role from Anacrites does not exactly help him maintain a glowing aura—somebody worked a flanker to be proud of," I commented.

Placidus beamed. "Terrible, isn't it?"

"Tragic! But you're stuck with him unless he or his father, or both if possible, can be discredited. That's my job. I'm partway there. I can finger them as ringleaders when the cartel was being mooted last month in Rome—though I can't put up witnesses. Of course they were both on the spot. Even young Quadratus had finished his agricultural clearances and gone home again to triumph in the Senate elections and the jobs lottery."

"Yes. He must have known Cornelius wanted to give up his

post; he and his father somehow maneuvered the quaestorship into their own hands. From here, it looks difficult to see why Rome fell for it."

"The graybeards in the Curia would approve. The family had interests here. The Emperor may have assumed the proconsul would be delighted by his catch."

"The proconsul soon told him otherwise. He was livid!" Placidus muttered. "I heard about it from Cornelius."

It sounded as though this proconsul liked breaking rules: he could spot a wrong move coming—and he was not afraid to dodge it. Not afraid of telling Vespasian he was annoyed, either. He was exceptional among men of his rank. No doubt he would live down to my expectations eventually, but at the moment it looked as though he was doing his job.

I returned to the main problem: "I'll be fair to Aelianus. Assume he meant no harm. He arrived in Rome with the report for Anacrites, all full of the importance of his mission. He was bursting with it, and could simply have boasted to the wrong friend in Rome. He may not have realized the Quinctii were involved."

"Did Cornelius tell him what the sealed letter said?" Placidus scowled.

"Apparently Cornelius used some discretion. Of course that only excited the lad's curiosity; Aelianus confessed to me he read the report."

Placidus was raging again: "Oh I despair of these young men!"

I smiled, though it took an effort. Pedants irritate me. "At risk of sounding like a ghastly old republican grandfather, discipline and ethics are not requirements for the *cursus honorem* nowadays . . . With or without the connivance of Aelianus, someone altered the report. Even with that done, they knew Anacrites would be taking it further. They decided to stop him. The results were disastrous. Somebody killed the agent who was on surveillance when the oil producers came to Rome—and they made a brutal attack on Anacrites too."

"Dear gods! Is Anacrites dead?"

"I don't know. But it was a serious misjudgment. It drew attention to the plot, rather than burying it. The investigation wasn't stopped, and won't be now."

"If they had kept their heads," Placidus philosophized, "nobody could have proved anything. Inertia would set in. Cornelius has left; Quadratus is installed. He can't be left on hunting leave forever. The financial affairs of this province are under his sole control. For myself, I expect every hour to be recalled to Rome, due to some quiet manipulation by the tireless Quinctius Attractus. Even if I stay on, anything I say can easily be dismissed as the ravings of an obsessive clerk with cracked ideas about fraud."

"You know how the system operates," I complimented him.

"I should do. It stinks—but gods alive, it rarely involves the murder of state servants!"

"No. That was arranged by somebody who *doesn't* know." Somebody inexperienced. Someone who lacked the patience and confidence to wait and let the inertia Placidus mentioned creep insidiously through the state machine.

Placidus was frowning. "Why are you so vague about the report, Falco? There ought to be copies of everything filed by the quaestor's clerk."

"He tried to find it for me. Gone missing."

"Why did you think that was?"

"Stolen to hide the evidence? Quinctius Quadratus is the obvious suspect. I'm only surprised he knew his way around the office."

"I bet he doesn't," Placidus retorted sourly. "But he will one day. Maybe it wasn't him. Maybe the documents have been removed by someone else to stop him seeing them!"

"Who do you suggest?"

"The proconsul."

If that was true, the bastard could have told me he had done it.

Placidus took a deep breath. When governors of provinces have to start prowling offices, censoring records in order to deceive their own deputies, order has broken down. Governors of provinces are not supposed to know how the filing system works (though of course they have all held lowly posts in their youth). Allowing them to fiddle with scrolls opened up frightening avenues. This was all filthier and more complex than Placidus had thought. "So what now, Falco?"

"A tricky piece of reconnaissance."

I explained about finding the dancer. The procurator did not know her, or was not aware of it if he did. He expressed a theory that men may watch, but do not learn the names of girls who entertain. Obviously his past life had been more innocent than mine.

"And where does she fit in, Falco?"

"I found evidence that she and her African musicians carried out the attacks in Rome on Anacrites and his man."

"What did she have against them?"

"Nothing personal, probably. I imagine that somebody paid her. If I find her I'll try to make her tell me who it was. And if his name happens to be one of those we have been discussing, you and the proconsul will be happy men."

I told him the address the two shipping tycoons had given me. Placidus said he believed it was a dangerous area of town—though inspired by the excitement of our conversation, he decided he would come along with me.

I let him. I believed he was straight, but I do have my standards; he was still a man who held a salaried government post. If I got into trouble with Selia and needed a decoy, I would cheerfully throw him to her as bait.

FORTY-SEVEN

Every town and city has its unhappy quarter. Hispalis might be a thriving hub of commerce, a producer of sculptors and poets, and a regional capital, but it too had potholed lanes where thin, dark-eyed women dragged screaming toddlers to market while very few men were in evidence. I could guess that the missing masculine element were all loafers or thieves, or had died of a wasting disease. Maybe I was prejudiced. Maybe I was just nervous. And maybe I was right to be.

Where the girl lived proved hard to find. There was no point asking directions. Even if anyone knew her, they would conceal it from us. We were too smart and too well-spoken—at least I was. Placidus looked pretty down-at-heel.

"This is a bad place, Falco!"

"Surprise me. At least with two of us, we can watch our backs in two directions."

"Are we watching for anything in particular?"

"Everything."

It was now late afternoon. The people of Hispalis were taking a lengthy siesta, much needed in the terrific heat of midsummer. The narrow lanes were quiet. We walked in the shade and trod softly.

Eventually we identified a lodging house, slightly larger and less grim than its surroundings, which appeared to match the directions Cyzacus and Norbanus had given me. A fat, unhelpful woman on a wonky stool peeling a cabbage into a chipped bowl agreed grumpily that Selia lived there. We were allowed up to knock on her door. She was out.

We went down and sat in what passed for a foodshop opposite. There appeared to be little to eat or drink, but a waiter was gambling furiously with a friend. He managed to break off long enough to ask us to wait until they finished the next round, after which he scribbled hasty sums on a piece of board, collected the dice again ready, then dashed together two beakers of something lukewarm and cut us two chunks from a loaf, before he and his pal reabsorbed themselves in their game.

Placidus carefully wiped the rim of his cup with the hem of his sleeve. I had learned to toss down a draught without touching the container. There would not be much point in hygienic precautions if the liquor itself was contaminated.

"This is a fine way to do work, Falco!" my companion sighed, settling in.

"If you want it, the job's yours."

"I don't know if I'm qualified."

"Can you sit in a bar doing nothing half the day, while you wait for a girl who wants to beat your brains out?"

"I can sit and wait—but I don't know what I'm supposed to do once she arrives."

"Keep well out of the way," I advised.

I was beginning to regret bringing him. The neighborhood was too dangerous. We were getting into serious trouble, and Placidus did not deserve it. Neither did I perhaps, but at least I had some idea what to expect and it was my job.

These tiny streets with cramped dwellings had neither

piped water nor sewerage. Ill-defined gutters in the stony tracks between hovels served to take away waste. In bad weather they must be atrocious; even in sunlight they stank. Depression was all around. A pitifully thin goat was tethered to a stick in the foodshop yard. Flies zoomed at us in angry circles. Somewhere a baby cried mournfully.

"You're not by any chance armed, Placidus?"

"You're joking; I'm a procurator, Falco!—Are you?"

"I brought a sword to Hispalis; I didn't expect to get this close to the girl, so I left it at the mansio."

We were badly positioned. We had come to the only place where we could stop and wait, but the alley outside was so narrow and winding we could see little of it. The few people who passed all stared at us hard. We sat tight, trying not to look as if our chins were barbered, and trying not to speak when anyone could overhear our Roman accents.

There were several battered lock-ups facing the path. One contained a man whittling at crude pieces of furniture; the rest were closed up, their doors leaning at odd angles. They looked deserted, but could just as well be in fitful use; any artisans who worked in this area were sad men with no hope.

After a while the waiter's friend left and two giggling girls arrived. They sat on a bench and did not order anything, but ogled the waiter who now had time to enjoy the attention. He had extremely long eyelashes; Helena would have said it was from batting them at women. After a short time the girls suddenly scuttled off, then a wide-bodied, bandy-legged man who could have been their father turned up and looked the waiter over. He left too, with nothing said. The waiter cleaned his fingernails with the knife he had used to cut our pieces of bread.

A redhead was walking past outside; she gave the waiter a faint smile. I have a strong aversion to redheads, but this one was worth looking at. We were seated below her line of sight, so we could peruse the goods unobtrusively. She was a girl who made the best of herself: a well-fitted soft green tunic above thongy shoes, earrings of cascading crescents, a chalk-white face highlighted with purplish coloring, eyes lengthened and widened with charcoal, and elaborate plaits of copper-colored hair. Her eyes were particularly fine. She walked with a confident swagger, kicking the hem of her skirt so her jingling anklets showed. She looked as though for the right reward she might show off the ankles they decorated, plus the knees and all the rest.

She also looked unlike anyone I had ever seen—though her best feature was that set of rolling brown eyes which did seem familiar. I never forget a shape either, however differently it may be trussed and decorated when I see it a second time. When the girl vanished somewhere opposite I found myself quietly finishing my drink. I said unexcitedly to Placidus, "I'm going across to check on Selia again. You stay here and keep my seat warm."

Then I hooked my thumbs casually in my belt and strolled over to the lodging house.

FORTY-EIGHT

The fat woman had gone. Nobody was about.

The building occupied a long, narrow plot running away from the street. It was arranged on two floors either side of an open-roofed passageway, then widening into a small terminal courtyard with a well in it. This was sufficiently confined to keep out the sun at hot times of year. At intervals pots were hung on the walls, but the plants in them had died from neglect.

The girl lived on the upper level over the yard, where there was a rickety wooden balcony which I reached by an uneven flight of steps at the far end. Outside her door was a pulley arrangement to facilitate drawing up water. There were wet drip marks on the balcony rail. A shutter now stood open, one which I remembered had been firmly closed before.

I walked around the balcony the long way, that is on the opposite side from Selia's room. I trod easily, trying not to let the planking creak. When I came back to the part above the entrance passageway a bridge crossed the gap; I guessed nobody used it much for the whole thing sagged worryingly beneath my weight. I moved on gently to her room. She had killed, or tried to kill, two men, so she had thrown away her right to modesty: I went straight in and didn't knock.

The red wig lay on a table. the green tunic hung on a hook. The dancer was naked apart from a loincloth. As she turned to stare at me angrily, she made an appealing sight.

She had one foot on a stool and was anointing her body with what I took to be olive oil. When I stepped through the doorway she deliberately carried on doing it. The body that received the attention was well worth pampering. The spectacle nearly made me forget what I was there for.

"Well don't be formal! Treat my place as your own!" She threw back her head. Her neck was long. Her own hair, which was an ordinary brown, had been pinned in a flat coil, close against her head. Her body was hard to ignore.

I cast a rapid glance around the place: one room, with a narrow bed. Most of the clutter was on the table, and it was predominantly female stuff. Occasional eating implements were jumbled in among the hairpin pots, cream jars, combs and perfume vials.

"Don't be shy; I've seen nudity before. Besides, we're old friends."

"You're no friend of mine!"

"Oh come," I remonstrated sadly. "Don't you remember me?"

She did pause, with one palm held flat to the oil flask. "No."

"You should do. I'm the man who went home from the Society of Olive Oil Producers of Baetica safely in one piece—because I had acquired a large amphora of fish-pickle, with two slaves to carry it."

She put her foot down on the floor. Her hand still moved slowly upon her gleaming skin, and as she massaged in the oil it was extremely difficult not to stare. She appeared not to notice that she was transfixing me. But the care with which she oiled her breasts told me she knew all right.

I waited calmly. When she jumped for the meat knife that lay among the cosmetic pots I grabbed at her wrist. It would have been perfectly effective, had she not been so slippery.

FORTY-NINE

Luckily for me the wrist I had seized was much smaller than my own; somehow I had encircled it. I felt her bones twisting in my grip and the knife flashed wickedly, but her weapon hand stayed held fast. It wouldn't last. Her all-over lubrication made her impossible to restrain for long.

I kept her at arm's length as she kicked out. Dancers have legs to reckon with. She was strong, but I had the advantage. Barging her shin with mine, I forced her to move back against the wall, making sure the corner of the table bruised her thigh. I banged her arm on the wall to shake the knife free. Spitting, she kept her grip on it. I thought of heaving her off, to spin her round and thrash her back into the wall, but she was so well oiled I would lose my hold. I smashed her elbow on the wall again. She gasped, and struggled to break free.

Her free hand cast behind me, grabbing at a soapstone pot to brain me with. There was no choice. I try hard to avoid naked women who are not my own property, but I had to protect myself. I went in close, throwing my body hard against hers then turning in my shoulder so I could break her hold on the knife two-handedly. This time I did it. The blade clanged to the floor. Instantly she went limp, then flexed herself violently. Her arm escaped from my grip.

I still had her pinned against the wall, but her writhing body was so slippery it was like trying to catch a live fish. I brought up one knee and stopped her reaching the knife again. She squirmed away from me, dropped to the floor, scuttled under the table, then stood up and tilted it. Vases and boxes crashed to the ground, in a hail of broken glass, colored powders, and thick scents. It didn't stop me, and dropping the heavy table lost her the second it took me to leap forwards and grab her by the only part I could circle with both hands: her throat.

"Keep still or I'll throttle you until your eyes pop out!" She thought about fighting. "Believe me!" I warned again, kicking out with one foot to free it from a tangle of cheap jewelry. To reinforce the message I was squeezing hard. She was choking. I was out of breath. She saw her situation was desperate. She stood still. I felt her jaw clench as she gritted her teeth, no doubt vowing to say nothing and bite me if she could.

"Well this is intimate!" Her eyes told me what I could do with myself. I was aware of her hands twitching, ready to go for me. I tightened my grip. She saw sense. "Now why is it that when I end up in the arms of beautiful girls with no clothes on they are always trying to kill me?" Her response was a look full of hatred; well, the question had been rhetorical. While she glared, I suddenly wrenched her around so her back was against me and I felt less vulnerable to frontal attack. I kept one arm tight across her throat; with the other hand I was reaching for the knife that I kept down my boot. That improved the situation. I let her see what it was. Then I tucked the tip under one of her ribs so she could feel how sharp the blade was.

"Now we're going to talk."

She made some sort of angry gurgle. I increased my pressure on her windpipe and she fell quiet again. I edged her over to the table that she had conveniently cleared, then I pushed her face down. I was lying on top of her. This possessed some attractions, though I was too preoccupied to enjoy it. Holding down women is nearly impossible; they're too supple. The gods know how rapists manage it—well they use terror, which on Selia had no effect. I tweaked my knife against her well-oiled side. "I can scar you for life, or just kill you. Remember that."

"Damn you."

"Is Selia your real name?"

"Get lost."

"Tell me who you work for."

"Anyone who pays."

"You're an agent."

"I'm a dancer."

"No, Spanish dancers come from Gades. Who sent you to Rome?"

"I can't remember."

"This knife advises you to try."

"All right; kill me with it then."

"Very professional! Believe me, real dancers give in much more easily. Who asked you to perform at the dinner that night?"

"I was the official entertainment."

"That was Perella. Stop lying. Who paid you for what you and your two cronies did afterwards?"

"The same person."

"Oh you admit you committed murder then?"

"I admit nothing."

"I want his name."

"You want your balls hacked off with a disemboweling knife!"

I sighed. "I'm sorry you're taking this uncooperative attitude."

"You'll be more than sorry, Falco." She was probably right there.

"Now listen! You may have killed Valentinus, but you underestimated what a thick skull Anacrites had. Simply cracking the Chief Spy's head will have worse consequences than killing him outright."

"You're never working for Anacrites?" She sounded surprised.

"You did leave him with a slight headache; he was allowed sick leave for a day or two. So you're right. Anacrites is not commissioning. I'm working for a man called Laeta—" I thought I felt her start. "Keep still, I said."

"Why?" jeered Selia. "What are you worried about?"

"Not a lot. I'm a professional too. Crushing a beautiful naked female on a table has its lighter side—but on the whole I like my women right side up, and I certainly like them affectionate."

"Oh you're all heart!"

"A complete softie. That's why you're face down against a plank of wood covered in bruises, and my knife's in your ribs."

"You're an idiot," she told me. "You don't know anything about the mess you're in. Hasn't it struck you that I'm working for Claudius Laeta—just like you!"

That sounded all too plausible. I preferred not to consider it. There was no immediate need to do so: we both abandoned comparing notes on our devious employer. Two things happened. I was unaware of lessening my grip on the dancer, yet somehow she wriggled suddenly and slithered sideways away from me. Then somebody else seized hold of my hair from behind and pulled me backwards in excruciating pain.

FIFTY

I thought you would never get here!" the girl snarled angrily.

Whoever had hauled me upright had me bowed over backwards with a torsion as tight as the throwing sling on a rock-hurling artillery mule. Once I realized, I began to react. Hair grows again. I wrenched my head free. I must have left behind a good handful of my bouncing curls, but now I could move. My eyes streamed, but I was bucking and thrashing. Of course he snatched at my wrist in the same way that I had previously grabbed Selia to make her drop her own knife; he was behind me so I closed my elbow against my side, resisting him.

Blows rained on my spine and kidneys, then I heard somebody else entering the room. The girl meanwhile was rubbing her bruises and finding a tunic as carelessly as if the rest of us were just flies buzzing around the window frame. Her bodyguards could do the work now.

I had managed to twist free. I jerked around so I could see my assailants: the two dark-skinned musicians from the dinner on the Palatine. It was the elder who had attacked me; he was wiry enough, and full of malice and energy. The other, more youthful, was burly, well-muscled and mean-eyed. I was in deep trouble. These were the men who had smashed in the head of Valentinus and left Anacrites for dead. I was fighting for my life.

"Sort him out!" Selia ordered. She had pulled some clothing over her head, but left it around her neck. She had paid these toughs sufficient to be sure they would kill for her. They looked as if they would enjoy it too. So much for the refining effect of music. Apollo was a thug, according to these two.

It was too small a room to contain four of us. We were close enough to smell each other's breath. Impetuously Selia herself went for my knife arm, grabbing hold and biting me. The others plunged at me too and with three to contend with in such a confined space, I was soon overpowered. Selia took possession of my knife. Her assistants each had me brutally by an arm; they were turning to rush me forwards against the farther wall when the girl complained, "Oh not in here!" A person of taste: she shrank from having my brains spread over her living space.

As they manhandled me towards the door I grunted in annoyance, "Just tell me this, Selia—if we're both working for Laeta why in Hades does he want you to remove me?" I ignored the two brutes, who for a moment stopped bundling me out.

"You're in my way," Selia responded offhandedly.

"Only because I don't know what's going on!" I was stalling. This group had killed. In no circumstances were they on the same side as me. "Anyway you take too many risks!"

"If you say so."

"The Parilia!" I reminded her. "You should have been lying low, not showing your face."

"Oh yes?"

"And I went to a daft lads' party afterwards where everyone knew you had gone home to Hispalis. You leave too many tracks. I found you—and so can anyone."

The heavies again started dragging me out, but Selia halted them with a raised hand. "Who's looking?" she demanded.

At least I was collecting my strength. The longer I could hold off any final battering, the more hope of escape. I ignored Selia's question. "If you really are a home-loving Hispalis girl, however did Laeta discover you?"

"I went to Rome, for someone else. I'm a dancer. I went to Rome to dance."

"So it wasn't Laeta who sent you to that dinner in your little Diana costume, then?"

"Find out, Falco!"

"Did Laeta order you to attack Anacrites and his man?"

"Laeta gives me a free hand." I noticed it wasn't an answer.

"You're in trouble," I warned her. "Don't trust Laeta to support you if the water heats up too much in his own pot."

"I trust no one, Falco." She had pulled down her dress and was calmly applying new paint to her face. She stroked it on with a spatula, swiftly and thickly. Before my eyes she was turning back into the archetypal Spanish castanet girl (the one who only exists in men's dreams), the blue-black hair she wore for dancing for Romans had been combed out on a stand. When she bent forwards and pulled it on the effect was as dramatic as when I saw her on the Palatine.

"I hope Laeta paid you. You won't see a sestertius if you're living out here."

"I've been paid," she said, perhaps glancing at the heavies to reassure them she would look after them too.

"So what in the name of Olympus is Laeta trying to do?"

"You tell me."

"Discredit Anacrites? Take over the spy's work?"

"Looks like it."

"Why does he need two of us?"

"One wasn't good enough."

"Or wasn't ever meant to be! You mean Laeta's used me as a noodle—and he's using you to hamper me!"

"An easy game, Falco!"

"Easier than playing around with palace politics. But you're lying anyway. Laeta knows Anacrites is a cheap buffoon who could be put out of action with a bit of simple intrigue. Cracking heads wasn't necessary. Laeta's not vicious. He's not crude. He's quite clever enough to outwit Anacrites, and depraved enough as a bureaucrat to enjoy finessing him. Laeta wants a classic power struggle. He wants Anacrites alive, so he *knows* he has lost the game. Where's the art, otherwise?"

"You're just delaying," Selia said. "Get him out of here!"

I shrugged and made no attempt to cause trouble. The two musicians walked me onto the balcony. Just outside I glanced behind and said calmly to the older one on my left, "She's calling you."

He turned back. I threw myself forwards and spun my shoulder hard. The man on my right was pitched straight over the balcony.

The other yelled. I kneed him impolitely. He folded up; I chopped down on his neck with a double fist. He crumpled to the ground and I kicked him in the ribs until he lay still.

Below in the courtyard I had heard the crash and a cry as the first man landed. It was only one floor down, so he might still be mobile. There were confused sounds which I could not interpret, but by then Selia had rushed out.

First she flung a tambourine, edge on. I parried with my arm, but it cut my wrist. I hauled up the man at my feet and held him as a human shield while she then threw a knife—mine. He flung himself aside, dragging me. The blade clattered on the boarding, then with me cursing it tumbled over the edge.

The girl came at us; I barged the man into her. She dropped another weapon, then suddenly muttered something and ran towards the stairs. Her groaning bodyguard came back to life enough to grab the new weapon. It was the kind of cleaver girls who live alone keep in their rooms to shorten flower stems, hack up pig carcasses and discourage lovers from leaving early. I'd be afraid to have one in the house.

He set about me again, keeping himself between me and the girl. It was her I wanted; we all knew that.

I managed to dodge the swooping blade. Then I let off a high kick, flummoxed him, and shoved him backwards. I set off around the balcony, sprinting lightly on my toes. I was going the long way, the way I had first come to Selia's room.

The elderly fellow was tougher than he looked. I could hear him chasing after me. At the passageway bridge I slowed my steps. He was gaining, which made him pound harder to catch me. Once across, I turned back just in time to see the bridge give way. With a crack of splitting timber, the musician fell through. The wood was not rotten, just too flimsy for its intended purpose. He was left dangling, trapped between the broken planking. Blood dripped from his wounds where he was impaled on huge splinters of wood. When he tried to move he screamed.

To save time, I flipped over the balcony, clung to the rail, lowered myself as far as possible then dropped. I had just missed the well. (I had forgotten about that.) Neat work, Falco.

In the courtyard to my astonishment I found Placidus, fighting the other bodyguard, who was limping and nursing a broken arm from his fall. Placidus was keeping him under control, though only just. The procurator himself had a long gash in his side. My dagger, which had fallen from the balcony, lay near them, still bloody.

"The girl—" Placidus gasped, as I took over and stopped his opponent with a well-aimed kick. I got one arm around Placidus and leaned him on the well. "I could have handled this one—" If he was a freedman now, he had been a slave once. Even in the imperial palace that meant a sordid early life. He knew how to take care of himself. "I just didn't expect her. The girl slashed me before I could square up to her—"

"She got away?" I asked, retrieving my knife. He nodded disconsolately. I was peeling back his tunic gently to reveal the wound. "Save your strength. Don't talk. We've caught these two gruesome characters anyway." I was annoyed about losing Selia, but I did not let it show.

Placidus had put himself out for me. He looked pleased with his success, but he had paid a dangerous penalty. His wound was deep and nasty. "What's the damage, Falco?"

"You'll live—though once the pain sets in you're going to know all about this."

"Ah well, the scar should be interesting."

"I can think of easier ways to excite rumors!"

"I'll be all right. You go after the girl."

If we had been anywhere respectable I would have done. I could not abandon Placidus in this seedy area where the dancer might have friends. A crowd was gathering. They were silent and still; I would not trust them. No one offered assistance but at least nobody tried to interfere.

I made the man with the limp stand up and walk ahead of me with my knife against his back. Supporting the procurator with my free arm, I slowly set off on a difficult trip to find the nearest guardpost of the local watch.

Fortunately it was not too far. Rather than have Placidus faint at their feet, folk did give us directions. The glare I gave them persuaded them to tell us right.

We limped there safely. My prisoner was locked in the cell. Officers went off to bring in his companion. Placidus was carefully stretched out, bathed and bandaged; at first he protested volubly, then he suddenly passed out and made no more fuss. I led a search that lasted the rest of the day, but Selia had slipped away somewhere. I am a realist. She could have gone in any direction, and would be miles from Hispalis by now.

At least I knew something about her. She had lied about most of it, but sinister patterns were emerging. Events had moved on. Suspects had laughed at me and beaten me up, but I had sized up the opposition—including the man who had commissioned me.

If her claim to be working for Laeta was right, Selia and I took our wages from the same soiled hands. I had no real job; I could not rely on being paid. On these terms I was not even sure I wanted to be.

It was time to return to Corduba. I badly needed to discuss all this with Helena. And if she agreed, I could ditch the whole filthy business and go home to Rome.

FIFTY-ONE

I rode back to Corduba even faster than I had come. I was glad I was not journeying in July or August, but even so the weather was uncomfortable enough to remind me this was the hottest part of Spain. Around me, covering the alluvial plain to the south of the River Baetis, lay the finest olive groves in Baetica. For oil rather than fruit, maybe the best olives in the world. Beyond the river even in the baking sun all the hills were green. Trees and shrubs flourished. I was crossing a bowl of abundant fertility, yet my mood remained grim.

For one thing, I was worried about Helena. There was nothing I could do about that. At least I was on my way back to her.

And I now had a new problem. I had not told poor Placidus, who was in enough misery with his wound, but what I had learned from the dancer filled me with dread. If Selia really had been working for Laeta, the attacks in Rome made one kind of sense: I was involved in a power struggle—as I had all along suspected—between two arms of palace officialdom. It looked darker and more bloody than I would have expected, but it was internal.

Whatever was going on here in Baetica might not matter to anybody back in Rome. The oil cartel could merely be the excuse Laeta and Anacrites used to perpetuate their rivalry. Or Laeta had used it on his own. Much as I loathed Anacrites, he was beginning to look like an innocent victim. He might have been just doing his job, decently attempting to protect a valuable commodity. Perhaps he was unaware of the threat from Laeta. When I saw them together at the dinner they had sparred verbally, but there was no sense that the spy suspected Laeta might actually be preparing to pick him off. Him and his best agent—a man I reckoned I would have liked.

I could walk away from the palace intrigue—but the dead Valentinus would continue to haunt me.

The scenario stank. I was furious that I had ever become involved. Helena's father had warned me that whatever was happening among the Palatine magnates would be something to avoid. I should have known all along how I was being used. Well of course I did know, but I let it happen anyway. My mission was a bluff—if Laeta hired Selia to attack Anacrites, he must have brought me in merely to cover his own tracks. He could pretend publicly that he was searching for culprits, though all he wanted was power. He must have believed I would fail to find Selia. Maybe he even supposed I would be so entranced with the importance of investigating a provincial cartel, I would forget to look for her at all. Did he hope I would be killed off in the attempt? Well, thanks, Laeta! Anacrites at least would have shown greater faith in my tenacity.

Perhaps instead Laeta wanted *me* to kill *Selia*, because she would know how he came to power.

As for the quaestor and his bumptious senator father, they looked like mere adjuncts to this story. I could only warn the Emperor that Quinctius Attractus was assuming too much power in Baetica. The proconsul would have to deal with Quadratus. I was treading on sliding scree, and I could risk nothing more. No informer accuses a senator of anything unless he is sure of support. I was sure of nothing.

I decided I did not want Claudius Laeta to acquire more power. If Anacrites died, Laeta could take over his empire; once in charge, whether he was bothered about the price of olive oil looked doubtful to me. I had heard for myself how Laeta was obsessed with the trappings of success with which Anacrites had surrounded himself: the suite in the palace of the Caesars, the villa at Baiae. Laeta's personal ambition looked clear enough. And it relied on undetected maneuvering. He certainly would not want me popping up in Rome to say *he* had paid Selia to eliminate Anacrites. Vespasian would never stand for it.

Maybe I would have to use this knowledge to protect myself. I was perfectly prepared to do so, to secure my own position—yet dear gods, the last thing I really wanted at this point in my life was a powerful politician nervous about what I might know.

I would have to fight him ruthlessly. It was his own fault. He was leaving me no choice.

I spent two days riding hard with muscles that had already ached and a brain that swam. I was so tired when I reached the mansio at Corduba I nearly fell onto a pallet and stayed there overnight. But I needed to see Helena. That kept me on my feet. I recovered the horse Optatus had lent me to come into town, and forced myself to stay upright on it all the way home to the Camillus estate.

Everything looked normal. It was dark, so the watchdogs set up a hectic yammering at my approach. When I led the horse to the stable a slave appeared to look after him, so I was spared that. The slave looked at me shiftily, as most villa rustica staff do. Without a word, I left my baggage roll and limped slowly to the house.

Nobody was about. A few dim lamps lit the corridor. I was

too weary to call out. I went to the kitchen, which was where I expected to find everyone. Only the cook and other house-slaves were there. They all froze when I appeared. Then Marius Optatus broke in through another door opposite.

He was holding a leash; he must have been to investigate what had disturbed the dogs. His face was gray, his manner agitated even before he saw me.

"Falco, you're back!"

"What's wrong?"

He made a vague, helpless gesture with the hand that held the dog leash. "There has been a tragic accident—"

I was already on my way, running like a madman to the room I shared with Helena.

FIFTY-TWO

Marcus!"

She was there. Alive. Larger than ever; still pregnant. Whole. Sound.

I fell to my knees beside the chair as she struggled to rise and took her in my arms. "Oh dear gods . . ." My breath rasped in huge painful gulps.

Helena was crying. She had been crying before I crashed into the room. Now instead she was calming me, holding my face between her hands, her light rapid kisses on my eyes both soothing and greeting me.

"Optatus said there had been an accident—"

"Oh my darling! It's neither of us." She laid my hand upon the unborn child, either to comfort me or herself, or to give the baby notice that I was home again. It seemed a formal, archaic gesture. I tickled the child and then kissed her, both with deliberate informality.

"I should bathe. I stink and I'm filthy—"

"And half dead on your feet. I had a feeling—I've ordered hot water to be kept for you. Shall I come and scrape you down?"

"That's more pleasure than I can cope with . . ." I rose from my kneeling position beside her wicker chair. "Stay and rest. But you'd better tell me about this accident."

"Later."

I drew a finger across her tear-stained cheek. "No, now."

Helena said nothing. I knew why she was being stubborn. I had left her. Something terrible had happened, which she had had to cope with on her own, so now I had lost my rights.

We gazed at one another quietly. Helena looked pale, and she had her hair completely loose, which was rare for her. Whatever had happened, part of her unhappiness was because she had been alone here without me. Well, I was home now.

In the dim light of a single oil lamp, Helena's eyes were nearly black. They searched my face for my own news, and for whatever I was feeling towards her. Whenever we had been apart there was this moment of readjustment; the old challenge was reissued, the new peace had to be reaffirmed.

"You can tell me I shouldn't have gone away—but do it after you explain what's been happening."

She sighed. "You being here wouldn't have changed anything. There has just been a terrible accident. It's young Rufius," she told me. "Rufius Constans. He was working on an oil press on his grandfather's estate when one of the quernstones slipped and crushed him. He was alone when it must have happened. By the time somebody found him he was dead."

"Yes, that's a dreadful thing to have happened . . ." Constans had been young and full of promise; I felt bitterly depressed. Helena was expecting my next reaction. I tipped my head on one side. "He was alone? Nobody else was with him?"

"No, Marcus," she replied softly. I knew that, trained by me to be skeptical in every situation, she had already spent time wondering, just as I was doing now. "No; I can see what you are thinking. But there is no possibility of mischief."

"No special crony lending Constans a hand with the oil press?"

"No. Quinctius Quadratus was out of action; I can vouch for that myself."

I took her word. I was too tired to concern myself with how she knew.

I held out my hand and now she let herself take it. "Have you been fighting?" Helena could always spot the damage.

"Just a few knocks. Did you miss me?"

"Badly. Was your trip useful?"

"Yes."

"That makes it all right then."

"Does it? I don't think so, love!" Suddenly unable to bear being apart from her, I tightened my grip to pull her up from the chair. "Come and wield a strigil for me, sweetheart. I'll never reach my own back tonight."

We had edged around my guilt and her withdrawal. Helena Justina held herself against me for a moment, her soft cheek pressed to my stubbled one, then she took my arm, ready to walk with me to the bathhouse. "Welcome home," she whispered, and I knew she meant it now.

FIFTY-THREE

The bathhouse at the villa was designed for hardy old republicans. I won't say it was crude, but if anyone hankered for the unluxurious days of dark, narrow bathing places with mere slits for windows, this was ideal. You undressed in the cold room. Unguents were stored on a shelf in the warm room, which was certainly not very warm at night; you got up a sweat by vigorously shaking an oil jar to try to dislodge the congealed contents.

A single stoker kept the fire alight and brought water in buckets. He had gone for his supper but was summoned back. Since the bath was reserved for Optatus, Helena and myself, plus any visitors, he seemed glad of a rare chance to show off his skills. We needed him this evening. The promised hot water had been used up by someone else.

"That's just typical!" Helena stormed moodily. "I've had three days of this, Marcus, and I'm ready to scream."

I was stripping, very slowly. I hung my foul togs on my favorite hook, tossing aside a blue tunic that had been left by some previous bather. Nobody was in evidence now, which was just as well. Helena insisted on kneeling to unstrap my boots for me. I helped her upright, then kept hold of her. "What's the matter, fruit?"

She took a deep breath. "I have about four different events to relate; I've been trying to keep them neatly arranged in my mind—"

"You're so organized!" I threw back my head, smiling at the anticipated luxury of listening to Helena. "A lot has been happening? You mean Constans?"

"Oh . . ." Helena closed her eyes. The young man's death had affected her profoundly. "Oh Marcus, I was with his sister and Aelia Annaea when the news was brought; I feel I'm part of it."

"But you said it was an accident. Truly?"

"It had to be. I told you; he was alone. It was such a shock. Everyone is very distressed. His sister is so young. I have not seen his grandparents, but we've all been imagining how distraught they must be—" She stopped, and suddenly became weepy again. Helena rarely gave way like that.

"Start from the beginning," I said, stroking her neck.

Taking a lamp, we walked through a heavy door into the so-called warm room. This part of the bathhouse was deadened to sound by the thickness of its walls, though somewhere at the far end of the hotter room I could hear vague shoveling sounds as the slave began replenishing the fire; the rattling and bumping noises traveled through the floor. Helena Justina rested on the low ledge against one wall as I worried a flask to extract a few dribbles of oil. She had presumably bathed once today, so she retained her undertunic modestly and forwent the full cleansing procedure.

She linked her hands and began rather formally: "The first thing, Marcus, was that I had a letter from home—from my brother Justinus."

"The lad! How is he?"

"Still in love with his actress."

"It's just a crush."

"So it's dangerous! Well, he's been working hard on Aelianus anyway, which he complains cost him a lot of drinks. Aelianus is feeling terribly guilty; his friend Cornelius, the one who wrote the famous secret dispatch, has written from Athens telling Aelianus not to talk about it to anyone called Quinctius."

"But Aelianus had already done that?"

"Apparently."

"He told me he fell out with Quadratus when your father was being cheated over the oil pressing."

"Well, quarrels don't last among lads. But Aelianus now says he and Quadratus did meet in Rome, though it wasn't a success. Their row in Baetica had soured the friendship so by the time of that dinner it had cooled permanently."

"Too late!"

"I'm afraid so. Justinus has found out that Aelianus has been bottling up a disaster. Before he went to the Palace, he had had the report with him at the Quinctius house. He left it with his cloak, and when he collected it the seal looked different. He picked it open again—as he confessed to you, he had actually read it once—the second time the letter had been altered to give a quite different assessment of how serious the cartel was."

I nodded. "So either Quadratus or his father Attractus deliberately tried to underplay the situation. Did Aelianus challenge his pal?"

"Yes, and that was when they quarreled again. Then Aelianus was frightened that he couldn't alter the scroll anymore without making a thorough mess of it, so he just handed it in to Anacrites and hoped everything would be all right." Helena sucked her lip. "I have strong views on Quadratus—which I'll come to next!"

"How has he been annoying you?"

"He'll annoy you too, because we've been landed here with the dreadful bull-necked, spoiled-brat, insensitive rich girls' delight 'Tiberius' himself."

"*Here?*"

"It's your fault."

"Naturally!" I know my place. Helena was clearly furious; I kept hold of the oil flask in case she let fly with it. "Even though I was a hundred miles away?"

"Afraid so." She had the grace to grin at me. I put down the oil flask. Helena Justina had a smile that could freeze all my capillaries. Our eyes met, a glance that was rich with feeling and memory. Only friends can exchange so much, so rapidly. "It was because of your horse, Prancer."

"Prancer belongs to Annaeus Maximus."

"And you lent him to Quadratus and Constans. Quadratus brought him back."

"I told him not to."

"Well, isn't that just like him?" Her voice grated. "And now the irritating creature has come to stay here, where everyone loathes him, and he's using all the bathwater!— If I challenge him about it he will apologize so politely I'll want to hit him with an oven hook. I can't prove that he does it deliberately, but he makes life a trial from morning to night for everyone around him."

I tutted. "He has to be a villain. I'll prove it yet!— But Helena, my heart, you still haven't told me: Why has this social woodlouse become our guest?"

"Your horse threw him. He has hurt his back."

"I won't hear another word against Prancer: the horse has taste!" I cried.

Growing too cold, we both stepped into wooden-soled clogs and braved the steam of the hot room. Helena took a bronze strigil and started scraping me down while I braced my aching limbs against her steady strokes. I could take as much of that as she was prepared to indulge me with, especially now that her mood had softened up.

"So Quadratus is bedridden?"

"No such luck. He can shuffle about. Everywhere Optatus and I try to go, he appears, making himself agreeable."

"That's disgusting!"

"He decided it was courteous to take an interest in my pregnancy. He keeps asking questions I don't want to think about. He's worse than my mother."

"The man's a complete lout. Worse than a girl's mother? That's as low as he can get! By the way, how is your pregnancy?"

"Don't bother, Falco. When you try to take an interest, I know it's all fake."

"You know I'm a fake you can trust."

"You're the fake I'm stuck with, anyway . . ."

She looked tired. I pried the curved strigil from her hand and took over ridding myself of sweat, oil and filth. Then we both sank onto the wooden bench to endure what else we could of the heat. Helena collected the damp strands of her hair and wound them into a clump, holding the weight off the back of her neck.

"Marius Optatus could go out in the fields and olive groves, but I've been stuck with our unwanted guest. I had to talk to him. I had to listen too—unendingly. He is a man. He expects to hold the floor. What he has to say is banal, humorless and predictable. He expects admiration in inverse proportion to content, of course." I was chortling. I loved to hear Helena condemning somebody else.

"Has he made advances to you?" I demanded suspiciously. I knew how I would react if I had Helena Justina to myself for days.

"Of course not."

"He's an idiot then!"

"He regards me as a mother-goddess, I believe. He pours out his heart to me. His heart is about as interesting as a burned cinnamon bun."

"Has he admitted he's a bad boy?"

"He doesn't know," said Helena, summing him up with furious clarity. "Whatever he does, he never even thinks about whether it's right or wrong."

I sucked my lower lip. "No fascinating hopes and joys? No undetected talents?"

"He likes hunting, drinking, wrestling—with opponents who are not too professional—and telling people about the future he has planned."

"He told me how good he was going to be as quaestor."

"He told me the same," she sneered. "I expect he tells everyone."

"I expect some are impressed."

"Oh lots would be," she agreed readily. "People think mere self-confidence equates to nobility."

She fell silent for a moment. "*I'm* confident," I mentioned, since she was obviously thinking it.

"You're confident for good reason. And when that's inappropriate you're filled with doubt. What Quinctius Quadratus lacks is judgment."

We were again silent. The slave had done his duty with a will, and the room quivered with steam now. Wetness streamed over my forehead from the hair flattened on my head. I scooped water from a basin and threw it over my face and chest. Helena was looking very flushed. "You've had enough," I warned her.

"I don't care. I'm just so pleased to be with you, to be talking to you."

It was too hot to touch another person, but I took her hand and we exchanged a slippery embrace.

"Why do we hate him?" I mused after more reflection. "What has he really done? Other people think he's wonderful."

"Other people always will." Helena had clearly had plenty of time to evaluate the hero.

"He's likable."

"That's what makes it so bad; he could be worthwhile, but he's chosen to waste his potential. We hate him because he is bound for success, which he doesn't deserve. He is an empty shell, but that will not prevent him rising."

"His underlings will buoy him up."

"And his superiors will avoid the effort of reporting his inadequacy."

"He'll introduce stupid procedures and make terrible decisions, but by the time the results show he'll have moved on up the ladder and be wreaking havoc somewhere else."

"And he will never be called back to answer for his mistakes."

"It's the system. The system is rotten."

"Then the system must be changed," said Helena.

Left to myself I would have sunk into a heavy sleep, but I managed to rouse us both enough to wash in the warm pool. "So what's the story of poor young Constans?"

"I told you most of it."

"You were with Aelia Annaea?"

"Tolerating Quadratus was becoming too much. Optatus took to finding excuses to ride into Corduba. Aelia and Claudia came to rescue me; we sneaked off in the Annaeus carriage, and then we spent the day at Aelia's house."

"This was today?"

"Yes. Then this afternoon a desperate message came for Claudia Rufina to rush home because of the tragedy. Her brother had been working on the estate; I think maybe there had been some trouble about the life he had been leading—that party you went to with Aelia's brothers has had its repercussions throughout the neighborhood. Anyway, Rufius Constans had promised to reform himself. Hard work was his way of showing it."

"What caused the accident?"

"New stones had been delivered for an oil press, and he went to inspect them. Nobody thought he would attempt to move them on his own. When he failed to return for lunch with his grandmother a servant was sent out, and he was found dead."

"An accident," I repeated.

"Nobody else had been there. As for Quinctius Quadratus, he was here; we all know it. Without question he is unable to ride. He could never have got to the Rufius estate. Besides, why would he harm his young friend?"

I shook my head, unable to suggest an answer. Then I did say, "I saw Rufius Constans before I left. He and his grandfather were at the proconsul's palace, trying to gain an interview."

Helena looked at me. "Intriguing! But you cannot ask Licinius Rufius what they were doing there. He and his wife will be heartbroken over their loss. So much was invested in Constans."

"And so much wasted," I agreed, in my most republican mood.

"They had probably gone to ask the proconsul for support in advancing the young man's career!"

That was not how it had looked to me. The old man had been too urgent in his manner, and the boy too sullen-faced.

Because of the cramped layout of the bathhouse, we had to return through the warm room to reach what passed for a cold plunge. It was in a kind of cupboard to one side, built off the cold room with the cloak-hooks. Even before we pulled back the curtain which concealed the pool, I had an inkling of something suspicious. Then Helena Justina exploded. "Oh really! I don't believe this thoughtlessness!"

I did. Somebody had bathed in the small pool so vigorously they had swooshed almost all of the water out onto the floor. Before I squashed down on the sitting ledge and splashed myself as best I could to cool down in the remnants, I glanced back into the outer room. There were wet footprints everywhere, and the blue tunic I threw on the bench had now disappeared. Whoever had used the cold water must have been lurking in the pool when Helena and I first entered. Whoever it was could have overhead all we said. Luckily the thick doors to the warm rooms would prevent sound emerging once we had passed through them.

Frankly, if it had been Quadratus eavesdropping, I found it hard to care.

I was pretty well incapable of movement now. When I struggled from the pool, dripping sporadically, Helena had to find a towel and dry me down herself.

"So are you going to tell me your own adventures, Marcus?"

"Oh mine are just horses, wine, men's talk, and women in their boudoirs getting undressed." Helena raised her eyebrows and I thought it best to produce a rapid, lightly censored version of my time in Hispalis. She was not best pleased with the part about Selia, I could tell. Being an informer had taught me to recognize growling and grinding of teeth.

"Bad news, Falco."

"I won't have that! I protest I'm innocent."

"I think you made up the whole story." She had guessed that I had pruned it. "What a puzzle your dancer is! Is she the killer? Is she seeking the killer for Laeta? Will her ravishing figure distract you from your family loyalties? Will she beat you up again? Or will she just beat you at your own game?"

I tried not to wince as Helena moved to buff up certain lower regions that preferred softer treatment. "Spare me the exotic massage . . . A procurator called Placidus had a dagger gash that proves what she wanted. Selia was not after my body, unless it was dead. I beat up her guards and captured them; they will stand trial before the proconsul on the basis of a report I've left with the vigiles about that night in Rome. I was supposed to stay—material witness—but I waved my pass from Laeta and pleaded urgent secret work."

"Dry your own feet please," said Helena. "I'm too large to reach—"

"You're adorable. Better than a Syrian bodyslave—"

"When have you been cosseted by a bodyslave?"

"They fling themselves on me all the time. Beautiful girls with terrific hands, and slinky boys with very long eyelashes . . ."

Helena's chin came up. "There's one more thing I haven't told you yet. The cook told me that while I was resting one day a woman came here looking for you."

"Selia?" Was she pursuing me?

"It can't be," Helena informed me coolly, drying her own hair. "This one was here three days ago, Falco—when according to you, you were pinning the unclad Selia to a cosmetics table in Hispalis. I had not realized you were so sought after."

"Oh gods! You know what this means: I'm not just being beaten up by one female agent—Anacrites' special charmer wants her turn as well!"

I was so depressed that Helena relented. She kissed me, fairly gently. Then she took me by the hand again, and led me away on stumbling feet to bed.

FIFTY-FOUR

Grief-stricken women seem to make beelines for informers. It must be our comforting manner.

"You have to help me!" wailed Claudia Rufina.

I was very tired. Normally I could mop tears, straighten a mourning veil, and stop hiccups by giving a sudden shock by way of loud noises, cold keys down the cleavage, or an unexpected pinch on the backside. Today I just sighed.

"Of course he will!" Helena soothed the distressed young lady. "Marcus Didius is deeply sorry about what happened to Constans; he will help you if he can."

I had been left to sleep in, but still felt like a half-stuffed cushion. After days in the saddle my spine, and all the parts attached to it, were on fire. I needed to be placed in the tender care of my trainer Glaucus and his fiendish masseur from Tarsus, but they were many hundreds of miles away in Rome, and a great deal of the distance between us was sea.

Worse, when I had crawled into the kitchen this morning the breakfast which the aged cook had lovingly prepared for me had been devoured by Quadratus. Of course the old dear rushed to bring me another plateful, but it was not the same. So let's be literal about this: my mood was absolutely foul.

I held up a hand like a masterful orator. Claudia Rufina fell silent, though Helena sniffed; she hated sham.

"Helena Justina is correct about the deep sympathy I feel towards you and your family. Nothing can mitigate the untimely death of a promising youth with the Empire at his feet." And so much money, I thought. I was extremely tired. My mood was truly low.

"Thank you," said Claudia, catching me out by responding with dignity.

"You are a sensible young woman and I believe you will respect frankness." I was not normally this rough. I noticed Helena's eyebrows shoot up. Guilt increased my bad temper. "Excuse me if this sounds harsh: I came to Hispania on a difficult mission. I received no assistance—no assistance at all—from the dignitaries of Corduba, including your own family. I have still to solve a murder in Rome, and write a long report on certain commercial matters here. I have to condense my efforts into far too little time, in order to be able to return to Italy before Helena Justina gives birth." We all glanced at Helena; by now she looked so large it seemed likely we were expecting twins. "Claudia Rufina, this is no moment for me to take on a private commission, especially when it's fairly clear we're discussing a very sad accident."

"Besides which," muttered Helena, "Marcus has had his breakfast eaten by that young man of whom everyone thinks so highly."

"Tiberius?" Claudia was looking down that unfortunate nose of hers. She still seemed drawn to the handsome and eligible quaestor—yet her expression had a closed look, as if her attitude might be changing.

"Yes, Tiberius!" Helena's smile was like the benign glance of a sibyl just before she prophesied universal war.

"Oh," said Claudia. Then she added in her serious way, "I

came in Grandfather's carriage. Would you like me to take Tiberius away?"

"That would be extremely kind," Helena answered. "You see, I am being frank too today."

"It's no trouble," replied Claudia quietly. "I would like a chance to talk to him anyway." That was when I started worrying about Claudia.

I was surveying our visitor more gently. She wore a dark veil, though she had it thrown around her casually as if a maid had persuaded her at the last minute. She had left the maid at home, traveling to see us set-faced and quite alone. Her gown was the blue one I had seen before, less neatly cinched in. Her hair was dressed as normal in a tight, plain style that emphasized the large shape of her nose. As a wealthy heiress she ought to be enjoying herself in elaborate funeral drapes pinned together with onyx jewelry. Instead she could be genuinely abstracted by grief.

"I think we'll send Tiberius home in our own carriage," I disagreed.

Helena looked annoyed. She was dying to be rid of him. "Marcus, Claudia Rufina said she wishes to speak to him."

"What about, Claudia?" I asked crisply.

Claudia looked me straight in the eye. "I want to ask him where he was when my brother died."

I looked straight back. "He was here. He is too badly hurt to ride. When he first took his fall, Helena Justina insisted that a doctor look at him. We know his injury is disabling."

Claudia's eyes dropped. She looked miserable and confused. She did not think of asking us why anyone should doubt that Quadratus had been hurt, or why we had already taken trouble to work out for ourselves that he had an alibi. She might have an inkling of our own doubts about him, but she still shrank from the full implications.

Helena linked her hands on her stomach. "Tell us why you came to see Marcus Didius."

"He investigates," Claudia declared with a proud tone. "I wished to hire him to discover how Constans was killed."

"Don't you believe what you have been told about it?" I asked.

Once again Claudia defied me with her stare. "No, I don't."

I ignored the drama. "Does your grandfather know that you have come to me?"

"I can afford to pay you!"

"Then be businesslike and answer the question I asked."

Claudia was growing up almost before our eyes. "My grandfather would be furious. He forbids any discussion of what happened. So I didn't tell him I was coming here, or why."

I quite liked her in this mood. She was young and spoiled, but she was taking the initiative. Helena had noticed my change of expression, and she was looking less critical. As gently as I could, I explained to the girl, "Look—people come to me all the time claiming that their relatives have died in suspicious circumstances. They are usually wrong about it. Most people who die unnaturally have been killed by close members of their family, so I don't get asked for help because they're hiding the truth. When I am asked to investigate I almost always discover that the person died because their time was up, or in an honest accident."

Claudia Rufina took a deep, slow breath. "I understand."

"It will be hard to face losing Constans, but you may just have to accept that he is tragically gone."

She was struggling to seem reasonable. "You won't help me."

"I didn't say that." She looked up eagerly. "Something brought you here today when you ought to have been grieving, and comforting your grandmother. Something troubled you sufficiently to drive you from home on your own; I take that seriously, Claudia. Tell me why you feel suspicious."

"I don't know." She blushed. At least she was honest. That was a rare treat in a client.

I had spent large amounts of time dealing with women who were holding back in one situation or another. I waited. I could tell Helena Justina thought I was being over-stern. I was just far too tired to be messed about.

Claudia Rufina glanced at Helena for encouragement then said firmly: "I believe my brother was murdered. There is a reason, Marcus Didius. I think Constans knew something about what you are investigating. I believe he intended to reveal what he knew, so he was killed to stop him talking to the authorities."

There were a number of questions I might have gone on to ask her, but just as she had finished speaking Tiberius Quinctius Quadratus (in a fetching blue tunic that I last saw in the bathhouse) tapped on the door politely—in case we were discussing anything private—then as we all fell abruptly silent he strolled into the room.

FIFTY-FIVE

He went straight to the girl. Considering he had admitted to me that the public were wrongly convinced he would marry her, it might have been kinder to keep his distance. But he was murmuring shock and regret. Then as Claudia collapsed in tears, he stooped over her chair, holding one of her hands and with his other arm gently around her hunched shoulders.

Young men are not normally so good with the bereaved. Maybe Helena and I were wrong about him. It is possible to take against someone, then continue to loathe them out of pure prejudice. Maybe Quadratus was a perfectly well-meaning lad, with a kind heart . . .

On the other hand, Claudia had not been crying until he spoke to her.

Claudia struggled to calm herself. She brushed away the tears and leaned forward to free herself from the young man's solicitous embrace. "Tiberius, I want to ask you something—"

I interrupted her. "If and when Quinctius Quadratus is required to answer questions, I'll deal with it." The girl caught my eye and fell silent. I wondered whether he noticed she might now have doubts about his probity.

Quadratus straightened up, remembering to put a hand to his sprained back. He was rather pale. His good looks were strong enough to take it. His physique was too sturdy for him to look anything other than bouncingly fit. "Falco, it's perfectly obvious you believe I have done wrong somewhere. I would like to answer your questions and clear things up!" Very good. Spoken like an innocent man, in fact.

"I have nothing to ask you, quaestor."

"You always use my title as if it were an insult . . . I wish to have these suspicions removed!"

"You are not under suspicion."

"That is clearly untrue." He sounded so pained, a court would free him on the spot. Juries love a man who goes to the trouble of bad acting. "This is all so unjust, Falco. It seems I cannot move in Baetica without incurring censure. Even the proconsul seems disinclined to work with me—I suppose he thinks I was appointed through influence, not on merit. But is it my fault if my family has strong connections with Baetica? I was as qualified for this quaestorship as any man in Rome!"

"That is perfectly true," I declared. So it was. Idiots with no sense of ethics are elected to the Senate every day. Some of them are bound to get dumped in important financial posts. "But be lenient," I teased him. "You do meet the occasional eccentric governor who criticizes his quaestor on the grounds that the lad has read Plato's *Academy* yet can't tell which way up an abacus should stand."

Quadratus was letting himself get snappy: "There are very competent people to do the sums, Falco!" True. And just as well, when the man who should be making decisions on the basis of those sums was unable to understand what the figures meant or whether his staff had fiddled them—and when he had told me he did not think there was any point in trying anyway. Quadratus ran his hands through his fine head of hair, looking troubled. "I have done nothing wrong."

I smiled. "Criminals say that every day. It makes life very hard for innocent men: all the good speeches are used up."

Quadratus frowned. "So where does that put me?"

I assumed an expression of surprise. I was enjoying myself. It was time to force the issue too: "Doing your job, I suggest." If my doubts about Laeta's purely personal interest were right, there was no point expecting him to pursue the Quinctii once he had snatched Anacrites' position. I may as well give this one a chance to damn himself in office. "Why not prove the proconsul wrong? You came to Baetica to fill the quaestorship. The efficient management of your function is the best way to demonstrate your quality. Just tell him hunting's lost its allure, and you're back in harness. Either he'll accept it with good grace, or he'll have to dismiss you and you can go to Rome to fight your case officially."

He looked at me as if I had just revealed the secrets of eternity. "By Jove, I will! You are right, Falco!" He beamed. The transformation had been slick. No longer the suffering accused, he was so used to his family brazenly grabbing whatever they wanted, he now burst with confidence that he could force the proconsul to act as he desired. The coming confrontation might be more interesting than Quadratus realized. "So you're not hounding me, after all?"

I smiled. Let him think that. "First, quaestor, I shall place my carriage at your disposal to return you to your father's estate."

"Of course; you must be sick of me. I'm sorry to be a burden. I've been looked after splendidly!"

"Think nothing of it," smiled Helena.

"But I can't possibly take your carriage."

"Well you can't ride Prancer again."

"That demon! I ordered Optatus to put him down—"

"Prancer does not belong to Optatus," I interposed coldly. "His owner is Annaeus Maximus, and his current trustee is me. He threw you; that is what horses do. You were hurt; that was your risk when you mounted him. I'm no horseman, but Prancer never gave me any trouble. Maybe you upset the beast."

Swift to back off, he answered quietly, "As you say, Falco." Then he turned to Claudia Rufina. "If I'm leaving, I can easily take you home at the same time."

"I wouldn't hear of it," I told him. If Rufius Constans had known something about the cartel, whoever wanted him silenced might wonder if he had talked about it to Claudia. If Claudia was correct in thinking her brother had been murdered, then she herself needed to be guarded—even from suspects with firm alibis. I was not having her left alone with the son of the man who was running the cartel. "Quadratus, you need to travel the shortest way, for the sake of your sprained back. Helena and I will escort Claudia in her grandfather's carriage—"

"Maybe Tiberius would be more comfortable in that one," suggested Claudia suddenly. "It has a seat that can be pulled out flat so he can lie at full stretch."

I accepted the arrangement. Helena and I would escort Claudia in our own carriage. We would be going by way of the scene of the accident—though I did not tell the charming Tiberius that.

FIFTY-SIX

We all set out together in a procession of two carriages, but I had instructed the Rufius driver to maintain a dead slow speed, in order to protect the wounded gentleman. That enabled Marmarides to move ahead and lose them. I felt better after that, even though for much of the journey we were driving through the spreading fields of the Quinctius estate. I had ridden on top with Marmarides, leaving the women together, though Helena told me afterwards they had made a silent couple, with Claudia Rufina staring numbly into space. She had probably run out of energy and been overtaken at last by shock.

The scene of the young man's death had been marked by a portable altar. It stood at the roadside, so nobody could pass without taking note of the tragedy. On the slab stood flowers, bowls of oil, and wheaten cakes. A slave we found slumbering in the shade of a chestnut tree was supposed to be on guard at the sad shrine.

I remembered the place. The Rufius oil presses were in a yard before the main house; it was attached to what would have been the original farm, a villa rustica in an older style that had been abandoned when the family became prosperous and opted for a larger, more lavish and urban home. The old house was probably now occupied by bailiffs and overseers, though in the daytime it was normally deserted as they were all out in the fields and olive groves. That was how it must have been yesterday when young Rufius came out here.

I jumped down quickly as Marmarides pulled up. The main estate road ran through this yard. Marmarides made the mules wheel and parked the carriage on the shady side, where a horse was already tethered; I patted the animal as I went past and found its flanks warm from a recent ride. A flock of white geese came strutting towards me menacingly, but the slave who was guarding the shrine took a stick and drove them away.

There were various outbuildings into which I glanced: stables and plough stores, a wine cellar, a threshing floor, and finally the oil production area. This was roofed, but the wall that faced the yard comprised huge folding doors, presumably to allow access for carts; in summer they were left standing open.

Two rooms were used for oil production, which was normal on most farms. The outer one contained two presses, as well as vats let into the floor. Here there was no sign of Constans' death. The vats would be used for ladling out the pressed oil, allowing it to rest and separate from its other liquid as many as thirty times. Giant ladles were hung on the walls, along with a large quantity of esparto bags. I was examining these when somebody ducked in through the arch from the adjacent room and said at once, "Those are used to hold the pulp as it is pressed."

It was Marius Optatus. Having seen his horse outside I was expecting him, though I wondered what in Hades he was doing here. He went on quietly, "About twenty-five or thirty bags are piled up, with metal plates between them occasionally to hold them firm—" He gestured to the further room from which he had come. "Constans died in there."

Behind me in the yard I could hear Helena and Claudia dismounting slowly from the carriage, Helena trying to delay the girl so I would have time to view the scene alone. Optatus heard them too and looked concerned at their presence. I stepped into the yard and called to Helena to stay outside. Then I followed Optatus into the inner room.

Light struggled to infiltrate through slits in the north-facing walls. I stood for a moment, accustoming my eyes to the half-dark of the small room. A faint rich smell remained from last year's olives. The confined space was quiet, though we could hear the remote sounds of voices from the yard. The boy's body had been removed. It looked as if everything else had then been abandoned as it was.

"This is where the first crushing takes place," Optatus explained. "The fruit is picked, and carried in deep baskets to the farm. It is washed, sorted, and stored in heaps on a sloping floor for a couple of days. Then it comes here for malaxation. The olives are crushed in this mill, to form a rough pulp, evenly mixed. After that they go next door for the oil to be pressed out."

The crushing mill consisted of a large circular stone tank, into which whole fruit would be dumped. A central column was supposed to support heavy wooden arms which ran through the centers of two vertical hemispherical stones; these were kept slightly apart from each other by a strong rectangular box into which the wooden arms were fixed. It was plated with metal and formed part of the pivotal machinery which turned and supported the grinding stones.

"Poles are attached through each stone," Optatus explained in his steady unemotional way. "Two men walk around the vat and turn the poles slowly, churning the fruit."

"So it's not quite the same as grinding corn?"

"No; cornmills have a conical base and cup-shaped upper stone. This is the opposite—a basin into which the stone rollers fit."

"They move quite loosely?"

"Yes. The aim is to bruise the olives and free the oil, to

make a slippery paste. But you try to avoid breaking the stones; they taste bitter."

We fell silent.

The old worn grinders were propped against a wall, one flat side out, one convex, both stained dark purple and badly misshapen. Pale new concrete had been used to improve the basin. One new stone stood within it in position, already fixed upright to the central pivot though it was held fast on blocks. Both stones had been supplied with brand-new turning poles, their wood still white from the adze.

"You see, Falco," my companion continued levelly, "the roller fits fairly loosely. In use the pole acts merely as a lever to move the stone around in the vat. The stones revolve almost of their own volition, due to the pressure of the fruit." Although the grinder still had wedges beneath it, he leaned on it to show me there was free play. Leverage on the pole would move the stone and tumble the olives against the sides of the basin, but not so tightly that the kernels were split.

I sighed. I fingered a collar, fitting tightly around the pole. "And this washer—which I presume is adjustable—is fixed here on the outside to keep the stone on?"

"It should be." Optatus was grim.

"Then I suppose I can work out what happened to the boy."

"You will!" Presumably Optatus had already thought through events, and did not like the result.

The second grinding stone lay on the ground. A pole had been partly thrust through it, but then smashed by a fall. Even in the dim light I noticed dark marks on the earth floor next to the stone; they looked like dried blood.

"So what do you reckon?" I asked Marius.

"The new grinders arrived two days ago but Licinius Rufius had not yet made arrangements for fitting them. I asked at the house, and apparently he intended to instruct the stonemasons who have been working on his new portico to do this job."

"Why didn't he?"

"He had had a dispute with them about a column they broke, and they had walked off the site."

"That's probably true. I saw the broken column when I was here before."

"Constans seems to have decided to surprise and please his grandfather. All he had said to anyone, however, was that he was coming over to inspect the new rollers before the bill from the supplier was authorized. Dear gods, Falco, if I had known his mind I would have helped him myself! I do wonder if he came over to ask me—but I had gone into Corduba to escape from Quadratus . . ."

"So they say he was alone—yet here we have the first new stone, already hauled into position."

"I have talked to the workers, and none of them was involved."

"This was some job to tackle! Rufius looked a sturdy lad, but he cannot possibly have moved the weight on his own."

"No, Falco. That is why I rode over here today; I just cannot believe what is being said about this accident. It would take at least two men to maneuver and fix these grinding stones—preferably four." The concern in our tenant's voice convinced me his motives were genuine. Like me, he was a practical man. The flaws in the story had astonished and dismayed him so much, he had had to see for himself.

"So what is the fixing procedure, Marius? Each stone has to be lifted into the basin—I presume you get it upright with a fulcrum, and use ropes to heave it in?" I glanced around. Now my eyes were more used to the light, I could make out discarded equipment.

Optatus confirmed how difficult the task would be: "It's heavy work, but raising the stone in the basin is really the easy part. Then the grinder has to be held upright, raised off the bottom, and wedged."

"To set it into position? It churns above the base of the tank?"

"Yes. Setting the height takes strength."

"And courage! You would know if a stone like that rolled over your toe."

"Or fell on your chest," growled Marius, thinking of what happened to young Rufius. "First you decide the position. Then somebody has to climb up and straddle the center pivot to aim the pole into its fixing on the column—I have done that, Falco, and unless you get lucky immediately, it leads to some raw cursing. The man who is to guide the end into position soon hates the man who pushes the pole through the stone. Making a fit is very difficult. You have to give clear directions—which your partner naturally gets wrong."

Optatus painted a neat picture of the joys of teamwork. I wished I could see him trying to organize a couple of my brothers-in-law in some simple household task.

"Maybe Rufius and his helper quarreled . . . Rufius must have been the one on the ground."

"Yes. The stone slipped, and fell out on him," Optatus agreed. "The estate workers told me they found him on his back with his arms outstretched, and the grinding stone right on top of him. It had caved in his chest, and crushed his stomach too."

I flinched. "Let's hope he died at once."

"He could not have lasted long. Even if the stone had been lifted straight off him, he would never have survived."

"The point," I said sourly, "is whether he could have avoided being crushed in the first place."

Optatus nodded. "I inspected the pole, Falco." He bent over it to show me. "Look, the cap has not been fitted. It looks as if very few wedges were being used to position the stone in the basin either; whoever was doing this job must have been a complete amateur—"

"Rufius was very young. He may never have seen rollers installed before."

"It was madness. Unplanned, unthinking incompetence. The grinding stone would have been wobbling around on the lever, very hard to control. Once it started to lean out at an angle, the man on the ground might have jumped out of the way if he was quick, but more likely he found its weight too much to resist."

"Instinct might have made him try to support the stone longer than he should, especially if he was inexperienced. Jupiter, it's ghastly— Wouldn't his friend up above heave on the top rim to pull the stone upright again?"

Optatus was blunt: "Maybe this 'friend' pushed the stone out instead!"

"You're leaping ahead— But that would explain why the 'friend' vanished afterwards."

Optatus became more than blunt; he was angry. "Even if it really was an accident, the friend could have got the stone off Constans afterwards. He would still have died in agony, but he need not have died alone."

"Some friend!"

A noise alerted us, too late perhaps, to the fact that Marmarides had just led in Helena and Claudia. Claudia's expression told us she had heard what Marius said.

Optatus straightened up at once and went to the girl. He placed both hands on her shoulders and kissed her forehead. The action was brisk and he released her immediately. Claudia gave him a half-smile, and unlike when Quadratus swamped her with condolences she did not burst into tears again.

Optatus explained in a few words what we had been discussing. "There is no doubt; Constans cannot have done this work alone. Somebody—as yet unidentified—was here helping him."

"Somebody killed him." Claudia's voice was now eerily controlled.

I had to intervene. "It could have been a terrible accident. But whoever was here *must* have seen your brother badly hurt, and yet they simply abandoned him."

"You mean he need not have died? He could have been saved?" A high note of hysteria showed how Claudia's mind was racing.

"No, no. Please don't torture yourself with that thought. Once the stone slipped and fell on him his wounds would have been too severe." As I spoke to her, Marius put a hand on her arm and shook his head, trying to persuade her to believe it. Now Claudia did begin to cry, but instead of comforting her himself Marius looked embarrassed and steered her to Helena. As a lover he lacked useful instincts.

Helena held the girl close to her, kissed her, and then asked me, "Marcus, who do we think this missing companion was?"

"I'd happily name one person!" Marius snarled.

"We know you would—but Quinctius Quadratus has an unshakable alibi: the bastard couldn't ride. Even if his young pal Constans had gone over to our estate to fetch him, he would still need to get home again after the accident. How are you suggesting he did that?" Optatus was silent, reluctantly conceding the point.

"Call it murder, not an accident!" insisted Claudia, breaking free from Helena's arms.

"I won't do that, Claudia," I said patiently, "until I can either provide evidence, or make somebody confess. But I give you my word, I will do all I can to discover what happened, and if it really was murder, whoever was responsible will be made to pay."

Claudia Rufina made a visible effort to control her emotions. The young girl was brave, but she was close to breaking point. At a signal from Helena I quietly suggested we leave the scene of the tragedy and take her on to her grandparents' house.

FIFTY-SEVEN

The great half-finished house lay silent. The builders had been dismissed and the estate workers kept to their quarters. Frightened slaves flitted among the pillars indoors. Time had stopped.

The body of Rufius Constans had been raised on a bier in the atrium. Extravagant branches of cypress decorated the area. A canopy darkened what should have been a space filled with sunlight, while smoking brands caused visitors to choke and rub their streaming eyes. The young man awaited burial swathed in white, smothered with garlands, reeking of sweet preservative oils. Busts of his ancestors watched over him. Laurel wreaths which he had never managed to earn for himself had been placed on tripods to symbolize the honors his family had lost.

Marius and I exchanged glances, wondering if one of us could keep watch while the other climbed up to inspect the body. The possible gains were not worth the risk of discovery. We chose to avoid the howls of outrage.

In an adjacent reception room Licinius Rufius and his wife were seated, completely motionless. Both were clad in black. Both looked as if they had neither slept nor eaten since they learned of their grandson's death. Neither showed much interest in the fact we had brought back their granddaughter, though they seemed to be pleased that the rest of us had come to share their grief. The atmosphere was stultifying. I sympathized with their tragedy, but I was still weary and short-tempered after my long journey to Hispalis. I could feel my patience ebbing fast.

Chairs were produced. Claudia sat down immediately with her hands folded and her eyes downcast, resigned to her duty. Helena, Marius and I took our places more uneasily. There was a good chance we could all imitate statues for the next three hours and not hear a word spoken. I was angry, and I felt such passivity would not help.

"This is the most terrible tragedy. We all realize how deeply you are suffering."

A slight reaction passed over the grandfather's face, though he made no attempt to reply to me.

"Will you come to the funeral?" Claudia Adorata, the old lady, asked me in a hushed voice. She belonged to that group of women who seek their comfort in formal events. Marius and I both agreed to go; I had already decided with Helena that she should excuse herself. Nobody would thank us if she caused a disturbance by giving birth in the middle of the drawn-out obsequies.

I had to speak out: "Licinius Rufius, Claudia Adorata, forgive me for raising unwelcome issues. I speak as a friend. It has been established that somebody who has not come forward must have been with your grandson when he died. The situation needs to be looked into."

"Constans is gone," Licinius dragged out. "There is no point. You mean well," he conceded in his autocratic way.

"I do, sir. I respect your wish for privacy—" I knew it remained possible that the young man's death had been a sad—but avoidable—accident. I kept my voice calm and respectful. "I would like to speak to you in private; it concerns the safety of your granddaughter."

"My granddaughter!" His eyes flew to me, and met a cool reception.

No doubt Claudia Rufina would be smothered with attention after the funeral, but at the moment she was not being granted her due. The old man was sufficiently formal to stop discussing her in what amounted to a public situation, so he stared at me, but then indicated I could follow him to another room. Claudia herself made a swift movement as though she wanted to assert herself and come with us, but Helena Justina shook her head surreptitiously.

Licinius sat. I stood. It gave him status; I did not need it.

"I'll be brief. Your grandson may have died because of a bungled task, or it may have been more than an accident. Perhaps that only matters if you want to know for your own peace of mind. But I saw you and Constans at the proconsul's palace; I have drawn my own conclusions about why you took him there. I strongly believe there are people who will not have welcomed Constans speaking out—and they will be feeling relieved now he has been silenced."

"You said you wished to speak about my granddaughter, Falco."

"This does affect her. Will you tell me what Constans knew?"

"I have nothing to say on that subject."

"If Constans was aware of something illegal—perhaps the cartel I discussed with you recently, or maybe something even more serious—then you should consider the position very carefully. I knew them only a short time, but it seemed to me that Constans and Claudia were very close."

"Claudia Rufina is deeply upset—"

"It's worse than that. She may be in danger. Other people, those who had an interest in your grandson's silence, may now be wondering whether Constans told his sister what he knew."

Licinius Rufius made no remark, but he was listening to me much less impatiently.

"Don't lose them both!" I warned.

The girl was not my responsibility. Her grandfather possessed ample means for ensuring her protection. I had seeded his mind, anyway. He rose, looking gruff though on principle. He hated to acknowledge that anyone else knew better.

As he started to leave the room he turned to me with a faint smile. "Your skills seem limitless."

"Not at all. I cannot, for instance, lure you by any method I know into discussing the proposed cartel."

At last he allowed me to mention it, though he still sang the old refrain: "There is no cartel."

"I may even end up believing that." I smiled. "Try this, sir: a group of you, chosen for your prominence in the business world, were invited to Rome by an influential senator. A suggestion was made which you rejected out of hand. Then somebody—not necessarily the senator himself—made a stupid mistake. It became known that the Chief Spy was showing interest in your group. Somebody lost his head and arranged a couple of murderous attacks. The rest of you recognized a dangerous bungle, one which only drew attention to the unpalatable plan. You left Rome fast."

"Convincing," Licinius Rufius commented coolly. He was now walking slowly, as if due to his age and his bereavement. This would allow us a certain period of discussion before we rejoined our companions.

"Then I turned up here, suggesting you were all still in the thick of the conspiracy . . . Actually, sir, I've changed my mind: those of you who were important enough to run a cartel are well placed, by your very prominence in the oil-producing world, to ensure fair prices. You could be the people who take a stand *against* price-rigging."

"I told you that was my view, Falco."

"Olive oil is a rich commodity? There will be enough for everyone?"

Licinius Rufius gripped my arm and stared at me keenly. "What's more, because the product has universal applications, including large consumption by the army, we producers should take care. Otherwise the whole industry may be taken over and state-controlled."

"Just as corn is! You are a man of sense—as well as probity."

We now reached the intriguing situation where it was Rufius who wanted something from me. He had stopped again. We were standing in a corridor. He seemed much more frail than when I first met him, though I hoped it was temporary. I could not press him to a seat, for there were none. I just had to hope I could squeeze him before the old chap collapsed.

"When I was in Rome, Falco, one of the arguments that was put to us was this: somebody at the Palace is extremely eager to assume the state control I mentioned. It was suggested that we all get together in a position of strength—" a position which sounded like the cartel to me— "Then we could resist that move—"

"By bribing the official?" I asked calmly.

He bridled, but replied, "Was that a reasonable suggestion?"

"You mean, would it work? Only if there was nothing more subtle in the official's mind."

"Is there?"

"I don't know. If we're talking about a particular official, then anything is possible. He has great power—and a mind like a Cretan labyrinth. Were you told his identity?"

"No. Do you know who it is?"

"I can guess." Claudius Laeta was the name that floated through my mind. I could still hear him gloating "*Liquid gold!*" when he and I were discussing olive oil.

Rufius was watching me closely: "If the threat of state control comes true—"

"As far as I know, sir, that is not current policy." I had seen a useful lever. Whatever Laeta might be intending, I had my own ideas about how I would report on Baetica once I returned to Rome. It was not necessarily Laeta who would be my first contact. After all, on other missions I had been received in private by the Emperor himself.

"Licinius Rufius, I am not empowered to make promises. But if I were putting forward official proposals, I might say that the oil producers of Baetica seem to me a responsible body of men who should be allowed to run their own industry." It would be cheap at least. Vespasian liked any system that cost the Treasury nothing. "Hispania has been a Roman province for a long time. We are not discussing some untrustworthy backwater full of savages in skins. And maybe it's time the Spanish provinces were thought about more carefully."

"In what way, Falco?"

"I can think of a number of provisions that Vespasian might consider. Granting wider rights of citizenship. Improved status for Romanized towns. Greater encouragement for Hispanians who wish to partake in the Senate or who qualify for equestrian posts in Rome."

"Would he do these things?"

"All I can say is that, unlike others, Vespasian listens to advice." And he knew the power of social bribes.

"You are very close to him, I think?"

"Not close enough for my own sake, sir!" I grinned.

I was still determined to extract his grandson's secret if I could. "You won't talk about Constans. I accept that, sir—" His protest died, fairly quietly. Perhaps his resolve was softening. "May I just ask you again about your visit to the proconsul?"

Licinius Rufius sighed. He breathed deeply and slowly. I let him take his time. "Falco, I had a long discussion with my grandson after the party given by the sons of Annaeus Maximus."

"You were angry with him for going to the party without telling you?"

"To start with. That became a minor matter. I sensed he was in serious trouble. He was afraid of something. He told me there had been a dancer at the party who was asking questions. It was rather confusing—"

"There are *two* dancers," I explained.

"So it seems. All I ever persuaded Constans to say was that he had political information involving one of them."

"Not the one at the Annaeus party?"

"I think not. There was another girl Constans and his friends had known, a local entertainer. I dread to think what class of girl—"

"Not a very good dancer," I told him.

"You know of her?"

"Her name is Selia; she comes from Hispalis." She had tried to kill me three days ago; I kept that to myself. "What's the story with Constans?"

"He had been involved in hiring her once. I cannot imagine how it came about; my grandson was a quiet lad—"

Light was dawning. "I think it was Quadratus who wanted her hired—but he had gone back to Rome for the Senate elections. So he wrote and asked Constans to organize this girl from Hispalis to dance at that dinner we all went to on the Palatine?"

"Something like that." Licinius was trying to avoid telling me. He had failed to appreciate how important it was. "It sounds perfectly harmless. My grandson paid her fare and appearance fee—though, as you know, he didn't even attend. It's annoying, and a waste of money, but young people do far worse things. Frankly, I could not understand why Constans became so exercised about it."

"And how did this come to light, sir?"

"Annaeus Maximus had ridden over here after his sons' drinking party."

"To complain about Constans being a guest?"

"No. Maximus came to warn me that his lads had seen fit to allow in a dancer."

"*Warn* you, sir?"

"The dancer had been asking questions—it is presumably the same woman who had already accosted me. She is taking an interest in what happened when we went to Rome. Well you must know who I mean! She's asking much the same as you, Falco; Annaeus and I presume you are working with her. She has been hanging around Corduba for weeks."

"I can see how that would have alarmed you all!" I avoided comment on the suggestion that I was part of some joint inquiry team. "And how did this frighten Rufius Constans?"

"What upset him, and made me persuade him to appeal to the proconsul, was that the dancer who performed for the Annaei had also been asking questions about the other girl. One of the Annaeus boys had then told her that it was Constans who paid for Selia's trip to Rome. On learning that, for some reason, my grandson became hysterical."

I could have told him the reason. Perhaps it was better to leave Licinius merely puzzled than to say that Selia's performance in Rome had included murder. Rufius Constans had been her paymaster. I could not believe he had known what he was doing. It seemed much more likely the poor boy was someone's dupe. But it looked bad—and had probably seemed worse to him. It would be easy to suggest that it had been Rufius Constans who panicked and paid Selia to start crashing inconvenient inquirers into Roman walls. My own view was that he was too immature to do that. However, his precise role called for examination, as the boy must have realized.

I could imagine his thoughts when he heard his grandfather and Annaeus Maximus—two men who were normally barely on speaking terms—anxiously discussing government inquiry agents, then revealing that one official had been told how Selia and Constans were linked. He probably thought he was about to be arrested—and so he should have been, both to protect him as a witness and to allow time to question him. Frankly, if he were still alive, I would be arresting him myself.

FIFTY-EIGHT

We made a slow and thoughtful journey back to the Camillus estate. I traveled in the carriage this time, and told Helena of my talk with the grandfather. Helena was feeling very tired but still had strength to worry about the bereaved family. "Something needs to be done for poor Claudia."

"What's her problem? I think she's seen through Quadratus."

"Quadratus may think much more of her though, now she's the sole heiress!"

I grinned. "I wouldn't worry. Claudia may have become a fortune-hunter's dream—though I'm sure her grandpapa is up to the situation. Anyway, as you said yourself once, the Quinctii will be looking for a bride with seven consuls in her pedigree and an ancestry she can trace on copper tablets all the way to the Seven Kings of Rome."

"Meanwhile Claudia," said Helena, "harbors serious ideas of using her inheritance to make endowments in the local community. She wishes to make her life as a female benefactress to Corduba—and now that she'll inherit the entire family fortune, she'll be even more determined."

"Commendable! Still, she's not averse to men."

"No," Helena agreed. "She is a good young woman with a fine character. She has been well brought up. She is honest, direct, serious, and loyal to those she loves. She ought to be head of her own household; she will make a chaste, intelligent partner and an admirable mother."

I knew my girl. "That's a set speech! What exactly are you planning, fruit?"

"She could be married with a clause in her dowry that says large sums are supplied for the comfort of her husband and any children—but that Claudia Rufina is to have a fixed annual amount to devote to the community."

"Married to whom, my darling?"

"How about someone from a rising senatorial family who are *not* snobbish about background, but who would be happy to offer their position and refinement—"

"In return for her glittering collateral?"

"Oh don't be crude, Marcus!"

"It was your idea," I pointed out.

"She already knows Aelianus," mused Helena.

"Of course she does," I answered, thinking how much pleasure it would give me to shackle that young man to a serious girl with a rather large nose whose funds he was forced to respect.

Helena looked pleased with herself. "She's a nice girl. Marius Optatus may not be too pleased with me, but I think I'm going to invite Claudia to Rome. Obviously she cannot stay with us—" No; our cramped, ill-decorated apartment was not the place to entertain a fabulous olive oil heiress. "So I shall have to ask Mother to take her instead!"

"Well I'm sure she'll conquer Rome with ease, my love—and her fortune should conquer your brother! Just give me a chance to clear up the residue of events from her own brother's disastrous visit to the Golden City first."

* * *

Our house was quiet and subdued that evening. Nobody took much enjoyment in dinner, and we dispersed quickly afterwards. I was sitting alone in the garden, trying to shape my thoughts into some sort of order, when Marmarides coughed.

"Something is not right with the carriage, Falco."

"That seems fairly typical of Baetica! Do you need a part fixed?" My heart sank. As I remembered his employer, the ex-legionary Stertius, his invention and prowess with machinery had far excelled mine.

"There is a difficulty with the hodometer," Marmarides confessed.

Well that was no more than I expected. Overelaborate gadgets always go wrong. In fact if I come anywhere near them, even simple ones, their rivets snap. "Do you want me to have a look at it?"

"Later, perhaps."

To my surprise Marmarides deposited his slight figure on my bench then produced a bundle of note-tablets from a pouch at his belt. He opened one or two; they were covered with slanting figures in a big, careful hand. Every line began with the name of a place. Some were dates.

"What's this, your travel diary?"

"No; it's yours, Falco."

"Are you writing my memoirs for me, or auditing my expense claims?"

Marmarides laughed his jovial laugh. Apparently I was a crack wit. Then he laid his tablets open on his knee and showed me how every time we took a trip in the carriage he listed it, with the date and the new mileage. When we came to make a final reckoning of how much I owed Stertius, the driver would be able to demonstrate our usage of the vehicle exactly, should I venture to disagree with his reckoning. Plainly his master Stertius thought of everything. Stertius must have dealt with argumentative types before.

"So what's up?"

"Today you went over to the Rufius house, stopped on the way where we all talked about the young man being killed, then I drove you home. Now it is evening. I feed the mules, clean the carriage, and sit down with my little stylus to make up the record."

"And?"

"The miles don't fit, Falco."

My first reaction was bored incomprehension. "Well, if you're slightly out I won't have a seizure. I can trust you on one or two discrepancies— Mind you, Helena Justina keeps my accounts and she's more precise."

"Falco, how far do you think it is to the Rufius house?"

"Four or five miles?"

"So don't you see, Falco?"

"I'm very tired still from my trip to Hispalis—"

"This line here," Marmarides explained stubbornly, pointing to his last written note, "is my count for your last trip that I know about—when Helena and you went into Corduba and you interviewed Cyzacus and Gorax. The day we all had a fight on the riverbank."

"I'll never forget. You fell in. I thought I would have to compensate Stertius for drowning his freedman . . . So now you have to add a new line about today?"

"I go to the hodometer and count the pebbles that remain."

"And you notate this column?" I indicated the final row, where the figures diminished with each entry.

"That's what doesn't fit. From the day you went to Corduba to now, there are twice as many miles as I expect."

"You allowed for the return journey?"

"Oh yes. The miles the carriage has traveled since Corduba," Marmarides told me with a beaming smile, "are enough for a journey to the Rufius house, there and back—then there and back a second time!"

I was impressed. It was immediately apparent what Marmarides meant. "This is your big chance to solve something for me," I said.

He beamed. "You talked about how the man with the bad back could have gone to help the young one fix the grinding wheel. He could have gone in your carriage, Falco."

I was keeping calm. "In agenting you have to work out everything, and make sure there can be no mistake. I thought Helena was out in the carriage that day? I thought she went with Aelia Annaea to her house?"

"No," he said. "Aelia Annaea came to visit in her own carriage, and Helena Justina left with her." Marmarides had really thought this through. "Marius Optatus went into Corduba, but he used an ox-wagon."

"So our carriage was in the stable?" He nodded. "The slaves were all in the fields and wouldn't see much, Marmarides. The farm is near the road, so anyone could drive off without drawing attention . . . Did you happen to notice whether the mules had been out? Were they sweating at all?"

Marmarides looked sheepish. "I never looked, Falco." Then he cheered up, able to exonerate himself. "I was not here. After Helena Justina left, I hitched a ride with Optatus to Corduba."

"What did you want in Corduba?"

He just grinned. There was a woman in this somewhere, and I decided not to explore it. Since neither Helena nor I had been here there could be no objection. It also gave Optatus an alibi. "All right. You observed Quinctius Quadratus with his bad back during the time that he was here. If he couldn't ride, do you think he would have been able to drive a two-mule carriage a short way?"

"Probably. He would not have been much use as a partner in a heavy lifting job though, Falco."

"Whoever was partnering Constans was certainly no good, we know that."

If it was Quadratus, maybe he did not let the stone fall deliberately. Maybe his back just gave out. Maybe the boy's death was a genuine accident—one that should never have happened, caused by bungling incompetence. It was cowardly of Quadratus not to own up to his part in the stupidity, but it was not a criminal act.

So perhaps the worst that had happened that day was that Quadratus got bored—or maybe Constans, panicking about Selia, had appealed for his advice. For one reason or another Quadratus went to see his dear friend Constans. Then two young men who should have known better got together and decided to do a job for which they were poorly qualified. The work was too hard for them. Quadratus was unfit; the grinding stone fell on poor Constans. Quadratus was the elder and should have behaved more responsibly. That would make him the more reluctant to admit he had been there. Besides, he must have been badly shocked by what happened.

"We have to be sure," Marmarides decided firmly. He had picked up a few phrases from me, apparently. "You must come with me to the stables and we will recount the pebbles that are left in the hodometer. Then you will have firm evidence."

He was in charge. So we walked over to the stables, crouched down at the back of the carriage and inspected the Archimedes hodometer. Marmarides counted the pebbles that remained on the upper gear wheel. Sure enough, there were several less than there should have been according to his notes: a rough count of the missing mileage confirmed that it would equal two trips to the Rufius estate: there and back for Quinctius Quadratus, plus our own drive out and back today.

Solemnly we made a note on the tablet, explained our deductions, and both signed as witnesses.

FIFTY-NINE

The funeral took place next day. There were no distant relatives to summon, and Baetica is a hot locality.

The necropolis which the wealthy Cordubans used lay nearest to us on the south of the city, this side of the bridge. Naturally it presented the best aspect. The wealthy did not inter their smart relations among the middle class or paupers, least of all with the gladiators in their multiple columbarium outside the western gate. Across the river from the noise of the town each family possessed a gracious mausoleum, lining the important road that passed through to the fertile plain and the sun-drenched slopes of their rolling olive groves.

I did wonder why they didn't build their tombs in complete privacy on their own land instead of crowding into a necropolis which was passed daily by carriages and carts. Maybe people who socialize madly in life know their dead will still want friends to mingle with in the afterlife.

The Rufii had not yet become so extravagant as the family who had constructed a miniature temple complete with Ionic columns around a little portico. Grandeur would come, no doubt. For the moment theirs was a simple brick-built, tiled roof edifice with a low doorway. Within the small chamber was a series of niches containing ceramic urns. Wall plaques already commemorated the parents, son and daughter-in-law of Licinius Rufius. These were somber enough, though nothing to the new panel planned for the grandson. We were shown a maquette, though the real thing would provide half a year's work for the stonemason. The text began, "*O woe! O lamentation! Whither shall we turn?*" and ran on for about six grim lines: longer than I could force myself to read. Sloths like me were soon provided with assistance, for Licinius gave an oration on a similar basis which lasted so long my feet went numb.

Everyone was there. Well, everyone who owned half a million upwards, plus Marius Optatus and myself. For the rich, it was just an extra social occasion. They were arranging dinner-party dates in undertones.

Only one notable person was missing: the new quaestor Quinctius Quadratus. His sprained back must be still inconveniencing him. Absenting himself looked amiss, however, since he had been the dead young man's close friend.

The proconsul had deigned to be brought over in a litter from his praetorium. As we all stumped around trying to fill in time while the corpse heated up in the cemetery oven, his honor found time for a muttered word with me. I had been looking for someone to share a joke about whether they used the embers in the oven to warm hot pies for the mourners afterwards—but with him I confined myself to a reverent salute.

"What do you make of this, Falco?"

"Officially—a young lad who foolishly attempted a job for which he was unqualified while trying to please his grandfather."

"And between ourselves?"

What was the point of condemning Constans now? "Oh . . . just a regrettable accident."

The proconsul surveyed me. "I believe he tried to see me,

when I had gone out to Astigi . . ." This was not an invitation to speculate on the reason. "A statue is to be erected in the civic forum, I believe."

"It's all work for the stonemasons, sir."

We did not discuss my mission; well, I never expected to.

The women had clustered in a huddle. I was in a mood for avoiding them. I expressed my formal sympathy to Licinius in the routine handshake line. Optatus made himself more agreeable; I saw him among the Annaei at one point. Then he came back and whispered, "Aelia Annaea asked me to tell you that Claudia wishes to speak to you privately. Licinius must not know."

"Maybe her friend can arrange something—"

I might have given more precise instructions but just at that moment a hurried messenger came from Helena, asking me to return to her at once.

SIXTY

It was a false alarm.

I sat with Helena, holding her hand, and we both said nothing. The pains which had frightened her seemed to be coming to nothing, but the next occasion could well be different. We were safe today, but seriously alarmed. We had run out of time.

A couple of hours passed. As we began to relax again, we pretended we were both sitting silent in the garden purely in order to enjoy each other's company.

"Marcus, nothing is happening. You can leave me if you want."

I stayed where I was. "This could be my last chance for the next twenty years to enjoy an afternoon in the sun completely alone with you. Savor it, my love. Children make it their sole ambition to interrupt."

Helena sighed gently. The earlier excitement had left her subdued and shocked.

After a while she murmured, "Don't pretend to be dozing under the fig tree. You're planning things in your head."

I was in fact mentally packing bags, consulting maps, debating the virtues of sea against land travel—and trying to reconcile myself to absconding from Baetica with my task only half done. "You know what I think. There's no time to waste. I want to go home now."

"You think it's too late already! It's my fault," she shrugged. "It was my idea to come to Baetica."

"Everything will be all right."

"You know how to lie!"

"And you know how to joke— It's time to leave. Good time, I hope. Anyway, I'm coming with you."

"You're wonderful!" Helena said. Sometimes she almost sounded as though she trusted me. "I love you, Didius Falco. One of the reasons is that you pursue a cause relentlessly."

"Well! And I thought it was because I had momentous brown eyes and a body you want to grab . . . So you really think I'm looking for a chance to bunk off after some villain and let you down."

"No," she retorted, with her old spirit. "I think you're lusting after a set-to with some half-naked female spy!"

"Oh discovery! No; let's be honest. You're bound to be annoyed to find I've ended up tangling with devious female agents—but you can count the peas in a pod. You know it's not my fault there seem to be women everywhere—but you think I'm spinning out the job in Hispania purely because I want an excuse to avoid being with you when you start producing the child. I'm famous for breaking promises. I know that."

"No," said Helena patiently. "You're famous for finishing what you start."

"Thanks! Now I've started on fatherhood— So we are going home?"

The fight seemed to go out of her. "I'll do what you decide, Marcus."

That settled it. If Helena Justina was being meek, the poor girl must be terrified. I took a manly decision: I was not up to reassuring a woman in the last stage of her pregnancy. I needed my mother; I needed Helena's mother too. We were going home.

Marius Optatus came riding back shortly, and I told him of my decision. He had the grace to look sad at losing us. Immediately afterwards a carriage appeared, bearing Aelia Annaea and young Claudia. There were some sturdy outriders who made themselves at home in our kitchen; Licinius Rufius must have heeded my advice about protecting the girl.

"Marius told us Helena might be having the baby. We said we were coming to help—"

"Just a twinge," said Helena. "I'm sorry to be such trouble—"

They looked disappointed. My feelings were more mixed. I wished it was all over, though I was dreading the event. Helena's eyes met mine, full of tolerance. The requirement to be sociable with our visitors would be good for both of us. But our afternoon together had brought us very close. Those moments of deep, private affection stayed with us as powerfully as if we had spent the time making love in bed. In fact our mood may have communicated itself, for both Marius and Aelia Annaea looked at us rather quizzically.

Since the others had just come from a funeral they needed space to settle their own emotions. They had the customary mixture of anticlimax and revival. The dead young man had been sent to his ancestors; the living could pursue daily routines again. They were tired after the ceremony, but the immediate pressure of grief had been eased, even for Claudia.

Helena ordered mint tea. That's always good for covering any awkwardness. No one has time for anything but finding space to put the strainer and making sure they don't slurp from their beaker or drop crumbs from their almond cake.

I was still sitting close to Helena; Claudia was placed at my other hand so she could tell me whatever she had come about.

Marius Optatus seated himself with Aelia, all set to pretend to admire the lily tubs if anything too scandalous was being discussed.

We progressed through the necessary ritual. I apologized for rushing off. Fuss was made of Helena. There was a swift review of the funeral, including the size of the turnout, the quantity of the garlands, the affecting style of the eulogy, and the comfort of knowing that the departed was in peace. I thought Constans had left behind a little too much unfinished business for that, but in the hope that his sister might be intending to right some of it, I was prepared to extend some charity to the lad.

Claudia reached the point where she felt she could talk to me. She squirmed. She blushed. I tried to look encouraging. "Marcus Didius, I have something to tell you," she finally blurted out. "I have to confess that I have not been telling the truth!"

I was leaning forwards, trying to look happy drinking from a dainty terracotta bowl. I stirred my mint tea with a tiny bronze spoon, flipping out a leaf onto the ground.

"Claudia Rufina, since I became an informer I have talked to many people who have told me one thing—only to realize they should have been saying something else." Sometimes, in wild moments I longed for a witness who would break the pattern and surprise me by croaking—under pressure of conscience or perhaps my own fingers squeezing their neck a little too tightly—that they were sorry to cause me extra work but they had mistakenly given me *accurate* answers. No doubt adding that it was quite unlike them, a moment of sheer madness, and they didn't know what came over them . . .

"You are not the first person who ever changed their mind," said Helena softly.

The girl was still hesitating. "It is better to have the truth in the end," I stated pontifically, "than never to learn it at all."

"Thank you, Marcus Didius."

There was no point being cruel to her. I could have said, sometimes truth that emerges *so* late in the day is too late to help. But I'm not that kind of dog.

"This is very difficult."

"Don't worry. Take your time."

"My grandfather has forbidden me to talk about it."

"Then we won't mention this conversation to him."

"Constans told me something—though he made me promise never to reveal it to anyone."

"You must believe it's important, or you wouldn't be here now."

"It's horrible."

"I thought it might be. Let me help you: has it to do with some violent events in Rome?"

"You know!" I needed her to tell me. Finally she forced herself to come out with it: "When my brother was in Rome he was involved in killing somebody."

That was more than I expected. All the others were keeping silent and still. I too handled the situation as calmly as possible. "My dear, you cannot change what Constans did. It's best to tell me exactly what you know. What I most need to hear is who else was involved? And what exactly happened?"

"It was to do with the plan to regulate olive oil." Regulate was a nice new word.

"Did your brother give you details of the plan?"

"Tiberius and his father were in charge. My grandfather and some other people had gone to Rome to discuss it, though they all decided not to become involved."

"Yes, I know that. So be assured your grandfather is safe; he retains his position as an honorable citizen. Now I want to talk about what happened in Rome, Claudia. Your brother was there; he was of course a very close friend of the younger Quinctius? Quadratus was older; they were like patron and client. I already know that your brother, at the request of

Quadratus, had arranged a special dancer to appear at a dinner where the olive oil plan was being discussed."

"Yes."

"Your brother and Quadratus did not attend that dinner. Is this what you want to tell me? Did Constans tell you where they were instead?"

"They stayed away from the dinner—because of what was going to happen." Claudia's voice was now barely a whisper. "There had been a discussion at the Quinctius house about certain officials who were aware of the plan and taking too close an interest. The father—"

"Quinctius Attractus."

"He said those people had to be stopped. I think he meant just pay them some money to go away, but Tiberius thought it wouldn't work. His plan was to hire someone to attack them instead."

"Just to frighten them, perhaps?" I suggested.

Claudia, who had been staring into her lap, now looked up at me. She was a straightforward girl. "Marcus Didius, I don't believe we should pretend. They were meant to be killed."

"Who carried out the attacks?"

"The dancer, and some men who helped her."

"Were your brother and his friend there?"

"How did you know?" I just raised a rueful eyebrow; Claudia steeled herself and finished her story: "Quadratus persuaded my brother to be present—first when he hired the people to do it. Then—this is the gruesome part—they both hid in the shadows that night and watched as the first man was killed. My brother was horrified and ran away. Quadratus went with him. They got drunk somewhere, and later went home and pretended they had been to the theater."

I replaced my cup on the table in front of us. The tray wobbled; Helena reached out quietly and adjusted it.

"So Quinctius Quadratus and Rufius Constans were present during one of the attacks. Do you know which one?"

"No."

"Did either of the young men strike the victim at all?"

"Not as far as I know. Not Constans, I am sure of it."

I linked my fingers, still trying to sound calm. "Thank you for telling me, Claudia. Is that everything?"

"That is all my brother told me. He was hysterical about it. I helped persuade him to go with Grandfather to admit everything to the proconsul—but they weren't able to have an interview. What should I do now?"

"Nothing," I said. One step at a time. I might later want to ask her to consider becoming a court witness, but there were difficulties about calling a woman, especially one of refined birth. Somebody male had to speak for her; it always weakened the case.

Helena glanced at me. She had realized that her plan to invite Claudia to Rome might be doubly useful now. We could get the girl there without antagonizing her grandfather, then maybe ask Claudia to make a statement for the investigating judge, even if she was never called into court.

"Have I done the right thing?"

"Yes. Go home now, Claudia. I shall have to interview Quadratus, but I won't tell him where I learned my information. You need not even tell your grandfather you talked to me, unless you feel you want to."

"So everything is all right!"

Nothing was all right. But we called for her carriage and her armed guards, then we sent her home.

Dawn is the classic time to surprise a villain, though I never knew why. You run a great risk that his doors are locked. While you are kicking them in he wakes up in a sweat, realizes what is happening, and gets his sword out ready to run you through.

It was still early evening. I decided to tackle Quadratus at once.

Aelia Annaea stayed behind with Helena. Marius Optatus came with me. We took his strongest male slaves, plus Marmarides. I strapped on my sword. The others were armed with whatever came to hand, mostly rakes and sticks.

The Quinctius estate was much like others I had visited, though it bore signs of the absentee landlord at his most astute: abundant flocks, tended by the fewest possible shepherds, and secondary cereal crops growing below the olive trees. Everything looked in respectable condition. Moneymakers don't neglect their land. Believe me, there was a great deal of land.

The house had charm and character. Thick walls to keep it cool in summer and cozy in winter. Vine-clad pergolas leading to statues of coy maidens. A separate bathhouse. A terrace for airy exercise. It spoke of wealth, yet wealth possessed by an honest country family. Long harvest lunches taken with the tenantry. Girls with pink cheeks and boys who were keen on horseflesh. Life lived with a constant supply of fresh fodder and an old earthenware jug of home-produced wine always ready to hand.

Amazing. Even their damned house lied.

We told the escort to wait quietly but to rush in like ravening wolves if we signaled them. In the event even bringing them proved unnecessary. Quadratus was not there. He had listened when I advised him to take up his job as quaestor. The same day he came home from staying with us he had packed some note-tablets, taken a litter and a pack mule, a personal bodyslave, clean tunics and a mapskin of the area, then he had told his servants he was going on a surprise tour of the Corduba mines. The procurator whose job was to look after them, and who was probably perfectly competent since he had been appointed by Vespasian, would not be too happy at an unannounced official visit. Nor was I, come to that.

Our trip to the estate was not entirely fruitless. I sensed that the staff there had almost been expecting me. They were surly and clearly nervous, and eventually one of them told me they had just been about to send over to fetch me from the Camillus farm when I turned up anyway. Somebody had left a message on the Quinctius premises, a message personally addressed to me. I could tell from the slaves' expressions I was not going to like it, even before they led me and Marius to the stable where this mysterious missive had been scrawled on a hitching post.

All it said was *For Falco*, followed by a neat pictogram of a human eye.

Lying on the straw below the drawing was the dancing girl called Selia. She was dressed in outdoor clothes, including a wide-brimmed traveling hat tied on over her own loosely knotted brown hair. She was dead. Her skin felt cold, though her limbs were still limp. She had been killed quickly and neatly by pressure to the neck. It was clearly carried out from behind before she realized what was happening. She had been lying here for a few hours. Unless Quadratus had sneaked back unobserved, the killing certainly happened after he had left for the mines. I could not believe he did it. The method was too professional.

If somebody was killing agents who had worked for Laeta, that could well mean they would now try to kill me.

SIXTY-ONE

Even before I explained what had just happened at the Quinctius estate, Helena Justina had lost the idyllic tenderness she displayed towards me earlier. She was cool. I did not blame her but I could have coped better with solicitude. We were in thc garden again. I had hardly even started to discuss what I planned to do next, but we were close to quarreling.

"Not the mines, Falco!"

"Just think of it as a tour of the local industry."

"That's what you were going to say, I suppose—had Marius Optatus not told me the whole truth before you could stop him!"

"I don't lie to you."

"You hold things back—if you believe you can get away with it!"

"I'm a man, Helena. I have to try. I tell myself I'm protecting you."

"You're annoying me," she snarled.

I said nothing. Pleasing honesty had failed: time to keep quiet.

"Marcus, I'm in an impossible position now! I don't want

you to go—but I don't want you to stay with me unwillingly, just because of my condition; I won't be made an excuse. You'd never forgive me afterwards—maybe I wouldn't forgive myself! Besides, I know just how badly you feel about the mines. You suffered all the torments of Hades once in a silver mine; it's too much for you to volunteer again."

"I won't be digging for ore again. All I need to do is to apprehend Quadratus and haul him back to face a trial. But you're right. I'm not irreplaceable. Someone else can go."

Helena frowned. "You think anyone else will bungle it."

"I don't care."

"Of course you care. And I care too!"

Helena's passionate belief in justice was one of the reasons I first fell for her. Single-minded girls are always dangerous. A man can float along for years being cynical and flippant, then some fierce tyrant (who happens to have the advantages of a sweet mind, a delicious expression and a body that is crying out to be entwined with his) sneaks under his defenses; next thing he finds himself taking a stand on some issue he would once have crept away from, simply to impress the girl.

"I am about to be a father. That is my sole priority."

"Oh Didius Falco, you have so many priorities you need an abacus to count them. You always did. You always will."

"Wrong. You're going home, Helena—and I'm staying with you."

"Wrong yourself. You have to finish your work." She had made up her mind now. "I hate it, but that's the only way. You know I can't bear to see you nobly pretending not to fidget, while all the time you're in agony because the bastard has got away."

"I will not break my promise to you."

"I release you from it—temporarily. Marcus, I don't complain. You never pretended to be other than you are, and I never dreamed of reforming you. I love your persistence, though you know how hard it is for me just now . . . Go and find him, and arrest him. Then dear gods, Marcus—" There were tears she could not resist. "Please promise that as fast as you can you will come back to me."

Tomorrow was the Nones of May. I could still remember clearly that hot night last August in Palmyra which was probably when our baby was conceived. May was only six days old. The child might not be born until the end of the month. I told myself there was still just time to do it all. I told Helena, and hugged her. While she tried not to cry so much that I wouldn't endure it, I in turn kept her close against me so she would not see the gaunt expression on my own face.

I was starting to hate this garden. Helena must have stayed here when we went over to the Quinctius place, as if she was worried that just moving indoors might start the pains again and cause the birth to begin. Her anxiety only increased mine.

While I had been absent Aelia Annaea had kindly kept Helena company. She was still here. When Marius Optatus foolishly created a crisis by confessing that he thought I was now intending to ride after Quadratus, Aelia had quickly drawn him off the scene for a walk in the orchard while Helena tore me to shreds. Aelia seemed to be waiting around to give us the support of a friend when we reached our decision.

Now she walked back to us, leaving Marius. He mooned in the background, as if he had been given definite orders to wait. Aelia Annaea was quiet, but brisk. Owning a gold mine gives a woman distinct confidence. I liked her, perhaps almost as much as Helena did.

She drew up a folding chair, left from our polite afternoon with Claudia. Smiling, she surveyed our present mood. "So everything is settled."

I scowled unhappily. "Are you asking us, or telling us?"

Helena dried her eyes. "Careful, Aelia. Marcus hates bossy women."

"That must be why he lives with one!" Rich widows can be

very provocative. I had suffered clients like this—before I learned to turn them down. She grinned at me. "Well I have come to offer suggestions, that is all."

Helena and I both gazed at Aelia; we must have looked pretty wan-faced.

"Marcus Didius has to find Tiberius." Even now from habit Aelia retained the informal use of his name. "Helena, if you intend returning to Rome, I think you should start out gently straightaway. I have been discussing this with Marius, and I'm going to talk to Claudia. Claudia is very unhappy at home. I think she would like to accept your kind invitation to visit Rome."

"I haven't actually asked her—"

"No, but I will! It will be hard to leave her grandparents so soon after her brother's death, but if she waits she'll never go. The excuse will be that she is accompanying you, Helena; you will obviously need help on the journey. So!" Aelia Annaea was direct and well organized. "While Falco goes after the fugitive, you can travel very slowly by road. I'm going to come with you myself as far as the Tarraconensis coast. Claudia will be with us too. We shall take my carriage, which is spacious and comfortable, and I will return in it afterwards. This fellow—" She indicated me—"can ride after us as soon as he is ready, then take you home by sea."

Helena looked troubled. "Marcus may have to attend a court case."

"No," I said. "If there's a court case it will be in Rome."

There were special arrangements for senators-elect. Quadratus would have to be taken back home. There were probably even more interesting arrangements when two different branches of government service had concerned themselves with the crimes. Those arrangements probably featured provisions for silencing me.

"So!" Aelia Annaea exclaimed again brightly. "What do you think?"

I took and kissed her hand. "We think you're wonderful."

"Thank you," said Helena, clearly very relieved. "Aelia, would you enjoy a visit to Rome yourself?"

Aelia Annaea looked a little mysterious. "No, I don't think so at the moment, Helena. I may be busy doing something here in Corduba." She proudly accepted credit for her solution to our own problem, then stood up again, presumably ready to take her leave of us. Since she had originally come with Claudia I asked, "Is Marius Optatus intending to arrange some transport for you?"

"I expect so."

"Would you like me to speak to him?"

"No, don't worry. Marius and I are on good terms."

She smiled. Even without the jewels which normally weighed her down, she was a fine young woman, the more so when she felt cheerful and pleased with herself. Her veil fell back; her hair was loose for the funeral and the softened effect made her look even more appealing. She turned away and walked back to Marius, a slim figure with a firm step.

I was intending to find Marmarides, to tell him that our ways must finally part, thank him, and settle up for the carriage. First, I finally persuaded Helena to go indoors. She rose, a little stiff from sitting so long, her shape thoroughly awkward nowadays. I walked with her, taking her slowly to her room. Then, while she was washing her face in a basin, I went to the shutter and quietly opened it. I whistled under my breath; Helena came to look out with me.

Marius Optatus and Aelia Annaea were standing together under an almond tree. They were fairly close, talking quietly. Aelia was probably explaining her scheme for taking Helena to the coast. She had removed her veil and was twirling it casually from one wrist. Marius held onto a bough above his head; he looked even more relaxed. From his attitude, I suspected Marius was harboring masculine plans.

He spoke. Aelia responded, perhaps rather pertly for she

tilted up her chin. Then Marius slipped his free arm right around her waist and drew her to him while they kissed. It seemed a popular move with Aelia. And when Marius slowly let go of the almond bough to embrace her even more closely, it seemed that his love for the lady's gold mine might actually be slightly less important than the love he felt for her.

SIXTY-TWO

I told myself it was not going to be like the last time. Mines are simply places where ores are produced. In that respect they are no different from glass factories or pig farms. Or even olive groves. There was no reason for me to start sweating with terror simply because I had to visit one or two mines. Time was short. I would not be staying. A couple of questions to ascertain the location of Quadratus—whether he was there, or had already called there, or whether the local foreman had heard he was on his way. Then all I had to do was say a nice hello to him, present him with the evidence, extract his confession, and lead him off. Simple, really. I should be feeling confident.

I could not help remembering what happened to me that other time. Something I hate to talk about. A nightmare to endure, then a cause of other nightmares for decades afterwards.

It had been my first mission for the Emperor. Britain. A province I had served in earlier. I thought I knew everything. I thought I would have everything under control. I was proud, cynical, efficient as an eagle stripping carrion. The first thing that happened was that I met a wild, contemptuous, patrician young divorcee called Helena and long before I noticed it, she had knocked every certainty of the previous thirty years from under me. Then I was sent undercover to the mines. For reasons that had made sense to everybody else, I was sent in disguised as a slave.

In the end it was Helena Justina who rescued me. She would not be doing that again. The last time her crazy driving of a pony cart had almost scared me more than all my sufferings in the silver mine as she raced me to a hospital before I died of exposure and cruelty; now she was herself being carried at a delicate pace along the Via Augusta to Valentia and then north towards a port called Emporiae. From there I would be taking her by sea around the southern coast of Gaul—a route that was famous for storms and shipwrecks, yet the quickest way back home.

Three years. Nearly three years I had known her now. I had changed and so had she. I liked to think I had mellowed her. But she had mellowed herself to begin with, when she let herself feel concern for a man she had at first heartily despised. Then I had found myself falling too. I recognized my fate; I plunged straight in. Now here I was, riding up into the hills of another mineral-rich province, older, mature, responsible, a seasoned state official: still stupid enough to take on any task, still put upon, still losing more than I ever gained.

It would not be like the last time. I was more fit and less fanatical. I distrusted too many people, including those who had sent me here. I had a woman and a baby to care about. I could not take risks.

I had visited the proconsul to tell him my intentions. He listened, then shrugged, then told me I seemed to know what ought to be done so he would not interfere. Same old routine. If it worked out well, he would want all the credit; if I got into difficulties, I was on my own.

The proconsul's staff, who did seem to have better orders

about helping me in my mission, had supplied me with a set of mules. Even better, I had been given a map, and what must be the briefing on mineral deposits that they had prepared for the proconsul when he took up his post. From it I learned in detail what I had previously tried to avoid knowing.

Whereas the silver mines of Britain had proved to be disappointing, the landmass of Hispania was blessed with enormous riches. There was gold, gold in fabulous quantities. It had been estimated that the great state-owned mines of the northwest produced as much as twenty thousand pounds of gold every month; they were protected by the sole legion in the province, the Seventh Gemina. Besides gold there was silver, lead, copper, iron and tin. In Baetica there were old silver mines at Carthago Nova, silver and copper mines near Hispalis, gold mines at Corduba, cinnabar at Sisapo, silver at Castulo; in the ore-laden Mariana mountains—to which I had been told Quinctius Quadratus was heading—there were hundreds of shafts producing the finest copper in the Empire and an extravagance of silver too.

A few older mines remained in private hands, but the Emperor was easing out individual ownership. Most of these establishments were now under government control. A procurator administered the sites; contractors or local mining societies could take a lease on identified shafts on payment of a hefty sum and a proportion of the minerals they produced. Presumably the keen new quaestor imagined he had tripped off on his scenic tour in order to audit the procurator. Unlike his cowardly action in abandoning Rufius Constans under the weight of a grinding stone, questioning the rule of a high-powered imperial career officer was decidedly brave. I myself was not even looking forward to telling the procurator—if I met him first—that Quadratus had devised such a plan. He might be a senator-elect, and the proconsul's deputy, but compared with the man he was venturing to spy on he was a mere temporary figurehead. Any ferret-faced freedman with equestrian status in a salaried post would wrap the quaestor round a scroll baton and send him home at the bottom of the next dispatch-rider's pouch.

I had to find Quadratus before this was done. I wanted him in one piece, pristine and unrolled.

I had crossed the river at Corduba. My journey would take me into the long line of gentle hills that had been a constant backdrop to our stay. In a gentle arc from west to east they closed off the Baetis valley on its north side, stretching from Hispalis to Castulo, and were pockmarked with mineral works almost all the way. Tumbling rivers with wriggling lakes ran through the hills. Transhumance paths, the ancient drove-roads for moving cattle every season, crisscrossed the terrain. I moved up into cooler air, amongst oak and chestnut trees.

I traveled light, camping out if it was more convenient, or begging a night in a contractor's hut where I could. There were two roads going east from Corduba. I was all too conscious that while I took the upper route through these pleasant hills, Helena Justina was traveling the lower, along the river parallel with me. While I was constantly nipping up byways to ask after Quadratus at isolated workings, she made a steadier progress not too far away. I could almost have signaled the carriage.

Instead here I was, miserable as death, barely in contact with humanity. I hated it when the stubbly speculators only produced morose grunts for me; I hated it more when they were hungry for gossip and wanted to delay me for interminable chats. I ate cheese and hard biscuit; I drank mountain stream water. I washed if I felt like it, or not if I felt perverse. I shaved myself, never a success. It was worse than the army. I was surly, solitary, famished and chaste.

In the end I realized Quadratus was not bothering with the smaller individual mines. Only the big show would do for the famous Tiberius; he must have gone straight to the huge silver mine with its complex of hundreds of shafts let to numerous contractors, which lay at the far eastern end of the mountain range. He probably traveled by way of the river road, and stayed in decent mansios. Still, he would not be as desperate as I was, and he lacked the verve and efficiency to cover as much ground. I might yet head him off.

It was a cheering hope. It kept me going for half a day. Then I knew I had to face the kind of scene I had sworn to avoid forever, and I felt myself break into a sweat.

It was the smell that turned my stomach first. Even before the appalling sights, that sour odor of slaves in their filth made me want to retch. Hundreds worked here. Convicted criminals who would slog it out until they died; it was a short life.

I could hardly bear to enter the place, remembering how I too once labored to hew out lead-bearing rocks with inadequate tools on a pitiful diet amidst the most sordid cruelty. Chained; flogged; cursed; tortured. The hopelessness of knowing there was no relief from the work and no chance of escape. The lice. The scabs. The bruising and the beatings. That overseer, the worst man I had ever met, whose mildest thrill was buggery, and his biggest triumph watching a slave die in front of him.

I was a free man now. I had been free then—only enslaved from choice and for an honorable motive, though there are no grades of degradation on a chain gang in a silver mine. Now I stepped down from a sturdy horse, a self-assured man with position in the world. I had rank. I had a formal commission with an imperial pass to prove it. I had a wonderful woman who loved me and I was fathering a little citizen. I was somebody. The mine perimeter was guarded, but when I announced myself I was called "legate" and provided with a polite guide.

Yet when that smell hit my gut I was nearly thrown back to three years ago. If I relaxed, I would be a trembling wreck.

I was led through a busy township in the shadow of mountains of slag. As we passed the cupellation furnaces, the smog and the ceaseless dints of the hammers left me almost demented. I seemed to feel the ground trembling under my boots. I was told how here the shafts reached over six hundred feet deep. The tunnels chased seams of silver underground for between three and four thousand feet. Deep down below my feet the slaves worked, for it was daylight. There are rules. No mine may work at night. You have to be civilized.

Below ground there would be huge polished mirrors to reflect the bright sunlight from above; beyond the reach of the sun the slaves carried clay lamps with vertical handles. Their shift lasted until the lamps ran out; never soon enough. The lamps used up the air and filled the tunnels with smoke. Amongst this smoke the slaves toiled to free the lumps of ore, then carried the backbreaking weight of esparto bucketfuls on their shoulders in a human chain. Up and down from the galleries, using short ladders. Pushing and shoving in lines like ants. Coughing and perspiring in the dark. Relieving themselves when they had to, right there in the galleries. Near-naked men who might never see daylight for weeks on end. Some endlessly trudged treadmills on the huge waterwheels that drained the deepest shafts. Some struggled to prop up the galleries. All of them coming a little closer every day to an inevitable death.

"Stunning, isn't it?" inquired my guide. Oh yes. I was stunned.

We came to the procurator's office. It was manned by a whole battery of supervisory staff. Men with flesh on their bodies and clothes on their backs. Clean-skinned, well-shaven men who sat at tables telling jokes. They picked up their salaries and enjoyed their lives. Visiting overseers cursed and complained as they took their breaks above ground, while they boasted about pacifying new convicts and keeping the old hands at their hard work. The supervising engineers, silent men scribbling inventive diagrams, worked out new and astonishing achievements to be turned into reality underground. The geometrists, who were responsible for finding and evaluating the seams of silver, completed dockets in between putting their feet up and telling the most obscene stories.

It was a room where people constantly came and went; nobody took any notice of a newcomer. Arcane discussions were going on, occasionally heated though more often businesslike. Huge movements of ore and endless shipments of ingots were being organized through this office. A small army of contractors was being regulated here, in order to provide a vital contribution to the Treasury. The atmosphere was one of rough and ready industry. If there was corruption it could be scandalous and on a massive scale, as I had proved in another province. But we had had a new emperor for two years since then, and somehow I doubted that more than harmless fiddling went on here. The profits were enough to cushion greed. The importance of the site ensured that only the best staff appointments were approved. There was an unmistakable aura of watchfulness from Rome.

It did not include supervision by the quaestor, apparently.

"Oh yes, Quadratus was here. We gave him the grand sightseeing tour."

"What? '*This is an ingot; here's an Archimedes screw*'—then sending him down the deepest shaft on a wobbly ladder and suddenly blowing out the lamps to make him shit himself?"

"You know the score!" the procurator beamed admiringly. "Then we bluffed him with a few graphs and figures, and booted him out to Castulo."

"When was this?"

"Yesterday."

"I should catch up with him, then."

"Want to look around our system first?"

"Love to—but I need to get on." I managed to make my refusal sound polite. Seen one, you've seen them all.

Castulo would be a day's ride away. Quadratus himself had told me his father had interests there, in the tight little mining society which had tied up all the mineral rights for a radius of twenty miles or more. The mining sites were smaller than here, but the area was important. Some of the wealthiest men in Hispania were making their fortunes at Castulo.

I nearly escaped without incident. I had left the office and was looking for my guide. Apparently he worked on the principle that if he got you in, you could find your own way out while he sloped off for a gossip with a friend.

Then a man came towards me. I recognized him immediately, though he did not know me. A big, shapeless bully, just as sly as he was merciless. He seemed heavier than ever, and shambled with even more threat in his ugly gait. His name was Cornix. He was the slave overseer who had once made a habit of singling me out for torture. In the end he had nearly killed me. Of all the pig-ignorant debauched thugs in the Empire he was the last man I would ever wish to see.

I could have walked right by him; he would never have realized that we had met before. I could not help my start of recognition. Then it was too late.

"Well! Well! If it isn't Chirpy!" The nickname froze my blood. And Cornix was not intending me any favors when he leered, "I've not forgotten I owe you one!"

SIXTY-THREE

He had two beats of time to reduce me to a jelly, but he missed his chance. After that it was my turn.

I had made a bad mistake with Cornix once: I had escaped his clutches and publicly humiliated him. The mere fact I was alive today was because in my time as a slave I had continually outwitted him. Since I had been shackled, starved, despairing, and close to dying at the time, it was all the more commendable.

"I'm going to smash in your head," he told me, in the same old sickening croak. "And after that, we'll really have some fun!"

"Still the tender-hearted giant! Well, well, Cornix . . . Who let you out of your cage?"

"You're going to die," he glowered. "Unless you've got a girl to rescue you again?"

This kind of delay—with its attendant danger—was the last thing I could afford. The girl who had once rescued me was heading for the coast, in a condition where she sorely needed me.

"No, Cornix. I am alone and unarmed, and I'm in a strange place. Obviously you have all the advantages."

I was being too meek for him. He wanted threats. He wanted me to defy him and force him to fight me. One or two people were already watching. Cornix was yearning for a big display, but it had to be my fault. He was the kind of rowdy who only picked on slaves, and then covertly in corners. His official role was as a tough manager who never put a foot wrong. In Britain his superiors had been told the truth eventually, and it must be due to me that after the shake-up I organized there he had had to roam abroad to find himself a new position. Just my luck he had found it here.

"I'm glad we've had this little chat," I said very quietly. "It's always good to renew acquaintance with an old friend!"

I turned away. My contempt was iron-hard and just as cold. Refusing to antagonize the bastard was the surest way to achieve it. There were tools and timber everywhere. Unable to bear my forbearance Cornix grabbed a mining pick and came after me. That was his mistake.

I too had sized up possible weapons. I caught up a shovel, swung it, and banged the pick from his grip. I was angry, and I had no fear. He was out of condition and stupid, and he thought he was still dealing with someone utterly exhausted. Three years of exercise had given me more power than he could cope with. He soon knew.

"You have two choices, Cornix. Give up and walk away—or find out what pain means!" He roared with rage and rushed me with his bare hands. Since I knew where Cornix liked to put his snag-nailed fingers, I was determined not to let him get in close. I used my knee, my fists, my feet. I released more anger than I even knew I had, though dear gods I had lived with the memories long enough.

The ruck was short. It was nasty. Slowly his oxen brain realized more was called for than he generally had to use. He began to fight harder. I was enjoying the challenge, but I had to be careful. He possessed brute strength, and he had no qualms about how he used his body. I was staving him off with punches and kicks when he bore down on me and grappled me. His roars and the familiar smell of him were churning me up. Then I broke free for a moment. Someone else took a hand. A bystander I had hardly noticed stepped forward adroitly, and passed me a gallery prop. The rough-hewn round timber weighed something terrible, though I hardly felt it. I swung the pole at chest height, with all my force. It felled Cornix with a pleasing crack of broken ribs.

"Oh nice! I learned that from you, Cornix!"

I could easily have brought the timber down on his skull. Why sink to his level? Instead, I raised the prop above my head and crashed it down across his shins. His scream sang sweetly in my ears. When I left he would never be able to follow me.

Suddenly I felt a lot better about a lot of things.

I turned to thank my rescuer and had a shock. For the second time I had escaped that brute's clutches through intervention of a female kind.

I knew I had seen her somewhere, though she lacked the kind of beauty that my brain catalogues. She was of an age where her age had ceased to matter, though clearly full of spirit and energy by the way she had helped me out. She looked nothing, just a dumpling you could see selling eggs on a market stall. She wore a brown outfit with extra swaddlings in unbleached linen, topped by untidy swags of strawlike hair emerging from a scarf. A battered satchel was slung across a bosom that wouldn't raise excitement in a galley-slave who had just set foot on land for the first time in five years. Eyes of an indeterminate color were surveying me from a face as lively as wet plaster. She showed no reserve about being here on a site that seemed otherwise exclusively for men. Most of them had not even noticed her.

"You saved my life, madam."

"You were coping. I just threw in some help."

"We must have met before." I was still gasping. "Remind me of your name?"

She gave me a long stare. While I blinked back at her she stretched out one pointed shoe, and drew a sign in the dust with her toe: two curved lines with a smudge in between them. A human eye.

"I'm Perella," she said matter-of-factly. Then I remembered her: the surly blonde who had originally been booked to dance for the entertainment of the Olive Oil Producers of Baetica.

SIXTY-FOUR

Without another word we turned away from the procurator's office, leaving Cornix writhing on the ground. No one made a move to help him. Wherever he went he was a man with enemies.

Perella and I walked right through the mine environs to the gate where I had left my mules. She had a horse. She mounted without help. I swung up with an element of slickness too. For once.

We rode single file—me leading—down the one-way road from the settlement towards the major cross-country route through the Mariana mountains. When we reached a suitable quiet spot I signaled and reined in.

"I've been dodging another Spanish dancer, name of Selia. Nice little mover with castanets, and even better with a cleaver in her hand. She won't be titillating men anymore though—or murdering them either. She's learning new dance steps in Hades. All the breath's been squeezed out of her."

"You don't say!" Perella marveled. "Persons unknown, would that be?"

"I believe so."

"Better keep it that way."

I let her see me looking her over. She was bundled up like a wet cheese. I could not see a weapon. If she carried one it could be anywhere. Her satchel, perhaps. But if she killed Selia, she had adequate skills even without weapons.

"I'm not after you, Falco."

"You've been trying to track me down."

"Only when I had a moment. You dodge about a lot. Falco, if we're intending to have a cozy chat we could get down and sit under a tree."

"Far be it from me to refuse to exchange sweet nothings with a woman in a wood!"

"You don't look happy on a mule."

Apt, though I was not sure I wanted to be cozy with Perella; still, she was right about me hating life in the saddle. I dismounted my mule. Perella jumped off her horse. She unwound a large sturdy shawl which formed one layer of her garments and spread it on the ground. Equipped for everything. Obviously if I wanted to vie with such a specialist I would have to improve myself.

We placed ourselves side by side like lovers on a picnic rug: lovers who had not known each other very long. Midges started to take an interest immediately.

"Well this is nice! All we need is a flagon of wine and some rather stale rolls, and we can convince ourselves we're a couple of skivers enjoying a holiday." I could see Perella was not one for lighthearted quips. "Last time I saw you I believed you were a regular dancer who had lost an engagement due to trickery. You never told me you were employed by the Chief Spy."

"Of course I didn't tell you. I'm a professional."

"Even so, eliminating the beauteous Selia just because she pinched your dinner-date seems to be taking your rivalry too far."

The woman regarded me with those mud-colored eyes. "What makes you think I killed her?"

"It was very neat. *Professional.*" I lay back with my hands folded under my head, gazing up through the oak tree boughs. Bits of leaf flittered down and tried to land in my eyes, while I felt that old forest dampness starting to seize up my joints. Going home to hold conversations sensibly in wine bars became an attractive thought.

She sighed, squirming on the rug so she could still see me. "Too flash, that Selia. So painted up that everywhere she went she was unmissable."

"Good intelligence agents know how to blend in, eh? Like informers! So the flash lass has had her lamp snuffed out by the decent working girl?"

Perella still managed not to admit it. "Her time was up. I reckon the young fool quaestor had sent for her from Hispalis to finish you off, Falco."

"I owe somebody a thank-you then."

She showed no interest in my gratitude. "My bet is, Selia thought he was losing his nerve and she intended to do for him as well. If he talked she would have been in trouble."

"Letting her remove Quadratus would have solved a problem."

"If you say so, Falco."

"Well let's be practical. Apart from whether it's likely anyone can persuade a judge to try him, when any judge in Rome is liable to have his inclination to do so suborned by large gifts from Attractus—somebody has to catch the bastard first. You're chasing round the mines now, and so am I. I'm definitely looking for Quadratus and you're either after him—or me."

She turned around and grinned at me.

"What was the game?" I asked in a dangerous voice. "You've been lurking around all my suspects—Annaeus,

Licinius, Cyzacus—they've all had a visitation. I gather you even made a trip to see me."

"Yes, I got to most of them ahead of you; what kept you dawdling?"

"Romantic mentality. I like to admire the scenery. You may have got to them first, but most of them talked to me for longer."

"Learn anything?" she jeered.

I ignored it. "You knew I was official. Why not make contact? We could have shared the work."

Perella dismissed my quibbles as mere prissiness. "Making contact with you took second place! Until I decided whether I could trust you I didn't want to give you any clue who I was or what I was there for. I nearly managed to get to you the night of the Parilia."

"Was it you who hurled that rock at me?"

"Just a pebble," she smirked.

"Then why make yourself invisible afterwards?"

"Because unbeknown to you, Quadratus was lurking up ahead."

"He had left in a carriage with two others."

"He'd stopped it, pretending he wanted to throw up. The girl—"Aelia Annaea—"was distracted, looking after the youth, who really *was* chucking his heart up. Quadratus had walked back slowly along the track as if he was getting some air, but it looked to me as if he was expecting somebody. That was why I flung the stone, to stop you before you blundered into him. I thought he was waiting for a meeting with Selia; I wanted to overhear what they said."

"I never saw you and I never saw him."

"You never saw Selia either! She was creeping up behind. In fact, Falco, the only one who wasn't hiding in the dark from you that night was Selia's sheep!"

"Did Selia make contact with Quadratus?"

"No, the girl in the carriage called out and he had to go off with her and the youth."

"I thought it might have been you dressed up as the shepherdess?" I suggested. No chance of that: Perella could not compete with the dead girl's glorious brown eyes.

She laughed. "No fear. Can you imagine trying to get Anacrites to sign an expenses chit for the hire of a sheep?"

So she still thought he was in operation, then.

"Let's talk about Rome," I suggested. "Double dealing is afoot; that's clear. It's in both our interests to explore who's doing what to whom, and why two thoroughly reasonable agents like ourselves have ended up in the same province on two different missions involving the same racket."

"You mean," mouthed Perella, "are we on the same side?"

"I was sent by Laeta; I'll tell you that for nothing."

"And I was not."

"Now that raises an interesting question, Perella, because I had worked out you were a staffer for Anacrites—but the last time I saw him he was lying in my mother's house with the fare for the ferrymen to Hades all ready in his outstretched paw."

"The Praetorians have got him in their camp."

"I arranged that."

"I saw him there."

"Oh so I'm dealing with a girl who mingles with Guardsmen. Now that's a *real* professional!"

"I do what I have to."

"Spare my blushes; I'm a shy boy."

"We all work well together." That's usually a pious lie.

"How fortunate," I said. Still, the intelligence service was attached to the Guard. "Did the Praetorians tell you he was with them?"

"I tracked him down myself, after you told me he had been beaten up. It was hard going, I admit. In the end I came to ask you where he was—" I remembered giving her my address. "You'd just left Rome, but someone put me on to your mother. She didn't tell me where he was, but she had a big pot of soup bubbling, and I guessed it was for the invalid. When she went out with a basket, I followed her."

"Ma's still taking Anacrites broth?" I was amazed.

"According to the Praetorians she regards him as her responsibility."

I had to think about that. "And when you took your own bunch of flowers to his sickbed, exactly how was your unlikable superior?"

"As tricky as ever." This was a shrewd lady. "He croaked and moaned as sick men always do. Maybe he was dying. Maybe the bastard was rallying and fighting back."

"And Ma's still nursing him? I don't believe it! In the Praetorian camp?"

"The Praetorians are great lumps of slush. They adore the maternal virtues and such old-fashioned tripe. Anyway, Anacrites is safe with them. If he survives he'll think your mother's wonderful."

I experienced a swooning dread that I would go home to Rome and find my mother married off to the Chief Spy. Never fear; she would have to divorce Pa first. They would never sort out arrangements while neither was on speaking terms.

"And you talked to Anacrites? What did he say?"

"Nothing useful."

"How like him!"

"You saw the state he was in. It was only a couple of days after you left."

"So who sent you here?"

"Own initiative."

"Do you have the authority?"

"I do now!" Perella laughed, fished down inside her satchel and held something up for me to see. It was a seal ring; rather poor chalcedony; its cartouche showing two elephants with entwined trunks. "Selia had it. I found it when I searched her. She must have stolen it when she clonked Anacrites."

"You searched her?" I inquired politely. "Would that be before or after you squeezed very hard on her pearly throat?" I received a sideways look. "I knew the ring was missing, Perella. Knowing Anacrites, I assumed he heard Selia and her heavies creeping up behind him, so he swallowed it to safeguard public funds."

Perella liked that. After she finished laughing she spun the ring in the air, then threw it as far as possible across the road and into a copse opposite. I applauded the action gently. I always enjoy a rebel. And with Selia dead, the ring was no longer useful evidence. "I'll tell Anacrites you've got it, Falco. He'll be on at you about it for the next fifty years."

"I can live with that. What are you doing here?" I demanded again.

Perella pursed her mouth and looked sorrowful. I was still trying to reconcile in my mind that this dumpy fright in her frumpish wrappings was a highly efficient agent—not just a damsel in a short dancing frock who listened in at dinners to earn herself a few denarii, but a woman who worked alone for weeks on end, who traveled, and who when she felt like it mercilessly ended lives.

"What's going on, Perella?"

"Did you know Valentinus?" she asked.

As her voice took a lower note, I felt a chill. For a second I was back in the Second Cohort's fire engine house, with Valentinus swinging stiffly in a hammock and that gruesome bucket beneath his head to catch his blood. "Hardly. I met him once, at that dinner; I really missed my chance to talk to him. The second time I saw him he was dead."

"He was a nice lad."

"He seemed so to me."

"We had worked together a few times. Anacrites had us

both on the Baetican case. It was all mine to begin with, but Quinctius Attractus must have twigged that we were on to him, and he arranged for me to be pushed out by that girl. So Valentinus had to do duty that night instead of me. When he was killed, I decided to follow up. I owed him that. Well, Anacrites too. He does his job in his own way—and it's better than the alternative."

"Claudius Laeta?"

Perella let her eyes narrow. "Obviously I have to watch my step, Falco—I know you're thick with him."

"He paid my fare, but I'm not in his pocket."

"You're independent normally?"

"Freelance. Like Valentinus. That's why I wasn't weeping when I found Selia dead. I recognized your pictogram too—Valentinus had one on his apartment door . . . I gather you share my skeptical attitude to Laeta?"

Perella hunched her shoulders. She was choosing her words carefully. The result was a colorful character appraisal, the kind he would not want to have read to the Emperor at birthday bonus time: "Laeta's a cheating, dabbling, double-dealing, swindling jumped-up clerk."

"A gem of the secretariat," I agreed with a smile.

"It was Laeta who told Quinctius Attractus I was keeping an eye on the Society; I'm pretty sure of it. You know what's going on among the palace bureaux?"

"Laeta wants to discredit Anacrites. I hadn't realized he was stirring the pot so actively, but the word is he wants to get the spy network disbanded so he can take over. The hidden power in the Empire. The watcher we love to fear."

"You could get a job with him, Falco."

"So could you," I retorted. "Decent operatives never lack work. There are too many duds out there messing up chances; the new work rotas will contain ample spaces. Laeta would welcome both of us. But do we want to embrace his slimy charms, Perella? It's still our choice."

"I'll probably stick with the dog I know."

"If he survives. And if his section survives too."

"Ah well."

"I'll work for myself as usual."

"Well we both know where we are, then!" she smirked.

"Oh yes. Under a tree in a wood in Baetica without a lunch basket."

"You're a misery, Falco."

We seemed to be talking frankly—not that I trusted her any more as a result. Nor did I expect Perella to trust me.

"If I level with you, Falco, can I expect the same favor?" I screwed out a half-hearted shrug. "I came to Baetica for two reasons," she announced. "I wanted to see Selia get it—but most of all, I'm going to sort this cartel nonsense and get the solution marked up as a credit to the spies' network."

"Outwit Laeta?"

"And you too, if you're on his side, Falco."

"Oh I was sent to block the cartel too; I think it's a dead duck now." I gave her a far from modest grin. "I dropped a few suggestions in a few relevant ears, so I'm taking credit for suppressing it!"

Perella frowned. "You'd do better to take a laxative!"

"Too late. Give up. It's fixed. Now there's just young Quadratus. He's crazy and out of control—just the right material for the Palace to use in its cover-up of the real mess. What Rome needs is a juicy patrician scandal to fill up the *Daily Gazette;* that's always good for taking the heat off the government. Putting Quadratus out of action on grounds of unspeakable misdemeanors caused by foolish youth allows the big men to escape with their pride intact."

Perella scoffed quietly. "There is a problem I don't think you realize."

"You mean the noble Quadratus belongs to a rich and ancient family? Do you think he'll dodge the indictment?"

"Who knows? I mean, the cartel was never just a scheme set up by a few notables in Baetica for their personal gain," Perella said. I thought she was referring to Attractus. He certainly wanted to rule far more than the cartel. Then I stayed quiet. Something in her tone was far too ominous. "Laeta wants the cartel too, Falco."

"Laeta does? Well I discovered a reason for that. He's suggesting to the oil producers that he intends the industry to become state controlled. Attractus is trying to bribe him into keeping quiet."

"I thought Laeta had another plan," Perella mused. "Oh if the oil market comes under state control, he certainly wants to be the man in charge—who creams off the golden froth for himself."

"It wouldn't surprise me. First he would have to persuade the Emperor to take over the industry and provide state funds for running it."

"I can think of a way he would manage that." Perella was enjoying her superior knowledge.

"All right, you've lost me." I could be frank. I was dying with curiosity.

"Laeta really wants the oil market cornered; he wants it for the Emperor."

SIXTY-FIVE

I gulped discreetly. Immediately she said it I could see there might be an appeal. Yes, Vespasian wanted to go down in history as an honest servant of the state. But yes too, he was notoriously personally mean.

He came from a middle-class family, Sabine farmers turned tax collectors: hardworking intelligent folk on their way up—but with never enough money to run on fair terms with the old patrician families. He and his elder brother had clawed their way through the Senate to the highest posts, always in comparative poverty, always having to mortgage last year's gains in order to move on to the next magistracy. When Vespasian, having made it to consul somehow, was awarded the governorship of Africa, his brother had been compelled to fund him—and while he was there in his exalted position, Vespasian became a legend: for what? For acquiring a monopoly in the supply of salted fish . . .

Why should he change? He inherited empty coffers from Nero. He had the new man's zeal to make his mark. Grabbing the market in a staple commodity could still be the Emperor's dream. He ruled the Empire now, but he was just as short of funds for the business of government and probably just as eager for cash in hand himself.

"There could be various ways this would work for Laeta," I suggested slowly. "The most basic is the one I mentioned—a local cartel is set up, stage-managed by Attractus, and Laeta agrees that the state will allow it to exist provided he gets a large personal bribe. The next stage, more sophisticated, is that he exerts even more pressure; he says the cartel will only be allowed to continue if *the Emperor* gets a huge percentage of the profits."

"That's what I thought," said Perella. "Both of those needed Anacrites wiped out. He was trying to stop the cartel."

"Such a simple soul! Wiping out Anacrites has an additional bonus for Laeta: *he* can then take over the spies' network."

"So you agree with me. That's it?"

"I think Laeta might be toying with even more elaborate plans. For one thing, I can't see him staying happy with Attractus as prime mover in the cartel. This probably explains why he hired me to expose the conspiracy: he specifically complained about Attractus getting above himself. So let's assume what he really wants from me is to remove Attractus. But what then happens to the cartel?"

Perella was rushing ahead. "Suppose the cartel is made public, and it's banned—and the estates of the conspirators are all confiscated. That would attract Vespasian!"

"Yes, but what would happen? We're not talking about another Egypt here. Augustus was able to grab Egypt, capture its wonderful grain, and not only accrue huge profits for himself but gain power in Rome by controlling the grain supply and using it for propaganda, with himself as the great benefactor ensuring the poor are fed."

Vespasian had actually shown that he appreciated the value of the corn supply by sitting in Alexandria during his bid for the throne, and tacitly threatening to keep the grain ships there with him until Rome accepted him as emperor. Would he contemplate a similar move with oil? If so, would it actually work?

"So why can't the same thing happen with Baetican oil, Falco?" Perhaps after all Perella belonged to the active type of agent, rather than the puzzle-solving kind. She was adept at strangling her rivals, but lacked a grasp of political functions. In the complex web of deceit where we were now stuck, she would need both.

"Baetica is already a senatorial province, Perella. This is going to be the problem. It may be why, in the end, nothing will ever happen. Anything in Baetica that's officially taken over, confiscated, or otherwise state controlled will simply benefit the Treasury. For the Emperor that would hardly be a disaster; the Senate's control of the Treasury is nominal and he himself could use the money for public works, sure. But the olive oil is never going to be a monopoly in his personal control, and he'll get no personal credit for producing an oil dole for the populace. No; better for him that whatever happens is underhand. That way there may be profits."

"So you're saying, Falco, the ideal result for Laeta is to destroy Anacrites, destroy the Quinctii—and yet keep the cartel?"

"Apparently!" I could see how it might be organized too. "I bet Laeta will propose something like this: in Rome the estate owners, and anyone else in the trade who joins in, will all become members of the Society of Olive Oil Producers of Baetica as a cover for their operations. The society will then make large personal gifts to the Emperor—and smaller, but still substantial ones, to Laeta of course. It will look like the kind of ingratiating behavior that's officially allowed."

"So what can you and I do about this?"

"It all depends," I said thoughtfully, "whether Vespasian has been informed of the devious plan." Remembering earlier conversations with Laeta I reckoned he would not yet have shared his ideas with the Emperor. He would want to be sure his proposals would work. It would suit Laeta to complete the scheme, then present it to his imperial master as a working proposition. He was assured of the credit then. While the cartel was being set up, Laeta could keep open an escape route in case anything went wrong. If that happened he could fall back on the straightforward move, holding his hand from personal involvement and gaining his credit by exposing the plot. But if everything went well, he could produce the more elaborate scheme for his imperial master with a splendid—though secret—secretariat flourish.

He would always have kept a secondary plan to cover snags. Me finding out too much, for instance, on the way to removing Attractus. So he had hired and kept Selia paid up, in case he wanted to eliminate me.

He had made at least one serious miscalculation: for this plan to work, the oil producers themselves had to want a cartel. If they sneakily took the honest route, Laeta would be nowhere.

The other problem would be if Vespasian decided that *he* preferred to keep his hands clean now that he was an emperor.

"Anacrites had seen what was going to happen." Perella was still talking. "He always reckoned Laeta wanted to put the cartel in place, then offer it to the Emperor as his bargaining piece. Laeta's reward will be power—a new intelligence empire, for a start."

"It's cunning. He will demonstrate that Anacrites has simply blundered in and threatened the success of a lucrative scheme—failing in his dumb spy-like way to grasp the potential for imperial exploitation. Laeta, by contrast, exhibits superb speculative nous, proving himself the better man. He is also loyal—so hands his idea to a happy and grateful Emperor."

Perella looked sick. "Pretty, isn't it?"

"Disgusting! And you're telling me before Anacrites received his head damage he was onto all this?"

"Yes."

"I've been told it was Quinctius Quadratus who lost his nerve and arranged for Anacrites to be beaten up. Is there any possibility that Laeta himself really organized the thugs?"

Perella considered. "He could be evil enough to do it—but apparently when he heard what had happened he went green with shock. He's a clerk," she said cruelly. "I expect he hates violence!"

"He did look flustered when he came to me about it."

"Maybe it finally struck him that he was messing with something more dangerous than scrolls."

"That hasn't made him back down from the general plan," I commented.

"No. You said it right, Falco. Everything depends on whether Vespasian has been told all this. Once he knows, he'll love it. We'll be stuck with it."

"So what was Anacrites intending to do to thwart Laeta's scheme?"

"What I'm still doing," she returned crisply. "The spies' network will produce a report saying, '*Look! People were planning to force up olive oil prices; isn't it scandalous?*' Then we show that we've stopped the plot. If enough people know, we force the Emperor to agree publicly that it was corrupt and undesirable. We get the praise for discovering the project, and for ending it. Laeta has to back off—from the cartel, and from us."

"For now!"

"Oh he'll be back. Unless," remarked Perella in a tone Laeta would not have cared for, "somebody wipes him out first!"

I drew in a long breath then let it out again, whistling to myself.

I had no opinion on whether Anacrites or Laeta was best for running the intelligence service. I had always despised the whole business, and only took on missions when I needed the money, even then distrusting everyone involved. Taking sides was a fool's game. With my luck, whichever side I ended up on would be the wrong one. Better to extract myself now, then wait to see what developed. Watching the two official heavyweights slogging out their rivalry might even be amusing.

I was growing stiff, sitting on the ground. I stood up. The woman followed, gathering up her shawl then shaking it to dislodge twigs and leaves. I was once again struck by how short, stout and apparently unlikely as a spy she was. Still, she didn't look like a dancer, yet everyone who had seen her perform said she could do that.

"Perella, I'm glad we pooled our knowledge. We underlings have to work together!"

"So we do," she agreed—with a pinch-lipped expression that told me how she distrusted me just as freely as I did her. "And are you still working for Laeta, Falco?"

"Oh I'm working for justice, truth and decency!"

"How noble. Do they pay well?"

"Pitifully."

"I'll stick with the network then!" We had walked to our animals. Perella flung the shawl across her horse's back then leaned on the saddle before leaping up. "So who goes after Quadratus?"

I sighed deeply. "I'd like to; I hate that young bastard—but Perella, I'm really stuck now. He's gone in entirely the wrong direction—back west towards Corduba. I've sent my girl to the east coast and I ought to go after her."

She looked surprised. My tenacity must be more famous than I thought. "You don't mean that, Falco!"

"I don't have much choice! I want to corner Quadratus, but I don't want to face Helena—let alone her enraged family—

if I slip up and let anything happen to her. Her family are important. If I upset them, they could finish me."

"So what then, Falco? Aren't you the man to take a chance?"

Irritated, I picked at a tooth, pausing for anguished reflection. "No, it's no good. I'm going to have to leave you to take the credit. Anacrites' group needs the kudos, and I just haven't the time to follow in the direction Quadratus has gone. I've found out what you need to know. You saw me at the silver mine? They told me at the supervisor's office that he had been there yesterday. He let them know he was going back to look at the mines near Hispalis."

"And you can't do it?"

"Well it's impossible for me. That's the wrong way. I'll have to give up on him. I've simply run out of time. My lady is about to pop a baby, and I promised to put her on a ship so she can get to a good Roman midwife. She's gone on ahead and I'm supposed to be following."

Perella, who may even have seen Helena looking huge at the Camillus estate in Corduba while I was in Hispalis, snorted that I had better be sharp, then. I gave her the customary scowl of a man who was ruing his past indiscretions. Then I swung up onto my mule again. This time it was I who managed it gracefully, while Perella missed and had to scramble.

"Need a hand?"

"Get lost, Falco."

So we parted in different directions, Perella going west. I meanwhile took the road to the east at a gentle pace, pretending I was headed for the Tarraconensis coast.

I was. But first, as I had always intended, I would be visiting the mines at Castulo.

SIXTY-SIX

This time fear had no hold on me. Old anxieties surged around as they always would do, but I was in control.

I found the quaestor very quickly. Nobody could mistake that handsome, wholesome appearance. He was standing, talking to a contractor; the other man looked grateful for my interruption and positively scampered off. Quinctius Quadratus greeted me with warmth, as if we were old dice-playing friends.

This was not one of the great underground workings, but virtually open-cast. We had met at the head of an entry to a seam, more of a cleft in the side of a slope than a real shaft. Below us open tunnels had been carved out like long caves with overhanging roofs. The constant chipping of picks reached our ears. Slaves were clambering up and down an ungainly wooden ladder, ribs showing, all skinny limbs and outsize bony elbows, knees and feet. They carried the sacklike sagging weight of ore-baskets on their shoulders in a jostling chain while Quadratus posed like a colossus at the top of their route, quite unaware that he was positioned in their way.

He had made no attempt to hide from me. In his eyes there could be no reason for him to act the fugitive.

"Do you want to talk indoors, quaestor?"

"It's pleasant here. What can I do for you?"

"A few answers, please." I would have to pose extremely simple questions. His brain had the consistency of a slab of lead. I folded my arms and talked in a straightforward way like a man he could trust. "Quinctius Quadratus, I have to put to you some charges which you will see are immensely serious. Stop me if you consider anything is unfair."

"Yes I will." He looked meek.

"You are believed to have been the sole mover, or to have assisted, in tampering with an official report on corruption which had been written by your predecessor Cornelius; you altered it significantly while the document was at your father's house after being taken there by Camillus Aelianus."

"Oh!" he said.

"You have also been accused of inveigling Rufius Constans—a minor who was under your influence—into supplying a dancer to the Society of Olive Oil Producers of Baetica. The girl subsequently attacked and killed an imperial agent, a man called Valentinus, and seriously wounded Anacrites, the Chief Spy. The charge is that you incited Rufius to join you in hiring the dancer to do the killings, that you took him with you when you arranged this, and that with him you hid in the shadows and witnessed the first murder. You then got drunk, and later lied about where you had been that night. Rufius Constans confessed everything to a witness, so there will be full corroborative testimony."

"That's a tough one," he said.

"There is evidence that you were with Rufius Constans when he was crushed under a grinding stone, and that you then abandoned him alone with his injuries."

"I should not have done that," he apologized.

"I possess physical proof that you took my carriage to visit him. I ask you to tell me whether or not you engineered the apparent accident?"

"Ah!" he responded quietly. "Of course it was an accident."

"The dancing girl Selia has been found strangled at your father's estate near Corduba. Do you know anything about that?"

Quadratus looked shocked. "I do not!"

Well, I believed that.

"There are those who believe you are unsuitable to be quaestor, though you will be glad to know that in my opinion mere ineptitude is not an indictable offense."

"Why would I want to do these things you mention?" he asked me in a wondering tone. "Is there supposed to have been some personal advantage to me?"

"Financial motives have certainly been suggested. I'm prepared to be persuaded most of it was caused by complete irresponsibility."

"That's a hard verdict on my character!"

"And it's a poor excuse for murder."

"I have a good explanation for everything."

"Of course you have. There will always be excuses—and I believe you will even convince yourself that the excuses are true."

We were still standing at the top of the exit from the seam. Quinctius moved aside abstractedly as a chain of slaves began to climb out via the ladder, each with his head down as he carried a basket of newly hewn rocks. I signaled the quaestor to walk further off with me, if only to give the poor souls room, but he seemed rooted to the spot. They managed to get past him somehow, then another lot descended the ladder, most of them going down like sailors, with their backs to the rungs and facing out.

"Thank you for your frankness, Falco." Quadratus ran his hand through that mop of luxuriant, smartly cut hair. He looked troubled, though perhaps only by the necessity to interrupt his self-appointed mission to inspect these mines. "I shall consider what you have said very carefully, and provide an explanation for everything."

"Not good enough. These are capital charges."

He was still standing there, a sturdy, muscular figure with a bland expression but a pleasing, good-looking face. He had everything that makes a man popular—not merely with women, but with voters, strangers, and many of his peers. He could not understand why he failed to win over his superiors. He would never know why he did not impress me.

"Can we discuss this later?"

"Now, Quadratus!"

Apparently he did not hear me. He was smiling faintly. He stepped towards the wooden ladder and began to descend. Ever incompetent, he had followed the method used by the more practiced slaves—facing outwards instead of first turning around to give himself a proper hold.

I had done nothing to alarm or threaten him. I can say that faithfully. Besides, there were plenty of witnesses. When his heel slipped and he fell, it was just as he said of what happened to Rufius Constans—an accident, of course.

He was still alive when I reached him. He had crashed down onto a ledge, and then fallen another ladder's height. People rushed up and we made him comfortable, though it was clear from the first he would not be recovering. In fact we left him where he was and it was soon over. He never regained consciousness.

Because a man has to stick to his personal standards, I stayed with him until he died.

PART FOUR:

BARCINO

A.D. 73: 25 May

In some parts of the city there are no longer any visible traces of bygone times, any buildings or stones to bear witness to the past . . . But the certainty always remains that everything has happened here, in this specific space that forms part of a plain between two rivers, the mountains and the sea.

Albert Garcia Espuche, Barcelona, Veinte Siglos

SIXTY-SEVEN

From Castulo to the northern coast is a long, slow haul, at least five hundred Roman miles. It depends not just on which milepost you start counting from, but where you want to end up—and whether where you do end up is the place where you wanted to be. I had shed my spare mule then used my official pass for the *cursus publicus* and took it in fast stages, like a dispatch-rider—one who had been charged to announce an invasion by hordes of barbarians, or an imperial death. After several days I hit the coast at Valentia. I had come pretty well halfway; then it was another long trek north with the sea on my right hand, through one harbor town after another, right past the provincial capital at Tarraco at the mouth of its great waterway, until at length I was due to reach Iluro, Barcino and Emporiae.

I never got as far as Emporiae, and I'll never see it now.

At every town I had stopped to visit the main temple, where I demanded to know if there was a message. In this way I had traced Helena, Aelia and Claudia from place to place, encouraged by confirmation of their passing through ahead of me—though I noticed that the brief dated messages were all written by Aelia Annaea, not Helena herself. I tried not to worry. I was closing on them fast, so I convinced myself our journeys would coincide at Emporiae as planned. Then I could take Helena safely home.

But at Barcino, the message was more personal: Claudia Rufina was waiting for me on the temple steps.

Barcino.

The one place on that heartbreaking, backbreaking journey that sticks in my mind. All the others, and the previous long cross-country and coastal miles, were obliterated from my memory the instant that I saw the girl and realized she was weeping into her veil.

Barcino was a small walled town in the coastal strip, a pausing place on the Via Augusta. It was built in a circlet of hills near the sea, in front of a small mountain that was quarried for limestone. An aqueduct brought in water; a canal carried the sewage away. The area was rural; the hinterland was divided into regular packets of land, typical of a Roman settlement that had started life as a military veterans' colony.

Wine-growing was the local commercial success, every farm possessing its kilns for making amphorae. Laeitana: the wine I had last drunk at the dinner for the Olive Oil Producers of Baetica. Wine export thrived so well the town had an official customs post on a bridge beside one of its rivers. The harbor was notoriously terrible, yet because of its handy location on the main route to Gaul, then onwards to Italy, the port was well used. Low breakers rolled unthreateningly on the beaches beyond the inlet. I could have cheerfully taken ship to Rome from here with Helena, but the Fates had another plan.

I had ridden in through the southeastern gate, a triple entrance set in the middle of the town wall. I took the straight road to the civic center, past unpretentious two-storied houses, many of which had a section devoted to wine production or handicrafts. I could hear the trundle of corn- and olive-mills, with occasional bleats from animals. I never thought that my journey would be ending here. I was now so close to Emporiae, which I had planned to use as our staging post; it seemed ridiculous that anything should intervene so late in the journey. I believed we were going to make it.

I reached the forum, with its modest basilica, tempting foodshops, and an open area dedicated to honorary monuments. It was here I saw Claudia. She was leaning against one of the fine local sandstone Corinthian columns in the temple, anxiously looking out for me.

My arrival had made her hysterical—which did nothing for my own peace of mind. I calmed her down enough to let her blurt out what had happened: "We stopped here because Helena was about to have the baby. We were told they had a decent midwife—though it seems she has gone to deliver twins on the other side of the mountain. Aelia Annaea has rented a house and she's there with Helena. I came to find you if you arrived today."

I tried in vain to compose myself. "What are the tears for, Claudia?"

"Helena has gone into labor. It's taking far too long, and she's exhausted. Aelia thinks the baby may have too big a head—"

If so, the child would die. And Helena Justina would almost certainly die too.

Claudia led me as fast as possible to a modest town house. We rushed in through a short passage to reach an atrium with an open roof and a central pool. A reception room, dining room and bedrooms led off it; I could tell at once where Helena was because Nux was lying at full stretch outside the bedroom, with her nose pressed right against the crack under the door, whining pitifully.

Aelia's rental was clean and would have been prepossessing, but it was full of strange women, either clamoring dolefully—which was bad enough—or doing routine needlework as if my girl's suffering merely called for attendance by the civic sewing circle. A new spasm of agonizing pain must have come over Helena, for I heard her crying out so dreadfully it shocked me to the core.

Aelia Annaea, ashen faced, had met us in the atrium. Her greeting was merely a shake of her head; she seemed quite unable to speak.

I managed to croak, "I'll go to her."

At last this male forwardness silenced a few of the wailing women. I was weary and hot, so as I passed I rinsed my face in the atrium pool—another sacrilege, apparently. The needles had stopped stabbing, while the hysteria increased.

I scooped up Nux, whose only reaction to me was a slight tremble of her tail. All she wanted was to reach Helena. So did I. I dumped the whining dog in Aelia's arms then I grasped the door handle. As I stepped inside, Helena stopped screaming just long enough to yell at me, "Falco, you bastard! How could you do this to me?— Go away; go away; I never want to see you again!"

I felt a wild surge of sympathy with our rude forefathers. Men in huts. Men who really were capable of anything. Men who had had to be.

Behind me Aelia gasped, "Falco, she can't do it; she's too tired. The baby must be stuck—"

It was all out of control. Helena looking ghastly as tears mingled with perspiration on her face; Aelia wrestling with the frantic dog; strange women fluttering uselessly. I let out a roar. Hardly the best way to regain calm. Then, infuriated by the noise and fuss, I seized a broom, and with wide sweeps at waist height I cleared the room of women. Helena sobbed. Never mind. We could panic and suffer just as well on our own; we could manage without interruptions from idiots. I strode to the door after them. Aelia Annaea was the only sensible one present so I rapped out my orders to her:

"Olive oil and plenty of it!" I cried. Adding thoughtfully, "And warm it slightly, please."

EPILOGUE

To L. Petronius Longus, of the II Cohort Vigilorum, Rome:

Lucius Petronius, greetings from the land of the Laeitana vintage, which I can assure you lives up to its reputation, especially when drunk in quantity by a man under stress. I solved the Second Cohort's killing (see coded report, attached: the cross-hatch stands for "arrogant bastard" but in the prefect's copy it should be translated as "misguided young man"). For the time being I am delayed at this spot. As you no doubt surmise, it's a girl. She's beautiful; I think I'm in love . . . Just like the old days, eh?

Well, old friend, anything you can do three times, I can manage at least once. Here's another report, which with any luck you will *not* be reading in the Forum in the *Daily Gazette*:

> *Hot news just in from Tarraconensis! Word reaches us from Barcino that the family of a close associate of the Emperor may have a reason to celebrate. Details to follow, but rumors that the baby was delivered by the father while the mother yelled "I don't need you; I'll do it myself, just like I have to do everything!" are believed to exaggerate. M. Didius Falco, an informer, who claims he was present, would only comment that his dagger has seen a lot of action, but he never thought it would end up cutting a natal cord. The black eye he acquired while attempting to ministrate has already calmed down. His finger was broken entirely by accident, when the noble lady grabbed his hand; relations between them are perfectly cordial and he has no plans to sue . . .*

Helena and I both feel completely exhausted. At the moment it seems as if we'll never recover. Our daughter is showing signs of her future personality; she closes her eyes on the crisis and goes fast to sleep.

ACKNOWLEDGMENTS: RESEARCH

While writing this book I learned of the death of Sam Bryson, who once gave me a practical demonstration of how Falco might thwart an assailant coming at him with a knife. We acted this out in a restaurant, which may have slightly surprised other people who were dining at the time . . .

Neither the books I have plundered nor the archaeology I have cribbed will ever be listed as formal sources, because the Falco series is fiction, and meant purely to entertain. But even apart from librarians, authors and tour guides whose job it is, people have always been generous with their interest and help; this seems an occasion to mention just a small sample—for instance, Sue Rollin for reassurance on the Decapolis, Mick McLean for a list of metals that I *will* use one day, Janet for steering me to hypothecs, Oliver for the rude joke about the camel, and Nick Humez for the even ruder song (with tune). I have to thank Sally Bowden who not only published me first, but then thoughtfully brought up her son to be an archaeologist—and Will Bowden, who enabled a trip to the Domus Aurea, and doesn't turn a hair when asked if a descent into the sewers might be possible . . . Staff at London Zoo Reptile House were enormously helpful about snakes; then Bill Tyson described what a scorpion bite is really like . . .

For this particular story, I relied heavily on Janet Laurence who selflessly handed over all her own notes on olive oil, and Robert Knapp who responded most kindly to a request from a complete stranger for a copy of his authoritative book on Roman Corduba, not to mention Señor José Remesal Rodrigez, who sent me his papers on the Baetican oil trade without even being asked. Most devoted of all must be Ginny Lindzey, who catalogued for me every detail of Jonathan's birth, and the accidental damage to Jeff during Tobin's—only to have this sacrificed to the editorial pencil . . .

And as usual thank you Richard, who walks the streets, eats the meals, pours the drink, keeps the tone masculine, carries the fish, photographs the dog, rehearses the fights (and other technically difficult scenes), and inspires the best lines.

More

Lindsey Davis!

Please turn the page

for a special bonus excerpt

from

THREE HANDS IN THE FOUNTAIN

Available at bookstores everywhere!

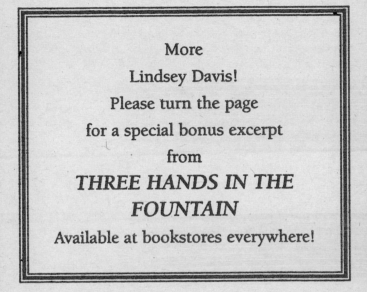

ONE

The fountain was not working. Nothing unusual in that. This was the Aventine.

It must have been off for some time. The water spout, a crudely moulded cockleshell dangled by a naked but rather uninteresting nymph, was thick with dry pigeon guano. The bowl was cleaner. Two men sharing the bottom of an amphora of badly travelled Spanish wine could lean there without marking their tunics. When Petronius and I sloped back to the party at my apartment, there would be no clues to where we had been.

I had laid the amphora in the empty fountain bowl, point inwards, so we could tilt it on the edge when we wanted to refill the beakers we had sneaked out with us. We had been at it awhile now. By the time we ambled home, we would have drunk too much to care what anybody said to us, unless the wigging was very succinctly phrased. As it might be, if Helena Justina had noticed that I had vanished and left her to cope on her own.

We were in Tailors' Lane. We had deliberately turned round the corner from Fountain Court where I lived, so that if any of my brothers-in-law looked down into the street they would not spot us and inflict themselves upon us. None of them had been invited today, but once they heard I was providing a party they had descended on the apartment like flies on fresh meat. Even Lollius the water boatman, who never turned up for anything, had shown his ugly face.

As well as being a discreet distance from home, the fountain in Tailors' Lane was a good place to lean for a heart-to-heart. Fountain Court did not possess its own water supply, any more than Tailors' Lane was home to any garment-sewers. Well, that's the Aventine.

One or two passers-by, seeing us in the wrong street with our heads together, assumed we were conferring about work. They gave us looks that could have been reserved for a pair of squashed rats on the highroad. We were both well-known characters in the Thirteenth District. Few people approved of either of us. Sometimes we did work together, though the pact between the public and private sector was uneasy. I was an informer and imperial agent, just back from a trip to Baetican Spain for which I had been paid less than originally contracted, although I had made up the deficit with an artistic expenses claim. Petronius Longus lived on a strict salary. He was the enquiry chief of the local cohort of vigiles. Well, he was normally. He had just stunned me by revealing he had been suspended from his job.

Petronius took a hearty swig of wine, then balanced his beaker carefully on the head of the stone wench who was supposed to be delivering water to the neighborhood. Petro had long arms and she was a small nymph, as well as one with an empty cockleshell. Petro himself was a big, solid, normally calm and competent citizen. Now he stared down the alley with a glum frown.

I paused to slosh more liquor into my own cup. That gave me time to absorb his news while I decided how to react. In the end I said nothing. Exclaiming "Oh my goodness, old pal!" or "By Jupiter, my dear Lucius, I cannot believe I heard that correctly" was too much of a cliché. If he wanted to tell me the story he would. If not, he was my closest friend, so if he was playing at guarding his privacy I would appear to go along with it.

I could ask somebody else later. Whatever had happened, he couldn't keep it secret from me for long. Extracting the fine details of scandal was my livelihood.

Tailors' Lane was a typical Aventine scene. Faceless tenement blocks loomed above a filthy, one-cart lane that meandered up here from the Emporium down by the Tiber, trying to find the way to the Temple of Ceres, only to lose itself somewhere on the steep heights above the Probus Bridge. Little near-naked children crouched playing with stones beside a dubious puddle, catching whatever fever was rampant this summer. Somewhere overhead a voice droned endlessly, telling some dreary story to a silent listener who might be driven to run mad with a meat-knife any minute now. We were in deep shade, though aware that wherever the sun could find access the August heat was shimmering. Even here our tunics stuck to our backs.

"Well, I got your letter at last." Petronius liked to approach a difficult subject by the winding, scenic route.

"What letter?"

"The one telling me you were a father."

"What?"

"Three months to find me—not bad."

When Helena and I and the new baby sailed back to Rome from Tarraconensis recently it only took eight days at sea and a couple more travelling gently from Ostia. "That's not possible."

"You addressed it to me at the station house," Petronius complained. "It was passed around the clerks for weeks, then when they decided to hand it over, naturally I wasn't there." He was laying it on with a mortar trowel—a certain sign of stress.

"I thought it would be safer sent to the vigiles. I

didn't know you would have got yourself suspended," I reminded him. He was not in the mood for logic.

Nobody much was about. For most of the afternoon we had skulked here virtually in private. I was hoping that my sisters and their children, whom Helena and I had invited for lunch in order to introduce them all to our new daughter in one go, would go home. When Petro and I had sneaked out not one of the guests had been showing any sign of leaving. Helena had already looked tired. I should have stayed.

Her own family had had the tact not to come, but had invited us to dinner later in the week. One of her brothers, the one I could tolerate, had brought a message in which his noble parents politely declined our offer of sharing a cold collation with my swarming relatives in our tiny half-furnished apartment. Some of my lot had already tried to sell the illustrious Camilli dud works of art that they couldn't afford and didn't want. Most of my family were offensive and all of them lacked tact. You couldn't hope to find a bigger crowd of loud, self-opinionated, squabbling idiots anywhere. Thanks to my sisters all marrying down I stood no chance of impressing Helena's socially superior crew. In any case, the Camilli didn't want to be impressed.

"You could have written earlier," Petronius said morosely.

"Too busy. When I did write I'd just ridden eight

hundred miles across Spain like a madman, only to be told that Helena was in desperate trouble with the birth. I thought I was going to lose her, and the baby too. The midwife had gone off halfway to Gaul, Helena was exhausted and the girls with us were terrified. I delivered that child myself—and I'll take a long time to get over it!"

Petronius shuddered. Though a devoted father of three himself, his nature was conservative and fastidious. When Arria Silvia was having their daughters she had sent him off somewhere until the screaming was all over. That was his idea of family life. I would receive no credit for my feat.

"So you named her Julia Junilla. After both grandmothers? Falco, you really know how to arrange free nursemaids."

"Julia Junilla *Laeitana*," I corrected him.

"You named you daughter after a *wine*?" At last some admiration crept into his tone.

"It's the district where she was born," I declared proudly.

"You sly bastard." Now he was envious. We both knew that Arria Silvia would never have let him get away with it.

"So where's Silvia?" I challenged.

Petronius took a long, slow breath and gazed upwards. While he was looking for swallows, I wondered whatever was wrong. The absence of his wife and children from our party was startling. Our families frequently dined together. We had even survived a joint holiday once, though that had been pushing it.

"Where's Silvia?" mused Petro, as if the question intrigued him too.

"This had better be good."

"Oh, it's hilarious."

"You do know where she is, then?"

"At home, I believe."

"She's gone off us?" That would be too much to hope for. Silvia had never liked me. She thought me a bad influence on Petronius. What libel. He had always been perfectly capable of getting into trouble by himself. Still, we all rubbed along, even though neither Helena nor I could stand too much of Silvia.

"She's gone off *me*," he explained.

A workman was approaching. Typical. He wore a one-sleeved tunic hitched over his belt and was carrying an old bucket. He was coming to clean the fountain, which looked a long job. Naturally he turned up at the end of the working day. He would leave the job unfinished and never come back.

"Lucius, my boy," I tackled Petro sternly, since we might soon have to abandon our roost if this fellow did persuade the fountain to fill up, "I can think of various reasons—most of them female—why Silvia would fall out with you. Who is it?"

"Milvia."

I had been joking. Besides, I thought he had stopped flirting with Balbina Milvia months ago. If he had had any sense he would never have started—though when did that ever stop a man chasing a girl?

"Milvia's very bad news, Petro."

"So Silvia informs me."

Balbina Milvia was about twenty. she was astoundingly pretty, dainty as a rosebud with the dew in it, a dark, sweet little piece of trouble whom Petro and I had met in the course of our work. She had an innocence that was begging to be enlightened, and was married to a man who neglected her. She was also the daughter of a vicious gangster—a mobster whom Petronius had convicted and I had helped finally put away. Her husband Florius was now developing half-hearted plans to move in on the family rackets. Her mother Flaccida was scheming to beat him to the profits, a hard-faced bitch whose idea of a quiet hobby was arranging deaths of men who crossed her. Sooner or later that was bound to include her son-in-law Florius.

In these circumstances Milvia could be seen as in need of consolation. As an officer of the vigiles Petronius Longus was taking a risk if he provided it. As the husband of Arria Silvia, a violent force to be reckoned with at any time, he was crazy. He should have left the delicious Milvia to struggle with life on her own.

Until today I had been pretending I knew nothing about it. He would never have listened to me anyway. He had never listened when we were in the army and his eye fell on lush Celtic beauties who had large, red-haired, bad-tempered British fathers, and he had never listened since we came home to Rome either.

"You're not in love with Milvia?"

He looked amazed at the question. I had known I was on safe ground suggesting that his fling might not be serious. What was serious to Petronius Longus was being the husband of a girl who had brought him a very handsome dowry (which he would have to repay if she divorced him) and being the father of Petronilla, Silvana and Tadia, who adored him and whom he doted on. We all knew that, though convincing Silvia might be tricky if she had heard about sweet little Milvia. And Silvia had always known how to speak up for herself.

"So what's th situation?"

"Silvia threw me out."

"What's new?"

"It was a good two months ago."

I whistled. "Where are you living, then?" Not with Milvia. Milvia was married to Florius. Florius was so weak even his womenfolk didn't bother to henpeck him, but he was clinging fast to Milvia because *her* dowry—created with the proceeds of organized crime—was enormous.

"I'm at the patrol house."

"Unless I'm drunker than I think, didn't this whole

conversation begin with you being suspended from the vigiles?"

"That," Petro conceded, "does make it rather complicated when I want to crawl in for a few hours' kip."

"Martinus would have loved to take a stand on it." Martinus had been Petro's deputy. A stickler for the rules—especially when they helped him offend someone else. "He went on promotion to the Sixth, didn't he?"

Petro grinned a little. "I put him forward myself."

"Poor Sixth! So who moved up in the Fourth? Fusculus?"

"Fusculus is a gem."

"He ignores you curled up in a corner?"

"No. He orders me to leave. Fusculus thinks that taking over Martinus' job means he inherited the attitude as well."

"Jupiter! So you're stuck for a bed?"

"I wanted to lodge with your mother." Petronius and Ma had always got on well. They liked to conspire, criticizing me.

"Ma would take you in."

"I can't ask her. She's still putting up Anacrites."

"Don't mention that bastard!" My mother's lodger was anathema to me. "My old apartment's empty," I suggested.

"I was hoping you'd say that."

"It's yours. Provided," I put in slyly, "you explain to me how, if we're talking about a quarrel with your wife, you also end up being suspended by the Fourth. When did Rubella ever have a reason to accuse you of disloyalty?" Rubella was the tribune in charge of the Fourth Cohort, and Petro's immediate superior. He was a pain in the posterior, but otherwise fair.

"Silvia took it upon herself to inform Rubella that I was tangled up with a racketeer's relative."

Well, he had asked for it, but that was hard. Petronius Longus could not have picked a mistress who compromised him more thoroughly. Once Rubella knew of the affair, he would have had no choice about suspending Petro from duty. Petro would be lucky even to keep his job. Arria Silvia must have understood that. To risk their livelihood she must be very angry indeed. It sounded as if my old friend was losing his wife too.

We were too disheartened even to drink. The amphora was down to the grit in the point anyway. But we were not ready to return home in this glum mood. The water board employee had not actually asked us to move out of his way, so we stayed where we were while he leaned around us cleaning the cockleshell spout with a disgusting sponge on a stick. When the plunger failed to work he burrowed in his tool satchel for a piece of wire. He poked and scraped. The fountain made a rude noise. Some sludge plopped out. Slowly, water began to trickle through, encouraged by more waggling of the wire.

Petronius and I straightened up reluctantly. In Rome the water pressure is low, but eventually the bowl would fill and then overflow, providing the neighborhood with not only its domestic supply but an endless trickle down the gutters to carry away muck for the streets. Tailors' Lane badly needed that but, drunk though we were, we didn't want to end up sitting in it.

Petronius applauded the workman sardonically. "That all the problem was?"

"Seized up while it was off, legate."

"Why was it off?"

"Empty delivery pipe. Blockage in the outlet at the castellum."

The man dug his fist into the bucket he had brought with him, like a fisherman pulling out a crab. He came up with a blackened object which he held up by its single clawlike appendage so we could briefly inspect it: Something old, and hard to identify, yet disturbingly familiar. He tossed it back in the bucket where it splashlanded surprisingly heavily. We both nearly ignored it. We would have saved ourselves a lot of trouble. Then Petro looked at me askance.

"Wait a moment!" I exclaimed.

The workman tried to reassure us. "No panic, legate. Happens all the time."

Petronius and I stepped closer and peered down

into the filthy depths of the wooden pail. A nauseous smell rose to greet us. The cause of the blockage at the water tower now reposed in a bed of rubbish and mud.

It was a human hand.